THE NEWLYWEDS

A totally addictive psychological thriller full of twists

KAELIN WENNERBERG

Originally published as *The Jameson Cabin*

Revised edition 2024
Joffe Books, London
www.joffebooks.com

First published in Great Britain in 2023
as *The Jameson Cabin*

This paperback edition was first published
in Great Britain in 2024

Cover art by Nick Castle

ISBN: 978-1-83526-339-6

This book is dedicated to my mother, sister, and fiancé who took the time to read my un-edited script and give me all their thoughts and recommendations. Especially my mother, Carla. Without you none of this could be possible. You were the one who always supported me in everything I did. I miss and love you more than anything.

TRIGGER WARNING

The following novel contains explicit content and subject matter. Reader discretion is advised.

CHAPTER 1

The sun gleaming on my closed eyes startles me awake from my short-lived nap. *Damnit!* It had taken me most of the car ride to fall asleep. I hadn't been on a road trip this long in ages . . . ever since I was just a child, it seemed.

Although beautiful, the blue and nearly cloudless sky forced the bright sunshine into the windshield. I lift my car seat forward and put the sun visor down. Soon afterward, I feel the familiar sensation of a hand on my knee. I look over at my fiancé — *Oops! Husband now* — and, as expected, he smiles lightly at me. This is often the grin I wake up to in the morning — like he hasn't seen me in a couple of days, and my presence had been the very thing he'd been looking forward to. Even though we haven't left each other's side much in the eighteen months we've been together.

A fast-moving relationship, I know, but he is the one for me. I knew it the day I met him. As corny as that may sound, my parents were the same way. Their relationship crumbled eventually, but the love they shared during the first five years of marriage was the stuff of dreams, and that's how I'd always pictured and prayed mine would play out. Without the Romeo and Juliet ending of my parents, of course.

Sunney Lane Jameson. Even his name makes my body shiver. He is one of the most compelling people I have ever met. Looking at him now, my eyes watch his every move as if he might disappear. He stares at me as if I have been gone too long while I gaze at him as if he might vanish in the blink of an eye.

"How was your nap?" he asks, his voice soft and gentle as if I am still asleep and he doesn't want to wake me.

This is another thing I ardently love about my husband. He always speaks to me calmly and softly — like I am some small animal he's caring for. His voice is deep, and rugged and direct when he speaks to others.

"Definitely not long enough," I whine.

Sunney checks his wristwatch and replies, "Almost a good two hours."

"Just about how much I got last night," I say with a wink, and Sunney immediately chuckles.

"You should expect that tonight," he says, his dark brown eyes blazing with desire and looking me up and down just like when we started getting closer.

I laugh, although I know it to be true. Sunney and I are insatiable when it comes to the bedroom. I can never see myself growing weary of witnessing his undeniable beauty or touching his naked body. Even better, I know he thinks the same of me. He treats my body like a temple, even when it isn't one. Even when I know he can find a woman with a body crafted with as much dedication and commitment as Sunney shows to his own.

He has classically handsome features — tall, sturdy, brawny and is one of the strongest men I've ever met. Maybe not in the way that he could go to the gym and lift a barbell that is quadruple his weight. More like he could survive stranded in the desert by exercising the pure will to live. He doesn't spend his days indoors at the gym; he spends them outdoors, engaged in all the things he loves — golfing, hiking, biking, and skiing.

"How much longer until we reach your special cabin?" I ask — the same question I asked before I took my nap and when we left this morning.

Frankly, I feel anxious. Since the beginning of our relationship, Sunney has always mentioned his quiet little cabin in the middle of the woods. He heavily adores it, and I don't blame him after seeing a picture. It isn't huge but it's exquisitely built with brand-new wood and furnishings. This is the first time I will be seeing it in person. He promised himself he would only take his wife to the cabin. In the eighteen months we've been together, he has visited it four or more times for fishing and hunting trips, never staying more than three days. A month before our wedding, he spent the most time — approximately a week — there.

"To make it perfect," he had explained. I assumed, and my work friends agreed, he was probably turning the man cave into an actual home.

"We'll be there soon," he reassures me, and I sigh in exasperation.

I feel impatient; I can't help it. I've been anticipating this honeymoon since the day we officially planned it all out. I remember I was sitting in Sunney's kitchen. I stayed at his place nearly every night, but we still didn't live together; I had three months left on a long apartment lease. I was wearing one of his oversized white button-up T-shirts and nothing else — it is how he likes me in the morning. I had been a little irritated because the previous night, he had told me he might not be able to give me a honeymoon immediately after our wedding due to work complications. I knew it was selfish to be angry, but I'd been dreaming of our honeymoon ever since I first started dating him. I had never expected to share this experience with the previous men I had dated.

While I was sitting at the table, trying to convince myself not to be upset, he came out of the shower and walked into the kitchen, wearing a towel around his waist. He looked at me the way I love, closed the distance between us in mere seconds, and kissed me. After I got a breath in from the fervent embrace, I asked him what had gotten into him. It was then and there that he surprised me with the cabin idea. Initially, I was a little dubious because I have never been much of an outdoor girl. I had imagined my honeymoon somewhere with the ocean right out front, like Hawaii or the Bahamas.

It took a bit of convincing on Sunney's end, but he eventually got me on board. It would mean one month of total isolation from anyone. He knew the area and said he'd have everything perfectly organized and better than any resort. Sunney had never lied to me before, so I had no reason not to believe him.

I wanted to push him more on our arrival time but, on second thought, decided not to. Annoying my husband this soon wouldn't start our marriage well. He isn't easily irritated, but I have seen it happen. He isolated himself completely in the rare few times we fought. Most men scream and holler or even punch a hole in the wall, but Sunney is different. He did whatever he could to momentarily isolate himself from me for a couple of hours at the most, returned, apologized, and hugged me tightly. It could occasionally be frustrating, but in the end, I knew it was the best thing I could ask for from a man — to be calm and collected when push came to shove.

Sunney tightens his grasp on my knee and says, "I'm looking forward to this just as much as you."

I can't help but wonder what he has in store for me. The possibilities are endless. Sunney has always been the romantic one in our relationship. I tried to outdo him with surprise gifts and dates, but his efforts always trumped mine. For example, I bought him a new bike on his last birthday because he complained his was worn down due to frequent use. I never had as much money to spend on him as he did on me, so buying this bike cost nearly a whole paycheck, but I was excited to give it to him. Then for my birthday, he bought me an engagement ring, proposing while out on a picnic he'd planned to watch a beautiful sunset. So yeah, getting engaged on my birthday was quite possibly the gift that would outdo anything I could ever give, no matter how expensive or thoughtful.

Another sleepless hour passes before Sunney pulls over at a small, red-painted gas station. A green sign bearing the name of only one town is on the other side of the road. It reads RUBICO 4, the town closest to Sunney's cabin. He has described it as small, mostly full of elder folks, perverted truckers, and a few families that wished to stay out of the big cities. I had never been to Rubico, but the area is beautiful. Fully grown pine trees surround it, and mountains in the distance still have little bits of snow on them, although it's August. The air smells fresh, as if it has just rained. We haven't passed a town or many other houses in over an hour, so it seems as secluded as possible.

The gas station, on the other hand, stands out like an abundance of garbage bins left in the middle of a beautiful scene. Trash is scattered everywhere. The building has a tacky firetruck red color with chipping paint that needs to be redone. The concrete it stands on is cracked with weeds and ant hills sprouting from it. The bathroom is at the back, and even without going inside, I know it will be filthy. My bladder doesn't care, though, as I need to pee. I go inside and ask for a key from the overweight attendant wearing smudged and tilted glasses who cannot take his eyes off my chest. Sunney's glare is the only thing that stops him from staring at my ass as I walk out the door.

I take a Kleenex from my purse, grab the bathroom door handle, and pull it open. It is somehow worse than I had pictured it. The floor is an old white and black tile, sticky and covered in dirt and used paper towels. The wall is white, or well, it used to be. It is now extremely crumbled and covered in sharpie written words. Mostly the stereotypical middle school jargon — *Josh fucked Lisa* or *Kelly's a hoe.*

I sit when I finally get enough toilet paper to cover the germ-ridden seat without using what little is left. As I pee, I read the ridiculous scribbles on the wall.

Don't fuck the inbreds down here.

They're all inbreds, it reads with an arrow pointed above.

I can't help but agree with these vile words, remembering the looks of the attendant.

Licky, sticky, the bitches here are icky, I read, shaking my head.

Call for a good time at 505-877-2617<3, 'cause why wouldn't you want the surely stunning men who crossed paths with this bathroom to call you?

Go to Dollz if you want to get AIDS.

What is Dollz? I ask myself.

Andrea and Sunney forever. 2001.

Hannah sucks cocks.

Hold up.

I stop and scan the text thoroughly. *Andrea and Sunney forever*? This can't be a coincidence. Sunney is not a common name or even a known name. 2001 was only a year before we met.

My mind races frantically, unable to decide what to think of this middle school bullshit. *Do I really have any reason to be mad? Did Sunney take Andrea to his cabin? Maybe that whole, 'Only my wife can come to my cabin' is utter bullshit.* For the first time today, I suddenly want to grab the bottle of Crown Royal stashed in my bulky hot pink purse. However, before I can, there's a knock on the door.

"Anyone in there?" a deep male voice enquires.

I quickly sit up, pull my pants up, and holler, "One second!"

I turn the faucet on, knowing full well that washing my hands will be pointless as soon as I touch the faucet or doorknob again.

Another knock sounds, and the voice says, "Come on, lady. I really have to take a shit."

I roll my eyes. Can't even get a full three minutes of silence to freak out about my husband's ex-girlfriend scribbling their names on the walls of a shitty bathroom. I reach into my purse, so annoyed that I decide to have one shot at cooling myself down. It's an essential evil I must deal with in my life.

I take a long swig of the Crown. It burns going down my throat but brings a momentary feeling of relaxation to my body. I pop a piece of gum in my mouth so Sunney won't smell the liquor on my breath, and after securing the bottle in my bag, I open the bathroom door. The man standing there is a lot different-looking than I had imagined. I was picturing a fat, creepy redneck. This man appears to be in his early thirties and is tall and ruggedly handsome. He has buzz-cut chocolate-colored hair and a well-groomed full beard to go along with it. He is broad-shouldered and has a nice square jaw that looks like it could take a hit with plywood. He is wearing a button-up, oversized red-and-blue plaid jacket. It's more of a winter jacket, although it's well over eighty degrees outside. I realize he must be wearing it to overcompensate because he is a brawny man. He is not fat by any means, but he certainly doesn't spend time watching his diet or in the gym. His size, however, suits his stature and makes him ten times more intimidating.

"Oh, woah!" he exclaims, his hazel eyes widening, not expecting me to be the person standing there. His cheeks flush red.

"Excuse me," I awkwardly reply.

He quickly steps out of the door's entryway and, with a soft cough, says, "Sorry about the er — language."

"Doesn't bother me. But a word of advice — work on your patience," I say, fake laughing so I don't sound like a complete bitch.

"You're right, thanks. You just passing by or from Rubico?"

Momentarily, I smell his breath. It smells like whiskey, which should disgust me, but instead it incites me to have a drink from my own stash.

"First time, if you couldn't tell," I say, looking down at my clothing.

By the confused expression on his face, clearly I've just made a stuck-up remark. Although not very polite, it is true. I'm wearing an expensive, chic, lilac-colored satin slip dress. I had purposely ordered it a size up so it would be comfy for the drive but sexy enough to keep Sunney driving as fast as he can get away with to get me into bed. However, I didn't anticipate that it would stick out in a shithole such as this.

"I don't know. You look pretty comfy to me," he says finally, smirking.

I raise my eyebrows, almost insulted. I decide, however, to keep my expression as stoic as possible. The old me would have wanted to insult him immediately, but alas, I had promised myself since changing that I would no longer stick to such immature tendencies.

"Not as comfy as you, that's for sure. A little chilly out today, huh?" I say, smirking back.

I expect this statement to insult this man, but it doesn't. He laughs.

"Gotta love a woman with a sense of humor and—" he exhales, takes a deep breath and looks me up and down — "such great curves."

My mouth opens a bit. *Wow.* It's my first time being hit on as a married woman. The old me would have loved this compliment from a good-looking, strong man. Not like many men are willing to say such things in a setting outside a bar. Then I think of Sunney and know I can't occupy my time with men like these anymore, nor should I want to.

"My husband sure loves them, yes," I say, raising my left hand to show off my pearly eight-carat white gold wedding ring.

The man raises his eyebrows briefly.

"Of course, he does. My apologies; I didn't realize."

I just nod my head, forgiving him. After an awkward couple of moments of silence, I walk past him. However, something in my mind begs me to stick around.

Before I get even three steps forward, he speaks up, "Well, it was nice to meet you—"

I turn around and offer, "Toni."

He extends his arm and says, "Quinn, Quinn Robins."

I shake his hand and smile softly. At least he is pleasant compared to most men when rejected.

After I let go, he chuckles and asks, "Isn't Toni a boy's name?"

This man surely is picking at straws for a conversation. It's not the first time I've been questioned about my masculine name.

"Women can also have it, same as the name Quinn."

Quinn chuckles again. He sure can take a joke as well as throwing one out.

"Right again, you are, dear."

I gulp. He just called me "dear." I really need to veto this conversation. I know I should, but still, my feet stay stuck to a spot only a few steps away from him.

"You and your husband just moved here then?" he questions.

Before I can answer, a familiar voice behind me asks, "What's the holdup, hun?"

Finally, my feet move from what seem like their glued state. I turn around and see Sunney swiftly walking my way. I almost had not recognized his voice. It has assumed a deep, angry-sounding tone — one he does not often use around me. I don't think I've been gone for more than a couple of minutes.

"Baby!" I exclaim, smiling as if I had something to hide.

He doesn't smile back or look at me. His eyes stay on Quinn's, with his thick eyebrows furrowed.

"What's up, man?" Quinn asks, a small smirk on his face.

Quinn's one of the first men I've met that hasn't been immediately intimidated by Sunney's sternness. Quinn is very intimidating himself with his larger stature, dirty hands, and scruffy beard. It's compelling to see two different-looking men being equally daunting.

"Don't think I've had the pleasure of meeting you like my wife has," Sunney says, a fake smile plastered on his face, briefly making eye contact with me like I'm a kid in trouble.

"No, you haven't. Name's Quinn," he says, extending his hand.

Strangely, he had given me his full name, but Sunney only got his first.

"Sunney."

Their handshake is so firm that just looking at it makes me wince. The fact Sunney also didn't offer his last name makes it obvious where this conversation will go.

"You new to Rubico?" Sunney asks, his eyes scanning up and down Quinn without care.

"New to New Hampshire, actually. Just moved to Rubico a couple of weeks ago."

"What brings you here?" Sunney asks.

"Came into some money, found a cheap trailer, decided to buy it along with some land, and fix it up."

"What kind of money did you get into?"

"Sunney, that isn't our business," I intervene, glaring at him, but he doesn't even glance my way.

I have always been the nosy one in this relationship. It's out of character to see Sunney ask such an impolite question. Why is he so interested in Quinn's personal business? He's met far more interesting people and asked far less.

"It's alright; I don't mind. It's a long story that I need a couple of beers to talk about," Quinn says, smiling lightly as he stares at my flushed face.

"Fair enough. It's just — not many people move to Rubico," Sunney points out.

"Don't they? I think this is such a charming town — from the three dive bars, one supermarket, rundown homes, and dainty little strip club," Quinn says, his eyes briefly finding mine before making eye contact with Sunney.

Strip club? I remember the writing on the wall mentioning a place named Dollz. *Perhaps that's the strip club. It would make sense.* I didn't think a town as small as this would have one. Most larger towns can barely keep one open.

It's completely silent, and I'm debating if Sunney will cuss him out or whether this will end in a fight. Quinn doesn't seem to shy down from a fight, either.

This is when I decide to intervene in the most subtle way I can. I grab Sunney's hand, lace my fingers through his, and say, "I think it's time we get going."

Sunney looks at me, expression cold and serious. But moments later, his somber face morphs into a bright smile. He tightens his hold on my hand a little too much.

"Of course, baby. It was nice to meet you, Quinn. Enjoy your new home. Maybe I'll see you around."

Quinn nods at Sunney, and, gazing at me, says, "Wouldn't surprise me if you did. Have a good one, you two."

Sunney wraps his arm around my waist and replies, "Will do."

He then turns us around, and we begin to walk away. I look back once more, offering a light smile that Quinn returns with a wave. Even after I turn around, I feel his hazel eyes on us.

I will spend the next month in a small cabin, excluded from everyone except my husband, but I have this sneaking suspicion that this is not the last time I will see Quinn Robins.

CHAPTER 2

Before

The Keelover, located in the depths of downtown, is one of my favorite bars. I love frequenting many others, but the Keelover is always my go-to when I'm shit-faced or planning on getting shit-faced. It's another average Friday night for me. No work tomorrow, and I'm ready to drink away all my thoughts. It's midnight, and I'm four shots of tequila and five Vodka-Crans deep. Although with my alcohol tolerance, which isn't much, I'm already off my rocker because I skipped dinner. It's my new tactic to not gain any weight — an ardent effort to undo my missteps due to all the alcohol I have been putting in my system over the last year.

The Keelover is by far one of the biggest dive bars in town. The people here have no morals, money, job security, or self-esteem — you get the drift. Mostly, it's a bar where I can sit and think while drinking away my troubles. If I'm in the market to find decent people *or a man*, I will try the cocktail bars scattered around the block. But it has been over a month since my relationship ended, so I'm not in the market to find another disappointing one. Tonight, I'm not looking for a future husband. Just one (or two) last shit-faced nights to get my mind off things.

My face is still healing from my last relationship and is nowhere near as black and blue as it was, but it still has a yellow tinge to it. My broken nose is nearly healed and thankfully isn't permanently deformed. Bruises and cuts always seem to scare nice men away. It makes them think you are either a druggie or in an abusive relationship. That would have been a correct guess one month ago. No more, though. I've concluded that chapter in my life. That and actively trying to build myself past the daily uppers, bottles of vodka, whiskey, and punches to the face. But I already know that alcohol will be the hardest to quit as it has always given me a haven from my never-ending thoughts of despair.

As I knock back the rest of my drink, I can't help but stare at the disturbing sight in the smudged mirror behind all the booze bottles. Myself. It has been a long, stressful month. My natural matte black hair, which was once thick, lustrous, and perfectly straightened, is now greasy, tangled, and wearing thin from all the past years of stress or from being pulled out — either by myself or, on occasion, my ex-boyfriend, Tom, depending on the mood he had been in. The back of my neck has droplets of sweat pouring down into my chest due to the bar's poor air conditioner. My skin is pastel-colored and dry from the lack of sun. My ice-blue eyes are bloodshot and have bags under them no concealer can hide. Lack of sleep is a hell of a bitch. At the very least, I have lost the twenty pounds I'd gained during the two years Tom and I dated. It's not just now I'm disgusted with my appearance; I have been for the past month. I could only stand to look at myself when my pupils were dilated and whatever I'd taken had kicked in.

I look down, clutching my empty, sick stomach, feeling the mix of the double drink I just finished, and the sight of myself almost makes me hurl. I feel on the verge of punching my stomach, so it no longer causes discomfort. Instead, I take a handful of peanuts sitting in a dirty ceramic glass and stuff them in my mouth.

At least my head hasn't started to bang yet. After the last dose I took two hours ago, I'm out of Tylenol, and a walk to the gas station a block down from my apartment is not an option for me at this point in the night. The creeps that hang out there didn't scare me when I was sober and clear-headed, but shit-faced like this, nearly everything scares me. And I no longer have Tom to escort me there.

Tom, Tom, Tom . . . I think. I remember the way I would call his name. In the beginning of our relationship, I would always try to say it sweetly, no matter how he treated me. I thought of the way he'd call my name, at first with love and admiration, and then, in the end, his words laced with pure disgust. Once the beatings started we both lost the love for each other. I had tried to keep mine but soon I could no longer hide my emotions.

"Don't puke at the bar again, Toni," the asshole bartender orders, obviously having noticed my head down and me clenching my stomach.

"Another Vodka-Cran, please," I ask, letting go of my stomach once the pain fades.

The bartender rolls his eyes but turns around and goes to the readily available bottle of Nikoli. My favorite. Cheap with a kick.

I know what he thinks of me — pathetic, drunk, druggie, and so on. He has been here long enough to know how most of my nights go. He also knows about the whole Tom situation. Most of the regulars know. How can they not? The event made news, and it has been a hot topic in the neighborhood. I avoided the news on TV like the plague, unable to even see the face of the man I once loved.

Every night I promise myself it will be the last night I'll drink my sorrows away. The last night I'll swallow some pills that make me feel fluffy and not depressed. Then the ever-lingering alone time in my apartment with the sound of the TV blaring and my thoughts bring me back here nearly every night. Here there's only one TV and it mainly blares sports events. This is my only safe haven from it all.

The bartender sloppily hands me my drink. I put a couple dollars on the bar and grab my glass, tossing the two neon colored plastic straws aside. After taking a hefty swallow, I can already feel the headache I'm going to have tomorrow. Thankfully, I won't have work to be hungover at. It's a miracle I haven't gotten canned yet. Thankfully, being a receptionist at a dental clinic isn't all that grueling. I've been there long enough; my boss is used to me being hungover at least three times a week. If I show up on time, don't smell like booze, and smile at the customers, he is content with keeping me.

"What can I get for you?" I hear the bartender ask nearby.

"Jack and Coke," a deep, masculine-sounding voice says.

I glance in the direction of the voice and notice a man sitting only a seat down from mine. He's well-dressed and extremely alluring, too handsome to be at a bar like this. He sits up straight, unlike all the hunched-over drunks here. He's wearing a sleek, black, brand-new-looking suit. It's his first time in the Keelover, I can tell that much by the way he nervously peers around the place. He is probably already considering his getaway. Once he's done examining the horrendous sight that is this dive bar, the bartender sets down his Jack and Coke. He squints his eyes in disbelief, looking down at it, probably expecting it to be served in a fancy rocks glass, and not a cheap clear plastic cup.

I can't help but be intrigued by this stuck-up-looking man. His gelled-back, curly, shoulder-length dirty blonde hair, and large dark eyes have attracted me in seconds. I've always been a sucker for blondes and moody eyes. Just looking at his thick hair as he runs his fingers through it reminds me of when I would lay with Tom on a lazy Sunday, running my fingers through his hair. Tom had always cut his hair short, and had hazel eyes, not black. Still, this man and Tom had instantly left me speechless before the first spoken words. Of course, the first time I met Tom, I looked like a decent human being, and not a drunken pathetic excuse of a woman as I do now.

I contemplate talking to him, wishing he would glance over at me. Notice me and not be repulsed. I feel like a teen girl at her favorite band's concert. Thinking if only one of them would look her way in the crowd of people.

I chicken out three times trying to say something, anything before finally thinking, *Fuck it!* What's the worst that can happen?

"First tim—" I begin to say, but suddenly, my gut stings again.

I instantly grab my stomach and cover my mouth, feeling like I might vomit if I don't multitask between the two. I want to escape to the restroom before he notices, but it's too late. His dark eyes are already on me. Thankfully, he's not smiling from laughter but has a look of confusion and pity. Now that I think of it, that may be much worse. This, this right here, is the worst that could happen.

I leave my seat and run to the bathroom with all my strength. As soon as my knees hit the dirty linoleum floor, I puke my guts out. Most of it is a red liquid along with the undigested peanuts I've eaten. Truthfully, as embarrassed as I am, I feel ten times more sober. I had planned on throwing up tonight, just not before trying to talk to an attractive man. There goes my chance if I even had one to start with.

I wipe my mouth and flush the toilet. Grabbing hold of the handlebar, I lift myself. I look down at my black heels, cursing myself for thinking that wearing them was a good idea. I hate heels, but they add to my average height and scare away all the losers from hitting on me. Once up, I exit the stall and approach the mirror. I wash my hands and try wiping away the tears under my eyes. I fix my messy hair, running my fingers through it, then tucking it behind my ears. Luckily, I am the only one in the bathroom and don't have to be embarrassed.

As I exit, I stop to stare both ways. To the left is the back door where I can escape all the embarrassment I'll feel returning to the bar. To the right is the bar with the alluring stranger and liquor. I curse myself for most likely making the wrong decision and turning right. As I walk back to my seat, nearly all the regulars stare at me. I avoid eye contact as much as possible. Once back in my seat, I force myself to avoid eye contact with the attractive man who is now staring at me. Even without nearly throwing up in my lap before him, I know I wouldn't have stood a chance. I am an absolute mess. It's been one month since I ended a toxic, abusive relationship, and I can't stop drinking. I'm not ready to meet another man. Nowhere near, in fact, no matter how attracted to him I am.

I hear a long sigh and look over at the man instinctively. He has a small smile on his face as he says, "Some bar, huh? At least the music is decent."

I hadn't even been paying attention to what was playing. I hear *Unchained Melody* by Elvis Presley playing. He is so overplayed, and I hate love songs, which is his entire oeuvre. I fake a smile, though.

"R–right," I say, my voice cracking.

Jesus, it feels like I'm in eighth grade again and can't talk to boys.

"I mean, I guess I can't complain. I got a double for a single price," he says, lifting the plastic cup and taking his last sip.

"They always serve their drinks double," I say, feeling my hands shaking.

"Good to know," he responds, lifting his empty cup, getting the bartender's attention, who speed walks over to him.

"Another, sir?" he asks politely.

Sir? He never talks to customers with such respect.

"Yeah, and two shots of the lady's choice," he says, winking at me.

The bartender looks just as surprised as me. My mind races, and suddenly, an alcoholic like me doesn't remember a single shot. I think of tequila, but my stomach can't handle another one of those. I need something sweet and subtle.

"Butt sex," I blurt out and instantly feel my cheeks get heated. *Fuck.*

The man smiles, showing a bright set of perfect white teeth and replies without waiting a beat, "Sure, haven't had that in a while."

The bartender, not nearly as amused as him, nods, and leaves to make our shots. The man gets out of his seat and moves down to the one at my side, and I get a sniff of his cologne. It smells like sandalwood — my favorite. I want to get closer and press my nose against his neck to smell him better.

"Hope you don't mind?" he asks.

I shake my head and say, "Of course not."

"What's your name?" he asks. His breath smells good — fresh and minty.

"T–Toni, you?" I say, nonchalantly placing my hand over my mouth because I know my breath smells of vodka and vomit.

He extends his hand, and as I shake it, he says, "Sunney Jameson."

I gulp. It couldn't be *the* Jameson, as in Jameson Life Insurance, the biggest insurance company in the city and possibly in the state. The one advertised on all the billboards around the nicer part of town.

"Yes, Jameson, as in Jameson Life Insurance. My father is the CEO, I'm his lapdog who runs it," he says like he had read my thoughts.

"You like it?"

"Keeps me busy and pays the bills. What do you do?"

I knew that question would come up and my answer would drive this high-class man away. I have never been ashamed that I'm not wealthy or don't have some insane-paying job along with a fancy degree. But, for some peculiar reason, this man evokes this feeling of shame in me. Maybe it's because he's the first man to speak to me who is wealthy.

Thankfully, before I can answer, our shots arrive. Sunney diverts his attention away from me and whips out his wallet. I can't help but notice it's stuffed full of bills. He takes out a twenty and hands it to the bartender.

"Keep the change, thanks," he says casually, to which the bartender smiles and nods in gratitude. This is probably the biggest tip he's gotten all night or even all week. People with that amount of money don't come here.

Sunney lifts his shot and exclaims, "To new friends!"

I laugh and grab the small plastic shot glass. We clink them together and take the shot. It's sweet, and I lick some of it off my lips. As I do, Sunney watches me, his eyes gazing at the rest of my body. Thankfully, I had put some effort into my outfit choice. I'm wearing my favorite tight dark jeans that have slits in the knees. I also wear my go-to dark blue V-neck crop top that is cinched through the middle and shows off my cleavage that, thanks to my nicest black push-up bra, looks bigger than it is.

"So — I got to ask. Are you old enough to be in here?"

I get that question often. Although my long dark hair helps me look above the age of eighteen, I have a youthful, baby-looking face. There is acne and freckles on my chubby cheeks. At the end of middle school, I had prayed I'd start growing into my body. All I had asked was to grow boobs like all my girlfriends and lose the chipmunk cheeks. Neither had happened. But these drawbacks didn't stop me from attracting the attention of my biggest crush when I was a sophomore.

"I'm twenty-three, thank you very much," I say, crossing my arms.

"That's good to hear, or I might have had to tell on you," Sunney says, pursing his lips.

"I'd like to see you try, tough guy."

"Is Toni short for something?" Sunney asks after nearly thirty seconds of looking me up and down and me staring off into the distance, pretending I didn't realize he was doing so.

"No, my parents were just assholes. What about you? I don't think I've ever heard the name Sunney before."

"Same."

I laugh, somewhat surprised. Sunney is almost as ridiculous a name as my own. I swear my parents wanted a boy, although, when I was a child, they always denied such a thing. Maybe their relationship wouldn't have crashed so hard if I had been a boy. My mother and I had been too similar for her to handle. If she could see me now, she would say we are doppelgangers.

"What brings you here?" I ask.

Sunney raises his eyebrows and, chuckling, asks, "Do I stand out that much?"

"That's not what I mea—" I begin to say, but stop myself because it's exactly what I meant.

"Truth be told, I was just looking for something new, something different. I get sick of the same short skirts and expensive ties."

The short skirt comment makes me wonder if he is sick of hooking up with rich plastic women and is now seeking a real one. I could deliver that want of his, if true.

"Does the Keelover deliver?"

He keeps eye contact with me and answers, "It sure does."

Just staring at this man and talking to him is arousing. I had promised myself I wouldn't have sex with anyone for a while, or at least until after I'm completely over Tom. I had already tried a one-night stand, and waking up alone in bed, knowing you'd just been used by someone who didn't care about you is not something I fancied doing again, especially since I was absolutely smashed, and the sex was god awful.

However, after barfing most of the liquor in my system out, I feel less hammered and want this man. It's just a feeling. I don't want just a one-night stand with him, but I know he is out of my league for anything but that.

We talk for the next fifteen or so minutes, never breaking eye contact. I avoid questions about myself while trying to summon the balls to ask if he would walk me home. My confidence is not as high in the absence of a hammered feeling. In these short minutes, I learn Sunney's dad founded Jameson insurance when he was only thirty but now Sunney mainly runs it himself. He's twenty-six years old, never been married and is an only child. He owns two homes, one of which is here in town, and one is a cabin six hours from here in the Gile Forest. He loves to bike, fish, and run. He's so fascinating and confident without being cocky. With every word he says, I'm drawn to him even more.

"So, tell me something about yourself, Toni. You haven't said much," Sunney asks, and I gulp.

"What do you want to know?"

Sunney shrugs and says, "Tell me what you want me to know. Tell me anything."

I struggle to find words and, after a couple of awkward moments of silence, just say, "I like to — uh, drink."

Sunney isn't amused by my answer and frowns. I think I have finally blown it.

"I'm sorry. I guess that is a pathetic thing to say."

Sunney takes a sip from his cup and replies, "I wouldn't say that. I just didn't think it would be the first thing you could think of. A lot of women drink. Tell me something else."

It's now or never — either expose myself for the mess I am or use any shred of confidence to hit on Sunney.

However, I do neither because, suddenly, my stomach churns again. *Seriously, now?* I don't have the time to properly excuse myself from Sunney before I turn around and run. I run out of the backdoor this time as the bathroom has a line outside of it. I hate going out the backdoor as it smells horrible from the dumpsters scattered everywhere, the men who constantly piss outside, and everyone else's vomit. To add to it, the alleyway is creepy and unsettling.

Luckily, it's lightly raining, and water engulfs the smell of the dumpsters. I vomit out more liquid, barely any at all. Just as I finish, I hear the backdoor open. I wipe my mouth quickly and turn around, expecting a concerned Sunney. But it's not him; it's a friend of Tom's. One of the short, stocky ones I can never recall the name of. I stand up straight and lightly smile, hopefully covering my vomit. The man glares at me, his arms crossed. He never liked me, not before or after the incident. Tom had probably told him anything to get him on his side.

"Hello," I say, wiping my mouth of any residue of vomit.

"Toni Lovette, the bitch that killed my friend. You have some nerve showing your face around here."

Shit! Tom is still causing me trouble from beyond the grave.

"What are you talking about?" I ask.

"Don't play coy. I knew Tom, and I think you're a lying bitch," the man says, stepping closer to me.

"Get away from me!" I shout, feeling my body shaking.

CHAPTER 3

Before

I am instantly transported to the night from a month ago. Images flash through my mind. I have already faced multiple panic attacks from this ordeal due to these persistent mental flashbacks. I take deep breaths in and out, knowing I can stop it if I try, but it may already be too late.

"You deserve to rot in prison!"

"Fuck you!" I yell back, anger instead of fear coursing through my veins for the first time.

"You bitch—"

Before he can finish, the door slams open, and Sunney walks out on cue, as if he already knew what was happening.

"Step away from the lady," he orders sternly, touching the man's shoulder.

The short man grabs Sunney's hand and throws it off. He tries pushing Sunney, who barely moves an inch and stands nearly a foot over him. I want to watch Sunney beat this man up. It's one hundred percent apparent Sunney would win by a landslide. He's more muscular, not fat like this man, and taller, not a near-midget.

"She's a fucking killer!" the short man yells.

"And how do you know that?" Sunney asks.

"He was a good friend of mine. I knew him personally, and he would have never hurt a fly."

"Do you not see the bruises on her face, you fucking moron?" Sunney says, looking over at me, our eyes meeting.

I had hoped that they'd be hard to see in the dim light, but apparently not. I should've worn more makeup.

The man turns around and examines me. He's silent as he finally notices them. His once-angry face turns soft and stoic at once.

"Get out of here," Sunney says calmly, although his fists are still balled as if he's ready for a fight to ensue.

The man, either not wanting to fight or maybe changing his mind at the sight of my bruises, quickly turns around and says, "Fine. Find a new bar, Toni."

He then whimpers on his way to the door as if Sunney has harmed him. Giving us one last look, he heads inside. Sunney and I stare at each other as soon as he's gone. I don't know what to be more ashamed of — the fact someone almost attacked me or the fact he called me a killer in front of this handsome man. Either way, I have to get out of here now.

"I'm sorry about all that. I need to go," I blurt out, looking at my hero probably for the last time, then scurrying down the alleyway.

"Toni, wait up!" I hear him yell behind me and then feel his hand on my shoulder.

Just the touch of him brings me to an immediate halt.

"I don't know what happened, but I'm sorry. You didn't deserve that. Can I walk you home?"

I want to say no, still embarrassed about everything, but I also worry that man could leave the Keelover any minute and spot me. I nod slowly, and we begin to walk. It's silent, and I want to say something . . . anything, but what? Hey, that guy was right. I killed my boyfriend because he was beating me. I stabbed him thirteen times with an old steak knife. It was dehumanizing and haunts me every minute of the day, but I swear I'm a good person. The police tried to keep my name a secret, but some people close to Tom had to know. Word spread eventually.

"About tha—" I begin to say.

"I know. The bartender told me."

"Oh."

"I can't possibly know how you're feeling, but you do have my condolences. It's sick to see how many women suffer from domestic violence."

Not many cases of women killing their assaulter.

I glance over at Sunney for the first time since we started walking. He is looking down at me. He's about six or more inches taller. It's dark and hard to tell, but his expression seems somber and sympathetic. Most people, despite their pity, are freaked out when they learn what I've done. Why wouldn't they be? It isn't every day you meet someone capable of murder, despite the fact their life had been on the line.

"The reason I didn't say any—"

"Stop, stop. You don't need to. We just met. When the time comes, and you're ready to talk, we'll talk."

I feel like my heart might have just blown up in my chest.

"So — you want to see me again?"

"I mean, yeah, what did you expect?"

What a ridiculous question. Why would I expect him to want anything but to run away from this situation as fast as possible? Is he just feeling an extreme amount of empathy for me? I have virtually nothing to offer him. No money, no good family, or a high-paying career. I don't even think I'm nearly as attractive a girl as he can get.

"I dunno, I just feel after everything, you would have run away by now."

"I never shy away from a cute girl — and I don't know, there's just something unexplainably interesting about you. Maybe we can try going on a couple of dates and so on. Then one day, this can be our crazy story," Sunney says, and I feel his hand rest on my lower back.

No matter how old you get, hearing yourself being called cute never gets old. I can't help but wonder if this is some sort of dream. Wealthy, extremely good-looking men don't just act like a woman's fucked-up past is nothing and can be forgotten — especially my fucked-up past. There has to be a catch. I don't want to press my luck, but there has to be something off about this Sunney. It's maybe just a romantic ploy to get laid.

"What's the catch here, Sunney?" I ask.

"Catch?"

"I mean, you are a wealthy, charismatic, good-looking guy. I live in a shitty apartment, work as a fucking receptionist at a dental office, and my last relationship, well—" I say, unable to finish.

"You work at a dental office? That's good to hear; I need a new dentist."

I want to laugh, but instead, I just glare.

"A catch? Hmm, I guess I sometimes forget to brush my teeth at night," he says, shrugging his shoulders.

I can't help but snicker before I give Sunney a light shove.

"Gross! That's my deal breaker," I joke, knowing I need to lighten the tension.

"You could always stick around to get me back on track with my — dental hygiene."

"It might be tough, but I'm up for the task."

At this point, we have made it to my shitty apartment building. I stop in my tracks and turn to Sunney.

"So, you aren't just interested in hooking up? You can be honest."

I'm not twenty years old anymore; I don't want to be led on — is what I really want to say but don't. Sunney seems to see through me anyway.

"As a man seeing this gorgeous woman before me — yes, I am. That's not it, though, no. You have my word; I won't try anything till you want me to."

I purse my lips and reply, "I mean, it would make more sense if you were some Patrick Bateman psychopath at this point."

"I'm not sure if I should feel insulted or happy by that. Insulted you think I'm a serial killer or happy you think I'm as good looking as Christian Bale."

"You're ridiculous, Sunney Jameson!"

"And you're beautiful, Toni — I didn't even catch your last name. Would it make me a serial killer to ask your last name?" he asks, touching my cheeks.

"Possibly, but I'll bite. It's Lovette."

Sunney smiles while still caressing my face.

We stare at each other in silence for a moment, and just when I think Sunney is going to kiss me, he leans over and plants a small peck on my forehead.

Removing his hands from my cheeks, he backs up and says, "Tomorrow here at 7 p.m., dinner?" Blushing, I look down and nod. He winks, turns around, and walking away, yells, "Now, when did Patrick Bateman ever give a girl a kiss on the forehead?"

CHAPTER 4

I expect Sunney to say something once we are on the road again, but he doesn't. He seems more tense than usual. His hands are tightened on the steering wheel, even though, for most of the drive earlier, he had been relaxed with one hand on my knee. Was it because I had talked to Quinn alone for a few minutes? Was he angry because Quinn had insulted Rubico in front of him? Sunney has never been a jealous type, but then again, I've never given him a reason to be jealous. Any guy that found out I was with Sunney immediately backed off. He has a known name and power in our town.

Suddenly, the radio starts to static, and Sunney immediately readjusts it. But the static continues. He punches it and scowls as his nostrils flare. Now there is no doubt he is annoyed and taking it out on the stereo.

"Piece of shit!" Sunney curses.

"What's wrong?"

"You've made friends fast," Sunney sneers.

I look at him dumbfounded.

"Not really. He nearly barged through the door when I was in the bathroom," I calmly respond, hoping to placate him. I do not want to start any sort of argument or, God forbid, fight on the first day of marriage.

"Where does he get off on talking to me that way?"

"How am I supposed to know? I don't know the man," I shrug.

"You were back there for quite a while, Toni. Had to be a bit acquainted. What were you two talking about?"

Sunney is pushing my buttons. It isn't like him to act jealous or even the slightest bit petty. I have spent plenty of time talking to other men that were friends of friends at social events. Never has he acted covetous of me. Neither have I, for the matter. I know Sunney meets many women, great-looking women, in fact, through work or while hanging with one of his many friends. I trust him. But then again, I haven't dealt with the heartache of being with an unfaithful partner. Just a violent one.

"Part of that time, I was trying to ensure I didn't touch anything in that grotesque bathroom. Quinn and I barely even spoke," I explain, tightening my fists, trying my best to remain as calm as possible. I would not lash out at him. I had to remain calm and kind.

"Oh! You're on a first-name basis now?"

I should've taken two swigs of that Crown Royal. I wonder how mad Sunney would get if I pulled it out.

"Sunney, you're being ridiculous. I did nothing wrong!"

"I'm not being ridiculous. You didn't see how he was looking at you," Sunney says, moving his hand to my knee and giving it an almost too-tight squeeze.

"Stop!" I exclaim, instantly moving his hand off.

"I didn't appreciate the way he was looking at you. What man would stand by idly while that happened?"

"He wasn't even looking at me that much." Quinn had barely glanced at me after Sunney appeared.

"He was looking at you like he wanted to fuck you," Sunney says, placing his hand on my knee again.

How one look can say all that is beyond me.

Keeping my face calm, I reply, "Well, if that's the case, I didn't notice. I only notice how you look at me, not other men."

Finally, he smiles, reassuring me that he's done being petty and jealous. We're quiet again as we drive down the last bit of highway to Rubico, and I stare out the window of Sunney's 2003 Red Chevy Silverado. He bought it brand new two years ago; I remember him picking me up on our first date and telling me. Men are weird that way, always so proud of their vehicles, whether it is something brand new and shiny or old and shitty.

I still drive a shitty 1992 Buick LeSabre. I could afford a newer vehicle, but my Buick was the last thing given to me by my father. My sixteenth birthday present. Even then, it was an older model, but I didn't care. I had wanted a car so badly. Anything to get me to my then-boyfriend's house and back. My mom hadn't agreed with the gift at all. She wasn't working at that point and needed the money he had spent on it for more booze and whatever drug she had been taking at that time. It was also one of my last birthdays before the news that completely ruined my family broke out. Remembering my father's grim-looking face in the principal's office that day still brings shivers to my body.

Five minutes pass before we make it near Rubico. It only seems to be twelve square miles in length. However, before we can get closer to the sign, Sunney takes a sharp left turn onto a dirt road. I stare at the town one last time before we disappear into the woods. I feel let down. I wanted to see this town Sunney seems so fond of.

"Are we not going to Rubico?" I ask.

"I don't see any point," Sunney shrugs.

"I wanted to get a look around it. See the hype."

"But I want you all to myself," Sunney says, tracing his fingers higher over my leg.

"Sunney," I protest.

"In a couple of days, we can. For now, I want you all to myself," he says, inching his hand further up my thigh near my groin.

I blush, already feeling my lower body quivering. Just a small touch from Sunney always does the trick.

Sunney keeps his hand inches from my groin for the rest of the drive, rubbing my thigh. Once we get there, I don't want to even get a look around. I want to go straight to the bedroom.

We drive another ten minutes, about three more turns, a less sturdy road with each one. Finally, we end up on a muddy two-track road with weeds and grass growing in the middle. Sunney doesn't let up the speed, either. With every rock we hit, I feel flung into the air. I grab my seatbelt, quickly fasten it, and then grab the handle above the door.

"Don't be scared. I know this road," Sunney assures me, trying to hide a smile at my fear.

"You should slow down a little, at least."

"If I do that, we won't hit the bumps as much, and I can't accidentally move my hand," Sunney says, and like clockwork, we hit another rock in the road as he quickly places his hand over my crotch.

"Sunney," I whisper, resting my head on the seat. At least with my eyes on the baby blue cloudy sky, all I feel are the bumps we're hitting and his hand on me.

I don't look down again until we come to a sudden halt. I am amazed by the view ahead of me. Sunney's cabin, our honeymoon destination, is much more beautiful than I had thought. The picture didn't do it enough justice — it's a two-story cedar-made log cabin.

Marveling at the sight, it takes me a couple of moments to finally take my seatbelt off. Before I can, Sunney swings open the car door. He smiles widely, obviously proud of himself over my reaction. He puts his hand out and I take it, grabbing my purse containing the Crown Royal with my other hand. He pulls me out of the truck effortlessly and leans over to kiss me on the cheek.

"Not too shabby, huh?"

"There is no way you built this all on your own."

"I had some help from a few buddies, but we did it. Like it?"

"I love it."

"Come on! Let's go inside, babe," Sunney says, pulling me forward.

"What about our bags?"

"I'll grab them later. Come on."

The front door looks nearly brand new with its frosted glass and burgundy wood. It has two brass-colored deadbolts along with the lock above the doorknob. *Seems a bit much for a cabin in the middle of nowhere*, I ponder. Sunney takes out a set of two silver keys, unlocks the button lock with one key and the deadbolts with the other, and stuffs them back in his pocket. I want to ask why the extra precaution, but he picks me up before I can. I blush and have an overwhelming feeling I'm the luckiest girl in the world. It's a cliché, I know, but he's the first man in the world who has made me feel this way over five times now.

The first time was when we first met. I was such a mess, but he showed interest in me anyway. The second was our actual first date. He had taken me to one of the nicest restaurants in town and let me order whatever I wanted. Most girls don't think anything of that, but after years of only dating broke men, it was refreshing to be taken out of my comfort zone of fast food and "movie" dates. The third was the first time we had sex. He ravished me for nearly three hours. It felt even better because I had made him wait three months. The fourth was just yesterday at our wedding. The whole day I felt like the luckiest girl in the world, but one moment had me feel extra special — our first dance as man and wife. He had surprised me by playing *Sea of Love* covered by the Honeydrippers — our song.

It is one of my favorite love songs. Sunney hadn't been aware of this as I mostly listened to 90s hit music when he was around or in my car. It was a guilty pleasure, obviously. Some women get all in the mood from listening to Brad Paisley or some other country love song. Before I met Sunney, I used to listen to *Sea of Love*. One of my ex-boyfriends, a science teacher, had always played slow crooner music at his house when we had sex. It was almost like a ritual for him, even though he was the exact opposite of the romantic type. Besides, having encountered fucked-up versions of how love and sex work in the real world, the beautiful melody of this song is forever ingrained in my head.

Sunney, a big smile plastered on his face, kicks the door open. I can't help but squeal a little. He carries me into the cabin. Hickory hardwood flooring covers the open living room and kitchen. The walls are a freshly painted burgundy color, matching the door. I've always loved the shade red, whether light or dark.

In the living room, the sofa and loveseat are a matching chocolate color with turquoise-colored throw pillows. A glass coffee table is centered from the couch, set with a burgundy tablecloth. There is a matching traditional beige blended-colored rug underneath the couch set, coffee table, and widescreen TV as well as a black wood stove and chimney at the far-left end of the living room.

I drop my purse by the front door, hoping I don't crack the bottle as it is the only alcohol I have brought with me on this trip. Sunney wanted our honeymoon to be mostly dry, as he had noticed my drinking problem when we first started dating. I wasn't a fan of him telling me that, but as my adoring husband is paying for our honeymoon, I have obliged to the best of his knowledge. I snuck in the Crown Royal just in case.

We walk through the living room, and I barely get a peek at the kitchen, which has a double-door fridge, stove, dishwasher, sink, and even a fancy-looking countertop/table in the middle. Beyond that, a glass sliding door leading out to a porch frames a beautiful setting sun. This day has been a drag, but now more than ever, I don't want it to end.

"Hey, let's go out there," I say, pointing outside.

Sunney chuckles, kissing my neck lightly. He says, "There will be plenty of sunsets we can watch. Right now, you are all mine."

"You're done being jealous?"

"I was just doing that to work you up, babe. Get your blood pumping."

I roll my eyes. We walk across a long hallway, passing a large, I'm guessing, master bathroom, closet, and spare bedroom. We turn to a set of stairs, and as he walks up, I hold tightly onto Sunney as if he might drop me, even though I know he wouldn't dream of doing such a thing. Once we are upstairs, there are only two rooms — one a smaller bathroom and the other the master bedroom. *Our room.* The bed is a king cedar canopy with a burgundy comforter. A mix of red and black rose petals shaped into a heart has been artfully arranged on the cover. Sunney walks to the bed and gently sets me down on it. He moves over to a nightstand and, opening the drawer, starts taking out candles.

"How are the roses so fresh when you haven't been here for some time?"

"I had a buddy come down and set it up. Anything for my wife."

"Sunney," I gush.

"Shhh," he says as he makes his way to a tall cedar dresser with a large, attached mirror. He places the candles on it and starts lighting them up.

I can't place the exact reason, but brown — nice or cheap-looking — dressers always remind me of the one my parents had in their bedroom. I remember how cluttered it used to get with all the used glasses, liquor bottles, and my mother's clothing and jewelry lying on top. Then one day, when I was young, they got rid of it for no reason.

Returning to the nightstand, he takes out a mini remote.

"I placed speakers everywhere so we can always play our favorite music," Sunney explains, pressing a button. *Can't Take My Eyes Off You* by Frankie Valli plays from a black speaker in a corner.

"Baby, do I get a proper look around the cabin?" I ask.

"Soon enough. You don't get to wear that sexy little dress around me all day and expect me not to want it ripped off when we get here."

I laugh, and before I know it, Sunney jumps on the bed and kisses me. His hands find my waist as he gently pushes me to lie down. He kisses and lightly nibbles on my neck — my absolute biggest turn-on, and he knows it. Just as I feel my body begin to really heat up, he jumps off me and pulls me to stand up. As if on cue, *Sea of Love* begins to play from the speaker.

"Finally, some proper alone time to really dance to our song," he whispers.

Sunney places his hands on my lower back and slow dances with me — the same way we danced last night at our wedding, except now we are all alone and not in front of a big crowd. I place my hands over the back of his neck and rest my head on the soft, navy-blue button-up I bought for him last month. This is the first time I have seen him wear it, so it's still freshly pressed and unwrinkled. Although soft, I'd much rather it off and my hands on his slightly hairy chest.

We continue to dance, hardly moving at all. I can feel my heartbeat increase pace, and I'm a little embarrassed I still get nervous around him. I still fear he'll realize he could be married to some model with a tiny athletic frame. It's not that I'm not petite, but I certainly am no model. I don't count calories and don't have orthorexia. I had gotten into the habit of counting my calories when we first started dating when meeting all his buddies' beautiful tiny wives, but as the love grew, I became more comfortable in my body.

"I still don't know why you chose to marry me," I whisper.

"Because I love you, silly."

"I was such a mess when we met. You were perfect."

"No one is perfect. Something about you caught my eye. I've told you this. You're the one, Toni Marie Lovette," Sunney says, kissing my neck softly.

"Toni Jameson. I will never be Lovette again," I correct him.

"You got that right."

Sunney and I slow dance for the rest of the song. When it fades out to another, he grabs the bottom of my dress and slips it over my head. He then eyes my body like it's the first time he's seeing me half-naked. I fold my hands behind my back to reach my mega push-up scarlet-colored bra and unclip it. It was bought by Sunney and loved by me, no matter how much it stuffs my small breasts up uncomfortably. He places his hands over the straps and drops it to the floor.

He guides me back to the bed and kisses my neck again. His soft lips and his hand on my thigh cause my body to heat up like it had in the car. After last night's hours of sex, I thought my body might need a break from this insatiable man, but I was wrong. I lust for his dick and mouth so much now. Like a light switch, my sore vagina is wet and ready.

"I want you every day. This whole month," I say, feeling my body quiver with just the thought of being alone with him the next few weeks.

"Yes, ma'am."

CHAPTER 5

Three hours later, we are finally out on the deck. The sunset has long since gone and been replaced by the dark sky, stars, and a half-moon. I am wearing a black satin robe that Sunney gifted me last night. I had squealed excitedly because I had never owned an expensive robe. I told him it would be my daily outfit throughout this trip. Sunney had replied that as long as I kept the belt loose, he was okay with that. A deal I had readily agreed to.

I promise myself, *I will love this sight, night or day, sunrise or sunset.* I mean, as long as Sunney is by my side. I stare at him for a full minute — his long, dirty blonde hair ruffled up from me grabbing and pulling at it. He is only wearing gym shorts (my request) because I can never get enough of his chiseled body. He rocks us back and forth on a white double swing set on the side of the back porch — another gift for us.

"What's on the agenda for tomorrow?" I ask, yawning.

"Hmm, pancakes with strawberries for breakfast. For lunch, I'll have you; for dinner, we'll have rib-eye with homemade mashed potatoes; and for dessert, you'll have me," Sunney says, winking.

"I didn't ask for a menu," I reply, laughing.

"Why can't we just bask in each other's love on the first official day of our honeymoon?" Sunney asks, already knowing I'm a bit antsy to see Rubico.

He's right; we should spend the first couple of days basking in each other. I want to learn more things about Sunney and explore this haven of his. I'll save Rubico for another time. As an answer, I simply lean over and kiss his cheek.

"Okay, but you better cook my steak how I like it."

"Roger that."

"You can also answer some questions about yourself I am curious about."

Despite looking a tad bit uneasy, Sunney nods.

One of Sunney's flaws is that he has always been short and sweet with his past. He believes the past is the past and should stay that way. The one thing he did say was that he had only had two girlfriends before me, and none had fit into his future. *Why?* I wondered, but never really got an answer.

Suddenly, my mind remembers the events of the day. *Andrea and Sunney forever.* I widen my eyes, wondering how I had forgotten this. The whole Quinn thing has thrown me for a loop. I want to question Sunney, but I can't, not now. It'll come off wrong. I must wait. It might be weird to question him about his ex-girlfriends, specifically their names.

"For the record, it's almost a deal breaker that you like your steak well done, psycho," he answers, obviously not noticing the distant look in my eyes.

"It's delicious, and I don't like the sight of blood," I protest. We go through this every time he cooks steak for me, which has frankly been a lot.

Ever since Tom, any blood, even on a dead cooked carcass, reminds me of his body on our dirty linoleum floor. His eyes staring holes into mine even though he was long dead. Dead and gone, unable to hurt me any longer.

"Ready to get some sleep?" Sunney asks, interrupting my thoughts.

Sunney and I get up and head back to the bedroom. His hand is on my ass the whole time, but my mind is elsewhere.

I'm angry with myself for not only letting my mind go to Tom, especially on my honeymoon when I'm supposed to be happy, but also forgetting about those damn words on the bathroom wall.

When we return to bed, the silk sheets seem to envelop my body completely. I fall asleep with Sunney spooning me, his hand over my bare breast and my mind wondering who this Andrea is and if she had once lain with my husband in this same spot.

CHAPTER 6

It's only eight in the morning, and the sun is shining brightly over a cloudless sky on Sunney's and my first official day of honeymooning at the cabin. Apart from a few rainy nights, the weather is expected to be warm the whole time we're here. I couldn't be happier with that. I love rain and the sun. New Hampshire is known for having hot summer months and small bouts of wet weather, especially in August.

I talked Sunney into letting me go for a little jog this morning. I informed him I'll need to work off all the food he's planning to cook me this month. He seemed mostly concerned with me being in these woods alone because I "wasn't familiar with them". New Hampshire doesn't exactly have the scariest wild animals, I decided. I promised him I'd only be gone thirty minutes at the most. I need the fresh air and alone time. I don't want to talk to Sunney about it, but I rather enjoy having my alone time now and again. Before we met, I had spent too much time drinking at the bar, afraid of being alone, but now that I barely even think of the night's events with Tom, I once again love my own company. To keep Tom out of my head, I need to occupy it doing other things like reading, watching TV, or going for a run. Every day it seems to get easier and easier to expel those bad memories.

Although I can make a home of Sunney's beautiful new cabin, I also need time to think how I might ask about Andrea, if she even existed. It doesn't bother me that Sunney has ex-girlfriends, but to lie about having them at the cabin is another thing. What if he brought all his girlfriends to this cabin? Or worse, was it was some fuck shack where he brought women in general?

Sunney always denies being a womanizer even though he has the physique, flawless facial features, and charming personality to be one. I hear the way he talks not just to girls, but everyone. He can have any girl wrapped around his finger, including me. It was the very reason I decided to make him wait three months before we had sex. After our first date, I was already so enamored with him. I didn't want it to be easy, and it was one of the best decisions I ever made. I fell in love with his personality first.

Although unable to do much real running due to the uneven road and mud, it takes me only eight minutes before I make it to the nearest second turn. I take a breath and look down, wondering where it goes. Sunney told me no one lives remotely near us. We are as alone as it gets, he said. It's a bit creepy, and I wonder how Sunney could stand to be so isolated out here. Anyone could just show up and pull a home invasion-type shit-show.

Just as I am about to turn around and return to the cabin, I hear a vehicle down the lonely road. I step back off the path, my body shivering. I want to hide in the trees, but it's too late. An old-fashioned red Jeep Wrangler is in the distance, barreling down the road at fast speed. It's probably just some hiker or local.

I begin to casually walk on the road again. There's no need to just stand and stare like some weirdo, after all. As the jeep nears, I expect it to maintain the same speed, but, to my surprise, it slows down. *It's just because they're nearing a turn*, I remind myself. With my back turned and pace fast, I hope they will be gone the other way soon.

Once they approach the turn that doesn't even have a stop sign, I hear the engine. It's loud and needs to be replaced soon. I sneak a peek behind me when I don't hear it driving down the road to Rubico. The jeep has stopped at the crossroads. It's covered in mud, so I can't make out who's in the vehicle. I get chills even though it's hot and humid out. This would be the perfect place to hide a dead body.

For once, I wish I had a cellphone, not that the damn thing would have service out here anyway. Sunney brought his Nokia with him, but I didn't often bother with carrying one myself; too expensive and a pain to keep track of. While Tom and I were together, I had a Motorola to call him from when I was at work or he was out. I thought he was always hiding something.

The jeep turns toward the road I'm on. That's not right, though. There's no reason someone would want to drive this way; it's a dead end to Sunney's cabin. I quickly look forward and start jogging, my body shaking. I know if anything remotely bad were to occur, at least Sunney knows I'm due to be back in twenty minutes. The jeep slowly creeps forward but stops completely when it's at my side. *Wouldn't It Be Nice* by The Beach Boys blares through the radio. Seconds pass, and the driver turns the engine off, along with the music.

I look at the muddy passenger door window as it slowly rolls down. Once it's down, my fear vanishes into thin air as soon as I recognize who is in the jeep.

"Well, isn't that a familiar face!" Quinn Robins exclaims.

I knew I'd see him again, just not a day later. Despite his smile being so white and welcoming, I can't help but glare at him, angry.

"You scared the bejesus out of me!" I yell.

"Who is bejesus, and why was he in you?" Quinn says, cackling. His laugh is annoying and loud, but cute.

I cross my arms and ask, "What, are you stalking me?"

He lets out another cackle and says, "No, I live down the road. Are you my neighbor?"

"I guess. Sunney owns the cabin down the street."

"I was here before your pretty boy husband and you, so technically, it's you stalking me."

"Sunney has had a cabin here for years," I quickly shoot back.

"Well, shit, in that case, I'm stalking your husband, and you're stalking me. Stalker much?"

I shake my head and say, "Sunney told me no one else was living nearby."

"Well, *Sunney* is mistaken. I just moved here."

"Where's your place at?"

"Just down the road, a little over a mile from you. But I bet you already knew that, Mrs. Stalker."

"How do you know you're a mile from us?" I ask, ignoring Quinn's comment.

"I may have accidentally, uh — driven down your husband's road when I arrived here for the first time. Beautiful place, way better than my dump," Quinn explains with a big grin.

"You live in a dump? That's a shocker!" I mutter, but Quinn hears me and chuckles.

"I'm guessing that cabin is some vacation home. How long are y'all out here for?"

"Just a month. We're on our honeymoon."

Quinn raises his eyebrows and says, "How'd he talk you into that? Most women want to honeymoon on paradise islands and shit."

Quinn is right. That is where I had always pictured my honeymoon. But it wasn't like we wouldn't vacation another time. We had our whole lives to go on vacation. I can't help but wonder if Quinn has ever been married. He is charming, good-looking, and seemingly in his early thirties. Most men that aren't married by their thirties always have some sort of commitment issue. I stop myself from questioning him on this. *He's just a stranger,* I reason.

"I'm perfectly fine with being here," I reply simply.

"Why are you running out here by your lonesome? I'm surprised your husband didn't accompany you. He seems like the type of man who likes to run marathons or triathlons."

He is trying to insult Sunney; I can tell by his smirk and tone.

"You were staring at his body long enough to make that assumption, huh?"

"It isn't exactly hard to catch."

"If you're trying to insult him, you are failing terribly."

"Who said I was trying to insult him?"

"Just came off that way with that smirk and condescending tone of yours."

Ignoring my quip, Quinn smirks again. We're silent for a couple of moments, and a part of me knows I should just head on my way, but another part wants to stay; to stay and continue being rude to Quinn. I can't quite explain it, but I feel more comfortable being mean to him than I do with Sunney. With Sunney, I always want to be sweet and kind. It's almost like back when I was in high school and role-played as an innocent virgin with my first boyfriend (even though I wasn't a virgin anymore). It can be exhausting to pretend to be pleasant and softhearted all the time. With Quinn, although I barely know him, I feel comfortable being my normal spiteful self. I don't care if he knows I am not some lovely innocent woman, almost like how I became with Tom, even if that relationship turned violent beyond reason.

"What do you think of cute, small Rubico?" Quinn says, stepping out of his jeep.

What if he knows I want to stay and talk to him? That must be why he's getting out. Why is he resting his forearms against the hood of his jeep while staring me up and down? my mind races. Today he's wearing a dirty, very tight white cotton T-shirt. It exposes the top of his chest and the large biceps that he's flexing.

Realizing he can see me looking him up and down, I blush, embarrassed. I'm no better than him.

I look down and say, "Haven't been yet."

"Your husband sure seemed keen on the town. I mean, how couldn't he love all its cute little abandoned houses and pothole-ridden roads? I'm surprised he hasn't jumped at the chance of showing it to you."

I've had enough of that sarcastic tone.

"You know, if this town is so small and shitty, why did you even move here?"

"You really are good at reading sarcasm. I don't know; I just wanted to escape into the wild again. Like in my twenties when I was just a young'un like you."

"Again?"

"Yeah, back in my early twenties, you know? I'm sure Sunney was the same way."

More sarcasm. Sunney isn't the complete bore Quinn is making him out to be. I wonder why he is trying so hard to be such an alpha male. Sure, Sunney spent most of his early twenties building his career by attending business school. However, that didn't mean he was a bore. He played rugby and spent his spring breaks and summers traveling to other countries. He could have easily spent his vacations in country clubs instead.

"I'm sorry, how old are you? Forty?"

Quinn is not insulted by my question. He just laughs.

"Thirty-two."

"Sorry, I misjudged. You just have a persona that makes it seem as if you've lived forty years since you're so knowing."

"Oh, it does seem like I've been alive that long. How old are you, missus? Wait! Don't tell me. Twenty, twenty-one perhaps?"

I walk over to the opposite side of the jeep that Quinn still leans against. As he does, I rest my forearms against the jeep, imitating him. I notice his muscles are now starting to shake from the constant flexing. He didn't need to flex to still appear muscular.

While leaning against the dirty jeep, I peek into the windshield, which is so dirty that I can barely see through it. However, I catch a bottle of Jack resting on the passenger seat. It's more than half empty, and I can't help but wonder if Quinn is drunk right now. It's still early morning, so maybe he's a bit of an alcoholic. That must be why we get along so well. He mentioned that he would need a couple of beers before talking about his personal life.

Feeling his eyes on me, I quickly look back up at him. I want to ask if he's been drinking and driving, but I stop myself. I barely know this man, so it's not any of my business.

"Do I look that young to you?" I ask, pursing my lips.

"You got a young Meg Foster vibe going on. What can I say?"

I widen my eyes, unsure if he's kidding or not.

"I do not," I disagree.

"Have you ever seen *Ticket to Heaven*? It was way before your time, I guess."

I clench my fists and say, "I was born in '80. I'm twenty-four, smart ass."

"You look great for your age; I didn't guess you were a day over twenty-one."

I stare, trying not to smile. I cannot let Quinn think I'm flattered by his words.

"Tell me about yourself."

"Why?" I ask, a little uneasy now. *Why would he care?*

It isn't every day some man who you barely know, who also knows there is no chance of getting you into bed, gives a shit about you. Quinn's kind eyes and tall demeanor draw me in. I can't deny that. Hell, maybe he's just lonely and wants a friend. I don't have any male friends. Tom and I started dating when I was only nineteen, and we were too jealous to let each other be friends with the opposite sex. With Sunney, I directed my full attention and time to him. I lost touch with the few female friends I had. Our wedding was mostly attended by Sunney's large and happy family and a few messed up ones from mine. Pathetically enough, I had invited work colleagues to be my bridesmaids.

"We're neighbors. Why not?" Quinn asks.

"It's just a little weird."

"Well, if you don't tell me, I'll just take a gander at you myself."

I squint my eyes, unsure if he's joking or serious. This man has no idea who I am as a person — or the messed-up shit I've witnessed.

"Good luck with that."

"Thank you, but I don't really need any luck. You're a born New Hampshire girl, maybe even Maine. I can tell by your southern accent or lack thereof. You're from a small town. You were not born wealthy, but you sure did marry wealthy. That one is a given. You weren't the popular girl in high school because you avoided playing sports or whored around, but that doesn't mean you weren't pretty. You were; you just didn't know it and didn't find out until years after high school. But, by then, you were trapped in a toxic relationship. You wanted to go to college, but your relationship hindered you from that too, and now you feel it's too late. By the way, you froze seeing the Jack in my jeep. You're either frightened by the idea of someone drinking and driving or a recovering alcoholic. I will go with the latter as you don't seem boring or prudish. That and a prude would have called me out on my reckless behavior. Just getting warmed up here. How well am I doing so far?"

I can't even answer. I've never felt so insulted or creeped out in my life. Quinn has been spot on, the bastard. He grins at my now uncomfortable face. *How the fuck could he get that from just two meetings with me? Was he some Hannibal Lecter fuck? Did I need to tell him to point that high-powered perception at himself, or would that be corny?* Glass didn't keep us apart here, and Quinn wasn't a genius cannibalistic convicted serial killer. Just some creep that read me easily.

"What the hell is wrong with you?" is all I manage to ask.

Quinn scoffs, "I'll take that as a yes."

"You're something else; you know that? I have to go." I feel embarrassed and fully over the conversation.

Without waiting for a goodbye, I turn back toward the road leading to Sunney's cabin and start jogging again. However, before I make it past the end of the jeep, a hand grabs me by my shoulder. I stop and turn around, only to come face-to-Quinn's chest. Standing only a foot away, I smell his cologne. It's strong and smells of rosewood. A cheaper and more bitter choice than Sunney's, but I can't help but want another whiff. Now this close with my head inches away from his chest, I notice hair poking out. It reminds me of the one hairy man I'd dated. I gulp, erasing all bad thoughts in my mind, and stare up at Quinn's hazel eyes, looking down at me intently.

"Sorry, I didn't mean to offend you. It was just a joke," he says softly, and I immediately get a whiff of his breath, which smells exactly like Jack.

I shouldn't have let him see I'm upset. Just goes to show how spot on he is, even more so. It couldn't have been a joke; this man can read people. His keen judgment is the exact opposite of mine.

Shrugging his hand off my shoulder, I casually respond, "Don't do that."

"Don't do what?"

"Lie to me. You weren't joking. What was all that about?" I say, finally backing up, knowing if I stay too close, I'll want to ask for a sip of that Jack.

Quinn looks down at the ground, biting his lip like he's ashamed of the truth.

"I'm not exactly the smartest man in the world, but as far back as I can remember, I've always been able to read people."

"What do you mean? Like Hannibal Lecter?"

Quinn shrugs. "In a sense, yeah, except the actual cannibal part. It's always been easy for me to pick up quickly on people's behaviors — how they act, walk, or talk."

"Okay, what about my body language told you I was in a toxic relationship?"

"I caught that yesterday — the way you acted when Sunney approached us. You changed, stiffened. It's almost like you are used to changing who you are when your partner comes around. Some women can be happy and smiling while in conversation one minute, and then the next, they have no emotions."

"Sunney isn't toxic. He treats me perfectly," I say, insulted.

"I didn't say he was. You're accustomed to acting like that from a previous relationship."

How the fuck is he even getting all this? I have never met someone capable of such perception from the simple actions of people. He's pretty spot on, except he didn't pick off the fact I act a certain way toward Sunney so as not to expose my real self. I don't plan to stay around for Quinn to discover the part of me that I've carefully hidden.

"I should be getting back."

"If it means anything, I can tell you're a really good person."

Maybe his perception isn't all that great.

"Thanks, you too."

"You said no lying."

"I wasn't lying. You seem to have some hidden shell of goodness in you."

"Can I expect you to be here again tomorrow morning?"

"What? In this exact spot?"

Quinn smirks and, shaking his head, says, "I mean running, smart ass."

I want to say no because I hadn't planned on doing much running on my honeymoon. This had just been a spur-of-the-moment sort of thing.

"Because hell, maybe you could teach me a thing or two. I need the exercise."

Without thinking twice, I nod. "Sure, I guess you can tag along. Just try to keep up."

"Yes, ma'am," Quinn says, his usual smirk plastered on his face.

I mock his smile by mimicking it, and with one last look in those hazel eyes, I turn around and run back toward the cabin. Once again, like our first meeting, I can feel his eyes watching me as I leave. When I am out of view, I finally hear his jeep roar and drive off.

CHAPTER 7

Why had I said yes? It's too late not to show up now; that would make me a liar. It's not that Quinn doesn't deserve it. Deep down, I want to judge him as accurately as he analyzed me. Let's see how he likes being at the receiving end. Obviously, he is an alcoholic or going through tough shit to drink Jack at eight in the morning. The fact he just moved here and said it required some beers to talk about it is another clue that confirms these assumptions. *Fuck running! Just share some drinks with him.* My inner thoughts prod at me, and I quickly shake them away. *Like Sunney would want his wife drinking with a stranger.*

Even before I open the front door, I smell pancakes. I imagine Sunney standing there without a shirt, just boxers (the navy-blue ones he had been wearing when I left) and his dirty blonde hair messy. Once inside, I hear the faint tune of some music playing upstairs, but not clear enough to make it out. The living room and kitchen are empty, but as I approach the silver granite countertop, I see two plates on it. Both have two pancakes, over-easy eggs, and two slices of bacon. A tube of butter is out with a knife stuck in it. Just looking at it, I want to grab a fork to dig in. I stop myself somehow, my conscience telling me I should find Sunney first.

I head upstairs, walk down the hallway, and hear the music coming from the bathroom. The door is open, and the water from the shower is running. I lightly knock at the door, but the music is too loud, I'm sure, for Sunney to hear. Getting no response from the other side, I walk in slowly and immediately hear a loud grunting noise and see a shadow on the cream-colored curtains.

"Sunney?" I ask and slowly open the curtain.

Standing there, his back to me, very close to the corner, is Sunney with one hand on the beige porcelain shower wall and the other very vigorously moving up and down below his waist. He's masturbating. I'm too shocked to say anything, but Sunney notices my shadow before I can get out of the bathroom and turns around.

I try to play it off and laugh. "What are you doi—"

Before I can finish, Sunney yells, "Get out!"

"What?"

"Get out!" Sunney repeats, grabbing the curtain and closing it in my face.

In shock and unable to grasp what's happening, I depart from the bathroom. Just as I turn my back for a second, the door slams shut.

I slowly walk across the hallway to the bedroom, stepping on the rose petals from last night that haven't been picked up yet. The blankets and sheets are in disarray. I want to sit down, but I start making the messy bed instead. It's an old habit to keep my hands busy when bad or unusual things happen. This was not necessarily a "bad thing," but Sunney has never raised his voice like that at me. I hadn't even heard his voice get that high before.

As I pull the sheets up, I remember all the bad things that have happened to me, causing me to develop the habit of making a messy bed. The first was when I was only ten. My dad had yelled at me for spilling apple juice on the new living room carpet when he had specifically told me to keep drinks in the kitchen. I had pouted and run to my room.

For some reason, fixing my pink Cinderella blankets to go unevenly over my pillow had calmed me. I had done it several more times, getting in trouble as a youth, but the second major instance when I made a bed, it wasn't mine. It was my science teacher boyfriend's shitty double bed right after he had dumped me. I had never had my heart broken until that point, so the feeling had urged me to make the bed even as he screamed at me to get out. The third and most recent was after I stabbed Tom to death to stop him from choking me. As blood oozed from my broken nose, I made the bed on which we had slept together many times.

I just finish pulling the soft silk sheet over the pillows when Sunney rushes into the room. He has a towel over his waist. I try not to make eye contact with him and continue what I'm doing. I don't know what I'm angrier about. The fact he shouted at me for the first time or that he felt the need to masturbate on our honeymoon.

"Toni, baby, I'm so sorry I yelled at you," Sunney says, his voice modulated. He always manages to sound calm and sweet right after an argument. This time, however, it isn't me being petty or angry about something ridiculous.

I tightly close my eyes, knowing I might lose my cool if I look him in the face. I might lose control, and I don't want Sunney to witness that. I continue with the burgundy comforter, moving to the end of the bed to grab it. As I do so, I feel Sunney's eyes watching me.

"Babe, can you stop that for a second?" he asks, following behind me.

I don't stop at first, but then I feel Sunney's large hands over my waist. I instantly freeze and get shivers all over my body. *Damnit.*

"Why–why did you do that?" I ask, my voice low and a bit shrill.

"I–I can explain. I had just finished making breakfast, and I started thinking about you while waiting. Then before I knew it, I was turned on and needed a release, I guess." It was the same modulated tone. It wouldn't work for me.

"I don't care about that. I'm upset because you yelled at me for no reason."

There's a moment of silence, and then Sunney's hands tighten on my waist, pinching me a bit before moving off. I turn around, and his arms are crossed now.

"Toni, I said I was sorry. I'm sorry; I just prefer privacy and not being barged in on." His voice still has the same damn calm tone except with a hint of sternness.

"I said your name. The music was just loud," I counter.

"And listening to music while showering is wrong?"

I'm silent momentarily because I'm unsure how to communicate my hurt. I'm rusty at quick-witted ridiculous arguments. I feel my heart rate accelerating as the moments pass. Tom and I always had foolish arguments, and I was good at throwing fuel into the fire. Of course, toward the end, those incidents quickly escalated from simply who ate my food in the fridge to punching and pushing.

"Screaming at me for not knocking is okay, then?"

"I was hardly screaming. Don't you think you're being a bit melodramatic?"

"I don't know if you know this, but in the year we've been together, I have not heard your voice get that high even once. I think I know what I'm talking about."

Sunney chuckles, "It's *my* voice, so *I* think I know what I'm talking about."

Once again, I'm ready to argue more, but I can't help but look down at a large object below me, lingering around Sunney's waist. There's a bulge. He has an erection. I instantly place my hand over my mouth to cover it. Noticing me looking, Sunney smirks.

"What is wrong with you?" my muffled voice says, leaving my hand over my mouth because I want to laugh now.

How is he still turned on while we argue?

He snorts, "Why do you say that?"

His damn, white-toothed smile always has me smoldering. Somehow this man can make me angry, turned on, and laugh all at once. I feel less angry as the seconds pass, and my heart rate goes down. Besides the whole yelling part, it is a little hot — the fact that he had felt the urge to do that because of me.

"We're arguing. Why are you hard?" I ask, finally taking my hand off my mouth.

Amused by my question, Sunney shrugs. "It's not like I got to finish."

I lightly shove him. "You're a pig."

"I shouldn't have started without you."

I shake my head, all anger gone. Tom never had this effect on me. If he made me angry, I stayed that way all day or possibly for a week. He, however, was nowhere near as charming or had as beautiful a smile as Sunney. Also, when we argued, he had most of his clothes on, so I wasn't distracted by his body, unlike Sunney, at this moment.

"Why did you? I mean, we're on our honeymoon. Who does that? And why the shower?"

"Got pancake batter all over me cooking us breakfast, and the rest, well, the rest is history."

I know instinctively that his reply nowhere near answers my question as to why he was masturbating. Maybe it's just a hormone thing. I have never been on a honeymoon, so I don't know if other men do it on theirs. I'm right; he is a pig, and right now, that's sort of hot.

"Anyway, breakfast is getting cold, so we should probably eat," he says, leaning in and kissing my forehead.

"Let's finish what you started first," I say, looking down again and biting my lip.

"Yes, ma'am," Sunney answers, and, for a moment, I remember Quinn saying that to me less than twenty minutes ago. The way his lips had looked and how his breath had reeked of Jack almost made me think of how they would taste on mine.

Before my mind can wander to the dark side, I feel Sunney's big soft hands over my upper hips, resting on the sweaty fabric of my tank top. I quickly shake free of my immoral thoughts and get down on my knees, skipping a kiss with Sunney so I don't have to wonder what Quinn's would taste like instead.

CHAPTER 8

Quinn Robins

As Quinn Robins walks down the freshly mopped (but no wet floor sign anywhere) tile floor in Rubico in one of the two grocery stores, he ponders on whether he has it to live in this hillbilly town. No stranger to small towns; but this place seems too tiny. People constantly looking, wondering who the new, large, strange man is. Nearly every person, young or old, veers to stare at him everywhere he goes, especially here. But that might be because he is wearing muddy boots and leaving footprints all over the floor. All the Jack while cruising this morning has blurred out any remorse for being a dick.

Quinn has worked hard his whole life not to end up in a place like this. He spent the better years of his life working in the oil fields like his father, saving for the day he met a woman and wanted to settle down. That had always been the plan, and practically all had worked out until six months ago. Now, that blissful illusion is so long gone that it might as well be on another planet. He doesn't have a girlfriend or a wife to settle down with. Not anymore. And it is all his doing.

With a pound of burger, buns, and ketchup in his hands, he has everything he needs for dinner. He knows he could grab more, at least a week's worth of food, but his mind — the part that feels lonely — doesn't want to do that. It is the part where, with every sober second, he can't escape his thoughts, which endlessly repeat all the wrongs he's done. So even if it is just a trip to the rundown local grocery store while nursing a mid-day buzz, it is enough for him not to completely lose his mind.

A couple around his age are ahead of him in the check-out line, buying spinach, chicken, and a bunch of low-calorie frozen meals. Quinn can't help but feel a bit judgmental of them. Neither have wedding bands, but it seems they've been dating for a while. Both of them are heavy set (love weight), buying all that healthy food they won't eat. He already knows nearly everything about these two. They've not been married yet because this man most likely isn't completely in a relationship. He is still waiting for his soulmate to come along. Quinn can tell this by the way he casts glances at the cash register girl's tits, and every time his girlfriend runs her hand by his, urging him to hold it, he places it in his pocket instead.

"Forty dollars and twenty-four cents, please," the girl says, perking up her chest a bit for more attention from the man who leaves his hands in his pockets, indicating it is the woman's turn to pay.

They are obviously the type of couple that takes turns in their transactions, such as dinner dates or gas. So, the relationship isn't tightly bound by undying love. Quinn hasn't been a wealthy man his whole life, but he always tried to pay for every date he went on. Some girlfriends fed on that, but some insisted on paying occasionally. The ones that are like that are keepers. It meant they were independent, and Quinn found that sexy. However, despite his principles, he can't keep his mind off a woman that is the exact opposite of independent.

The girlfriend reluctantly reaches into her small purse and starts scavenging through it, pulling out a couple of fives, a debit card, and the exact change. Seemingly embarrassed, she peers up at Quinn, who casts his eyes down immediately.

Not one to care if he muddies a freshly mopped floor, he hates watching people's embarrassment. He judges the dick of a boyfriend more than the woman.

"Put the cash toward it, then run the card for the remainder, please," she implores, and the cash register girl nods, looking like she wants to mutter.

Once the couple is gone, Quinn looks up and puts his food on the conveyor belt as it inches forward.

The cash register girl smiles, looking Quinn up and down, and says, "Hello, sir. How is your day?"

Small towns have a thing for women going gaga over new men. By the look of this attention-seeking girl, he can tell she's excited about a possible new dick to sit on. Quinn could take the bait, especially his more confident, half-drunk self. It has been over three months since he's gotten laid, and this gal is decent looking enough. She has smooth dirty blonde hair that lands just below her chest, with bangs above her eyes. Glancing at her small but perky breasts, Quinn understands why the last man had looked. Her pink V-neck blouse is tucked into her jeans so they poke out more. Her name tape on the right side of her shirt reads Heather. She is begging for attentive eyes, and Quinn will oblige.

"Good," Quinn says, barely meeting her eyes and keeping a straight face.

He can't be too nice of a guy for a woman like her. Women such as these expect him to take them on plenty of dates before even getting a blowjob. It's not that Quinn doesn't like treating girls well. He just knows this girl (and most, for that matter) wants an asshole and is nowhere near ready to settle down, even though, after every failed relationship, they sure did like to complain and sulk about being single.

"Find everything okay today?" she asks, slowly checking his items, obviously wanting him to stay as long as possible.

"Uh-huh," he says, smirking, ensuring not to show his teeth because they aren't close to his best quality.

"I don't think I've seen you before."

"What, in this exact spot?" he asks sarcastically.

The girl instantly laughs out loud, not at all annoyed by his smartass remark. He remembers the beautiful woman who had used that line on him this morning. *Toni.* He had found it quite corny but funny at the same time. Women, in his experience, weren't exactly the funniest people. He hadn't expected Toni to be at first. She had come off a tad bitchy and serious. But when not on edge so much, she was actually quite goofy and cute. Crazy how the difference seemed to be her husband being around versus him not being around. Toni seemed so easily readable, but today she had surprised him with how differently she acted, especially by agreeing to go running with him.

Although coming off as easily readable the first time they had crossed paths, Quinn still could not stop thinking about her — something about that content but dejected look in her big doe-like, ice-blue eyes. That sexy dress would make anyone believe she had a massive amount of self-confidence, but her poor posture said otherwise. Quinn could read she was putting up a front to impress her stuck-up husband. He must've been her hero from some past trauma. Upon meeting her, Quinn strongly liked her, but he also knew he should stay away, as the last woman he had liked had ended up in the morgue.

"No, silly. In town," Heather says, faking a giggle.

"I just moved here about two weeks ago. Have only been in town a couple of times now, trying to fix my place up to living quality." In reality, he has been to the bar buying Jack and driving shit-faced around town afterward.

"You live out of town then?"

People in small towns are so invasive.

"Yeah, the dirt road four miles out of town near the old gas station."

The girl's eyes light up, and she asks, "The road that leads to Sunney Jameson's cabin?"

Quinn immediately recognizes that ridiculous name. Toni's stuck-up husband. He had acted so high and mighty the one time they met. He looked as soft as his hand-shake, completely readable within the first minute. He was unquestionably a trust fund baby sailing off his parents' successes in life. The way he had eyed Quinn, his gelled-back shiny blond hair, and Calvin Klein labeled clothing promptly gave him away as some pussy businessman.

Then that goddamn pristine cabin you couldn't even see unless directed to it. Quinn has never been one for not taking great care of his home and things, but that place is straight out of a goddamn HGTV show. He can tell it was blueprinted, designed, and built from the owner's mind, which costs a lot of money. Most people who build cabins, such as him, place them on the lake or some large mountain to be shown off and have a great view. Sunney's cabin, on the other hand, is surrounded by trees — the only puzzling thing about him. Why would he not boast that he owns such a high-quality place?

Quinn wants to lie to her; afraid she would tell him they were neighbors if Sunney and her were close friends. He hadn't shared that information with Sunney. He wonders what Toni would think of her husband being friends with some hot, barely-of-age broad.

Deciding to milk this for as much information on that asshole as possible, Quinn asks, "Sorry, Sunney Jameson? That a girl or guy name?" A *valid question. Who would ever want to fuck a guy named Sunney?* Quinn thinks, trying not to chuckle.

The girl smiles and says, "It's a guy. He lives in a cabin on that road you live on. He's so charming, handsome, and sweet. He used to date my friend Andrea at my other job until she cheated on him."

"If you don't mind me asking, what's your other job?"

She blushes and subtly presses her arms tighter to pop out her tits even more. She replies, "The strip club. I have been working there as a dancer since my eighteenth birthday over two years ago."

She must have added that last part to indicate she may come off underage and wants him to know she isn't. Twenty still is a hell of a lot too young.

"And things didn't work out between your friend and this — Sunney then?" Quinn's nosiness takes over.

"Hell, no! Sunney ended things after that. Then she just skipped town without telling anyone. Sunney was so heartbroken. It was tragic. He's just *such* a good guy."

Deciding to press his luck, Quinn asks, "And how long has he had a cabin out there?"

Thinking momentarily, Heather says, "I think he had it built a little over four years ago. Shortly after he started dating Andrea, all the girls thought she was so lucky to snatch the most eligible bachelor in town. After that, Sunney started coming to town less and less."

So perfect man Sunney dated a stripper who ditched town out of nowhere? First, the pristine cabin in the middle of nowhere and now this. Sunney seems more out of sorts than your typical rich pretty boy. Quinn might have been too hasty, thinking he's some basic, effortlessly readable man.

"I better get going," Quinn says, handing her his debit card, figuring he's gotten enough from her.

Seeming suddenly mortified for sharing that information, she grabs his card and looks down.

After paying, Quinn turns around to walk out, but before leaving, he feels pity for making her feel that way. That and she did seem like an easy lay. That isn't Quinn's usual game to go for, but the woman he would prefer to have is married, and the possibility of getting her isn't as high as this Heather. Not yet, anyway.

Turning around, he says, "I'll have to stop by sometime to see you."

"My name's Heather. You must request me," she says, biting her lip.

Quinn winks and leaves. He immediately thinks of what he will say to Toni about what he just heard. He wonders why he cares enough to mess around in this couple's honeymoon bliss. Maybe it's because his bliss is long gone, and he feels compelled to destroy others' happiness. He had had a kind heart long ago, but like any heart, it goes through enough heartbreak to quench putting others through that exact pain. He needs a distraction from all his other constant internal troubles in the meantime.

Digging into this couple's relationship might, however, get his name known around this town. This is the last thing he needs, especially if anyone were to find out where he last lived and what went down. That past needs to be buried deep down forever. He is now a reformed, good man.

Exiting the doors of the grocery store, Quinn crosses the street and approaches his Jeep. Just the thought of another sip of Jack nearly makes his mouth water. He throws his bags in the back and sits at the driver's side.

Closing the door, images immediately flash in his mind. It's his wife. Her long auburn hair wrapped around her shoulder as if she had just brushed it. Her eyes disapproving, as they had mostly been toward the end of their marriage.

"You really think what you're doing is right, Quinn?" she mouthed.

He didn't even need to hear it out loud to know what she was saying. She had always asked that question kindly and calmly. Maybe if she had shown more teeth, things wouldn't have gone south as they had. This time is different, however. She isn't discussing his drinking or anger issues. She is talking about interfering in the lives of the newlyweds.

He closes his eyes to expel her image. Waiting for moments to reopen them, he instantly reaches out to the bottle of Celexa in his glove box. Taking a couple out, he grabs the bottle of Jack, uses it to wash them down, and tosses the bottle under the passenger seat. He then goes for his can of the trusted long-cut Copenhagen and puts a big dip in. *Better.*

Starting the engine, Quinn looks down the main street. He thinks about the strip club and wonders if it would be a good idea to look at it now. However, that idea is immediately tossed aside when he realizes it's only one in the afternoon. He doesn't want to be the creep in a strip club on a Monday afternoon.

Before he can shift to reverse, a knock on his window stops him. He flinches, the sound startling him. Standing at his window, he sees a tall, lanky man with a big gold badge and a tan button-up shirt — a police officer.

CHAPTER 9

Quinn Robins

He instantly thanks the heavens he tossed his Jack under the passenger side. Taking a deep breath, knowing there's no way the one cop in this podunk town can catch him driving drunk in the middle of the day, he calmly rolls down his window. He has gotten out of way more sketchier situations before while being more intoxicated.

The cop has a baby-like face, light blonde hair, and a buzz cut. He's young, possibly in his early twenties, so he is likely not the sheriff. His button-down shirt is wrinkled and smells damp as if he had accidentally left it in the washer over a day. He also has a five o'clock shadow on his face, which means he hasn't shaved like cops are required to. Without looking at his left hand, Quinn can almost immediately tell he's unmarried and single. No respecting wife lets her husband go out in a wrinkled uniform, smelling of moldy clothes. The damp and wrinkled clothes and unshaven face could either be a good or bad sign. Good in that he doesn't have much respect for his job and probably isn't dedicated or accountable. Bad on the off chance he is just having a very off day, and is extremely pissed off for having to wear damp smelly clothes for a full shift of work.

"Hello, officer. What can I do for you?" Quinn casually asks, keeping his hands over the steering wheel and breathing as calmly as possible.

"I'm Deputy Adler, and I couldn't help but notice your plates are expired," the officer replies with a creepy smile plastered on his face, indicating he's not in a shitty mood after all.

"Oh shit! My bad, man. This whole move made it slip my mind."

Officer Adler raises his eyebrow as if he hadn't already known that and asks, "Ah! Rubico isn't known for many new citizens. Any reason you chose here?"

That's a damn good question. "Just needed a change, and I really loved this town's uh — landscape."

The officer just stares in disbelief.

"Where you from?" he asks the very question Quinn was dreading.

Thankfully, his driver's license still says Massachusetts, and not Vermont. Quinn had moved to Massachusetts for a few months before deciding to cover more ground away from Vermont. He had hardly met anyone or done anything besides hide out.

"Born and raised in Massachusetts, sir."

"A Masshole, huh? I bet you're a bad driver as well."

Quinn stares at the officer, unsure what to say.

A couple of awkward moments of silence pass with Quinn's intoxicated mind getting fuzzier and fuzzier.

"I'm kidding, 'cause they all call Massachusetts folk Massholes and bad drivers," Officer Adler says, briefly chuckling.

Quinn hadn't lived there long enough to know any of that. If he had been sober, he would have been able to fake laugh and pick up on sarcasm better.

Quinn quickly scans the officer, searching for anything to get him talking about something else, anything to keep his wandering eyes from looking under the passenger seat. His face is soft, jaw chiseled, his lips thin except his upper lip, which looks like he has something — CHEW in it.

Quinn wants to hit himself for not smelling it on his breath immediately.

"Is that long cut?" Quinn asks.

The officer smiles and gazes down at his feet, looking slightly embarrassed. Quinn immediately recognizes the sign — looking down at the feet implies someone is timid.

"That obvious, huh? It's just the mint pouch. Went cold turkey from long cut two months ago," he says, grabbing his lip and showing off the pouch.

What a pussy, Quinn thinks, but forces a small grin, which is returned with a big white smile from the officer. He is much cheerier than most police officers, especially with other men. Usually, they save all that cheerfulness for attractive women.

"Good for you, man," Quinn says with a thumbs up.

"Thanks, uh—?"

Quinn takes out his wallet and grabs his driver's license, giving it to the officer.

"Quinn Robins," he reads, taking a long look at the license before handing it back.

"You're a Libra, huh? I don't read that off you."

Quinn can't help but give him a strange look. After a couple more moments, he finally feels his gaydar going off. Most men didn't give a shit about their astrological signs, let alone other men's. They may pretend to if their wife is into it. It's not just the sign question; this whole conversation set him off. The timidness, cheery smile, and embarrassed look were all telltale signs. Quinn isn't homophobic by any means. Most of the time, in these situations, he'd immediately book it away with no explanation at all. That isn't an option here, and since he didn't want a DUI to attract unwanted attention to himself, he would have to play along.

"Really, now?" he says, forcing a smile.

"Yeah, I'm good at picking up that kind of stuff. I've pulled over a lot of people in my first year on the force, and for some reason, I'm super good at reading people from just their signs," he says, moving one arm up on the Jeep, expelling the smell of BO and damp clothes all at once.

Quinn, unable to think of anything to say, nods. He's surprised with himself for not picking up almost immediately that this man is gay. No cop would smile at civilians this hard unless they were attracted to them, which happens mostly with shady cops looking for women willing to get out of a speeding ticket with a quick blowie.

It might be painful, but Quinn will have to flirt or, at the very least, be aggressively nice to this man to save his ass. He can't go down to the station, as they might find out where he's really from and what happened there.

"So — you live in Rubico city limits or—?" Adler asks.

"No, about half a mile out of town. You turn on an old dirt road to get to it. Near the—"

"Near the Jameson cabin? Can't be. Only one person lives in that area," Adler interrupts, his eyes bulging.

Quinn is shocked that yet another person knows Sunney.

"I bought a small old trailer that has been sitting there over four years and fixed it all up. It was a pain in the ass but well worth it to live in peace," Quinn explains as he wonders if he should let Adler be aware that he knows he's neighbors with Sunney.

"I wasn't aware of that place," Adler says, seemingly in disbelief.

"I got the ownership papers, if you want to see them."

Damnit, stop being a smartass, Quinn reminds himself. It's hard for him not to be an asshole, especially when he has been drinking, and people treat him like an idiot or liar.

"Don't worry about it. Just unusual. You know Sunney Jameson, then?"

There is definitely a hint of jealousy in his voice. Quinn's gaydar is going off the hook on this guy now. He thinks up an idea to get rid of this cop for good.

"Not well. I just met him and his wife at the gas station the other day. Nice people."

Adler is completely emotionless and frozen for a couple of seconds. A grim smile replaces his creepy one. Quinn begins to think he has noticed Jack under the passenger seat.

"Who is his wife?" Adler asks.

Bingo!

"Toni — I think her name is. Nice gal. Do you have any more questions? I kind of have something I need to get to," Quinn says, hoping to wrap up this strange conversation as soon as possible.

Adler, clearly realizing he is still talking to a stranger and on the clock, shakes his head and says, "Get those plates up to date. Have a good day."

Before Quinn can reply, he has already turned around and started to speed-walk away from the jeep.

What a freak!

Chalking this encounter up to weird luck, Quinn backs out in his Jeep and drives away. He feels creeped out by how the officer reacted to that information, and he just about forgets to thank God that he has gone another day hiding in the shadows of this town so no one can ever find out about his past. Not that God could be on his side for all his wrong-doings in the last year.

Without a job and much of anything to do besides drink, he has his mind now set on two things — find out why everyone seems so obsessed with this Sunney and get to know Toni.

CHAPTER 10

It's only 7:40 a.m., and I am already ready for my run. The sun is in full swing, so I'm wearing running shorts and a loose-fitting tank top. I convince myself it's because of the heat that I'm wearing my shortest shorts, and not because I will be with Quinn. It will just be a casual run where I will do my best to set boundaries if needed.

Yesterday, Sunney and I "made up" in the shower, in the afternoon on the couch, and then after dinner on our bed. We hadn't spent much time outside that day, but I know it was for the best. I want to get used to the fact this will be my home for the next month. I plan on asking Sunney to show me around Rubico soon. My interest is still piqued at what made this town so holy to him. Perhaps Quinn could tell me about what he's seen in it.

Although I have forgiven Sunney for yelling at me for walking in on him in the shower, my mind keeps returning to that moment. It had been strange, and the whole situation was uncharacteristic of him. The music blaring, the yelling, and the arguing about it afterward. Such actions did not fit into Sunney's nature. Yes, we have had our little arguments here and there in the year we've been together, but nothing remotely involved screaming or yelling. I had left that part of me behind with Tom, and Sunney is the calmest man I've ever met. The whole incident made me want to take a couple of swigs of the Crown Royal in my purse more so than ever, or ask Quinn for some of that Jack he had in his Jeep. However, that would lead to a Toni I can no longer be.

Standing on the open porch outside the cabin with a cup of black coffee, I wonder where Sunney could have disappeared this morning. He had mentioned last night that he would be getting up early to go out in the woods for "man stuff," whatever that meant. I had been too exhausted to ask follow-up questions. A small difference between us is that he enjoys early mornings while I enjoy late nights.

There isn't much behind the cabin — just a homemade fire pit with numerous patio chairs surrounding it and a small, old-looking shed. It's about the size of an old carriage house, painted white but incredibly chipped and has no windows. It's as if Sunney had dedicated his whole budget to ensure his cabin was in a pristine condition and didn't spare a single cent on the shed. Earlier, my curiosity had bested me, and I had tried to peek inside, but it has a large padlock on the door. The padlock looks as if it possibly cost more than the shed itself.

As I swallow the last sip of my coffee, I see Sunney appear through the many tall pine trees surrounding the cabin. He is wearing a torn-up tank top and turquoise blue PJs, carrying a bunch of branches, which he sets by the firepit. He had mentioned wanting to sit outside one night, roast hot dogs and eat smores.

Walking out in the woods when it's dark is also on the schedule for this month, which I cannot lie is a bit frightening. The trees go on as far as the eye can see, giving me major creeps from all the horror movies I've seen. When I expressed this sentiment, Sunney had kissed my forehead and told me he had a just-for-safety pistol and knew these woods like the back of his hand. The perfect stargazing spot is what he wants to show me.

I set my cup down and jog down the stairs leading to the fire pit. Sunney immediately takes me in his embrace, looking me up and down like always. His sweat nearly douses me. Although his body is cold, I still feel the warmth I always do when I'm near him. Maybe I shouldn't go running with Quinn. It feels wrong as I gaze at my left hand and the wedding ring I adore so much. It reminds me of Sunney bending down on one knee while the sunset cast a perfect setting and asking me to marry him. It had caught me completely off guard as I wasn't expecting him to propose for another year or two.

I need to work on being a good person now that I'm married, and good people don't dress in provocative workout clothes and run with men they barely know.

They also don't imagine making out with another man instead of their perfect husband, my inner voice aims back at me.

Finally releasing me from our hug, Sunney looks me up and down again, except longer this time. It had to be my outfit. I can't tell if he's turned on by it or confused as to why it's so revealing. His squinting eyes seem to consider both options.

"Going running again?" he asks.

Those beautiful, almost suspicious-looking dark eyes convince me. *I can't go. But if I don't show up, what will Quinn do? Would he be angry and ballsy enough to come to the cabin and demand why I had ditched him?* He doesn't like Sunney already, and this sort of thing might incite him further, pissing Sunney off at my expense. I could deny it all if he decided to stop by. One thing I'm good at is lying. I must've inherited it from my mother.

New Toni has to do the right thing and prove that the inner voice is wrong.

"I was, but I think I'll just hang around here instead," I say, gulping.

"Why don't you run? It might be a good idea," Sunney quickly says, and once again his eyes analyze me. But this time, it's not the turned-on way like before.

"What do you mean?" I ask, raising an eyebrow.

"You have gained some weight these past couple of months. Running might not be such a bad idea," he answers casually, crossing his arms.

I am too stunned to answer immediately. Old Toni wants to slap his beautiful, unfazed baby face. New Toni wants to cry that her husband commented on her weight for the first time ever. I had caught him commenting on women's weight a couple of times with his buddies (*Wow, Bert's wife sure hasn't lost any of that baby weight, as he said*), but I had thought that it was just a thing men did because they had nothing else to talk about. Harmless. To top it off, I had only gained maybe five pounds in the past few months; it was nothing noticeable. *Or so I thought.* Love weight is harmless and should make your partner happy you're so comfortable with them.

"That was an extremely rude thing to say, Sunney," I remark, crossing my arms and expecting an immediate apology, even though it wouldn't undo what was just said.

Sunney grins as if I'm joking. *No, Old Toni, you cannot slap your husband.*

"I'm just honest, babe. Don't take offense," he says, leaning over and slapping my ass.

"What is wrong with you?" I ask, taking a step back away from his grasp.

"Oh, come on. Don't make a big deal out of this. It was just some advice."

I cross my arms, silent and still waiting for an apology.

"Well, I'm going to get more firewood. Have a good workout, and run well. Love you."

Before I can speak, Sunney steps closer to me, kisses my cheek, and then walks off. I'm instantly irritated with myself for checking out that perfectly shaped ass of his as he walks away. You feel the same irritation when you can't help but want to jump the bones of the popular boy in high school even after he calls you fat and ignores you for four years. Except with the popular boy, you get over him once you graduate and realize he is a dimwit buffoon. This guy is my asshole husband, whom I love. Turns out he could possibly have been that bully in high school.

It's a weird thing most girls do — wonder what their husbands were like in high school. I've always wondered about it myself. We like to imagine them being brooding and innocent. Hopefully, a virgin throughout high school, waiting till college, or if they did have sex with a girl, it only being in a longtime relationship. We imagine them as kind and thoughtful, but they were probably shallow assholes like most guys in high school.

I have little to no information on Sunney when he was in high school. He was a great baseball player, and his parents still have pictures of him in action at their house. The gallery also included a very striking prom photo in their stairwell, which I had noticed almost immediately because I hadn't gotten much information about Sunney's past girlfriends. He had a high school girlfriend. An obvious cliché — they were a sporty, popular couple, although Sunney denies this.

"We were just like any other couple," he had said when I poked at him.

She had long blonde hair, a slim body (which, I guess, is how he still must like them) and a stuck-up-looking, white-toothed smile. I now wonder if they liked bullying the outcasts while soaking up their good looks.

I frown, realizing my husband wouldn't have looked twice at me if we had gone to the same school. Not that he would have exactly been my type either. I was much more into older men back then, as I thought they were more mature. Silly Toni, all men are immature; it doesn't matter how old they get. They still think it's acceptable to hit their girlfriends or, in my husband's case, tell their wives they need to lose weight. I'll fucking show him.

On my way out the door, I grab my large purse with the Crown still hidden inside and sling it over my shoulder like I need to protect it with my life.

CHAPTER 11

It's nearly 8:20 a.m. when I check my watch for the eighth time since I left the cabin. I remind myself it's too early to assume I may be getting stood up, although my anger can be quite suggestive. With the events from this morning in my mind, I'm ready to kick two men's asses now, especially since Quinn was the damn one to invite me to run in the first place.

I am on the dirt road that leads to Quinn's place. I pace back and forth, wondering if it will be impossibly crazy to walk over there. I mean, what if something is wrong? *What would be wrong, though? What if something isn't wrong, and I'm the crazy married bitch at some stranger's cabin?* I chuckle, remembering my parents' warnings to never talk to strangers or go anywhere with them. But here I am, seriously considering going to a stranger's place of my own free will. They would be so ashamed of me.

Feeling my heart rate getting higher as the minutes pass, I walk over to the grass and sit. I reach into my purse and take out the Crown. It's piss warm from days of sitting on the heated cabin floor. As I open the cap, the smell makes me want to gag. I've never been much of a whiskey girl, as it's too strong for my taste. It belonged to Sunney and had been something I'd (or, should I say, Old Toni) grabbed hastily.

The morning before our wedding day, we were packing, and he had requested me to grab a bottle of his *Royal Brackla* (one of Sunney's personal favorites) whiskey for his bachelor party that night. I knew he wouldn't miss the cheap whiskey, so Crown had been my only option.

Holding my breath, I slurp down on the bottle for a moment. Once my nose doesn't burn anymore from the strength of the alcohol, I do the same again and again. By the third time, my belly feels warm, and my emotions de-escalate. It reminds me of my alcoholic days when I drank nearly every night. I had a better understanding of how Drunk Toni would behave. At the beginning of the night, only a few drinks deep, she felt like all her problems and everything she hated and was mad about would disappear. Add five more drinks, and she would either be crying or about to burst from all the pent-up anger.

"I must've missed the memo that this was going to be a party," a deep voice says, making me flinch and nearly drop my bottle.

I look over and see Quinn standing only a couple of feet away. I nearly burst out laughing at his current appearance and clothing selection. His short hair is in disarray as if he just rolled out of bed, his beard not neat like usual. From where I sit, I can see the exhaustion clear as day in his eyes. He wears a yellow laminated shirt that barely hangs over his stomach and appears to be two sizes too small. On the other hand, the off-brand shorts hang low and are two sizes too big instead. *How dumb to assume he could be in trouble or standing me up! He just overslept because he's hungover.*

Seeing my smirk, he asks, "What? What are you looking at?"

Placing my bottle on the ground and covering my mouth so I don't start cackling, I say, "Nice outfit."

"It's the only workout clothes I could find. Sue me," Quinn says, rolling his eyes.

I stand up too quickly, and all the alcohol directly goes to my head. Placing my hand against a nearby tree so I don't tumble to the ground, I use my other hand and place it over my spinning head *I really should have eaten breakfast.* Now it's Quinn's turn to try not to laugh, although his effort is nowhere near as good as mine. I hear him chuckling under his breath. The Old Toni in me is ashamed of being a lightweight in front of an obviously aged drinker.

"You don't want to run, do you?" Quinn asks, and I catch him eyeing me up and down. I can't tell if he's either judgmental of my current state or checking out my outfit.

"Do you?"

He's momentarily silent as if debating what to say or deciding if he should speak his mind. Taking a deep breath in and letting it out, he finally says, "Not really, I hate exercise if you couldn't tell. I just wanted a reason to hang out with you."

I look down, feeling my cheeks flushing for a moment.

"Why? You really that lonely?" I ask.

He shrugs and says, "I guess — and you're kind of cool."

"Kind of?"

"Shut up. You know what I mean."

Now it's my turn to be silent for a couple of seconds as I weigh my options on what to say. On the one hand, I am in no state to run and would rather drink for the rest of the morning. On the other hand, I should just tell Quinn we planned on running. That would be the better alternative to what we want to do instead.

"I do need the exercise," I say, remembering Sunney's words.

Quinn just chuckles and says, "You? You're joking. Have you seen this?" Quinn asks, grabbing hold of his gut and jiggling it.

Finding that a bit too attractive despite my better instincts, I purse my lips and say, "You're just a little stocky."

"Yeah, a little bit."

"To be completely honest, I'm in no state to run. How about a couple of drinks? If you're not too hungover anyway."

Quinn shows an open-mouthed smile and walks closer to me. Once again, we're inches away, but instead of the smell of Jack Daniels like yesterday, I smell minty toothpaste. *So, he had time to brush his teeth but not his hair?* He bends down and grabs my bottle.

Twisting off the cap at an impeccable speed, he just says, "I thought you'd never ask."

CHAPTER 12

Twenty minutes later, I am in a place I thought I'd never be — Quinn's cabin. I can no longer really call him a stranger at this point. I passed the very outer layer of the iceberg long back. I am nowhere near the core, however, as he hasn't shared much about himself. Then again, I don't think I'm even near the core of knowing my husband, nor the other way around. There's no way Sunney, in a million years, would imagine me in another man's home, sitting on his vintage floral sofa on the tipping point of drunk, laughing, and having a good time.

My heart rate is rising as I wonder if it's not too late to make it back to the cabin. If I'm lucky, he hasn't noticed how long I've been gone and is still dilly-dallying, chopping wood. Or, if I'm even luckier, he has noticed and thinks I may be hurt somewhere. He deserves a little worry for all the vile things he said to me. I'm still unsure what I will say when I get back. *Shall I be honest and say I went over to the neighbors, or just go the liar's route and say I got caught up in my run?* However, that lie wouldn't be very believable since I haven't sweated. It's not like going the honest route would be all that bad. At least I wouldn't be lying. Then again, I doubt Sunney would let me go on any runs again without him being there. I'm not doing anything bad, I reason, just trying to make friends so I have another person to talk to the whole month I'm here. Since Sunney is becoming more of an asshole with each passing day, I need an escape so I don't morph into Old Toni.

"I put your piss-warm whiskey in some ice, and now I believe I've earned something from you," Quinn states, interrupting my internal monologue.

I gulp, instantly wondering what he thinks he's earned by giving me a glass and some ice. Maybe I shouldn't have been too hasty to believe we could be friends. Most men aren't interested in that relationship.

"And what is it you've earned?" I ask, intrigued.

"You need to tell me two things about yourself."

I breathe a sigh of relief; glad he hasn't asked for what I thought he would.

"That talent for reading people hasn't already told you everything?" I tease.

Chuckling, Quinn shakes his head and replies, "First one — I don't even know your last name. What is it?"

"Jameson."

"Is that your maiden name or—?" Quinn asks, winking, causing a kaleidoscope of butterflies to fly into my alcohol-warmed stomach.

"No — it's Lovette."

As if soaking this in, Quinn inhales, exhales, and then repeats, "Lovette. I like that."

Obviously more than Jameson.

I smile lightly to express my gratitude.

"Any hobbies?"

"Hobbies?" I repeat the word, which sounds almost foreign to me.

"Yeah? Painting, reading, skydiving."

I think of that. My mind races through things I like doing. It's a small list that includes drinking and being in a toxic relationship.

"I'll have to get back to you on that one," I finally answer, knowing Quinn must think I'm a complete bore.

"Okay, next subject. May I speak freely about something I've gauged about you?"

I bite my lip, wondering what he's reading about me. I nod.

"Something must've happened with your husband. It's not my business, but I will ask if you'd like to talk or rant about it anyway."

I'm silent as I watch Quinn's probing eyes, wondering whether I should tell him. With his creepy perception abilities, it's surprising he doesn't already know the full story.

I know I shouldn't, as it's none of his business, but I want to get a man's opinion. Maybe I overreacted.

"He said something to me that was particularly rude and uncharacteristic of him this morning."

"May I dare ask what it was?"

"He recommended I go for a run as I've recently gained some weight, or at least he thinks I have."

Quinn's eyes bulge, answering my thoughts on whether I was overreacting. I wasn't.

"I don't think I've ever said anything like that to a woman before. That's a doozy. Pretty fucked up if I may say so."

I look away, slightly embarrassed I have just revealed this personal conversation with my husband. Momentarily, I wonder whether I'm compliment fishing now, urging this man to tell me I'm not fat and my husband was wrong.

"I don't know what you used to look like, but in my third-party opinion, he's wrong."

This brings a smile to my face. I grab my glass, taking another sip from it.

"I mean, I've gained some weight since we started dating, but he needs to understand that I am a real woman. I gain weight, get acne, and sometimes go days without wearing makeup."

"Is he more accustomed to women who are the complete opposite of you?"

"Yes! His friends always sleep with supermodels or wannabe actresses who eat ice cubes for dinner. If he wanted a woman like that, he could have easily gotten one."

Quinn chuckles, and I take another sip from my glass, realizing I'm closing in on a tantrum that would be better off shared with a female friend, that is, if I had any.

"So, what about you?"

"What about me?"

"Do you care about looks in men?"

I swallow, thinking that through for a couple of moments. The good moral version of me wants to say no right away, but the honest, somewhat self-entitled version screams yes. I do have to find men heavily attractive; however, not in the way Quinn is asking — in my kind of attractive. Not perfect in terms of beauty standards, but my own. Having dated and married a man like Sunney, I understand how that could be construed differently. Tom wasn't a Mr. Dreamy type. He was handsome, but after years of wear and tear of his body using drugs, he had lost some of the charm. I judged him for his appearance during the last few days of our relationship but mostly, I think it was all due to how unhappy I was.

"Yes and no. Like any other person, I do have to find them attractive. If they, however, change as time passes, become pudgy, or take less care of themselves, I wouldn't mind if I am still happy."

Quinn nods his head in agreement.

"And money?"

"Money?" I ask, understanding Quinn's question but still wondering if he's asking if I'm a gold digger.

"Yeah, do you care about how much money a man has?"

I shake my head, sipping my drink. It makes my throat feel dry but still, at the same time, calms my nerves.

"Do you have a job?"

"I did. I recently quit. I worked at a dental office. I'll probably look for another when I return home."

"But with your husband's income, it won't be needed, will it?"

I look deep into Quinn's eyes, trying to decipher if he's hoping to push me into admitting something. His expression remains unfazed and normal. If only I could read faces as well as him.

"No, but I'm not used to solely relying on a man's income. My last relationship was the opposite. So, if you're trying to trick me into admitting I'm a gold digger, forget about it," I snap.

Quinn chuckles. "Calm down, I wasn't. Just curious. Trying to figure you out is all."

More silence ensues as those captivating eyes continue to probe me. *What is going through his man's head?* It's almost fun making him work for an answer as his mind scrambles to figure one out. I continue sipping my drink, not wanting it to go empty or stop drinking it either. It feels like it's been too long since I've had a nice drink in my hand, even though I just had a swig a couple of days ago in the gas station's bathroom.

"He must not be much of a drinker."

"Why do you say that?"

"It's just how you reacted yesterday to seeing my alcohol and how you were already drinking at eight this morning. You obviously don't drink as much as you used to, and you have just gotten married. When people marry, they drink together on their honeymoon."

"How did you make this assumption?"

Quinn smirks, shakes his head, sips his drink, and replies, "Because I was married once upon a time, and my wife wasn't much of a drinker either. But even on our honeymoon, we drank heavily and enjoyed each other's company without needing to do it alone or with someone of the opposite sex."

My heart rate increases, and I feel a dabble of regret coursing through my veins. *Does he want me to feel like trash for being here, or does he want me to feel like trash because my husband made me angry enough not to be with him while I drank?*

I place my glass on the coffee table, nearly spilling it, stand up, and cover my face with my hands.

"I'm a terrible wife. I shouldn't have come here," I say, running my fingers through my hair.

"Shit! That wasn't what I was trying to say," Quinn says quickly, standing up and putting his hand on my shoulder. It feels warm, and even though I'm mildly annoyed with him, I don't push it away immediately.

"I was trying to say that, from my viewpoint, it seems like your husband isn't being the greatest to you, and it's fucked up of him to force you to want to drink."

"Every day, I just feel like he is becoming more and more of an asshole for no reason. The first day I met you, I found some girl's name and his written on the bathroom wall when he told me he had never brought another girl to his cabin. I don't want to sound crazy, so I haven't confronted him yet. After we met you, he was overly jealous, and the next day I went running—"

Just as I'm working up some steam, about to tell Quinn about the shower incident, he interrupts me. "Was the name Andrea?"

I blink a couple of times, trying to register what he just said. I heard that right. He had to have seen the names.

"You saw it too?"

"No, I sort of heard about their relationship in town yesterday. She was a stripper. A friend of hers said she left town after their split, and Sunney was heartbroken. Your husband is quite the popular one in Rubico, actually."

So, I'm not being delusional. Sunney really had lied about me being the only woman he had invited to the cabin. And she was a stripper. *Why would he just lie to me like that?* He had always been so vague about past girlfriends. It all made sense now.

"I shouldn't have said anything," Quinn says, and finally his hand leaves my shoulder, reminding me it was there for a while.

"Then why did you?" I ask, feeling my face flush hot.

"Huh?"

"Why would you tell me this? What are you getting out of it?"

"Nothing. Are you trying to accuse me of something?"

I know I need to stop, but I can't help but feel my morals weakening The alcohol has caused my anger at Sunney to suddenly shift to the messenger boy, Quinn. It's anger I haven't felt in a long time. I remember feeling it before killing Tom and nearly every day before that.

"Are you noting down information on my husband to turn me against him?" I ask, facing Quinn and pointing at him wildly.

Quinn's eyebrows turn into a V, and his nose wrinkles. It instantly reminds me of when I would accuse Tom of ridiculous things.

"Why would I do that? I barely know y'all."

"I don't know; maybe it's because you are lonely and want to fuck me."

Quinn doesn't flinch at this accusation like I thought he would. He crosses his arms and says, "Don't flatter yourself, hun. I chose to live here alone, away from crazy women like you. And trust me, I can fuck any woman I want. Why would I choose a married recovering alcoholic with a conniving shitty husband?"

Unable to control myself, I gasp. Without thinking twice, I raise my hand to slap him, but before my hand can collide with his bearded face, he grabs me by the wrist, stopping me. We stare at each other in silence for a couple of moments, and instead of wondering why I almost struck a man I barely know; I admire his features — his dark caterpillar eyebrows flared into a V, creating three wrinkles on his forehead. He sports a lot of large pores just above where his beard starts. If my hand had not been firmly held, I'd almost want to reach out and feel them.

God, I really am losing it. One moment wanting to slap that face, and the other, tempted to caress it.

Quinn finally drops my hand and says, "I think you should leave, Toni."

He's so calm, considering he just had to stop me from striking him. He should be angry. What I did was wrong, not like New Toni one bit. I should have never brought that Crown. It's already turning me into the woman I despise the most.

I quickly pace to the front door and, opening it, I turn to look at Quinn. He's still calm and staring at me.

"I'm sorry about trying to hit you. That was — that was wrong," I say.

I leave as quickly as possible, and it's not until I am a couple of yards from his house that I realize I left the Crown Royal. I'm better off without it, but still, I curse myself for leaving it behind.

CHAPTER 13

The first half of the walk back is miserable. My anxiety has practically flooded my mind. That and I can barely walk a straight line. My stomach rumbles from all the alcohol I consumed and no food. It's funny, as it was a daily thing for me at one time, but now not so much. *I must quit drinking*, I decide. It makes me too reckless and prone to do something horrible.

Quinn could have pressed charges for me attempting to assault him, scratch that — he still can. He has every right to. Even worse, he could have beaten the fuck out of me and called it self-defense. Although that wouldn't hold up in a court, he towers over me by nearly a foot and weighs at least eighty pounds more than me. I bet the courts would love another self-defense case where I was the perpetrator. I had already got so many judgmental stares from the police who'd handled Tom's and my incident. You'd think most would be on my side, considering I had a broken nose and bruises all over my face.

Once I make it to the end of Quinn's road, I sit near the same grassy area I had been in less than an hour ago. I want to return to the cabin more than ever, but I don't want to face Sunney. I know I still have some fire in the pit of my stomach, ready to be unleashed. Sadly, I hadn't unfurled it all on Quinn. Maybe I would've if I had gotten to hit him.

I press my palms to my face, my mind running through everything that has happened today for the tenth time. Our chat, the Crown Royal I swirled in my mouth before swallowing, and Quinn's every feature. I shouldn't have lost control in such a manner. It's unlike me to do so, not that early on into knowing someone.

Not long goes by before I hear a vehicle approaching. My heart rate increases, and I immediately think it's Quinn driving after me to make up. I look up eagerly and freeze at once, seeing Sunney's Red Chevy. He's driving so fast I quickly stand up and dash past the tree line, feeling I might get run over if I don't move immediately. He slams on the brakes only a couple of yards ahead of me. The door swings open and out comes Sunney, now wearing dark wash blue jeans and a tight grey and red baseball T-shirt.

"Where the hell have you been?" he asks, his face twisted in a scowl, looking me up and down.

I cannot let him know I'm drunk. I cannot let him know I'm drunk. I'm angry with him and don't need any blame getting turned toward me.

Standing up straight, I say, "Running, just as you wanted."

"It has almost been an hour. I was worried sick about you. You don't know these woods as well as I do."

"I'm not an idiot, Sunney. I won't get lost."

It's been a while since I've tried to act sober in front of Sunney. It's a craft I am not good at. I feel a bead of sweat roll down my back, as I try not to slur my words and keep my back straight.

"You're not even sweaty. What the hell were you doing?"

"Can I not be alone for a measly hour without being interrogated?"

Sunney squints his eyes at me and takes a few steps closer. I keep my back straight and look at him as normally I can.

"I know that face. Where did you get it, Toni?"

"Get what?"

"The pills or alcohol. You're on one of them. Remember the last holiday party?"

It was my last misdemeanor. I had tried to act sober in front of Sunney. It had been only four months into dating, and he had invited me to this fancy work holiday party where most guests were rich and stuck-up. His parents were also attending. I knew sober me wouldn't fit in one bit. While getting ready, I made over four Vodka-Crans for myself. With my mixing skills, I had been drunk already, so when we got there to loosen up, I'd swallowed a couple of oxys in the bathroom. I'd mixed the two many times in the past but had taken a break from it because I was trying to be myself around my new boyfriend. I had ditched the party to hide in the bathroom for over an hour with a group of older housewives doped up on xannys and strawberry margaritas. They were the only ones around whom I had really been able to relax. Unfortunately, Sunney's mother had found us and promptly told Sunney's father, who then told him. After being escorted back into the party by Sunney, I overheard his father lecturing him and saying, "She's trash, just like the last one. Take care of it." I was almost sure that he would dump me that night.

Sunney's parents are stereotypical rich parents. They are neither happy nor impressed with the poor girl their son dated and then married. His mother isn't all that bad; she's very timid. She has probably said all of one hundred words to me throughout our relationship. She constantly tries to impress her husband, who is far more interested in talking to the attractive young interns who work for him. He was unabashedly flirting with his interns that night, but I hadn't told Sunney that. Neither had I told him that his mom had also taken a xanny in the bathroom, probably to forget her shitty husband's sins.

"I'm not. These are two completely different situations, Sunney," I argue.

"There's no difference in you trying to act normal and not plastered. You want me to stop treating you like an idiot, then stop treating me like one."

"I'm not on anything!" I yell, balling up my fists, trying not to shake.

I don't know if I'm more irked by the fact that Sunney thinks I'm taking pills again or that he can easily tell something is off about me. But I know things are going to take a turn for the worse when Sunney gets closer to me and smells my breath.

"I can smell the whiskey on your breath! Why are you lying to me right now?"

"Oh, you want to talk about lying. Tell me this: Who has stayed at your cabin besides me?"

Giving me a blank stare, he says, "What?"

"I'm talking about Andrea."

It's not too often that Sunney has a dumbfounded look in his eyes. He either knows how to lie perfectly or answers difficult questions with ease. It's one of the top reasons he's an amazing salesman.

"Who told you that name?"

"Does it really matter?"

He wipes sweat dripping down his forehead and says, "Okay, I had a girlfriend before you. I already told you I'd had a couple. I don't know why you're jealous; we obviously broke up."

"I'm not being jealous. You lied to me. You said you'd only ever bring your wife to your cabin."

"I said that to make you feel special. You would have never wanted to come here if you'd known I'd shared it with another woman. You should be thanking me."

"Thanking you? For lying to my face?"

"For putting your feelings first."

"How many others were there besides her, Sunney?"

Sunney rolls his eyes, silent. That is answer enough for me. There were many more. I mean, would it be so ridiculous? It's a fancy ass cabin in a small, poor town. What woman wouldn't want one nice night with the richest man in town? I'd fall for it myself.

"I can't believe you, you lying son of—"

"Excuse me?" Sunney interrupts me.

I can't take Sunney's attitude any longer without bursting again. To give myself some space, I start walking toward his cabin. Right now, I only want some carbs, a gallon of water, and a few too many ibuprofens to relieve my alcohol-induced headache. However, I only make it a couple of feet before my shoulder is aggressively grabbed, and my body twists around to face Sunney, who looks just as angry as me.

"Don't walk away when I'm talking to you, Toni," Sunney orders.

I instantly shrug his tight hold off me.

"I'm hungry and have a headache. I can't do this right now," I say, knowing I shouldn't explain anything to him, but New Toni wants to.

"Then get in the truck. We can talk at home. You're not walking back."

I want to ignore him and continue walking, but my headache and stomach equally hate me at this moment. This way would be faster. I can ignore Sunney. Just because he's giving me a ride doesn't mean he has won this fight.

I reluctantly get in the pickup without a word. Sunney gets in next, slamming his door. Once he's on the driver's side, we start approaching the cabin silently. I feel his eyes darting, and he looks at me nearly every second. He knows something's off, but two can play that game since he wants to keep shit from me. He doesn't need to know about me hanging out and drinking with Quinn.

"Did you get the alcohol from someone else?" he asks, interrupting the silence.

"What?" I ask, trying to sound insulted he would even suggest such a thing.

"I'm going to check my stash when we get home, so you might as well tell me right now. Some fucking hunter or hiker give you some? You two hit it off?"

"Check your stash. I didn't take anything, and I'm done with this conversation!" I yell, crossing my arms and looking out the window.

Frustrated at my dishonesty Sunney slams his hand against the steering wheel.

CHAPTER 14

When we arrive, I hurriedly exit the truck and walk in a fast pace toward the cabin. I walk into the kitchen and find a box of mac and cheese in the cabinet. I rummage around to find a pot and other ingredients. Sunney walks upstairs, disappearing for a few moments, possibly checking wherever he keeps his booze. I pour water into the pot and place it on the burner, and when I turn around, I see him lighting a cigar. I give him a puzzled look as he never usually smokes except when hanging with work colleagues at the country club. He's baiting me, and I bite reluctantly.

"You're smoking?" I ask.

"What about it?" he asks, sucking in deep and blowing a load of smoke out.

The smoke reeks, so I turn toward the stove, looking out the window. It's such a glorious day without a cloud in sight. I could be hiking or going into Rubico with Sunney. Instead, I'm drunk in the kitchen, making mac and cheese, disgusted with my husband's attitude. *Such a great continuation of this honeymoon,* I think ironically.

Twenty minutes of silence later, my food is cooked, and I'm so done with the cigar smoke in the air I take my meal outside to the deck. I sit and begin to eat as fast as possible.

My tummy instantly feels satiated. When I'm done, I go back inside for more water and see Sunney has gotten rid of his cigar.

"Are you ready to talk?" he asks.

"Talk about your ex-girlfriend or me allegedly drinking?"

"Allegedly? Are you shitting me?"

For the first time, New and Old Toni agree it is best to just ignore that question. If I answer, it will be a total disaster. Instead, I grab a glass, fill it with water, and head back outside to sit. This time, however, only a few seconds pass before the door swings open. I hear footsteps approach me. His hands go over my shoulder, and for a moment, my past trauma makes me think he will strangle me. He, however, starts rubbing my shoulders.

"What are you doing?" I ask, moving away from his grip.

"If you're not going to talk, we can at least do something that doesn't involve talking," Sunney says, leaning over to whisper into my ear.

He can't be serious. I can barely hold myself together enough not to move my hands around his throat, let alone have sex with him. However, he might like the first in conjunction with the latter. I have never been a fan of rough play, but Sunney springs it on me occasionally, sometimes more aggressively than I like. Thus far, I have gotten out of it by telling him my whole relationship with Tom had been too traumatic to do that stuff.

"Yeah, I'm not in the mood," I say, leaning forward in my seat, escaping Sunney's continued advances to give me an awkward massage.

There's a moment of silence, and then very unexpectedly, Sunney walks over to face me. His dark eyes look down at me with a flare of anger. Before I know it, his hand is on my throat, forcing me to sit up.

"I don't think I was asking," he says, pressing his lips to mine for a hard, wet kiss.

I push him away, which thankfully isn't difficult due to the sudden adrenaline rush I'm feeling from anger.

"Get away from me. I said no," I spit at him.

It's troubling that this isn't the first time I've had a hard time having to reject Sunney's sexual advances. When we first started sleeping together, we were both insatiable but after some time I grew a bit tired of it. Not that I was bored or any less attracted to him, it just seemed that's all we were doing, every single day. I wanted more time to talk—to get to know each other. When I did try rejecting him, I felt he would act as though I was disgusted by him. That I no longer loved him. I believed his words, felt guilty for making him feel that he wasn't desirable. Now, I feel idiotic for letting him talk me into doing things I did not want to do. New Toni just lusted so much for making her perfect man happy.

I would also overhear him talk to his male friends about how their wives stopped as they said it "putting out". Sunney would act as though the women were evil and most likely cheating. He would go off on the fact his friends were bringing home so much money while the wives only had three easy jobs. Cook, clean and fuck their husbands. I didn't agree with any of it but my mind diminished all the red flags because in my eyes my husband was perfect. That I should thank the heavens he had chosen me. Just guy talk. Letting off steam. It's natural for men to do. Or is it just plain misogynistic pigs?

Sunney's face is blank for a few seconds, but then he smirks.

"Sometimes I really don't get you, Toni," he says, turning around and returning inside. He then walks to the door, puts on a brown flannel-lined jacket — too warm to wear this time of year — and briskly places his work boots on next. Then, without even glancing my way, he opens the front door and slams it behind him. Only a couple of moments pass before I hear his truck start up.

I collapse on the swing set, tears filling my eyes. I really am losing control of this honeymoon.

CHAPTER 15

Sunney Jameson

Sunney Jameson always exceeds the speed limit on the dirt road leaving his cabin and opening onto the highway, but fueled by anger and frustration, he's surprised he doesn't end up with his chevy in the ditch. This trip is one of the fastest he has ever made, excluding two years ago when he found out his whore of an ex-girlfriend, Andrea, had been cheating on him by forming an emotional and physical relationship with a rich client at the strip club.

She had been off work that night at 2 a.m. and let him rail her in the alleyway at no extra charge. This had been the main source of anger for Sunney since he had bought Andrea nearly anything she had wanted and trusted her enough to work at the strip club for an extra income. His instincts had told him that dating and eventually falling in love with a stripper was foolish. But four months in, she had agreed to transition from being a stripper to a bartender, which had given him some ease.

Before meeting Toni, Sunney had gone through many women without ever dating any except his high school girlfriend. At first, he had thought Andrea was just another gorgeous face, but after talking to her and learning about her dysfunctional life, he wanted to be with her and help her. He couldn't explain his desire to fix women with problems. Until then, he hadn't met a woman like Andrea. Most of his type had included women with their daddy's money just wanting fun time in their extravagant life.

Ironically enough, his destination now is the same as it had been that night — Rubico's lone strip club — DollsNitetimeClub. From the outside, it seems like a major shithole, but it pulls a hefty amount of cash from the lonely townie men sick of their wives, or the rich, well-known men from out of town who do not want to be seen at a strip club in their territory. The moment Sunney had first laid his eyes on Dolls, its flickering, dim red lights and faded grey-colored brick building, he was immediately mesmerized. Not by the women. Most of them working there were skanks, and more than a couple pegs down from women he deemed good enough for his time. He was enchanted by how easy it could be transformed into a drug and sex front to pull in double the money.

Sunney had first found the small town of Rubico simply passing through it on his way to a business meeting in a larger town nearby. Rubico was smack in the middle between his city and this one. In both places, he knew a bunch of other businessmen who would be interested. They could cheat on their wives and do cocaine. It was small and quiet, ready to be filled with perverted rich men.

So Sunney had worked his charisma with the old sleazebag that owned the place. In the first meeting, he swayed the owner into letting him invest a large sum and promised that, if or when the money started stockpiling, he would receive 30% of the income, along with his investment back. With a couple of visits to his country and golf clubs, he had talked a couple of dozen men into going to weekend parties filled with enough cocaine, heroin, and strippers to make Chris Farley keel over if he hadn't already done so. His friends didn't take long to get the word around to other men.

Toni has no idea about this extra set of income. He knows it would be best not to let her in on it. Especially now that they are married, and he has finally talked her into quitting that waste of time job she had. She doesn't need to know the full extent of how he makes his money. She would only overreact if she found out. Although, out of all the women Sunney has dated, he feels Toni is the smartest. But she's still as dumb as a deer stuck in the headlights (how he likes his women).

Despite her being an idiot, he loves her very much, more than he has ever loved another woman. Although he has met and charmed many women in his twenty-eight years, he has only been in love three times. Once in high school (puppy love, of course, almost unaccountable), second to Andrea, and now Toni. All three had been lonely, tortured women — a fact Sunney quickly discovered upon meeting and dating them. Ready to crack mentally — it's Sunney's type to a T. He wanted a woman he could fix and make a project out of.

His high school girlfriend Stephanie had been a popular girl in front of the crowd, but behind closed doors, her stepdad was sexually assaulting her while her mother refused to believe her. He's sure she keeps in touch with her mother, who is still married to her pedophile stepfather. She had been the weakest. When he graduated and she stayed in their hometown, Sunney dumped her and went to his chosen college. Last he heard, she was married to the town's drug dealer and ready to pop out her third kid. He has no hate toward her but he's happy he ended things because she had put on at least fifty pounds the last time he saw her.

His second girlfriend, Andrea, nearly eight years after the first, grew up shooting any drug she could get in her system, too dumb to use her flawless body to make money until moving to Rubico and getting a job at Dolls. Like Toni, she had spent most of her life dating abusive losers, but instead of killing them, she let it happen until the men left her weak ass. She had been the dumbest. Sunney had dumped her the moment he walked through the back door of Dolls and saw her getting porked by the creep who he had gotten revenge on in the best way he saw fit.

Finally, Toni. She was utterly normal for most of her teen years, but everything came crashing down when she was seventeen. Her parents had had an untimely death upon her graduating from high school, thrusting her into a toxic and abusive relationship with a boyfriend she eventually stabbed to death (twelve times to be exact, according to a front-page newspaper article). Toni is by far the most unhinged among all his romantic interests. This is why Sunney decided she'd be the one for him forever. She battles her inner demons while trying to stay perky and perfect for her adoring husband — the perfect blend of weak, dumb, and unhinged.

However, the honeymoon he had so perfectly planned for Toni has not been going the way he had thought it would. He had pictured a month of exploring this woman's mind, seeing what made her tick. However, she has been the most reticent to reveal details about her life, and Sunney, being the kindest man he can possibly portray, cannot bug her about it. He had also planned on repeatedly fucking her. She has almost near as high a sex drive as himself, and this morning was one of the first times she rejected him for sex. Sunney hates rejection in all forms. It means losing, and he has been raised never to lose. So, fueled with rage over his wife going behind his back and drinking, he decides it's time for him to visit a place where he won't face anger or rejection.

Sunney needs to have complete control in his romantic relationships. However, with Toni, he has struggled to gain control of her drug and alcohol use. It had been utterly embarrassing seeing her get wasted in front of his parents and coworkers at his holiday party. Since then, he has promised himself not to let her get that out of control again. He started with some bullshit pep talk — he reminded her how her parents, if alive, would hate to see her doped up and drinking. Then he marked every one of his bottles so he could tell what she was drinking and when. He then installed a tracking device in her piece-of-shit car to follow her whereabouts while he was at work or they were apart. After Andrea he had developed jealousy issues, but since growing up watching his father (who often cheated himself) closely watch his mother's whereabouts and drinking habits, jealousy had been basically instilled in his mind as normal behavior.

It is slow at Dolls. There are only a few vehicles parked outside, and the sidewalks are filled with strippers on smoke breaks clad in their high stockings and push-up bras while guards protect them from the creeps outside. Tuesday afternoon is a great day for Sunney to end up here. It won't be busy with his friends or the strippers who crowd him whenever he visits, praising him for all his help. One of the best reasons behind his Tuesday visit is that Heather, his favorite stripper, will be coming in for work less than an hour from now.

Heather Morgan is a tight-assed, perky breasted, doe-eyed super fan of Sunney. She and Andrea had been best friends. After his fallout with Andrea, Sunney had wondered why he hadn't just dated Heather instead. She wouldn't have cheated on him. Perhaps that was it. She praised his very name. People didn't want what they could have so easily. They subliminally craved what would make them work for it. It's basic human instinct. Heather was too clingy and dick hungry for Sunney to call her his. Although Toni was willing to be his from the get-go, she still longed for her ex. Sunney could tell because she would barely utter a word about him, and the very sound of his name made her grimace. Yes, it was due to all the pain he'd inflicted on her, but humans also liked to fog out something that hurt them by replacing it with something shinier and newer AKA Sunney. For the entire course of their relationship, he has been working on no longer being a rebound.

Putting on a navy beaten-up ball cap, Sunney walks through Dolls' double, black-colored fiberglass door. He's greeted by the clerk's station guarded by cheap dark plexiglass and an overweight middle-aged creep. Sunney, for his life, can't remember the man's name, even though he has been working the front desk for over five years. He had been working the night Sunney barged in to catch Andrea and willingly pointed Sunney to where they were.

"Mr. Jameson," he says, a fake fearful smile plastered on his face. The kind of "Oh shit, the boss just walked in. Hopefully, no one's slacking" look.

Sunney nods his head, continuing to walk into the building. He opens the cheap, lilac-painted second set of double doors and crosses through them into the club. The air is awfully warm and humid, like it always is in the middle of a summer day. Two main stages showcase three women simultaneously, with six smaller stages for one woman apiece on weekend nights when the club is busy. On the far-left side of the building, closest to the front doors, is the bar filled with bottles of mostly vodka flavors or whiskey. Sunney had put in a pretty penny to upgrade their alcohol choices to be more exquisite for his wealthy buddies.

Sunney goes straight to the bar, where only a few men occupy the seats. A barely legal short gal who works the bar, obviously too new to recognize him, walks over. Sunney finds her cute but not stripper-like attractive, which is probably why she has been assigned to the bar. She has a chirpy smile and a perky set of tits which may put her in good standing though. She has to lose a couple of pounds, as the Dolls management mostly hires anorexic model types. His choices and demands are always respected around here. It's not because that is specifically his type, just that most of his friends go for girls like that. Rich men like their women how they like the anorexic, cocaine-addicted models they don't stand a chance with. This is why he hadn't understood Toni's anger over his comment on her weight earlier. She regularly heard what his single friends said about large women. He didn't want to be the laughingstock of his friend group by marrying a wife who got fat.

Sunney orders a Jack and Coke, and when the bartender brings him his drink, he says, "Let Mike know I'm here, please."

The girl looking him up and down nods with a faint smile.

He heads over to the rear left small dance floor. A tall blonde with hair in a too-high ponytail moves her hips from side to side while leaning against the pole. The music is soft and melancholy — *Lady in Red* by Chris de Burgh. It instantly reminds him of *American Psycho* and the last time he had watched the movie as Patrick Bateman picked just the right tempo and classy songs to murder his victims to, as casually as some would pick a song to listen to while at the gym or on their drive to work. Such simplistic madness to that man. He had been attracted to Toni from the moment she had asked if he were some Patrick Bateman type the first time they met. Sadly, he was nowhere near the madness of that man.

A couple of minutes pass as Sunney sits and watches the blonde while she undresses. A couple of other men sit by the stage, but her eyes never leave his. She knows who he is; that much is obvious. They've not exactly met or spoken much, but all these women are thirsty for the wealthy man who blasted their business into a fortune. She approaches him on her knees, stopping a mere inch from him and sitting up enough that her fake tits rub onto his face. He quickly pinches his silver wedding band off and slips it into his pocket. He doesn't plan on explaining his recent marriage to all the girls, not quite yet. Marriage changes the way people perceive and treat you — not always in a bad way, but with his position here, it might.

"Hey, is there a Heather in today?" a deep, familiar voice asks behind him.

Sunney feels his body tense up. He recognizes that voice.

CHAPTER 16

Sunney Jameson

Sunney, as discreetly as he can, turns away from the stripper and toward the voice. Standing behind him are a cocktail waitress and a tall, bearded man. It takes Sunney a minute to recognize him. Tall, a little chubby, arms the size of tree trunks, and a fully trimmed beard. The man from the gas station who had eyed Toni like she was a piece of meat while trash-talking Rubico. How could he forget? Quinn. The man briefly glances over to the head that just looked his way, but Sunney quickly looks down and lets his hat cover his face.

The stripper notices Sunney is no longer giving her the attention she wants and goes over to one of the other men sitting nearby. He looks pleased to finally be getting some attention. Sunney likes it better that way — the clients are the ones who need to have a great time, so hopefully they will come back with other friends of theirs. Most girls here know to do their best when Sunney is present, but some are so eager for him to notice them that they forget to serve the clientele.

"She should be in soon. Can I grab you a drink while you wait?" the waitress asks.

"Sure, a whiskey sour, double. Thanks," Quinn answers.

Unsurprisingly, Heather has already clawed her nails into a new guy. She always feeds off any remotely attractive new toy. This is probably one of the reasons she's so fond of Sunney — he has never stayed put in town long enough to be old news.

A couple of moments later and surprise, Quinn takes a seat only a chair down from Sunney. He gazes at the stripper with longing eyes and places his hand briefly over his crotch. They really do have the same taste in drinks and women. As if noticing he's being watched, Quinn turns his head toward Sunney. They make eye contact, and for a moment, Sunney wonders if he remembers him. By the way his eyes instantly widen, he knows for a fact he does. Still, it isn't the reaction he had expected. It's almost as if Quinn had been intent on avoiding him for some reason and had been caught red-handed.

There's a moment of awkward silence. Looking at Quinn's dilated pupils, Sunney squints in disgust, masking it with a thin smile. Sunney wonders if he should just look away, pretend he doesn't recognize him, but decides he would rather have a little fun.

"Quinn, right?" Sunney asks, keeping his voice casual, acting like he barely recognizes him.

Finally, Quinn blinks and with a forced smile reaches out his hand and asks, "Jameson, right?"

This fucking asshole, Sunney thinks, extending his hand and giving Quinn a handshake so tight it's as if his life depends on it, which Quinn aggressively returns.

"How's it going?" Sunney says once their overly hard handshake is over.

"Living the dream. Didn't expect to see you here."

"You were expecting to see me elsewhere then?"

Sunney wants to make Quinn wiggle a bit. But he doesn't. He just shrugs and says, "Rubico's a small town."

"How's the wife?" he asks when Sunney ignores his comment.

He's being as genuinely nice as possible while trying to import dominance and carping into his words.

It's time for Sunney to show his dominant and in-control side. This man may tower over him in size and height, but Sunney has the two things he doesn't — money and women.

Sunney takes a couple of twenties from his pocket, holding them up for the stripper to see. It doesn't take long before she is near him again, rubbing her body to his. Taking the twenties, she rubs them over her body, all the while giving Sunney the eye fuck as Quinn stares, seemingly surprised.

"Was being a bit of a bitch this morning. Needed a break. You know how women get, or do you?" Sunney asks after the stripper returns to the pole to dance.

Seemingly not affected by his words, Quinn lightly chuckles and answers, "Oh, I do — all too well."

"Girlfriend? Married?"

"Married, once."

"You don't exactly come off as the married type."

"That's funny. I was thinking the same thing about you."

In most cases, this would be when the men walk outside to start fighting, but Sunney and Quinn keep grinning like it's playful banter.

Thankfully, to cut the tension, the cocktail waitress returns with Quinn's drink. As if parched to death, he takes a long gulp as soon as he gets it. Sunney breathes in and out, his thoughts buzzing. *He's obviously an alcoholic or suffering social anxiety. It's most likely the first, as Quinn does not come across as an anxiety-prone person. That and he seemed adamant about getting a double.*

Sunney has been studying Toni's social anxiety since they started dating. She drinks heavily whenever she feels awkward in a social situation, much like when they went to his holiday party. To cope with her nervousness, she drank like a fish that night. When his dad found out about her taking pills, he had instantly advised him to break up with her. Although Sunney is usually always faithful to his dad, he didn't follow through with this advice. Toni's dark and deep past intrigued him more than any other woman's had. He had to have her as his own, no matter how much of an alcoholic druggie she was.

They sit silently for a couple of moments, watching the stripper as the song ends. Both take bills out of their pockets and throw them on the stage. It gives Sunney a surge of confidence when the stripper eye fucks him as she grabs her money and gets off stage. Although this gives Sunney the upper hand, he knows Quinn is questioning the intentions of the overly attached stripper.

Good thing that the possibility of Quinn relaying this information back to Toni is slim to none. Rubico may be a small town, but Sunney will ensure Toni won't be caught dead in it alone, unescorted by himself.

"You must be a well-known man here," Quinn comments, keeping his tone timid, but Sunney knows it isn't just the stripper that gave him that impression. He's been talking to people. He just needs to know why his name is the chosen subject.

"Why would you assume that? I mean, I'm not saying no, but—" Sunney says, his eyes squinted and a palm raised in confusion.

As if deciphering his words, Quinn takes a large gulp of his drink, clears his throat, and answers, "I've met a couple of people around town who had good reviews of you."

"Ah. Gotta love small-town chatter. What can I say? At least my reputation precedes me."

Before Quinn can answer, the waitress grabs his empty drink, and, with a large grin, stares at Sunney and asks, "Another, Mr. Jameson?"

Although his drink is only half done, he can't fall behind Quinn. Not quite yet, anyway. Taking a too-large gulp and choking it down, Sunney hands his empty glass to the waitress and replies, "Sure, sweetie. Thanks."

After she is gone and a couple of moments of silence follow as the next dancer walks on the stage and a new song starts to play, Quinn chirps in, "That was some drink. It makes me think you might be a drinker like me."

Ah, good ol' alcoholic small talk, Sunney sarcastically thinks to himself. He dislikes Quinn more and more with every moment that passes. He despises most alcoholics and finds the way they talk to each other pathetic. *"Joe, are you really drinking again?" "Ha-ha, well, Bob, you're here too, ha-ha!"*

Visiting the bar four times a week is not a personality trait. Even Toni had mildly annoyed him when they first met, but at least she had a reason for her heavy drinking. Dead parents and killing your abusive boyfriend justify an alcohol addiction. If not, you're a sociopath or Mormon. Quinn appears to have a reason to be a heavy drinker — one that Sunney hasn't guessed yet.

"I'm more of a social drinker," Sunney says, knowing Quinn is probably the type to sit at home alone and drink till he pisses himself.

"No way," Quinn sarcastically replies.

There are a couple more minutes of silence before the waitress returns, handing them their drinks.

"I got that round," Sunney says.

"You drink free here, Mr. Jameson."

Sunney knew this would happen; he just wanted Quinn to know.

"Thanks, sweetie," Sunney says, grabbing a twenty from his wallet and placing the bill in the waitress's shorts, leaving his hand lingering on her waist momentarily.

She bites her lower lip briefly before walking off.

Quinn stares, amazed. "You a regular here?"

"Why do you say that?"

"Strippers don't just treat any customer like that."

"Not exactly. I don't live in Rubico, you see. Let's just say I know the owner personally."

"How so?"

"You ask a lot of questions, Quinn."

"I'm a curious guy."

"Well, for every question I answer, you take a drink. Sound fair?"

"As long as it goes the other way around," Quinn counters.

"Why not?"

Once again, there are a couple of moments of silence in which the men stare at each other, wondering how far each can take this game. Sunney couldn't care less about this man's roots. He yearns to know where Quinn has heard so much about him. Why Quinn cares is another mystery in itself.

"I'll start. Any reason you chose Rubico to move to? Rubico isn't exactly a bustling city."

As Sunney gulps his drink, he sees Quinn thinking momentarily. He wonders if he's debating whether to be honest or not.

"No reason for this town, in particular. It's small, less drama, and a cheap lot that fit my budget was for sale."

He's just vague enough in his answer that it seems honest. Sunney should've asked *why* he moved here instead.

"Any reason you're at a strip club on your honeymoon? I mean, no judgment, but isn't that reserved for your bachelor party?"

Sunney chuckles and waits as Quinn drinks nearly half his drink. He must want some liquid courage to ask the questions he's curious about.

"As I said earlier, I argued with the missus. She was a cunt so I needed a break."

Sunney wants a reaction out of Quinn, maybe choking on his drink or laughing hysterically with wide eyes, but he gets neither. Just a half smile greets him, like he had been expecting Sunney to say that. This is surprising as, the first time they met, he had only come across as gentlemanly and guarded. Quinn's drunk, so maybe the word "cunt" is no stranger to his mouth when angry.

"How long were you married for?" *Drink, swallow.*

As if expecting that question, Quinn nods and answers, "About two years."

"So short."

Quinn shrugs. "Sometimes shit doesn't go the way you want. How did you get your name so well known in this town?"

Sunney has been anticipating this question. If Quinn wants to be vague with his answers, so will he.

"I used my money in the right places, said the right things to the right people, then sat back and relaxed. I'm a businessman. Wasn't hard."

"Hmm, I need some tips, I guess."

None that I'm going to be giving you anytime soon, dickhead.

"Kids?"

Quinn shakes his head.

"You?"

"None that I'm aware of."

"Does your ex-wife know you're here?" *Drink, swallow.*

"Nope."

Rubico gives shelter to many runaways or people looking to be in hiding. That answer is the least surprising one of all.

"How long have you been with Toni?"

Finally, he asked a question about his wife. Sunney expected her to come up sooner or later.

"A little over a year."

"You move quick."

"I saw the woman I wanted to make mine forever and did just that. I don't believe in wasting time."

"I respect that."

"You and your ex-wife?"

"Three or four years."

"Thought you respected what I said."

Looking back, Quinn says, "I didn't know about her immediately, I guess. Wanted to get to know her a little better. Women have many shells, hiding what they truly are."

Before Quinn can ask his next question, the waitress appears with two shots of Jose Cuervo Tequila with limes and salt. Sunney immediately knows it's the owner playing a joke on him. He knows how much he hates cheap liquor. He looks around until he spots him behind the bar, waving with a huge grin. Sunney gives him the middle finger and makes eye contact the whole time while taking the shitty shot, forcing himself not to look like a pussy choking it down.

"Friend of yours?" Quinn asks, watching them and taking the shot easily, skipping the lime and salt to add insult to injury.

This man really is an alcoholic. This must've been what attracted him to Toni.

"Just a business partner. Anyway — as you were."

Taking the last gulp of his drink, Quinn asks, "What kind of business are you in that's so secretive?"

"You aren't some sort of Fed, are you?"

Quinn shakes his head.

"Well, between you and me, and saying as little as I possibly can, I'm in the business of earning money through this place in the easiest and moral-*ish* way I see fit."

"Prostitution?"

"Only if they want."

Quinn raises his eyebrows and nods. He either understands everything or nothing.

In the next fifteen minutes, they ask each other more questions, and Quinn finishes another two drinks. Sunney only just manages to finish his third, already feeling the effects of the shot. He wants to stay sober for this conversation and not get dumb. Although his feelings toward Quinn are still somewhat cold, he respects Quinn for remaining calm and collected with the answers he gets. However, there is a weird feeling between the two. They shouldn't get along like this, like something invisible is standing in their way.

The questions Sunney had asked Quinn had been a bore. He claimed he was born and raised in Massachusetts and had a younger brother and sister, which was no surprise as he'd come off as the eldest child. He had worked in the oil rigs for enough years to collect a pretty penny to give his girl a nice wedding. Her name was either Michelle or Meredith, and he obviously wasn't ready to answer Sunney's question of why they weren't together anymore because he had opted out with a shot of Pendleton (Sunney's least favorite drink). Quinn had asked Sunney where he was from, how old he was, whether he had been married before Toni, and what he did for a living other than the strip club business. He had happily supplied the answer, given his revenue is a substantial amount more than what Quinn makes or has ever made.

At this point, Quinn is headed directly toward getting hammered at such a fast rate that Sunney knows he has to have spent the morning drinking. With Sunney's turn up next, he decides to ask just that.

"Either you're a lightweight, or I'm guessing these weren't your first drinks of the day."

"No, I find it nearly impossible to deal with people unless I start the day drinking," Quinn explains.

"Does Toni know about your business here?" Quinn asks.

What a stupid question! If Quinn has learned anything about Sunney during this conversation, it is that he wouldn't be foolish enough to tell her.

"Fuck no," Sunney immediately replies.

"My turn. Just out of genuine curiosity, who exactly did you hear about me from, and how did I get brought up?"

Quinn's cheeks are immediately flushed. There's something he doesn't want to say.

"I heard about you twice. The other day from a stripper here. Heather, and some cop. Can't recall his name, overly friendly type."

He should've guessed it would be those two — two individuals who never seem to get him off their minds. Both are enamored with him. Instead of speaking his thoughts, as Sunney doesn't want many people to know a gay cop is in love with him, he nods. Adler's infatuation with him has been a major help when it comes to getting the police on his side, whether for his business or personal life.

"Heather a side piece of yours? No hate if she is. I get it. Men have needs."

"No, I don't believe in cheating. I've known her for some time. It started before I met Toni. The women in this town love men like me. I have money, looks, and am nice enough."

Now Sunney wants to find out why these individuals brought up his name. If there was any reason or whether, just like high school girls, they have no other personality trait and feel compelled to talk about their crush.

"Why did Heather and Adler start talking about me?"

Quinn bites his lip as if he has been hoping this question wouldn't pop up and that the earlier answer would've put the subject to bed.

"Because it seems we're sort of neighbors."

Sunney stares in disbelief. "I don't have neighbors."

"I didn't think I did either," Quinn says, shrugging.

"How close are we?"

"I'm not sure. Close enough that people know."

Interesting. He couldn't be close enough to him to matter. That dirt road his house was on went for miles upon miles out. Most of it was state land, except his and two other men who owned a few acres. Brian Peters must've rented his land out to Quinn. That idiot is always looking for ways to make an extra buck, and he owns a couple of shitty cabins sporadically laid out on that road. Most have been abandoned for a while, though. Quinn must've gotten a good deal. He really is hiding from something. People don't just buy shitty property in the woods because they want to. The wife he doesn't want to discuss must've had something to do with it.

"So, you say you don't believe in cheating. You don't count anything you do here as cheating?"

Sunney stares blankly at Quinn. He understands the question as it's been asked of him many times, by his friends mostly. They constantly cheat on their wives or girlfriends and ask him why he wouldn't because half the things he did could be construed as cheating. However, he doesn't see it that way. Sure, he watches his friends fuck a lot of models and strippers while also getting a couple of grabs of them, but if there isn't any emotional connection, or penetration for that matter, it is not being unfaithful.

"I didn't mean to offend. I'm just curious," Quinn says, sipping his drink while looking at the ground, seemingly awkward.

"No offense taken. In my mind, no, this isn't cheating. While I've been with my wife, I've never kissed or fucked another woman. Sure, I stare and sometimes grab a piece of ass, but that's harmless. It's all in fun. I don't care about any of these women. I don't go home to them. I don't care about what they have to say. But I care about Toni; I do. She's one of the only women I care about. All these others are just eye candy."

Sunney can tell Quinn doesn't agree with him. But his disapproval doesn't matter because other men don't need to agree with him. His views go when it comes to Toni and his relationship. Quinn and other men can have their views on cheating. He is practically a saint in his world compared to all the other men in his life.

"Shit, I'm buzzed. How about one last question?" Sunney asks.

Quinn nods, his eyes briefly watching the cocktail waitress deliver another drink.

"You find my wife attractive?"

Quinn's face finally shows some emotion. His eyes widen, and his eyebrows perk up.

"Err — what?"

"It seemed like you did at the gas station," Sunney says, raising his glass and taking a swig.

"I don't want to offend you."

"You won't, I promise."

Quinn thinks a couple of moments more, his stance changing from relaxed to awkward and slightly off like he's hiding something.

"I mean, initially when I saw her, yeah, I found her — good looking," he gulps, "but, generally, when I see a ring on the left hand, I stop looking. Out of respect, you know? I didn't like men staring at my wife."

"Fair enough."

"I got one last question for you," Quinn counters.

"Shoot."

"You're obviously a well-off man — charismatic, young, and wealthy. You just don't come off as the settling-down type. I don't know about any other men, but I would not be ready to settle down if I had what you have."

"Well, don't get me wrong. Settling down has been hard. I've had many gorgeous women in my time, but one night I just met the perfect woman for me."

"Perfect woman?"

"This may sound crazy, but I have a very specific type. When it comes to their looks, to be attracted to them, I also have to see some resemblance between them and a Bond girl."

Quinn squints his eyes, confused.

"So, when I was growing up, my dad used to love the old Bond movies. I watched them religiously as a child — I had gotten into them since I wanted to do anything to get to know my mostly cold father. I think I was maybe twelve and about to start puberty, when I started growing very fond of those movies strictly due to the gorgeous women James Bond wooed. My dad obviously noticed this, leaned over and told me, and I quote, "Don't stop searching till you find your perfect Bond girl, son — your favorite of them all."

"Well, after really staring at her and all her features, my wife Toni reminded me of my favorite Bond girl and, quite honestly, the most beautiful woman in the world — Jane Seymour from *Live and Let Die*."

Quinn is silent for a moment, probably processing what he just heard. Generally, Sunney's rule regarding women made people silent once they heard it. He has had the rule since high school. He didn't believe in settling for a less-than-perfect woman in his eyes, not just physically but also mentally.

"You know, I actually thought she looked like Meg Foster with her eyes and all," Quinn says.

"So, you thought of my wife long enough to compare her to a celebrity?"

"Oh no — no — no I—"

"I'm just giving you shit, man. I get it. All men do it. We all search for a woman that'll remind us of a woman we can never have. Me? I'm just a little more open about it, so I don't sound like a complete shallow prick. I also heavily look at their mental state and personality."

"Their mental state?"

"Well, I like the women I'm with to be hopelessly dumb and a little unhinged with a difficult past life. I like to be the man that rescues and takes care of them. I like them to be dumb because I can do as I want without them suspecting a thing."

"That excludes cheating, though?" Quinn asks, clearly not convinced about that aspect.

"Absolutely not. I get many chances to do it, but it just seems so immoral to me. It's almost worse than murder."

Quinn stares dead-eyed at Sunney for a couple of moments.

"You asked, man."

Quinn continues to stare. To the rare few with whom Sunney shares that tidbit, it is generally their expression.

"Fuck, man," he whispers, making Sunney chuckle. "And how is Toni messed up exactly?"

"She's a recovering alcoholic as of now, but when we met, she was a full-blown fucked-up alcoholic and an opiate-obsessed depressed individual. All her life has been elegiac. Her parents both ate it early on. Her mother was a major whore and alcoholic, which fucked with her loving father. She doesn't talk about that much, which I understand. And that's just the high school years. Her adult life is a bit more fucked. She dated a narcissistic, physically and emotionally abusive man for three years. When she tried ending the relationship, he tried killing her, and she stabbed him to death to protect herself."

Quinn's mouth is wide open. His eyes are huge as if he has just discovered this information about a close friend who had slid it under a mat the whole time. In his defense, most people in their lifetimes don't meet murderers.

Before he can speak, there's a loud squeal from across the club. "Sunney?"

Sunney immediately downs the last of his drink and turns his seat around toward the sound of the voice. The hot cock-hungry brunette, Heather, runs as fast as her four-inch heels allow her. She's wearing a black silk robe tightly wrapped around her small frame. She hasn't changed one bit since the last time Sunney saw her. If anything, she has gotten much hotter.

He receives a tight hug, her tits pressed nearly right in his face and her ass in the air. Her favorite style is to hug men. She's still a tease at heart, even if they have already been together. Sadly enough, he has only fucked her several times over a span of three days during a trip Sunney had taken before formally asking Toni to be his girlfriend. The sin of being unfaithful was just something Sunney couldn't quite understand himself and this fact got under his skin. Coming here, his boundaries were often tested, as most women here would fuck him in a heartbeat.

"Where have you been? Why didn't you call?" Heather asks Sunney, letting go and trying to sound perky and happy, hiding her hurt.

Knowing Quinn is eavesdropping, Sunney half-grins and says, "Busy time to be me, dear. I've been good, though, missed the hell out of everyone."

"We all missed you too, especially me. Well, shit — I have thirty minutes till I dance. Want to come to the back and catch up? All the girls want to see you."

Sunney briefly peers at Quinn, who is sipping his drink and staring at the current dancer. Seeing Quinn and Heather close by, he suddenly remembers Quinn had been asking for her.

"Sure, oh! My friend over here asked for you. Be a doll and say hi."

Heather quickly turns around, and recognizing Quinn only takes her a few moments. *They must've just met recently,* Sunney realizes. She immediately goes to Quinn and gives him a less tight but still nice squeeze of a hug. It is Sunney's turn to stare at her ass as she bends down. He also notices Quinn keeps his drink in his hand, and the other touches the left side of her shoulder. In contrast, most men would instantly go to her ass or lower back at the very least.

"Quinn, right? We met in the supermarket just yesterday." She beams.

"I came by like I said I would."

Heather smiles while Quinn awkwardly nods his head.

"Be a doll and give Quinn a nice dance. He deserves it. My treat."

Quinn shakes his head and says, "Oh no! I couldn't do that to you, man."

Sunney raises his hand and says, "I insist. It's the least I could do for making you sit here and bullshit with me the last hour."

Sunney takes a couple hundred-dollar bills from his pocket and, leaning over, places them in Heather's robe pocket, briefly caressing her side.

"I thought we were going to talk," Heather asks, her doe eyes enlarged and on Sunney.

"We will. I got to take care of some stuff first anyway. Work stuff. Remember, I've been gone awhile."

Sunney finishes the remainder of his drink and stands, and Quinn does the same. They stare at each other for a few moments before extending their arms for a tight handshake.

"It was nice talking to you. Thanks again."

"Not a problem. Be seeing you around, Robins."

The conversation had done very little but give Sunney more questions about his new neighbor. He would find answers soon enough, he decides.

As Heather grabs Quinn's hand and leads him to the back, Sunney takes out his Motorola and dials Officer Adler's number. He knows he's on duty now, which will work perfectly for what he wants.

"Adler, it's me. I need a favor. What? Yes, I missed you. Hold up, what happened?"

With the too-loud music and Adler's natural ability to overreact and talk fast, Sunney misses half of his words.

"We can talk tonight after you're off work. Right now, I need a favor. I need you to do a background check on someone for me."

CHAPTER 17

I wake up from a post cry-fest nap to a pounding noise downstairs. My heart rate is instantly out of control as I throw the blankets off my body and get into a sitting position. My head is still pounding from my drinking earlier today. I really am getting soft. I had cried myself to sleep, which I know, in my many years of doing so, often gave me baggy red eyes and a headache.

The pounding, which starts up again, is exacerbated by the doorbell going off. My mind instantly imagines some intruder trying to make their way in. But it wouldn't make sense to make a commotion and wake me up. Then again, would it matter, considering we're in the middle of literally fucking nowhere. They could make as much sound as they wanted, and only the house owners would be around to hear it.

I get out of bed, grab my robe, and wrap it around my body, as I'd only worn a thin tank top and shorts to bed. I hustle downstairs, stopping at the bottom to listen for more sounds. As my heart continues to beat at an excessive rate, a thought finally comes to mind. *Sunney hasn't come home.* Maybe it's him at the door, locked out. It's dark out, with the moon adding little light to the dim house. I walk a few steps to glance at the clock on the oven. It's five past ten. Sunney has been gone about ten hours now. If that is him, he'd better have a damn good excuse for where he's been. Going to the bar to have a couple when you need airtime is one thing, but it's another to disappear for nearly half a day.

I discard my fear of the possibility that there's an intruder and head to the door. However, just as I get to it, another couple of knocks ensue. I look through the peephole and nearly gasp when I see who it is. Not Sunney, but Quinn.

His eyes look around frantically as if he expects someone to come up behind him any minute. He must have walked here because he's wearing a thick brown bomber, and his jeep is nowhere in sight. He's also swaying back and forth, so he must be drunk — that or he's cold from his walk over here.

"Quinn?" is all I can get out.

He straightens up, as if trying to hide his intoxication.

"Toni, I know it's late, but I need to talk to you."

I feel an uneasy tingle in my stomach. Although I'd eagerly agreed to be alone in this man's home and ended up safe, the thought of letting him into my own feels wrong. Perhaps he'd thought over the whole situation and is back for revenge. He isn't a big fan of Sunney and could easily cause an argument between us, telling him I was alone with him this morning.

"I am sorry about earlier today. It wasn't right trying to slap you, but you shouldn't be here. Sunney would be furious—"

"This is about Sunney," Quinn says, staring through the peephole. It almost feels like we are face to face.

I put my hand over the first lock on our door, but I stop myself from unlocking it. Sunney isn't home and could be in danger. What if it has to do with Quinn? What if I'm letting some psychopath in, who wants to butcher me? But then I reason, *if this man wanted to kill me, he probably would have done it already, right?*

"One sec," I say and head over to the kitchen.

I grab one of the largest knives from the knife block and return to the door. I hide the knife behind my back and open the front door with a deep breath.

I am instantly greeted by a cold gust of wind that blows my robe up slightly, which Quinn notices. I want to wrap my arms around my waist out of embarrassment, but the knife in my hand, which I've hidden behind my back, stops me from doing so. We stare silently at each other for a moment, and I notice how good Quinn looks in the dim light of the waxing crescent moon. It's a dark night, but the stars and moon add enough light to make out the features of this attractive drunken man. I can't help but let my mind wander to all Quinn could do if he wanted — from grabbing me and choking me to death or grabbing my neck while we passionately kiss.

"Hey, sorry to wake you up. Have — have you been crying?" Quinn says, squinting as he looks at my face, and it takes a couple of moments for me to realize he has noticed the puffiness of my eyes.

"No, I'm just — tired. You really shouldn't be here," I say, taking one hand from under my back and rubbing my eyes, hoping to fade the puffiness into oblivion.

"I saw Sunney today."

I widen my tired eyes. "Where?"

"Strip club."

"What?"

As if nervous about what he's going to say, Quinn looks at the ground, takes a deep breath, and says, "I know it is none of my business, but Toni, you seem like a good person. Even though you tried to slap me and accused me of trying to fuck you, I like you. This is why I need to tell you all the fucked up shit your husband was saying and is doing currently."

"How — how did you guys even start talking?"

"He recognized me, I guess. I tried to hide, but he saw me. Then, for an ungodly hour, I had to talk to him."

I gulp and ask, "Do you know where he is now?"

"Probably still there, Toni. He knew A LOT of the people there."

An aching fury instantly replaces my fear.

"What are you saying?"

"He was practically gloating about the fact he's in cahoots with the owner doing some sort of shady shit."

"What shady shit?"

"I don't know. He didn't specify, but I know it's illegal. If I had to guess, some sort of drug dealing, or maybe even prostitution."

My mind spins on the idea that Sunney would do such a terrible thing. The man who, just four days ago, I could hardly imagine parking in a handicap parking spot because of how wrong he thought that would be. Now it's possible that he is running an illegal operation. It would make sense as to having a cabin in a small town.

"Wait — how the hell could he even get away with all that?"

"I'm pretty sure he's using a cop in town to get away with it, but I really don't know. All I know is things are weird there. A stripper especially seemed to have a great fondness for him. He made her give me a lap dance, and the whole time she was doing it, she was asking about him. He didn't even have his wedding ring on, for Christ's sake."

The possibility of Sunney being unfaithful has come to my mind many times due to his undeniable attractiveness and charisma but never had I thought he would follow through with anything like that. So, this is the reason he has never really been in relationships. He wanted to enjoy being single and doing what he wanted until the right person came along that would change him and the bachelor lifestyle. Of course, the thought of how easy it would be for him to cheat had crossed my mind, but I had decided not to give in to my jealous instincts after Tom. There had been plenty of toxic jealousy in that relationship to last a lifetime.

I take a deep breath and try to slow the anger filling up my body. I need to save up my anger for Sunney, and not Quinn.

"Okay, why did you come here this late and tell me? It's not that I'm not grateful you did, it's just—" *It's not something someone who nearly got slapped by the person they were telling would do.*

"Well, for one, I didn't like how things ended between us, and second, I felt like you deserved to know. He, uh — told me about your parents, last boyfriend, and what happened," Quinn says, his eyes on the ground after the last part.

Without meaning to, I drop the knife I was holding to the ground. I should care that Quinn now knows I had thought he might try to harm me with his visit, but I'm too shocked. I hate people knowing about Tom. People don't look at you the same way once they find out you have killed someone. Most of Sunney's family are great examples of that. They looked at me like I was some freak the day I saw them after Sunney had told them. After that, I made him promise not to tell anyone else as I wanted the incident to go away. But something like that never truly can.

Ignoring my deceived mind for a moment, I notice Quinn's eyes are gloomy.

"I'm sorry. I was just scared you were here because of the whole slapping inside—"

But before I can finish explaining, Quinn wraps his arms around my waist. Although it's chilly outside, his body is warm like a heater, and I feel his hot breath on the back of my neck. It must be the booze. His body pressed against me slows my heart rate.

"It's okay. I understand, Toni. You've been abused, and men scare you. I can't imagine living with that."

I let out a deep breath, my heart rate slowing down even more. He's not angry with me for suspecting him of having ill motives. It's strange because I know Sunney would be furious, and so would I. Quinn's mind really does work differently than that of most men. I wonder if he was this calm and collected with his wife. What could have possibly caused this man to not make his marriage work?

Finally, he lets me go, and without really thinking twice, I ask, "What happened with your wife?"

Quinn is immediately frozen in place, obviously not expecting that question.

"Come on. You know my deep dark secret. What's yours?"

"It's not really a deep dark secret. I was just an alcoholic."

Quinn's leaving something out, and I want to call him out on it but decide not to. At least not for now, because I know damn well if he asks me questions about Tom, I wouldn't give him a completely honest answer. Then again, I never give anyone a full explanation of that and hopefully never will.

"And you moved out in the middle of nowhere because?"

"To get away from it all. Start fresh. Is that so hard to believe?"

"No, I get it. How long have you and your wife been separated?"

Thinking for a couple of moments, Quinn says, "Six months."

It is still fresh, which explains why he is being so vague. Hell, in ten years, I know I will still be vague about Tom.

"Sunney also — uh, told me about your parents. I can't completely understand that, but my mom left the picture when I was young, and my dad was an alcoholic dirtbag. I don't talk to either of them."

"My parents weren't always awful if that's what Sunney told you. Their failed marriage and eventual death were mostly my fault."

"What happened, if you don't mind me asking?"

I should mind, but for some reason, those sad hazel eyes of Quinn's make me want to tell him almost everything about my past. I can't even blame the liquor, which would usually cause oversharing. I am sober and trust this man. However, at the thought of this story, I do want a little something to take the edge off. Although it is wrong, I suddenly don't care. My husband is out getting plastered with strippers. Why would a simple drink and story make me such a bad person?

"Hold on. I need a drink if I'm going to tell this one," I say, and Quinn chuckles.

I turn around and head for the kitchen, unsure if I'll find anything. I check the cupboards next to the fridge and find a couple of bottles of Sunney's high-end whiskeys. I hope that won't be my only option. After rummaging around, I check the fridge and in the back behind all the food, I find a half-empty bottle of white wine. Strange, I never knew Sunney drank wine. His mom does a lot, but I remember him complaining about its dry taste. He could not have been saving it for me as it has already been opened. Maybe his last girlfriend liked it, and he forgot to throw it out when they broke up.

I pop the top off and take a long chug. It has a dry licorice taste with minimal sweetness. I want to yak it up in the sink but force it down my throat. If I can handle straight Crown, I can handle expired white wine.

"Wine, huh?" a voice says behind me.

I quickly whirl around to see Quinn standing at the kitchen counter, his elbow resting on it. Still in a thick jacket, his arms somewhat bulge like he's again flexing. Before I can begin to fawn over his muscles, I catch sight of the kitchen knife I had dropped and forgotten to pick up in his hand. My heart rate increases again as I look at it. It reminds me of the last night of Tom's life. He had a much cheaper steak knife in his hand as he ate the dinner I'd prepared for us, and it ended up being the same one with which I stabbed him to death when he tried suffocating me on our cold, dirty linoleum floor.

Noticing my blank expression, Quinn sets the knife down on the counter.

"Sorry, I just didn't want to leave that on the floor."

I tightly shut my eyes for a few seconds while taking another gulp of the wine to blur out that goddamn night.

Opening my eyes, I smile and say, "I'm not normally like this. I promised myself I would not let that night forever be ingrained in my mind."

"Hey, we all have a traumatic memory ingrained in our heads, right? Some — some are just worse than others."

"Care to elaborate?" I ask.

"Do you?"

I take another sip of the wine and walk over to the front of the counter to stand directly across from Quinn. I set the bottle on the counter and push it in his direction.

"Good point. Drink?" I offer.

"That looks refreshing, but I actually have my own," Quinn says, reaching into his back pocket to pull out a silver flask.

I nod, grabbing the wine bottle. I want another drink to tell this story, but my tastebuds hate the sour wine. I almost want to do it to spite Sunney for being at the place he is now. If it had been Tom instead of Sunney, I know exactly how I'd react, but I also know exactly what the consequences would be. More than ever, these past couple of days have led me to the brink of transitioning into the Old Toni.

"I don't want to make you talk about something you don't want to," Quinn says, interrupting nearly a full minute of silence.

"No, I want you to know. I don't want you believing some backward ass story my husband told you."

Quinn nods.

"So, my parents met and married after only a year of knowing each other. They were totally and utterly in love, and soon after getting married, they decided to have me. Because my mom's pregnancy was apparently very painful for her, and she suffered from a severe eating disorder after I was born from all the pregnancy weight, she got her tubes tied. She was always that way — obsessed with her body image. She also had a heavy drinking problem and couldn't be faithful to my father. My poor father was so in love with her he didn't even know. It went on like that for quite some time. Until I turned sixteen and did just one thing to break their marriage in shambles."

I stop speaking as I realize I usually skip the part of the story I am getting to. I have not even told Sunney about this. All he knows is the story of my mom and dad's failed marriage and their eventual death. Quinn looks at me, puzzled. I know I should not go ahead, but what will I lose from telling him? I haven't shared it with Sunney because he might think less of me. With Quinn, I don't think he would. He seems to have just as fucked up, if not more so, a life than I do.

"I–I met someone during my sophomore year in science class. He was the new teacher. Mr. Nortec was thirty years old, unmarried, and totally handsome. I found myself purposely failing assignments and tests to get his attention. I even started seeing the most obnoxious boy in class because I knew he would lecture me about it, and he did. I eventually located him and showed up at his house one night. Psychotic, trust me, I know. I just felt I had to have him. It worked, and I lost my virginity to him. After a couple of months of secretly dating, I fell in love with him. After my seventeenth birthday, my mom caught me sneaking out a couple of times to see him and found and read a diary I kept. It was filled with details of everything we were doing. Do not ask why I would keep that sort of stuff in a diary — maybe because I fully did not believe it myself and had to write it all down. That is where the disaster started. My mom reported what she read in my diary to the school. The school, in turn, found a pair of my underwear I had left in his desk. Since I was underage, the cops got a warrant to search his house and found naked pictures of me. He got out on bail, but before his court hearing, he hung himself. My parents started fighting about how and why I did such a vile thing. Eventually my dad found out about her multiple infidelities. Once he did, she immediately filed for divorce—" I blink hard, and a few tears roll down my cheeks. "He shot himself one night while I was sleeping over at a friend's. My mom came home to find all the evidence, and she only lasted maybe another year — long enough for me to graduate high school — before drinking herself to death."

Although my puffy eyes sting from the tears, it feels good to let the truth free for the first time in years. I have kept that story hidden for so long that I almost don't believe it myself. Mr. Nortec, my first love, was the beginning of all my fucked-up views on relationships. I have blocked out most of our relationship. However, something I couldn't erase from my mind was the look my parents gave me, or everyone in the school who called me a slut during the rest of the year.

"Jesus, Toni. I'm sorry."

I take another sip of my wine, wiping tears from my eyes.

"It's not often I meet people with a more fucked up life than my own."

"Are you ever going to tell me what's so fucked up about your life?"

"Toni . . ."

"I mean, you know about me fucking my science teacher, being at fault for my parents dying, and killing my ex-boyfriend. What could be so fucking worse than that?"

Quinn looks uneasy and breaking eye contact, says, "None of that stuff is your fault. You were only sixteen. Your teacher was a groomer. With your ex-boyfriend, you were just protecting yourself. He would have killed you. None of what happened was your fault. It is just incredibly bad luck. What I did — is different. It was my — my—"

"Fault? What did you do? Quinn, you can talk to me. I won't judge you."

Thinking hard momentarily, Quinn takes a deep breath and says, "I cannot tell you. Not here anyway, not like this. Meet me tomorrow night for a run. I will have my jeep."

I hear the word "night" and automatically say, "I can't."

Quinn reaches forward and puts his hands over my cheek. It's cold at first, and I cringe, but seconds later, the feel of his fingers is warm and comforting on my puffy cheeks. It's exactly how I wanted to be touched while crying myself to sleep. I wonder what my future holds with Sunney if all Quinn told me tonight is true. Would I just end up like his mother? A sad snail of a human being while my husband is the life of the party and a bachelor in his mind? I mean, like father like son, right? Maybe this whole time, he's been putting on some facade to woo me and now, once married, he has decided to treat me like trash.

"Meet me at 2 a.m., please," Quinn says, pursing his lips and twisting his head as if begging like a puppy would for kibble.

Just like I had when I agreed to run with him before, I say without thinking, "Okay."

"You will not regret it, Toni. Thank you," Quinn says and, letting go of my face, walks around the counter in my direction.

Soon we are only inches apart, like we have been multiple times, but it feels different. His breath still reeks of Jack, of course, but this time my mind is not going through how what I'm doing is wrong and what Sunney would think of it. I don't care about that now. Now I want to be near Quinn, talk to him, and know his past.

"I can't help but wonder what things would have been like if only we'd met just a little earlier," he says.

"You wouldn't have liked me. I used to be drunk."

"I'm drunk, and you like me," he jokes.

"I guess our vices mesh well," I say, tipping the wine bottle up to take another drink, nearly spilling it all over my face due to my trembling hands.

Seeing this, Quinn gently grabs the bottle from me and sets it on the counter.

"You do not need to be afraid of me. I will not ever use or hurt you as they did."

I bite my lip, swallowing the cold wine that had settled into my gums.

"I'm not afraid of you."

"I can't explain it, but there's something special about you. I have this feeling you need protection."

"Protection from what?"

Quinn thinks for a couple of moments before saying, "The world. It has been unkind to you."

I bite my lip again so hard that I feel a sharp pain. Old Toni says that I deserve all the pain I've endured. She thinks the world should be worse for me. That it already isn't cruel enough.

"Sometimes I wonder if it's actually me that's been the unkind one to the world," I mutter, thirsting for another sip of wine to wash my anger away.

"Your mind is playing tricks with you. You are not unkind, not in the slightest."

I reach my hands over to rest on his chest. I wish he did not have his jacket on so I could feel him through the thin t-shirt. Quinn cocks his head to the side, reaching his hands up to grab my arms, pulling me closer.

Oh god, is this really happening?

Before I can answer any of those questions, we hear a vehicle's door closing outside. *Sunney.*

CHAPTER 18

I immediately clench my hand on Quinn's jacket.

"You have to go," I quickly say and pull Quinn to the back door leading to the porch.

I hastily unlock it and pull the sliding door open. Then, without meaning to, I push Quinn outside. Just thinking about what would happen if Sunney caught him here, especially if he's drunk, brings me a world of panic.

"What? Can't I just hide in the closet?" Quinn jokes.

I want to laugh, but my adrenaline levels and fear are too high.

"Quinn, I'm serious. You have to go," I repeat.

"I'll see you tomorrow night?" Quinn asks.

"Yes," I answer and quickly shut the sliding door, closing the blinds.

Seconds later, I hear the front door open. As fast as my tired legs allow me, I run up the stairs just in time to hear it closing. Running down the hallway, I remember the stupid wine bottle. Hopefully, Sunney will go straight to bed and not linger in the kitchen, giving me time to sneak downstairs later to hide it. Once I get to the bed, I remove my robe, quietly get in, and wrap the blankets over my body. As each moment passes, I get antsier, imagining Sunney discovering the bottle or even finding Quinn.

A couple of minutes pass until I hear footsteps coming up the stairs and straight into the bathroom. He's in the bathroom for only a minute or so before he exits. I hear rustling as he staggers, taking off his clothing. I feel his body get into the bed and wait for him to possibly wake me up or touch me. None of these things happen, so I creep my eye open to see him laying down, facing away from me. Internally outraged, I want to shake him awake and demand to know where he has been all night and see if he lies or tells the truth. It's not like I can tell him I know where he's been without outing Quinn.

I fight every stab of anger in my body to say something, anything to him. Instead, I close my eyes and try to let sleep take me instead. Although my body is begging me to rest, my mind keeps thinking about tomorrow night, Quinn, and my already crumbling marriage. If I see Quinn, I may regret it, but I also know if I don't go, I may regret it even more. It's an inner battle with my morals and the enticing need to see this man I barely know. If I do go, which my brain has already confirmed will happen, how am I going to sneak out that long without Sunney knowing? It'll be late, but how can I be sure he will even be asleep by then?

Sleeping pills, Toni. Drug him.

No.

Quinn's kind, hazel eyes flash in my mind. He talks to me like he's the damaged love interest from a romance novel. I want to know his secrets; I want him to feel comfortable to reveal his past. I bite my lip. Okay, sleeping pills it is. Not a lot. Just enough to knock him out so I can sneak away. It's the only safe option.

I wait ten minutes until I hear Sunney begin to do his quiet snore. It confirms he's asleep, so I sneak to the bathroom to find the pills in the bathroom cabinet. I don't take them, but I know Sunney occasionally does to help him sleep when he's stressed about work. He's got some potent ones from his doctor. But the chance of him taking some on our honeymoon is slim.

Entering the bathroom, I open the cupboard and scan everything in it. I let out an instant sigh of relief when I find a small bottle labeled Zolpidem. I open the bottle and frown when I see there are only three remaining. I have never known Sunney to take prescription drugs for sleeping. Hopefully, he won't notice they're gone — at least not immediately. If he does notice it eventually, I can take the blame.

I place the bottle back in its place, stuff the pills in my pajama pockets, and exit the bathroom. Then I run downstairs and hide the pills in one of the kitchen cabinets, so I'll easily be able to crush them and place them in his dinner or drink. Before leaving, I remember the bottle of wine I forgot to put away and realize it's no longer on the counter. So, he did find it. I look at the trash, immediately thinking he must have tossed it. Nope. Probably opted instead to hide it from me.

Fucking asshole. He can go out all night to a strip club, but God forbid I have a glass of wine.

I go back upstairs and, once again, as slowly as possible, get back into bed. I fight the urge to wake him and tightly close my eyes, before my body finally lets me fall asleep.

CHAPTER 19

The next day I don't crawl out of bed until nearly eleven. I know it'll be difficult to face Sunney and not choke him while hiding guilt over my plans to drug him. I thought there would be a chance that a good night's sleep might awaken some sense in me about this crazy plan, but I still feel the urge to go through with it. Old Toni is taking over me again.

I take a long shower, staring straight ahead as the water dowses me for more than ten minutes. I imagine Sunney being there with me if our honeymoon hadn't gone to shit and he wasn't out doing God knows what today already. He hadn't even felt the decency to wake me up and talk things over or at least kiss my forehead like he did most mornings. It's like a switch flipped the moment we were married.

After my shower, I dry off and put on a plain red sundress. Looking at myself in the mirror, I wonder if I will wear this when meeting Quinn. It'll probably be too cold, but considering the way the dress hugs my curves, I want to bear through it. With most of yesterday looking and feeling like a mess, I want to look somewhat decent. If Old Toni were to take over, I want to at least keep New Toni's ability to look attractive.

Taking slow, short steps downstairs, I spot Sunney sitting on the living room couch, eating a burger, which is surprising as he normally skips lunch or eats something moderately healthy. The TV is also on, which is another surprise as he limits his TV time to mostly at night, if ever. He doesn't like how it turns people into lazy slobs. Now that I'm angry with him, it sounds rather condescending.

We make eye contact, and swallowing his food, he says, "You're finally up."

I badly want to ignore him, so I don't start yelling. Instead I nod my head, and once down the stairs, move to the kitchen. I bite my lip, knowing I cannot ask him about last night. All I can do is act clueless about the fact that I know where he truly was. My stomach feeling miserably empty, I decide to make myself lunch. I halfheartedly expect Sunney to say something or get up to talk to me, but instead, he continues eating.

"If you want an argument, I'm not going to give you one," he finally says, and I can't help but stop what I'm doing almost right away to turn around and glare.

Now is when I start to look him over in a more analytical manner. He's wearing beige cargo shorts and a loose light grey tank top. Even with comfy clothes on, I still can't tell if he's hungover. Although he is growing a little facial hair, his face is still clear, and his eyes are not baggy.

"I don't want an argument. I want you to tell me what you could have possibly been doing all night," I say, turning away and continuing to make my lunch.

"I had a couple of drinks with some buddies and then went for a drive. Felt it was for the best we got some time apart to calm down."

Fucking liar. I bite my tongue to keep myself calm.

"Okay, Sunney. Whatever."

"Real mature."

I feel my hands begin to shake from anger. I can't do this; I'm going to explode. I finish preparing my sloppily made sandwich quickly and head back upstairs.

I sit in bed and wolf my food. I desperately want a bottle of vodka to wash it all down. It seems so long since I've craved liquor this heavily and often.

After eating, I toss my plate on the floor and wrap the covers around myself. As I lay in the darkness, I wonder what tonight might have in store for me. It now dawns on me that I know nothing about Quinn. He's hiding something big, but what is it? How bad could it possibly be? He seems one of the most genuine and honest people I have ever met. But I am just starting to realize that looks can be deceiving. I have to go through with this drugging plan. If I fail or get caught, who knows what the consequences might be?

CHAPTER 20

Quinn Robins

As Quinn turns the ignition to his jeep on and drives down to the intersection going to town and Sunney's cabin, he feels his whole body peppering with goosebumps. He cannot tell if it's due to the cool air coming through his open window or his nervousness about the fact he will be meeting a married woman at two in the morning to do God knows what and that he has the news clipping from that fateful night to show said married woman.

Last night while tossing and turning in bed for hours on end, he had decided he would tell Toni what he was hiding. She had told him about her past, after all. Whether she would understand or freak out and possibly tell the police is the biggest question. Although they barely know each other, there is something in the depths of those sad, ice-blue eyes that indicate she wouldn't tell anyone. No one had discovered his deep dark secret in the six months and two moves since it had happened.

As he drives slowly, never going faster than ten miles per hour, he stares at the crescent moon and the starless sky behind it. Something about this makes him feel wistful;

surely a night like this with so much on the line should at least be a full moon. If he freaks Toni out and she leaves forever, he could drink himself away to a beautiful-looking sky, maybe even get lucky and finally catch alcohol poisoning. It is what he should have gotten that night six months ago when his wife died.

When he approaches the intersection, he parks near the tree Toni had been standing by the other day. The large oak tree blocks the already dimly lit moon and brings darkness inside his jeep. He turns his headlights off to make it even darker in the chance anyone drives across this otherwise isolated road, although the likelihood is low. As he sits and waits, he grabs his now nearly empty bottle of Jack and takes a swig to hopefully get rid of the jitters. He doesn't want to make Toni nervous. This is why he drove to town that morning and bought her a bottle of Crown Royal since she seemed to enjoy it that day they had hung out. It's not that he wants to get her drunk and take advantage of her; just to loosen her senses up a bit. Drunk people either take bad news a hundred times better or worse.

He tosses the Jack back to the passenger side floor when he sees a dark figure walking in the background. He immediately gets the jitters again, now nervous at the off chance that Sunney and Toni had had a change of heart and she had told him everything. Not that he thinks Sunney would be able to overpower him in a fight, but something about the little fucker gives him the impression he isn't a fair fighter. He is possibly the wealthiest and most powerful man in this shit town, so it would not be easy having him as an enemy.

Now overwhelmed by his sudden anxiety, Quinn turns his lights back on to flash the figure and maybe get away if need be. Not that he could get far, as this last move had taken most of the money from his wife's life insurance.

Illuminated from the Jeep's high beams is not the figure of Sunney. Flaunting her curves in a dress similar to the one she'd been wearing when they met, is Toni. She looks nearly the best Quinn has ever seen her. She's wearing a tight, form-hugging red sundress that goes down to her upper thighs with a low V-neck exposing her small breasts. She raises her arm, blocking the glare of the headlights, and Quinn wants to turn them off, but he doesn't want to stop seeing her.

He forces himself out of the jeep, although his legs suddenly feel like jello. He can only manage to stand there and watch as she walks in his direction. During every other meeting, he has been trying his best not to watch her like some creep, but it was damn near impossible this time. Her curly pitch-black hair is down instead of in a ponytail. It falls to right below her chest; she clearly isn't wearing a bra, so her hard nipples are exposed. Quinn reaches his fist up to his mouth and bites it, trying to contain all his dirty thoughts of lowering that tight dress just a couple of inches to get a look at them.

Finally, when they are only a couple feet away, Quinn gets out of his head and realizes how cold she must be. He takes off his oversized plaid jacket and hands it to her. Her cheeks flush red, and she places it over her shoulders.

"You came," Quinn says.

She nods and says, "You asked me to."

"Right."

"And I suppose I kind of wanted to. Were the lights in my face really necessary?"

Quinn wants to be honest and tell her he had his doubts it was her coming. He thought it might be her husband with a pistol ready to murder him, but he wants to keep the conversation off that man.

"With these woods, I had to be sure you were coming."

"Did you think I was a bear?" Toni jokes back.

Quinn chuckles, feeling awkward like a prepubescent boy seeing an attractive girl.

"Let's get you out of the cold," Quinn says, walking over to the vehicle's passenger side and opening the door.

Once they're both in the jeep, taking one last glance at Toni, Quinn shuts his headlights back out. He still has the jitters that Sunney might be approaching any moment to gun him down for being with his wife — not that he didn't deserve it.

"Cold?" he asks.

Toni shakes her head, her eyes on the radio with a somewhat amused face.

"I haven't heard this song in ages," she says, increasing the volume.

Quinn, who has forgotten that the radio has been playing, recognizes the song immediately. He'd been replaying the same songs on his CD for months. They were the only songs he could relax to. This song, *Wild Horses* by the Rolling Stones, always reminds him of being a teenager and sitting on the hood of his car with his high school girlfriend, watching the stars. Back when the world moved so much slower, his problems consisting of when his girlfriend would finally sleep with him and if he would pass that science test next Friday. When he had drunk only to do fun things with his friends instead of drinking till he couldn't feel anymore.

"It brings back such a nostalgic feeling, you know? Like back in the day when everything was so normal," Toni says, and Quinn watches as she stares off into the darkness, her eyes glistening.

"You just read my mind."

Toni continues smiling, drumming her small fingers against her thigh, either due to nervousness or to keep up with the song's beats.

"Hey — I got you something," Quinn says, reaching down under the passenger side seat and briefly brushing his hand on Toni's bare leg, causing her to flinch.

"Sorry," he immediately apologizes, his cheeks flushing.

"What did you get me?"

He lifts the bottle and hands it to her. He worries she'll be annoyed, thinking he's trying to get her drunk or take advantage of her. Something about how she carries herself tonight differs from the other times they met. When she flashes a light smile, it gives him major relief in the pit of his stomach.

"Thought you might need something other than old shitty wine, and I sort of drank all of your last bottle."

A couple of moments of silence pass, and Quinn's nervousness takes over him, so he quickly says, "I'm not trying to make you drink or get drunk. I just thought—"

"This is great, thanks," she says, interrupting his blabbering.

She opens the bottle and takes a long swig. Her eyes are closed as if enjoying an extra sweet dessert that you know you shouldn't have ordered.

"You know what would make this even better? A cigarette."

"You smoke?"

"Not normally, but hey, when in Rome."

Reaching into his jockey box, Quinn recovers a box of Marlboro lights. Although chewing is usually his nicotine of choice, sometimes drunk him calls for a nice smoke instead.

Once he hands over the box to Toni, her face lights up. It's rare to see her smile this much. Although wielding a beautiful set of plump lips and white teeth, it still seems half-fake — like she's smiling to forget her sins. Something must have happened before their meeting.

After placing a cigarette in her mouth, Toni puts her ice-colored eyes on Quinn's.

"Got a light?" she mumbles.

He lights the cigarette for her, their eyes holding contact the whole time.

"I don't smoke much, but always keep a lucky lighter on me."

"Oh, yeah? And how's that luck going?"

"I'll have to get back to you about that later."

They sit in silence for a couple of moments. Toni rolls her window down and takes long drags of her cigarette, blowing the smoke out into the dark. For someone who doesn't smoke, they go in and out smoothly like she's a seasoned smoker. Quinn can't seem to take his eyes off her, and it unnerves him to realize how attracted he is to this woman. There must be something in the air tonight. His dick, already rock hard, is thankfully covered by his jeans and the darkness.

"You're staring, Quinn Robins," she comments.

"Sorry, I just — this may sound creepy, but I can't stop looking at your eyes. They keep me wondering what's going on in that head, and it's extremely difficult to tell if you're happy or want to kill someone."

"It switches up a lot."

"Your hair complements them even more."

Like a cheesy movie scene, Toni grabs a piece of her hair and smiles, her cheeks turning a light shade of pink.

"Really? I always sort of wished I could have been a blonde. Guys always went for the blondes when I was in high school. I got so pissed when my mom wouldn't let me dye it. Now I understand her reasoning."

It isn't much, but Quinn feels excited to hear a little about Toni's past life that isn't painful but normal.

"I always prefer dark hair on women."

"Was that your wife's hair color?"

Quinn hates talking about his wife. Not that she had been a bad person — more so that he had been such a bad person to her that even speaking about her feels wrong. She deserves better than to be spoken of by a monster.

Feeling Toni's eyes blazing into him, he says, "More so auburn, actually."

Still slightly unsettled by how long it took him to answer a simple question, Toni nods.

"Beautiful?" she asks.

Quinn nods, his stomach in knots just thinking about her and their failed marriage. He hadn't meant to cause her so much pain. Their relationship had been in the hole for months prior, but just one dumb night had really tightened the nail in the coffin.

"Yeah, she was. Way out of my league. I don't know how I get such beautiful women around me."

"You should be more confident, you know?"

"Says you. I just hope Sunney gets his shit together. He's lucky to have you."

Toni chuckles and, having finished the cigarette, tosses it out the window.

"Trust me. He's not all that lucky. I'm a mess."

"Everyone's a mess. You just have to find that person worth putting up with it all to be with you."

Watching Toni's eyes as they seemingly stare into his soul makes him reach into his jeans pocket and clutch the newspaper clipping. It's now or never. He has to tell her everything.

But before he can, she leans over and rests her head on his shoulder. The feel of her soft hair touching his neck makes his body shiver. He can't help but peek down her dress, her breasts slightly moving up and down as she breathes. Her heart must be going crazy by the looks of the movements to them.

Quinn tightly closes his eyes, realizing what a dog he's being. He looks away out the window and, clearing his throat, asks, "Anything you want to talk about with Sunney?"

"I feel he's become a completely different person since we got here."

"I mean, I only met the guy twice, but he sure seemed different the first time we met compared to last night. It was kind of eerie, you know? He came off as some plain rich yuppie, but a new personality emerged yesterday. I've been able to read people well my whole life, and it's not often you see someone do a complete one-eighty to that degree."

"What was he like? I doubt he's shown this side of himself to me, ever."

"He was the alpha dog in the room, the hot commodity, and he knew it. It doesn't end there. He wasn't a snob to me like during the first meeting. He was overconfidently friendly. He made it a very clear point he had you as a wife and that every woman around him fawns over him. It's almost like money and women hold the same value to him. To be completely frank, that is the kind of man who may not cheat on you at first but eventually will get bored. You are not a wife. You're a possession, Toni."

"I don't know if that's true. He lived his bachelor life for a while before meeting me."

"Some men never change."

"He's against cheating in every way."

"He said that. I don't know; it just seemed like a gimmick to me."

"But you said he was being completely honest last night. Wouldn't you have been able to read whether he was lying?"

"He was. I'm not saying he's cheating on you now. I just think it might happen in the future. He married you because you are not overly obsessed with him. He likes the chase more than the catch. He wants someone who won't ever fully be his."

"How do you know I won't?"

"Toni, look where you are right now."

Damn, word vomit.

Toni sits up straight and puts her hands over her face. She looks like she did the day they were drinking at his place before she exploded. Her emotions are the most bizarre out of the emotional bandwidths of all the women he has ever met. If it weren't a complete dick move, he would ask her if she had bipolar disorder.

"God, you're right. I should go. This — this isn't right."

Before he can speak, Toni gets out of the jeep and walks away without closing the door.

"Damnit!" Quinn mutters under his breath before getting out of the car and running to her.

"Toni, wait!"

"This is wrong, Quinn. I've done something terrible," Toni says, turning around and brushing away tears from her cheeks.

"What do you mean?"

"I did something awful to be here tonight."

For a split moment, Quinn wonders if she has killed her husband.

"What did you do, Toni?"

She seems to read his mind.

"I did not kill him, if that's what you're thinking. Jesus."

"I didn't say that."

"You were thinking it," she says, a small, nearly disguised smirk on the corner of her mouth.

"Okay, so you didn't kill him. What did you do?"

"I drugged him — with Zolpidem."

"The sleeping pills?"

"Yeah, his. I put some in his whiskey during dinner."

"Not enough to kill him, right?"

Looking offended that he would dare ask her such a heinous question, she answers, "No! Just enough to put him to sleep so I could meet you."

This is the most sweetest gesture thing Toni has done for Quinn. He hadn't expected that in the slightest. At least he does not need to worry about Sunney finding the two of them anymore. For the first time tonight, he truly feels alone with her. It's such a relief that Quinn starts laughing hysterically.

Furrowing her brows, Toni asks, "What's so funny?"

Quinn holds a fist up to his mouth to muffle his laughter.

"This isn't funny, Quinn Robins," Toni says, crossing her arms.

"Not in the slightest. If anything, it's sort of romantic. I've never had a chick drug someone for me."

"I hate you," Toni replies, smirking.

Quinn approaches her now that the air is clear between them. He holds her hand and pulls her toward him. Their bodies are now touching. The low hum of the song playing in the background while he looks deep into her scared doe eyes gives him a magnetic feeling of ease. Like all his wrongdoings mean nothing. She wouldn't run away, scared, if he told her all his deep, dark secrets.

He reaches into his pocket for the news clipping but finds nothing. *Damnit! It must've fallen out of the car.*

"Toni, I have to te—"

But before he can finish, Toni closes her eyes, puts her free hand over his cheek, and places her lips on his. The kiss is extremely soft at first as if she's unaware of what she's doing, but it doesn't take long to deepen. Soon the kiss is hard, and her tongue is in his mouth. She tastes like a mixture of mint toothpaste and the Crown Royal. He knows he should stop her, but her tight hold over his cheeks and the strong intensity of the kiss prevents him. It reminds him of a wet dream he'd had after the second time they met. He had had her naked body sprawled on the hood of his Jeep, and of course, before anything good could happen, he woke up with a raging hard-on almost as big as the one he currently has. He knows it's now pressed against her leg, but he doesn't care.

Deciding he wants to recreate that dream, he lifts Toni's body and carries her back to his Jeep. She shrieks mildly after he places her on the hood, probably feeling the chill of the steel on her plump thighs. However, with her legs wrapped around his waist, Quinn feels the heat she illuminates. He so badly wants to get on his knees and feel the heat on his face instead. But, as he wants to take it as slow as possible without scaring her away, he doesn't. They continue to make out, their tongues rubbing against each other the whole time.

"Take me to the back seat," Toni whispers into Quinn's ear a few minutes later.

Without a moment's thought, Quinn lifts Toni and heads to the back of the vehicle. She feels so light, like almost nothing to him. He does as she requested and stridently opens the back door, throwing her on the seat.

"Are you sure about this?" Quinn asks, praying she does not change her mind but wanting to know she's okay with what is about to happen.

Breathing heavily, she touches his chest and says, "Yes, but no one can know."

He feels a minor tinge in his heart because he knows Toni will most likely regret this afterward, and they will never be the same. His conscience begs him to stop, but seeing Toni's naked body and the possibility of pushing himself inside her is too enticing. It reminds him of when he was just a boy, and his mother would lecture and warn him not to eat the sweets she kept above the fridge, especially before dinner, but damn, was he a sucker for sugar back then.

Quinn climbs on her, running his fingers through her hair. He'd wanted to do it since last night, as her hair looks as soft as an angel's. It doesn't take long for them to be completely naked. Even in the dark, Toni's body does not disappoint one bit. He marvels at it as long as he can, taking mental pictures. He wonders if she is doing the same as she doesn't stop exploring his body with her wandering hands. The touch of another person brings him a kind of happiness he hasn't felt in months. Like that feeling you get when you realize you are falling for someone, and for a moment in time, the world isn't a complete and utter shit-show.

"You are so beautiful, Miss Lovette," Quinn whispers in her ear.

He has just incorrectly pronounced her married status. He knows, but doesn't care. The world would be better if she were single. If Sunney wasn't in the picture, they would just be two lost souls that had run into each other in this shitty town. Quinn wants to imagine them in this manner to help ease his morals.

The sex doesn't last long — about ten minutes. Quinn feels embarrassed, but he hasn't been with a woman to whom he is so attracted in so long that he couldn't last another second. The whole ten minutes, they had never broken eye contact. Her moans were low and innocent, as if she was worried that someone would hear them. Quinn, on the other hand, who had mostly been silent while having sex his whole life, moaned louder than he ever had. After finishing, he had snuck one last kiss on her sweet lips, getting a sour feeling in the pit of his stomach imagining it being their last. Even though short, it was the most passionate sex he'd had in years.

As they both redress, Quinn can't help but smile when he looks at Toni as she slides her dress over her body. His smile doesn't last long when he sees her eyes are wide and regretful.

"That was great," he says, gently touching her knee, worried he'll startle her. She seems to be in such a trance.

"It was, but it can't hap—"

"Wait. Before you finish, I want to say something, Toni."

Finally making eye contact with him, she nods.

"Sunney doesn't deserve you. Something is wrong with him. This isn't just jealousy coming out. I read it in his eyes at the strip club. Money and power are all he is out for. If you stay married to him, you will regret it the rest of your life."

She closes her eyes tightly and says, "I knew you would do this, Quinn."

Reaching to touch Toni's chin, he says, "I'm serious, Toni. You and Sunney, you don't match. You're not like him, and if you leave here tonight, you will continue to form emotional relationships with other men to fill that void in your heart he can't fill. I don't want to force you to be with me, but you and I, well, you'd never have to pretend with me. I will love you for all you are, and not what you're not. He may be able to make you happy materialistically, but me, I can—"

"You can what? Turn me into a drunk mess again like I was before Sunney? Quinn, we don't have anything in common other than the fact that we both like to drink and a past relationship fucked us up mentally," Toni interrupts.

"You're wrong."

"You don't even know me, Quinn. *We* don't know each other. You won't even tell me what happened to your wife. For all I know, you could have been abusive to your ex-wife. I mean, you are an alcoholic."

Now Quinn feels his temper flare. Although he has no qualms about telling people how he guessed them to be, hearing it from someone else just did not sit well with him.

"Maybe you are right. I guess I don't know you. All I have been trying to do this entire time is help you and be your friend, and every single time you've been nothing but cruel. I thought you were a sweet girl. I should've just stayed away from the both of you."

Taking a deep breath, Toni says calmly, "You're right. I am a mess. I get that. But you must admit this was fucking wrong, no matter how bad of a person Sunney may be."

Shocked by her relaxed mood, Quinn nods. She is right. He had known what he was doing with Toni this whole time was wrong in many ways. He didn't care, though. He wanted this screwed-up woman to be his own. It was like his wife and him when they met but flipped. He had been a depressed alcoholic (worse than at the end of their marriage), and she had been a sweet daisy of a woman determined to fix him. And she had done just that for the first three years they were together. After he lost her, he must've unknowingly adopted her fixer mentality.

"Okay, and I can deal with that on my conscience, I guess. Can you?" he asks.

Without hesitation, Toni says, "I have to live with a lot more than that. So, yes."

Quinn shakes his head, wondering what could give a person the lack of morals to be okay with being unfaithful to someone they love. Quinn had been a lot of things in his life but unfaithful was not one of them. Maybe that was the one thing Sunney and he had in common. Oh, and their taste in broken women.

"What do you have to live with that's worse than this?"

"I can't—"

"Can't tell me? Why?"

Toni looks out the window, seeming like she would rather be elsewhere than here. Quinn feels like he has just been used. He is the first of many men with whom Toni would get close to ignore her horrible husband. She's a classic rich man's housewife. He feels sick knowing he'll never forget her, but she'll move on with the next guy who gives her the tiniest bit of attention.

"Just because someone hurt you in the past and you had to protect yourself doesn't make you a monster."

"I've always been a monster, Quinn."

"That's not true," Quinn says, touching her chin to turn her face back toward him.

"How would you know? You don't know me," she replies coldly, moving her face so Quinn's hand drops.

"I should go. Please don't tell Sunney. I — just need to think things over," Toni says, and a second later, the Jeep door is opening.

"Will I see you again?"

Looking intently at the ground, Toni shrugs.

"Well, before you go, take this." Quinn reaches over and grabs the bottle of Crown Royal, handing it to Toni before saying, "You're going to need it."

CHAPTER 21

My heart is racing so much as I open the screen door and slide through it that I feel like I just did a line of cocaine. Part of me anticipates that Sunney will be sitting in the living room, demanding to know where I have been. I want to believe the lights still being off is a good sign that isn't the case. At this point, I don't even know what excuse I would give if he were to be up. My eyes are wet from crying, my hair is in disarray, and my panties are still soaked. It's a perfect display of someone who just got fucked in the back seat of a Jeep. Although uncomfortable and short-lived, it felt phenomenal. I had gotten off quickly, just knowing that anyone could catch us any minute, and we were in a somewhat public setting. For some reason, I turned into a horny, amoral bitch during those ten minutes. Thankfully, I had the decency to make him take me to the back seat instead of having sex right on the hood.

Before heading upstairs, I slip my dress up and over my head, and digging through the trash a little, I stuff it in there. Quinn had hastily grabbed for it when finishing. I knew I would never be able to wear it again, regardless. I didn't even want to face myself in the mirror with it on, knowing what I had had in mind when putting it on — turn Quinn on as much as possible and wait for the rest to happen without any pullbacks.

For good measure, I toss my wet panties and the full bottle of Crown Royal Quinn had given me in the trash as well, but not before taking one last long chug strong enough to cause my nose to tickle. I then go upstairs and into the bathroom, not turning the lights on until after the door is closed.

As I pee, I worry I may have contracted a UTI. Quinn hadn't smelled the best, so I can safely assume that he hadn't showered in a few days. He had masked it by heavily spraying cologne on his clothes. Although gross, his unsanitary body and scent had turned me on. It had been a long time since I had been fucked by such a drudge, dirty man. When Tom had a job and did twelve-hour construction shifts six days a week, we were still in our honeymoon phase, so even though he had come home smelling of sweat and concrete mix, I still usually wanted to fuck his brains out.

It's too early to tell, but I'm genuinely worried about contracting a UTI. I can't take any chances. Time to do another immoral thing to ensure Sunney doesn't find out about Quinn. It's been a couple of days since Sunney and I last had sex, so I would have to have sex with him again not to arouse suspicion. I go to the mirror and feel nearly the same as I did the night I met Sunney — like an utter piece of garbage, both in terms of looks and my mind. I take a washcloth and wet it with warm water. Then I scrub my crotch for a couple of minutes, hopefully getting any scent of Quinn off me. Finally, I brush through my hair and proactively avoid eye contact in the mirror.

Hopefully he'll go for this, I think, shutting the bathroom light off and opening the door. Hopefully, those sleeping pills didn't completely knock him out (or hurt him). I had only used a couple and placed them in his whiskey while he was in the bathroom. It had felt so shameful, but I still went through with it. From there, it only took an hour, maybe two, for him to pass out. I then waited another hour before leaving just to make sure he really was asleep, laying as still in bed as possible the whole time and getting out as slowly as I could. I moved so carefully that I ended up being late to meet Quinn. The walkover was so chilly and nerve-wracking.

New Toni urged me to turn around and go back, but Old Toni argued that I wouldn't do anything bad, just hang with Quinn. Lying to myself is becoming one of my worst habits.

I go to the edge of the bed where Sunney lies. I can't see him due to the darkness, but I can hear his slow breathing. I slowly get on top of him and, with my hands over his bare chest, kiss his neck. It takes a couple of moments for him to wake up, and I know he can feel my heavy thumping heartbeat on him. I pray and hope he doesn't throw me off, but Sunney has never been one to turn down sex.

He doesn't say anything but moves his hands to my waist. I look up and see his eyes are still closed, but his lips are tightly pressed together. Knowing it would be too wrong to kiss him while he is half asleep, I wait until his dick becomes hard. I force myself not to start crying as my thoughts curse me and call me a whore for all my wrongdoings.

Just as I am almost unable to listen to my thoughts anymore and get off, Sunney tightens his grip on my hips, moving them up to my back. His nails pierce my skin, and I squeal from pain but don't speak. He must still be angry with me from all our fighting. I consider the pain as my punishment for betraying him. He lightly moans, running his fingers into my back and thrusting himself inside me repeatedly. The sex feels dirty, like we both hate each other.

After it is over, I roll back to my side of the bed. Sunney doesn't say a word, which should worry me, but he is usually silent when we have sex in the middle of the night or early in the morning. I roll over to my side and wrap my arms around his waist. Feeling his warm skin against mine momentarily brings me a small amount of relief. It brings me back to before we got married, when everything was normal and I wouldn't dream of looking at, let alone fucking another man. Now everything is different. I am a cheater, and no matter how easily I can play the role of a normal wife for my husband, it will always be at the back of my head, gnawing at me. It takes nearly an hour to fall asleep with the pain and feeling of blood dripping from my scratched-up back.

CHAPTER 22

I had finally managed to fall asleep, my arms draped over Sunney's waist nearly all night. The feel of his skin on mine and his slow-beating heart had calmed me into a deep sleep. It seemed to be a pattern of mine, doing something terrible and then having some of the best sleep to hush the voices in my mind. First, sleeping with my teacher. Second, stabbing Tom to death, and third, cheating on my husband.

Sunney, of course, isn't in bed when I wake up. He's probably downstairs, I reason. I want to go down immediately and see if he has anything to say, but I take a quick shower instead. I desperately need to clean all the signs of my sins off my body.

As I shower, washing every inch of my body, I can't help thinking about Quinn. The way our eyes never left each other. He'd pressed himself deep inside me, passionately, yet somewhat quickly like a jackrabbit. I want to call it fucking, but the passion I had felt, the way all the windows had fogged up, how I had even done a *Titanic* moment and rubbed my hand against the fogged-up window during, wasn't just fucking. We had made love.

"Morning, baby."

I immediately grab one of the showers handles to stop from falling. A second later, the curtain pulls back and

Sunney is standing there, a wide, white-toothed smile plastered on his face. He is nude and holding a cup of coffee in one hand, and in the other, he has a pale pink kimono robe.

"Surprise," he says, his smile never ceasing.

"What's this?" I ask, looking at the robe.

"With all that was going on, I forgot to give you this. I got us some matching robes, and I know how much you like pink, so I got yours in that color. But it's light enough so that I can make out that sexy body."

I'm so flabbergasted I don't say anything, but I don't need to as moments later, Sunney sets his cup down on the sink and lifts the robe to expose the back. In porcelain colored sewn-on cursive letters, it reads *Mrs. Jameson*.

"I got a matching one for me that reads Mr. Jameson. Feel it; they are so soft. They are imported from France if you can believe it."

I reach out and feel my robe. It's so silky smooth that it reminds me of Sunney's Egyptian sheets back home.

"Babe, this is too much. I don't deserve it," I say.

"You deserve the world, babe. Now move over. Let me in," he says, hanging the robe on the shower hook and stepping into the shower.

Once he's in, he wraps his arms around my waist and leans in for what I think will be a kiss on the lips, but he bites my neck instead.

"Sunney," I wince, leaning away.

"Last night was awesome. I really enjoyed it."

"Me too."

I turn around, washing away the shampoo on my hair. When I do, Sunney gasps, placing his hands on my back.

"I scratched you up bad," he says, chuckling.

I flinch from the pain of his palms grazing over the scratches. Turning around, I know I am in no place to be mad at this man, even if he did go overboard on the scratching.

"It's okay," I say, faking a laugh.

"I am sorry for being a bit of an asshole these last few days. You don't deserve that. I want you to know that I would never do anything to break our trust in this relationship. I wasn't out the other night with any woman. I do business here in Rubico but be rest assured it's all so we can make a comfortable living as man and wife. All this is ours, babe. As they say, what's mine is yours," Sunney says, rubbing his hands up and down my waist.

Business in Rubico. I remember Quinn mentioning that to me the other night. He had suspected it was prostitution, but I didn't want to remotely think that was possible. Sunney already made a good amount of money with the insurance company. Why bother needing more? Maybe this fancy cabin is more expensive than I could imagine. I'm not an architect, so I don't know what this cabin or even his nice three-story house back home could cost.

"Why have you never mentioned this business?" I calmly ask, knowing I have no right to be anywhere near mean to this man for years and years after what I did.

"It's just a bit of a secret. But now that we're married, I promise to tell you soon."

"Is what you are doing illegal?" I know I'm prodding, but I can't help it.

"Let me wash your hair. Babe, turn around."

"I already shampooed it," I argue.

"Then I'll condition it, sweetie," he says, turning me around.

Soon his fingers run through my hair and gently rub my scalp. Some soap runs down my forehead into my eyes, but I ignore the burning, not wanting to stop Sunney from anything he might talk to me about.

"I will tell you soon, I promise."

"Are we in any danger?"

"I would never put you in danger, Toni. I love you more than you could ever know."

With every second that passes, my heart burns more and more remembering my betrayal. I have my first real argument with my husband, and my first instinct is to cheat on him. What if Quinn was right when he said I would always be like this, forming emotional relationships with other men? No, I wouldn't, *I couldn't.*

"I love you too," I whisper.

We finish our shower about ten minutes later. When we get out and dry off, I drape myself in the robe he got me. It feels smooth over my now-clean body. The bathroom's double sink and mirror allow us to get ready in silence, like back at his house. He shaves, I blow-dry my hair, we brush our teeth, and so on. I try to remain as normal as possible, but looking at myself in the mirror this long is difficult. However, I notice my skin looks bright and rejuvenated.

"Thanks for taking the trash out this morning. But please remember to shut the screen door all the way. You left it cracked open," Sunney casually mentions as he slaps on aftershave.

I freeze and immediately look wide-eyed at myself in the mirror. I almost drop the brush I have in my hand. Took out the trash? Is he referring to the trash with the Crown Royal, the slutty sundress which probably smells of Quinn's jizz, and my wet panties? I didn't take it out. That's a fact. However, that would have been a genius idea. My anxiety immediately begins to go through the roof, making me shake.

"Oh—" I gulp, "Sorry."

"No problem, baby. I just worry a bear could've moseyed inside, eating all our food," he says, chuckling.

"No doubt," I add.

When Sunney finally leaves a few minutes later to make us a late breakfast, I press my back to the wall and slowly slide down to a sitting position. I have to sit before my anxiety takes over. There must be a logical explanation behind this. It couldn't have been Quinn. He isn't crazy enough to do something like that.

He had said, *I don't want to force you to be with me* and *I will love you for all you are, and not for what you're not.*

Quinn's words reverberate in my head. *Would he have been angry enough about me leaving him immediately after we had sex to want to get back at me?* The trash would have been evidence enough for Sunney to know something was up.

Whether he took it out or not, I have to see him again. Talk to him and beg him not to tell Sunney. I can hopefully convince him to hand over the contents of that trash to me and burn it like I should've done in the first place. I could tell Sunney I was going on a quick run this morning. It would be a lot easier to reach Quinn during the day than at night, that's for sure. *Safer as well.*

I step out of the bathroom and go to the bedroom. I'm surprised to find Sunney sitting on the bed, reading a *Men's Health* magazine. It's the newest edition, July, with a picture of Seann William Scott clad in a form-fitting white button-up shirt. The similarities between the two men make me smile — dirty blonde hair, a strong jaw, and an amazing body. I'm the biggest idiot in the world for cheating on such a man.

"I thought you were going to cook breakfast," I say, making him lower the magazine.

"I was, but then I realized that you, my dear—" Sunney stands up and walks over to me, "—are a much better cook and can help me out."

Sunney has rarely ever complimented my cooking. Not that it is bad, just by no means chef status. Sunney prefers his cooking, even if he'd never say it.

"I was actually thinking of going on a run this morning."

Sunney frowns and, looking around the room briefly, says, "We both know what I said the other day was wrong. I apologize for that. See, always being with the guys joking around, and then suddenly not being around them was a bit of a shock. I made a joke to you that was not okay."

"That's actually not why I want—"

Before I can finish, Sunney places his index finger over my mouth, hushing me.

"You're beautiful, and it's our honeymoon."

I want to argue with him but know I can't. If I do, it'll just seem suspicious.

We go downstairs, and with Sunney's cooking compliment on my mind I shut off all my worries for a moment while I cook. We make veggie omelets with homemade hash browns.

Sunney even has a small bouquet of little blue flowers at the counter with a yellow pistil that I cannot place the name of.

While we eat, I concoct another plan to get to Quinn's place. *How would I get over there without Sunney finding out? What would I even say? Would he even talk to me?* The way he had looked at me before I left makes me almost certain we will never see each other again. I wish I could take it all back.

"Did I tell you about the weirdest encounter I had the other day?" Sunney asks, interrupting my thoughts.

"No, what happened?" I say, looking over at him as we each take a big bite of the hashbrowns.

"I saw that fellow from the gas station — I can't place his name. Uh—"

Not wanting Sunney to know I remember his name, I put on a puzzled face.

"Oh yeah, Quinn. Do you remember him from the bathroom? The one who had the hots for you."

Something like that.

"I don't think he had—"

"Anyway, I actually saw him the other night, and we had a couple of beers together. Quite the interesting guy."

"How so?" I ask, keeping my poker face on.

"Well, remember he said he would explain why he moved to Rubico over a beer? Funny as that was not the case at all. He was as vague as they get. Just said it was random and that he was married for a short while, but now he's chasing after one of the strippers here."

What stripper? Quinn hadn't mentioned that part. I want to know more, but I can't seem too interested.

"How long did you even talk to him for?"

"Like an hour. I also learned from a cop buddy he has quite the shady record."

Shady record? It's becoming nearly impossible for me to stay stoic.

"You have a cop buddy?"

"Yeah, he lets me know the ins and outs of new people that move to Rubico."

"Why does it matter?"

"Because this town gets a lot of strange people that sometimes need looking into. This Quinn seems chill on the outside, but he's a weirdo on the inside."

"Sunney, be nice."

"I'm being serious. The guy got a restraining order from an ex-girlfriend like eight years ago and got arrested for not leaving her alone. He has been arrested due to his drunken disorderly antics three times. That's not all. He has multiple assault tickets and get this — his ex-wife requested a divorce from him before getting in a wreck that took her life."

I drop my fork from shock. It clatters to the floor and nearly takes a century to stop rattling. Sunney chuckles as he watches me bend over to grab it.

Goddamnit.

"You good?"

"Yeah. It sounds terrifying for the women involved with him." *AKA me.*

I want none of this to be true, but why would Sunney make all this up?

I nod and look down at my half-eaten food, wishing it was gone already to escape this awkward conversation. I don't think I can even stomach it anymore. I'm not acting as ordinary about things as I need to. *What if everything I thought I knew about Quinn was a lie?* A restraining order, an angry drunk, an assaulter, and a dead ex-wife. That list alone worsens my fear that he broke into the cabin and took out the trash. Maybe he wants to use it to blackmail me instead of telling Sunney. He knows Sunney has a lot of money.

After breakfast, I slowly wash the few dishes, all the while wondering about ways I could make it to Quinn's as soon as possible. Anytime today wouldn't work. Maybe it would have to be another night trip. It couldn't be more than half an hour out of risk of Sunney waking up to see me gone. At this point, it's the only option I really have left.

CHAPTER 23

The rest of the day goes by in a blur. Sunney and I take a walk in the midafternoon. I get chills walking by Quinn's and my spot. I have to force small talk with Sunney, which I've never been good at doing. My heart never ceases to beat at a seemingly 100 mph speed thinking Quinn's Jeep will drive by us. Thankfully, he's nowhere to be seen. When we get back, I stray outside for a couple of minutes to find our dumpster and rifle through it. No luck, as it's mostly empty or has old trash.

We have a late dinner at 8 p.m., which Sunney has to almost force me into eating. I tell him I just don't have an appetite, but it's the stress inducing my sickness. *What if everything Quinn said was bullshit?* It might have been just a ploy to get me to sleep with him so he could blackmail me. This whole time he had seemed so hateful toward Sunney. He wouldn't mind taking a chunk of change from him.

After dinner, we settle into bed, and Sunney turns on his sound system to listen to our favorite music. I remember every moment we listened to or danced to each song. From the first holiday party to our wedding song.

As we cuddle, I feel so much guilt and regret. It's all I can think about. New Toni begs me to tell Sunney, let the truth free, but Old Toni forces me not to. She reasons that I would lose the one good thing in my life. I would be jobless, homeless, and, worst of all, husbandless. New Toni counters that if I don't tell him, I would have to live with the guilt for the rest of my life.

Surprisingly, it doesn't take long for me to feel drowsy. I force myself into the bathroom to brush my teeth and change into pajamas. Sunney puts on a pair of boxers with his matching robe over it. I do the same with velvet satin sleep shorts and a kami tank underneath. If I sneak out tonight, it'll be freezing if I just wear my robe. When I walk back into our room Sunney's eyes are already closed, and as I get into bed, I find myself praying he doesn't want to have sex tonight. My guilt from having sex with him last night is already too overpowering. I don't think I would be able to handle it again. I am exhausted from all the stress and lack of sleep.

After ten minutes, it feels like I might pass out any second. Just then, I feel Sunney's arm go around my waist and his lips gently kiss my cheek.

"Tired?" he asks.

"Yeah, you?"

"Yeah. I promise tomorrow will be more fun, babe."

"I–I'm sure it will."

"I love you," he says, turning his body away.

Hopefully, by tomorrow, I will have this whole Quinn situation resolved. I will get a couple of hours of sleep in before heading over there. Sadly, I can't rely on an alarm clock, but my body, like clockwork, almost always wakes me up a couple of times every night.

CHAPTER 24

I wake up in a bed of sweat, feeling weak. My body hasn't naturally woken me up. It was the loud sound of something breaking downstairs. At first, I wondered if it was just a dream, but only a couple of moments later, someone's hands are on my shoulders, shaking me.

"Toni, wake up! Wake up!" Sunney shouts.

I sit up straight, rubbing my eyes. Our room is nearly pitch dark aside from the feeble light coming through the window and smells heavily of sweat. I glance at the alarm clock on Sunney's side of the bed. *Three a.m.* I slept for nearly five hours.

"What's going on?" I ask.

"I think someone broke in downstairs. Get up!" Sunney exclaims, jumping from the bed.

So, I hadn't dreamt that. I force myself out of the bed, my whole body on fire from fear. Quinn immediately comes to mind. It can't be him. It must be an animal. We're in the middle of nowhere. *Who would want to break in here?*

"What do we do?" I ask.

Before Sunney can answer me, there is another crash downstairs.

"Go to the bathroom and lock the door. I've got a pistol downstairs," Sunney says, grabbing my hand and pulling me out of the bedroom.

"No, Sunney. You can't leave me alone," I argue, my voice already shaking.

"I have to, Toni. Just give me a couple of minutes. It's my house, and I know the layout better than anyone else."

Sunney gently pushes me into the bathroom, and although the lights are still off, the moonlight shining through the bathroom window allows me a look at his dark, widened eyes. He looks so confident and calm. *Everything will be okay. Sunney will take care of it.*

He leans over and kisses my forehead before slowly shutting the door. I quickly turn the lock over. Besides the bathroom's small window, I am in complete darkness, too frightened to even dare turn the light on. What would I do if someone breaks in? There is a chance I could fit through the window, but it would be tight and take me to the roof. What then? Jump down to break my legs?

I go to the mirror and see that my cheeks are flushed red even though my eyes are still drowsy. I turn on the sink, splashing cold water on my face.

Time to get your shit together, Toni.

When Tom attacked me, I didn't freeze. I was ready, so I survived. I might have to do the same tonight if it's not just some wild animal down there. If it is Quinn gone crazy, my chances are low. He's so much bigger and brawnier than Tom and Sunney. He could take me out with one single punch.

I go to the door and press my ear to it. I clutch the doorknob tightly when I hear loud voices.

"Whoever the fuck you are, get out of my house! I already called the police," Sunney screams.

Has he? I know there's at least one house phone in the cabin, but it's in the kitchen. I hadn't spotted one in the bedroom. I knew he wouldn't get cell service out here, and I hadn't even brought my shitty phone.

"Step away, or I'll fucking shoot you," Sunney yells again.

Before I can even process what's happening, the loud sound of one shot erupts. I fall to my ass immediately from shock. I try to get up but fall again. Tears already stain my cheeks, and I'm imagining the worst already. I finally get up, but the doorknob starts twisting frantically as soon as I do. My heart nearly stops, wondering who could be on the other side. The intruder then starts knocking, banging, and rattling the door.

Don't freak out! Don't freak out! my mind urges me.

Too fucking late for that.

CHAPTER 25

"Toni, it's me. Open the door," Sunney says moments later.

I let out a sigh of relief and unlock the door, my hand shaking so much it's difficult to turn the knob.

I immediately gasp at what I see. Standing against the door frame is a terrified, chalk white faced Sunney. He's holding a blood-soaked white towel over his head and leaning against the wall. His blonde hair is drenched with blood which is dripping droplets from his forehead. I wrap my arms around him, my heart thumping fast as I pull him into a hug, to which he grunts from pain and gently pushes me away.

"What happened?"

"As soon as I walked into the living room, some psycho hit me in the head with a rock or something. Thankfully, I grabbed my pistol in time."

"Did — did you shoot him? What did he look like? Is he still here? Did you call the cops?"

"I warned him I would shoot him if he attacked me again. He took a shot at me but I was able to dodge it. After that, he ran off. I don't know what he looked like. He was wearing some old clown mask. He busted the house phone, so I couldn't call the police."

Sunney, although bleeding profusely, is handling his fear-o-meter so much better than I am. Every answer he gives me drives a new level of terror into my body. Thank God for Sunney always handling stress so breezily. I, on the other hand, feel on the verge of hyperventilating.

"I don't understand why this is happening. What if he comes back?"

I want to warn Sunney so badly that Quinn may be doing this, but I can't do that without having to tell him why I suspect him. I don't plan to let that truth out unless I know it is Quinn for sure. I mean, he's done some bad things but is he really capable of something like this?

You've literally known him for less than a week, my brain curses me.

"Toni, to be honest, it may be one of my business competitors."

"At the insurance agency?"

"No, here in town. Let's just say I may have pissed some people off."

I've been so self-absorbed that I keep forgetting my husband is in some shady mystery business. It's becoming clearer that it's extremely illegal, and possibly life-risking.

"Sunney, I don't understand. What do you do?"

"Now isn't the time to explain all that. We need to get out of here."

He's right. I nod. Sunney runs back to our room, hastily pulling on a pair of blue jeans. He then grabs his cell, and we run downstairs. With each step toward the front door, I look everywhere in the darkness, ready for someone to pop out. When we reach the front door, I press my body close to Sunney's, terrified I'll be grabbed and taken away. When we get outside, he tightly holds my hand, and we run toward his truck.

"Shit!" Sunney curses.

"What?" I ask.

"He slashed the two front tires," he whispers, his grasp on my hand tightening.

I look down, and my heart shrinks.

"What do we do now?"

Sunney looks around for a couple of seconds, the way he usually does when he's stressed and his brain is in overdrive.

"There's a hill behind the cabin that I usually can get service on. It's less than a mile away. We can run there."

I don't even have shoes on and can feel my body shivering from the breeze already. It's like the night with Quinn all over again. The idea of running out into the middle of nowhere is even more disheartening. If I weren't almost certain this was Quinn's doing, I'd rather risk running down the road to his house for help.

"What if they follow us?" I ask.

"I have my pistol," he says, lifting his robe to reveal the pistol tucked into his pants.

We run from his cabin and into the darkness of the trees. Each step stings my bare feet, and I curse myself for not slipping on a pair of shoes before going outside. I hold in my complaints, knowing Sunney is still sporting a nasty gash on the back of his head and taking it like a champ.

As each moment passes and we venture further into the woods, I realize how similar everything is starting to look. The towering pine trees are all only a few feet apart, forcing Sunney and me to dodge each one as we run. I wonder how easy it would be to get lost out here. Luckily, I have counted all the fallen-over trees we've passed and the turns we've made. I'm not exactly adventurer supreme. I don't want to be an idiot and rely on Sunney to know his way around these woods.

Eventually, we reach a small hill about twenty feet high covered in tall barnyard grass. On the top, a thick navy-blue blanket has been laid out. Sunney must have come here to stargaze recently. A couple of smaller trees have lanterns hanging from them. For a couple of moments, I imagine how nice a dinner date here would've been instead of whatever we are doing now — scared and running for our lives from a possible crazy enemy of mine or Sunney's.

Sunney pulls his cell phone out of his pocket and lifts it in the air, searching for a bar. He turns his back on me and walks a couple of feet forward. I press my palms together, praying for this to work. Tears begin to stream from my eyes from the wind blowing on them. I wipe them away and look at Sunney, who watches me intently. His eyes look tired.

"It's going to be okay, baby," he softly reassures me, almost whispering.

For a moment, his sweet voice makes me fully believe his promise. But only a second later, we hear a loud shot. Sunney screams, and falls to one knee. Dropping the phone, he places his hand over his right thigh, which is now stained with blood. I try to scream, but nothing comes out. Instead, I drop to Sunney's side, thinking I'll be next.

In the distance, I can hear the sound of grass being trampled by footsteps. I cringe and look toward the direction of the noise. Standing behind a medium-sized pine tree only ten yards away is a figure. They're dressed in a thick black parka with the hood up and a plain plastic mask with red markings around the eyes. In one of their hands is an old revolver — the weapon they had just shot Sunney with. It's hard to tell with them hiding behind the tree but to me, they look tall. Maybe as tall as Quinn.

"Sunney, look," I whisper, moving out of Sunney's way.

He immediately moves his body to shield me from the figure and then reaches into his jeans to grab the pistol. Both of his hands clasped over the pistol shake profusely as he aims the weapon in the figure's direction. His grasp on the gun looks even worse than his aim, as his slippery hands are stained with new and old blood. I never knew Sunney to be anything of a marksman. I'm sure the one he wields was bought for slim to no protection reasons.

"What the fuck do you want?" he yells.

Saying nothing, the dark figure moves to the other side of the tree and extends a black-gloved hand to point at me. My heart feels like it has just stopped. I must be mistaken;

the figure could be pointing at either of us. But my brain tells me, *not if it's Quinn behind that mask*.

Sunney puts his cell phone in my hand and whispers, "Call 911."

I quickly dial 911 and put the phone to my ear. After a few moments of not hearing any dialing sounds, I look at the screen.

"There's no service," I say, showing him the screen as fresh tears roll down my cheeks.

"Shit," he whispers, grabbing the phone from me and moving it up in the air.

I look at the figure again and see him shaking his head at us.

"Toni, listen to me carefully. I need you to run back to the house. I'll take care of this prick. Whatever you do, do not leave that cabin without me."

"I can't leave you."

"I'll distract him and be right behind you."

"Sunney, no—" I begin to say, but before I can finish, another shot erupts, the sound so loud this time, my ears ring.

I look down at my body, searching for blood and waiting for the pain. I've been slapped and punched plenty of times but I have no idea what kind of pain to expect from a gunshot. A lot of people get shot and go into shock, or their adrenaline levels are so high they don't even notice it.

Sunney retaliates, shooting right back at the figure who hides behind the tree. Not that it matters. Sunney's hand is so shaky that the shot goes right past. *How can I leave him like this, injured with obviously no clue how to use the gun in his hand?* I could always go to the cabin and grab another source of protection. A kitchen knife — I've used one of those to protect myself before.

"Go, Toni. This is my fight, not yours."

I wipe my tears decisively. I've never felt so scared in my life. Considering my past, that really is saying something.

"I–I don't know where we are. Sunney—please don't make me—"

"Go straight and take a right in twenty or so yards. There will be a large sugar maple tree we passed. It has an old lantern on it. Keep running past the tree and you should see the cabin. Hide under the bed," he says, kissing my forehead hard.

"Okay, I'll see you in a couple of minutes," I say, touching Sunney's hot cheeks.

There's a burning feeling in my stomach that makes me feel like I'm lying to him. At least if the man goes after me, Sunney can shoot him if he gets a decent aim.

With one last look at the figure which has peeked its head out from behind the tree again, I turn around and run in the direction Sunney had instructed me. I expect to immediately hear shots fired at me or, worse, one hitting me in the back, but it doesn't happen.

If it is Quinn, there's no way he would want to end me so easily. He would want me to know it's him doing this. Look him in the eye and regret ever getting involved with a psychopath.

The trail the way down had been downhill so it takes me much longer than anticipated to make the run back to the cabin going uphill. Once I didn't hear anyone following behind me, I stopped and took my breath. I then continued forward and searched for the sugar maple tree. Sunney had been right, there was an old copper lantern hanging from a branch of the rather large tree. After that I had trenched forward and found the cabin with the aide of the moon light showing over it.

I run to the front door and open it, thanking God it's not locked. After I run inside, I slam the door shut and press my back on it, catching my breath. I hear another shot as soon as I can feel my lungs refilling, ready to give me the energy to run upstairs. Like in the bathroom, like deja vu, I flinch so hard I fall to the ground. Wiping the never-ending tears streaming down my face, I force myself to get up and run to the kitchen, grabbing one of the knives.

Once upstairs, I shut the door and lock it. I go to the only window in the bathroom and open it. I hope to create the illusion that I have jumped from it for the intruder. However, looking down, I realize a fall will likely break my legs. So, I crawl under the bed like Sunney had instructed. I already know the lock on our bedroom door will not last more than a few seconds against a strong man and his boot. Also, my hiding spot has to be one of the worst and clichéd ones, but the silver lining is that I can catch a glimpse of the door if someone breaks it open.

As I lie on my stomach, my heart beats so hard in my chest that I swear it shakes the carpet. I wonder where the shot came from. Sunney's pistol or the cloaked figure's. It was just one shot, so whoever made it must've hit what they wanted. If it was Sunney, he should've already made it back, but that shot to his leg would slow him down.

Just as I am on the verge of crawling out to go out and look for Sunney, the doorknob turns and then, when it doesn't open, the person on the other side begins to shake it. As I had fatally guessed, it doesn't take long before the door is broken through. I see brown, mud-smeared cowboy boots with pieces of stuck grass. They are not Sunney's. I have never once seen him in boots like that.

An instant later, a terrifying image flashes into my head. Last night with Quinn, we were in his back seat, removing our clothes. He had trouble removing his jeans due to the massive brown boo—

Oh no, no, no. They couldn't be his. It was dark that night, and anyone in these backwoods could own a pair of brown cowboy boots.

When the boots finally begin to walk, I clasp my hand over my mouth and nose to stop any sound of breathing. I want to scream for Sunney because the intruder being here could only mean one thing. Sunney couldn't protect himself or injure them. What if he is bleeding out in the woods, needing my help?

The boots walk over to the dresser and stand there for some moments, facing away from me. I hear them fussing with something, when suddenly music starts to play on the speakers.

"*You're mine, and we belong together. Yes, we belong together. For eternity*," the lyrics go.

I instantly remember the song. I have recently heard it without really listening. It had been playing in the background somewhere. This is not Sunney's taste in music, that's for sure.

Another memory soon swamps into my mind. Same night. Same place. Quinn's Jeep. The CD he played. This was one of the songs that was playing when we had sex.

Oh shit! It is him. The trash disappearing, the screen door being left open, the boots, and now the music. It can't be any damn coincidence. But why is he doing this? We have only met five times — and all of them mostly brief encounters. Even the sex was quick. Is he really a psychopath? He started by getting in a couple of bar fights, escalated to stalking an ex-girlfriend, somehow killing his wife, and now murdering a married couple because the cheating wife fucked him? It was all too cliché but made perfect sense.

The feet circle back to the bed and sit on it. He doesn't make a single sound other than heavy breathing. After a minute or so on the bed, he finally gets up and walks right out of the room. I wait, see him check the bathroom and then descend the stairs. A few minutes later, I hear the front door open and close. Maybe he decided to check outside. A part of me wants to hide all night until the sun comes out or until Sunney magically appears to rescue me, but I know I can't do that. This is my mess, and I have to fix it. I really don't know if I have it in me to kill another person, but if it comes down to saving my husband, anything is on the table.

I crawl out of bed, glancing at the stereo that is still blaring music from Quinn's CD. I want to smash it, but that might bring him back, so I decide not to. As I descend the stairs, the music follows me, playing through the speakers in the cabin. The music was relaxing and romantic at first, but now it makes my spine tingle and blocks out any other noise that could be heard downstairs. Quinn Robins might sneak up behind me and stab me in the back.

I peep over my shoulder with every step, expecting someone to pop out until I finally reach the door. I place my hand over the doorknob and turn it, ready to flee outside, but it only moves halfway before stopping. My heart stops, and I continue attempting to turn it. It can't be locked from the inside, so someone must be holding it.

CHAPTER 26

Before I can put my thoughts to action, the door swings open, knocking my body to the ground and my only weapon, the kitchen knife, from my hand. The door bangs against my head and I am on my ass again. Choking on air and my chest burning from the blast, I look up at the door, hoping against all hope that it'll be Sunney standing there.

Seeing the white clown mask and black-cloaked body with the night sky in the background induces more pain to my chest than the door that hit it just a few seconds ago. I try to get to my feet to run, but before I can, the man takes a gun out from behind his back. I gulp, seeing it's not the same as before but — Sunney's. His hand is now dripping blood, along with the blood splatter specked across the cloak.

"What do you want?" I ask, slowly sliding my body back.

He lifts the gun and points it at me.

"Quinn, please stop. I'm sorry. Don't do this," I shout, trying to crawl backward on the floor, but my body feels like it has lost all motor control.

The figure, relishing my helplessness, moves closer to me, pressing the gun to my temple as I slowly crouch on my knees, keeping my face to the ground.

"You don't have to do this. I didn't mean to hurt you," I beg.

He doesn't lower the gun even slightly, and I know this has to be the end. I tightly shut my eyes, trying to imagine Sunney's face one last time. Before we got here, fought, and I cheated on him. Maybe this is what I deserve. I mean, adultery is a sin. Could this be God punishing me?

Just as I anticipate my end, I peer up and behind Quinn's figure I catch the sight of blonde hair. It's Sunney, his dark eyes blazing with terror and adrenaline. Blood is splattered over his face, and it has completely soaked through his nightshirt. There's no pistol in his hand or I'm guessing he would have shot Quinn by now. On a closer look, I see he has a pillar of wood in one hand and that he's gripping a bloody spot on the side of his waist. Quinn notices my wide eyes have shifted behind him, but Sunney swipes the wood pillar over the back of his head before he can do anything. He instantly falls to the ground, landing only inches away from me. Sunney's pistol lands near my left foot, and I kick it away, not wanting to give Quinn a chance to grab it.

Sunney drops the wood and limps to my side. His body looks like it might break down at any moment. He kneels near me and places his bloody hand over my cheek. It's silent momentarily as I try to make out any words. I'm still in shock over the realization Quinn would have shot me if Sunney hadn't intervened.

After a couple of moments, Sunney and I slowly stand up. I stare at Quinn's motionless body, praying he doesn't get up for round two.

Sunney, whose hand is firmly clasped over my cheek, says, "I told you to hide under the bed. You're not safe down here."

"I had to come to check on you. Oh God, Sunney, I thought you were dead. I heard a shot, and then you didn't return and—" I weep, unable to finish, wrapping my arms around him for a tight hug as I bury my face in his chest.

"Not quite. The fucker shot me in the side but thankfully thought I was dead. He took my pistol and then ran back to the cabin. I don't know what he could want with you. You're innocent in all this."

My face was buried in his chest, tears soaking his shirt. I know it's time to tell him it's not his fight but mine. It's all my fault this is happening. If this is all God's doing to punish me for what I've done, maybe, the truth might at least save us.

"Sunney, it's not who you think it is."

"What do you mean?"

"I need to tell you something."

"We don't have time, Toni. We need to get—"

"Please, just listen."

"Wha—?" he begins to ask but stops talking abruptly, his body seemingly limp.

I finally lift my head from his shoulder and scream, seeing the sight before me. Quinn is on his feet, and he's standing directly behind us.

"Sunney, run!" I scream.

Sunney's eyes, now even wider than before, stare at me. He presses both hands over his stomach, more blood protruding from it. Just then, Quinn vigorously moves his hand behind Sunney's back. Sunney falls to his knees, and I rush to grab him. I peer up to see Quinn standing only a few inches from us with a bloodied kitchen knife.

"Run!" he mumbles. Sunney's eyes close as he flinches away from my touch.

I look back at Quinn, the knife still tightly held in his hand mockingly.

"Go," Sunney breathes, finally going limp in my arms.

I let him go and dart toward the pistol I had kicked away. Running would only get me so far. I have to end this the only way I know how. As I plunge toward it, Quinn drops the knife and jumps, but he's only a couple of inches behind me. I grab hold of the pistol. As soon as I have it pointed in his direction, my finger on the trigger, I pull it.

But nothing goes off. It just clicks. It's empty. Quinn, still silent, shakes his head mockingly. I make an exasperated sound and chuck the pistol at him as hard as possible. I manage to hit him in the mask and he is momentarily blindsided. I jump up and run for the sliding door but stop when I notice it has a chain and a large lock wrapped around it. When did he have time to do that?

I don't look back because I know the sight of Sunney's lifeless body will break me even more. I run up the stairs, slipping and falling on my face halfway through. I'm shocked Quinn isn't there to grab my ankle and pull me down. I must've thrown that pistol at him harder than I had thought.

I run to the bathroom, knowing going to the bedroom would be pointless since the locks are already broken. I rummage through the room for anything that can be used as a weapon. Not long passes before there's a knock at the door. I yank Sunney's electric shaver from its plug, unable to find anything else. My ideas are wearing thin, and I start peering out the one small window in the bathroom. I know the chances of me fitting through it is slim. If I do jump, I also risk breaking a leg.

"Toni," a soft, weak voice says behind the door.

It's Sunney's voice. I drop the shaver and run to the door, unlocking it. He's on his knees, both hands covering his blood-soaked stomach. Looking down at him, I realize this may be the last time I see him alive. It's a miracle he hasn't bled out at this point. The thought sickens me, and I want to beg for forgiveness because he'll never know why and who killed him. I could tell him now, but any courage I had mustered earlier has vanished into thin air. I can't let him leave this world hating me.

"Where is he?" I ask, leaning down to Sunney's level, our eyes making contact as I try and take in every second we have alone.

"He disappeared outside, probably to get a different gun. Here, take this," he says, giving me the kitchen knife.

I take it, knowing it may very well be our last chance. However, some old knife will be no match against a revolver.

"What should I do?"

"I'm not—" Sunney cringes in pain, grinding his teeth before continuing, "going to — make it much longer, but I have an idea. I'll sit at the bottom of the stairs — you hide behind the couch. When he walks over to me, stab him."

Although that might have sounded like an easy job merely moments ago, now the thought of killing another human terrifies me.

"Sunney, I can't—"

"Just pretend it's Tom. Tom, who tried to kill you, who abused you repeatedly."

My mind flashes to that fatal night. The dining room where it happened. The knife. Tom was laying on the ground, with me on top of him. He had attacked me moments before, punching me repeatedly, and shifted his eyes away to a kitchen knife near my grasp. The very knife that saved my life.

"We don't have much time," Sunney urges.

I tightly close my eyes and say, "Okay."

If I do this, maybe I can get Sunney in Quinn's Jeep. It has to be at his house still. That means over a mile I'd have to run. I can't carry Sunney that long but on foot I could make it there and back in the Jeep in less than fifteen minutes. What if the keys aren't in the ignition though? It's the only plan my scattered brain can think of, so for now I have to prey the key will be there. I can drive Sunney to the hospital before he bleeds to death. Just maybe.

We slowly descend the stairs with Sunney's arm over my shoulder and mine around his waist. His full weight on me makes every step painful, but I grit my teeth through it all till we are on the last step. I gently set him down and run behind the couch, crouching out of sight. A few minutes pass, and I begin to wonder if Quinn will be returning. But soon enough I hear the front door open. Sunney and I make eye contact briefly before he looks up toward the door. His eyes, which had previously looked fatigued, were now wide, like he is looking at something he hadn't anticipated seeing.

"Where is she?" says a voice I instantly recognize. *Quinn's.*

"You're never going to see her again, you son of a bitch," Sunney says.

I hear the floor creak as he slowly walks forward. I feel distressed, all the possibilities of me messing this up making my body shake excessively, but I center myself to avoid making any sound or letting the knife slip from my overly sweaty palm. I can do this. No, I have to do this.

I tightly close my eyes, seeing Quinn's face in my mind. I remember all the sweet things he had said to me. The way I felt we had a real connection. All of it was a lie. He is just some psychopath ready to kill Sunney and me just because I left him. It doesn't make any sense.

I open my eyes, peering above the couch. Quinn is no longer wearing the black cloak or mask. He has an oversized black hoody and dirty jeans on. With me already knowing his identity, he must've ditched the masked identify get-up. His brown hair is frayed, as if he has just run through the woods like a madman. He's slumped and looks on the verge of tumbling over.

"What did you do?" he screams at Sunney, who sits still, the tiniest grin on his face. It must be because he knows his death won't be in vain.

I tighten my grip on the knife and slowly stand up, but, as I take my first step forward, the floor emits the tiniest creak. Quinn, obviously already on edge, turns around. The revolver I now notice is in his shaky hand.

"Toni?" he asks, his voice much softer, unlike when he was talking to Sunney.

"Toni, kill him! Kill him!" Sunney screams at the top of his lungs.

Quinn turns his body back to stare at Sunney before lifting his revolver and pointing it at him.

"What the fuck did you do?" he asks Sunney.

I charge at him, but not before Quinn presses the trigger. Just as I penetrate the kitchen knife directly into the middle area of Quinn's back, I notice the revolver clicks, like it was empty this whole time. But hadn't he gone out to grab more ammo?

Quinn drops to his knees instantly, and thinking he might get back up, I take the knife out from his back, ready to stab him again. He twists his body slowly before laying down, looking into my eyes.

"Why?" he breathes, blood from his mouth splattering my face.

I drop the knife, horrified.

Why?

Sunney begins to roar with laughter as Quinn slowly falls to the ground, and I catch him in time, resting his body on the ground.

"Quinn, I'm — I'm sorry. I had to," I say, tracing his neck with my hand.

Sunney continues laughing as he watches us. My heart beats so loud I feel I might have a heart attack. Their words just before had sounded so off. Quinn had sounded so angry at Sunney. He'd asked him what he had done.

"Toni, you have to get out of here," Quinn says, more blood coming out from his mouth.

I feel tears streaking down my cheeks and they drop on his face.

"What?"

"Sunney — he knows. I'm sorry I couldn't save you," Quinn says, and his eyes slowly look away from me and fixate on the ceiling.

His body goes limp.

What have I done?

CHAPTER 27

I killed Quinn Robins. His blood is literally and figuratively on my hands. And on my face, I notice when I lick my lips and get a metallic taste. I can't even move. My body feels numb, like time has stopped. My husband laughs like a hyena, staring at the corpse just inches from him. It's nearly a full, excruciating minute of hysteria until he stops and finally looks at me with the biggest smile as I sit beside Quinn's body.

"I didn't think you'd have it in you."

I open my mouth to answer, but vomit comes out before words can. I heave on the ground, and Sunney starts laughing *again*. The vomit is mostly liquid and, I assume, is a delayed response to the murder that I just committed. I sit on all fours, retching.

When I regain some air after gagging, I use my sleeve to wipe my mouth. Before I can ask Sunney what is happening, I hear more laughter from the front door. It's female, high-pitched, and sounds innocent — almost like a Disney princess talking happily with animal friends.

When I look round, I see a woman walking through the front door. I've never seen her before. She looks slightly younger than me and wears an oversized black hoodie and pants. Her hair is straight, medium length, and a honey-brown color. She actually resembles a Disney princess with her small, oblong-shaped head and huge, brown-colored bunny eyes. In any situation other than this, she would have come across as someone I would immediately distrust and dislike. Now I just wonder who she is and why she's here. We only make eye contact for a moment, and the glare I receive is harder than I might have expected from a stranger. It's almost as if she knows me quite well.

"Gross," she says, eyeing my vomit.

"Who are you?" I ask, my hand still gripping the knife with which I'd just killed Quinn and pointing it in her direction.

She starts giggling, not one bit moved by the knife, before beginning to undress. She easily slides off the black hoodie and dirty black pants. Underneath, she's wearing a lemon-colored skin-tight silk nightgown with a slit up the leg. She no longer resembles a princess with her fake tits nearly popping out of her attire. I'm not much better with my sleep shorts, tank, and kimono still on. Looking her up and down, I notice she's also sporting a pair of brown cowboy boots — the same as Quinn's.

"Well, this is going to be awkward. Sunney, do you want to introduce us?" she asks, looking at Sunney with pining eyes.

"Sunney—" I begin to ask, looking back, but before I can turn around, I feel a hand aggressively yank on my wrist, twisting it until I drop the kitchen knife.

I yelp in pain, looking quizzically at Sunney as he lets go to fetch the kitchen knife from the floor. He takes a Ziploc bag from the back pocket of his shorts, drops the knife in it, and then walks toward the woman, barely limping.

"Toni, this is Heather. Heather, Toni. She's a brilliant actress," Sunney says, placing his arm around her waist.

"You did just as good." The girl beams, looking up at Sunney like she's meeting a celebrity.

"You are amazing."

I want to throw up again. That or I'll pass out and wake up in bed like this was all a sick lucid dream. I mean, it must be a dream. The shit happening right now seems too fucking insane.

"Sunney, I don't — I don't — understand—"

"Understand what's going on? Yeah, we kind of planned for that. I can explain everything, but you might freak out. I need you to take some relaxants," he says, walking over to the coat rack and grabbing one of his black briefcases.

He walks back over to Heather and places the briefcase in her arms, face side up, before entering the combination. Once it's opened, he takes out a white washcloth with a brown-colored glass bottle of chloroform. I'm unsure about what's happening and don't have time to think about it before Sunney opens the bottle and pours a hefty amount on the rag.

"Get away from me, you fucking freak!" I shout, lifting my hand into the air.

"Calm down, Toni. You need to relax," Sunney says, using the very soothing voice he would use when holding me while sick.

I step back as he walks toward me. My only option is to run upstairs, as the back door is padlocked. I only make it a few feet back before tripping over something. I land on my ass and realize it's Quinn's corpse. My stumble has caused his head to shift to the side. I let out a scream as his eyes stare into mine. I also notice now how much he reeks of alcohol, almost like he drank a gallon of it or had a gallon of it dumped on him. Sunney and Heather laugh at my comical fall. Their laughs pierce my ears as I again attempt to regain my footing. Just as I'm up, Sunney runs toward me. Now that I'm near him again and breathing normally, I notice his "blood" smell differs from Quinn's. While Quinn's smells heavily of rust, Sunney's mostly smells like old rotting milk.

Sunney grabs me by my arms, stopping me from running up the stairs and pinning me on the floor. I try to fight him, kicking at his legs and wiggling my arms away from his grasp. Moments later, Heather is by my feet, rag in hand. Before she can get near, I kick her in the legs. She falls to the ground and her face instantly flushes red from anger.

"You bitch!" she screams.

"Calm down. I got this," Sunney assures her. "Toni, you can do this willingly, or I'm going to have to hurt you, and

I don't want to do that, at least not yet," he warns me, his hand's grip tightening over my wrists.

I feel pain as his nails penetrate the thin skin on my wrists, but I refuse to quit. Who knows where I'll wake up if he gets that chloroform over my mouth?

"Why are you doing this?" I ask, looking at Sunney, whose eyes are too busy concentrating on my body as I continue to wiggle, gritting my teeth to cope with the pain emanating from my wrists.

"Because you cheated on me," Sunney says, finally looking into my eyes.

I momentarily stop squirming once I hear those words. With everything going on, I had forgotten about that. It still doesn't make sense. Sunney is doing all this for that?

My spell is broken when I notice Heather by my side. Leveraging my frozen body, she forcibly shoves the rag over my mouth and nose. Looking up, I can see she has an evil smile on her innocent, pale face. I feel like a dog that has just bitten its owners, who feel forced to put it down. Both smile in the same way as everything goes numb, and my vision goes completely blurry. My strength is gone. As Sunney stands up, looking down at me, it all goes black.

CHAPTER 28

When I come to, I'm unsure how much time has passed. I hear old jazz music playing through the speakers at a lower volume than earlier. It's Al Bowlly, the jazz guitarist from the early 1930s, popular for his old-timey songs. I remember a song of his playing from Quinn's CD the other night.

My eyelids feel heavy as I open them and look at the still-padlocked screen door. Looking down, I see I'm currently seated on one of the kitchen chairs, my arms over the armrests, tied down tightly with rope. I try to move my legs, but they're also tied down securely.

I'm still in the living room but now in the spot where the widescreen TV had once been. Sunney and Heather are nowhere in sight. Quinn's body is still laying on the ground, with a large pool of blood underneath him. The blood Sunney had left on the stairway is gone, along with the blood near the front door, and my vomit has been cleaned up.

Almost all the damage done to Sunney must've been fake, considering how easily he held me down and the rancid smell of the fake blood. Is Sunney capable of doing all of this to take revenge on me for cheating? How did he even find out about that? Where did he meet this woman, Heather, to join in? I know nothing about her. She has to be associated with his shady job somehow.

As I wiggle my hands, trying to get out of this rope, I hear the sound of footsteps descend the stairs. I'm ready to see Sunney and beg him not to do whatever he's planning, but instead I see Heather. She's wearing the same nightgown but now has on white stockings which go up to her thighs and black, Mary Jane platforms (stripper shoes, as I would call them). Although she's a short woman, the heels make her a few inches taller than me. Her long brunette hair hangs in two pigtails like some Harley Quinn lookalike. I dislike this bitch more and more every passing moment. I can see how Sunney could charm his way into getting her involved in this revenge plan.

"She's awake, baby," she yells once she's in the living room. She jumps over Quinn's body like some little girl jumping over her toys.

Baby. I grit my teeth, happy I kicked her when I'd had the chance. I hope it left a bruise. Old Toni would have beaten this little girl's ass any day. But I can't let Old Toni show right now because if Sunney has lost his marbles over my infidelity and I can no longer reason with him, maybe I can convince Heather not to go through with whatever they have planned. Convince her to let me go.

"I don't know what Sunney told you, but I don't deserve this. You can let me go right now, and I won't—"

"You don't deserve this? Deserve what? We haven't even done anything to you. You just wait, bitch!" Heather snarls at me, crossing her arms.

"Trust me. This isn't worth it. Just let me go," I plead, knowing Sunney will descend the stairs any second, and then any chance I have of convincing this stupid bitch to let me go will be gone.

"Sunney, she keeps pleading for me to let her go!" she yells up the stairs as if she's a sibling tattling on me to our parents.

Losing patience, I hold in my anger by biting my lip and say, "You guys won't get away with this. You'll both go to prison. Just let me go, and I won't say a thing."

It's not the purest of truths, but now I put on my innocent face, praying she'll buy it.

Heather rolls her eyes, paying no heed to me. Soon enough Sunney comes down the stairs. He's now changed from the fake bloodied clothes from the night before and appears to have showered. His hair is still wet and already neatly styled. He's wearing a pair of silk plaid navy-blue pajamas, a white cotton T-shirt, and a matching robe. He has a whiskey glass filled with ice and a dark liquid in his hand.

"Thanks, beautiful," Sunney says, wrapping his arm around Heather and kissing her left cheek, never leaving eye contact with me.

Oblivious to Sunney's intense glare at me, Heather shuts her eyes tightly with a small grin plastered on her face. I remember doing the same thing when I received that attention from him when we first started dating. Once he lets Heather go, they walk toward me.

"You're probably wondering what is going on, huh?" Sunney asks me.

"I mean, I have a pretty good idea, but I'm hoping this is all some sick joke you're playing. Revenge, maybe?"

"Sick joke? Not at all. This is all very real, and I wouldn't exactly say revenge. I would classify it more as punishment."

"Quinn wasn't trying to kill me, was he?"

I already know the answer; I just need to hear Sunney say it. I killed him for nothing.

"Nope."

"Did he do any of that awful shit you said?"

Sunney chuckles, sips his drink, and then reaches into his robe pocket, taking out a crumpled piece of newspaper. He walks closer to me, putting the clipping in my reading view.

"I found this baby on the ground at Quinn's and your little fuck spot. It seemed he had intended on showing it you, but he dropped it before he got the chance."

I look at the clipping. There's a picture of a car upside down rammed right into a tree. It's dated six months ago, in February. The description underneath the photographs reads:

> *Car accident causes the tragic death of one individual with two survivors. The driver drifted off the road early on the morning of February 10th, causing it to ram into a tree pictured to the right. The passenger was the only one not wearing a seatbelt and passed away from injuries sustained during the crash. The driver has been put into custody. Alcohol has been verified as a factor in the incident.*

I gulp, not clear why Quinn would be scared to show me that.

"I don't understand," I say.

Sunney shakes his head and takes out another piece of paper from his robe pocket. This one isn't crumpled but folded in half.

"I found this at your boyfriend's house. It looks like a suicide note from the day after you guys fucked. Interesting, right? Anyway—" he unfolds the sheet of paper and takes another sip. Then he fake clears his throat and reads:

> *"To whomever it may concern,*
>
> *I have decided to end my life with a very heavy heart. I cannot run from my past anymore. I have hidden the true events that unfolded on February 10th. If I am to die, I do not want to leave this world without the truth being set free. Not getting the justice I deserve may make me a coward forever, but I have made peace with that. My beautiful wife Michelle's death was not Bryan Henderson's fault. It was mine. We had left the bar all drunk in our senses, but Bryan had blacked out and was in no shape to even put keys in the ignition, even though it was his car we had taken that night. I insisted on driving. I had done it nearly a hundred times. What was once more going to do? But my assumptions were wrong. Although I had never touched Michelle, I had yelled at her about serving me divorce papers. She'd wanted*

to leave me for a while, I just never expected her to do it. She had finally had enough of my drinking. I think my yelling somehow made her forget to put her damn seatbelt on. She was always doing that; now I realize it wasn't intentional. She just didn't care about her life anymore. While driving, I think, she leaned over to try and calm me. It's all still sort of fuzzy. I looked away for a few seconds and slid on the ice on the road. It was not long before we rammed into a large oak tree only a couple of yards away from the road going over sixty miles an hour. When I came to, I saw the windshield was gone along with my wife, whose motionless body lay head-first in the dirt in front of the car. Without mourning my wife's dead body, I thought about all that would happen to me. Manslaughter, prison, felonies upon felonies. Bryan was breathing, but he was passed out in the back. I'd somehow managed to remember putting his seatbelt on over my wife's. In seconds, I made one of the worst decisions of my life. I switched spots with Bryan — put him in the front. I knew it would work, casting the blame on him — he already had three past DUIs. He didn't even realize I had done it. He was too drunk. I knew he'd do time, but I didn't think he'd kill himself. I wanted to fess up so many times. I just can't do it anymore. I want my wife's life insurance money to be given to her family. Tell them I'm sorry for all the pain I've caused them. One last thing — I want Toni Lovette to know I'm sorry for coming into her structured marriage and tearing all the pieces down. It's the last pain I'll ever cause another person.

Sincerely, Quinn Robins."

CHAPTER 29

I'm silent with my mouth agape, unsure how to comprehend what I just heard. So, Quinn committed vehicular manslaughter and blamed his friend in the backseat. No wonder he had moved to Rubico and refused to talk about his wife. Did he decide to end his life because I left so suddenly that night? Or had he imagined committing suicide before our encounter due to his guilt and shame? Although I'm angry at him, I can't deny that I'm also a murderer. No wonder we felt an uncanny attraction to each other. We were both tortured and constantly running from the past. Both of our failed relationships had ended in our significant others' deaths.

"Crazy what a little detective work will get you," Sunney says, folding the paper and placing it into his pocket.

"How — how did you find out about—"

"About you fucking our neighbor four days into our honeymoon?"

I nod, unsure I want to listen to the answer.

"It wasn't that difficult, Toni. You must think I'm some sort of idiot. You see, I ran into Quinn at the strip club the day before you guys fucked, and he called me by my last name. But I never gave him my last name the first time we met. So that raised the first red flag in my mind, but not a big one. Anyone could tell him that as I am well known in town. The second red flag was him informing me about the fact we're neighbors. That worried me because I do a lot of business at the cabin and didn't need some rat going and telling the police. I received all the shitty information from him and decided to maybe try paying him off. He wasn't a terrible guy. I enjoyed talking to him. I thought I could ask if he wanted to help me with the business. The third red flag, however, obliterated all that trust I had for him — or you — for that matter. You tried to drug me that night. You went to see Quinn, but funny coincidence, I caught you red-handed because I had planned on drugging you, using the same pills that night. I had planned on chatting with Mr. Popular that night as well. I was getting suspicious that he could be full of shit and had been sent by another competitor to sit and watch me, waiting for a slip-up."

"Why did you want to drug me? You had been out at the strip club most of the previous night. You could've just done the same."

"And risk you getting angrier with me? At this point, I still gave a shit about you and wanted our marriage to work. But, anyway, the minute I found that empty bottle of sleeping pills in the cabinet, I remembered having three pills from the last time I used it and was worried you were back to your druggie ways. Then I caught you trying to drug me with my whiskey of all things. You didn't even think to crush them until your back was turned and you were doing the act. Amateur shit is what it is, really."

I knew the way I'd given Sunney the drugs had been poorly planned. I had thought offering to grab him a drink would make him happy. I had never done that before, because the sight of whiskey made me want some myself, and I had spent most of our relationship avoiding liquor the best I could.

"I saw you drink it."

Shaking his head, Sunney says, "I had a couple of drinks, but the whole thing mostly got spit into the napkin resting on my lap. Who knew having manners would be my saving grace? When we went to bed, I played drugged-out husband and waited for you to get up and do whatever you had planned. I — God — to be honest, was scared shitless you would kill me to collect my life insurance, but when you got up, went downstairs, and left — that shocked me. My next thought was you would wander out in the woods by yourself. So, I followed you. I saw you get in that red Jeep and heard you guys talking. You got out of the Jeep soon, seemingly to leave, redeem yourself, and then in the flash of another moment, you kissed him. Then you let him fuck you."

"And you didn't intervene?"

"I wanted to. I wanted to shoot both of you in the back and skull fuck you. It was arduous not killing you when you returned and immediately had sex with me. I have never felt more disrespected, hurt and angry in my life. But this wasn't my first rodeo with a cheating whore. My last girlfriend had done the same thing. I had managed that maturely and as logically as I saw fit. Getting angry makes you do rash things. I might not have gotten away with it if I had killed you both there. After he, luckily for me, dropped that news clipping and the wind blew it my way, I returned home to ideate the ultimate revenge plan."

Had Andrea cheated on Sunney too? Did he kill her? Now it doesn't seem completely out of the question. He could get away with doing it again scot-free if he had done it before.

"Is this why you convinced me to think Quinn was trying to kill us?"

"Getting you to think it was Quinn was simple. I mentioned the trash mysteriously being taken out and leaving the screen door open to get you on edge. Then I asked Heather to stand behind a tree on a stepstool to replicate Quinn's stature, make you see she's wearing Quinn's boots he wore the night you guys fucked, and then play that romantic little mixtape you guys listened to. I figured that by planting the thought that I was bleeding out and needed immediate medical attention, you'd take the bait and kill him. Get the world to think he tried to kill us after becoming obsessed with you. Finding the suicide-slash-confession note was the icing on the cake. It proves he was unwell. Your cum rag of a dress and prints all over his Jeep prove you guys had a sexual relationship. He becomes angry after you end the relationship and decides to kill us before offing himself. He breaks into our house and kills you before trying to kill me, and I grab a kitchen knife and kill him instead."

"Do you think the cops are going to buy this? It's clear you're the jilted lover who murdered us, and the cops are immediately going to see through the ruse. Please, Sunney, if you just let me—"

"You see, I thought of that too. It's too fishy. But what if a young, loyal cop somehow showed up on the scene just as I am forced to kill this man and can vouch for seeing him attack me? A cop who got a concerned call from an exotic dancer," Sunney points at Heather and continues, "claiming two nights prior, as she was giving him a lap dance, that he wouldn't stop talking about a married woman he had been seeing and how he just needed to get her dirtbag husband out of the picture."

"Why would he just tell that to a random stripper?"

"Good question. I'm sure he would, as he's a man who currently has dozens upon dozens of empty liquor bottles and prescriptions for anti-depressants not prescribed to him scattered in his house and vehicle. Once again, clearly, he's not well at all."

Goddamnit, Quinn. He made the perfect murderer.

"Okay, and how will you get this so-called cop to lie?"

I hope, if I mention enough holes in this crazy scheme, Sunney will listen and let me go. Although this one seems less probable, as I remember Quinn telling me about a cop Sunney might be in cahoots with.

"By paying him a good sum with the life insurance money I'll get from your death."

Shit! My life insurance.

After I had killed Tom I had signed up for life insurance believing one of Tom's wacko friends who believed he was innocent would come after me. I wasn't close to any of my family but with my father's grandparents still alive I wanted to leave them a little something. Something to make up for being the only ones who still checked up on me even after my father's death.

Before Sunney and I got married he convinced me to change my coverage to Jameson Life Insurance for a better rate. With my grandparents nearing their eighties I had even changed my beneficiary to Sunney's name.

He would be a suspect as most husbands are in disappearance cases are but my signature is on all the documents. He's just in charge of the company that runs the insurance. He could charm the police just as he charmed me into signing all those documents.

"And he's in love with you and thinks you guys are going to ride off into the sunset," Heather says playfully.

Sunney has two so-called lovers wrapped up in this mess. I am fucked. Who knows who he's been fucking behind my back this whole time, if it was so easy for him to make two people follow him blindly? Maybe I can't get out of here by pointing out holes in this genius plan, but there might be another way. I can tell him how much of a hypocrite he is and how crazy it is to kill me over something so frivolous. Sunney isn't an idiot and still might be feeling betrayed.

"So, you can go fuck her and whoever you want, but because I did it, you're going to kill me?"

Sunney raises his eyebrows and glances over at Heather.

"We haven't had sex — since you've been together anyway. Your husband is about as loyal as they get. It wasn't until he found you with Quinn that he came to me. We've known each other since he dated Andrea, and the sexual tension has always been there. If it weren't for your wickedness, we would've been together by now. But I never gave up on Sunney. I always knew I wanted him to be mine," Heather says, running her hand over Sunney's back and looking at him like he is the reincarnation of Jesus.

He does have his hooks in her. It doesn't surprise me; he can talk nearly anyone into something he wants. Those looks and charisma are irresistible. They can make any woman swoon. It's the same feeling as being noticed by a superstar. Going to the first work party with Sunney made me feel that way. Everyone knew him. All the women who walked by were gazing at him with big eyes and glaring at me. Who knows what power he holds in this shitty little town?

Sunney and Heather stare at each other with horny, loving eyes. But I'm far more sickened by the sight of Quinn's dead body. It makes me want to vomit as I gaze at it. Our last meeting had ended on such a sour note, so much so that I had believed him being capable of murder. I want to be mad at him because what he did was terrible, but I'm no better. I killed Tom in self-defense, but deep down, I know very well I could have run out and gotten help after stabbing him that one time. After everything he did to me, I couldn't, though. I couldn't let him go about spreading lies about me. I had to end him.

"Sucks. He was probably the last person who could've helped you. And you killed him," Sunney says, noticing my eyes on Quinn.

I take a deep breath, not wanting to cry again in front of them.

"He didn't deserve any of this," I say, and Sunney once again chuckles.

"You are ridiculous, Toni. First, you let yourself get groomed by your science teacher—"

"How did you—"

"I research the women I am with, Toni. It's not hard to find out about such an event. You were groomed by your teacher and got caught. He hanged himself because of it all. There's the first blood on your hands. Then your dad killed himself because your mom whored around before she then drank herself to death. I will admit it was idiotic of me not to realize — like mother, like daughter. There's the second blood on your hands. Then your third—"

"Shut up, just shut up!" I yell, not wanting to hear anymore, as tears finally begin streaming down my face.

Sunney walks over to me and places a hand over my neck, cutting off my breathing.

"You are going to hear all I have to say about you, you fucking bitch."

Just as I start gasping for air, he lets me go, walking back to Heather.

"Where was I? Oh yeah, your third victim. The abusive ex-boyfriend. You stabbed him to death, leading to more blood. Last but not least — Quinn Robins. You killed him in cold blood. Four people, well, five, counting your mother, who would have otherwise been alive if it weren't for the likes of you."

These people's blood is not on my hands. I can't believe that. I was in love with — or thought I was in love with — my teacher. I couldn't help that he decided to end his life. My parents died when I was very young and naıve. Their marriage was bound to crumble from their own decisions. As for Tom, I had no choice in killing him. If he'd survived, he would've physically abused other women. I've been beating that into my mind for over a year now. *It's the truth.*

As for Quinn, I was tricked into killing him. I want to scream this at Sunney, but it's no use. He's no longer listening to me.

"Just tell me. I just want to know one last thing. How did you even get Quinn to come to our place? What did you say — or do to him?" I ask.

Heather and Sunney glance at each other briefly before looking back at me as if debating whether it's worth their time to tell me.

Shrugging his shoulders, Sunney says, "I made him spend the last hours of his life regretting sleeping with another man's wife."

"What did you do to him?" I ask.

A mischievous smile appearing on his lips Sunney says, "So, after drugging you with the wine at dinner, waiting for you to pass out, I—

CHAPTER 30

Quinn Robins: Before

After Quinn Robins sloppily signs his name for the last time on his suicide-slash-confession note, he folds it neatly before placing it into an envelope titled *To Whomever it May Concern.* He could have made it out to a specific name but he could not think of anyone who might be concerned with his death.

At a younger age, he had always thought of suicide as a selfish thing to do. He still does, in fact, but it's only selfish when you have people who care about and rely on you. Since losing his wife and best friend, he has isolated himself from everyone.

After placing the envelope on his coffee table, he sits on his couch, grabbing the last bottle of Celexa and popping a couple into his mouth. He washes it down with a chug of a bottle of Crown Apple he decided to have as his last drink. *Here's to you, Toni.*

He knows he would take her back if she showed up right now. He would discard the suicide plan and beg her to love him and make him better. But, as the saying goes, two wrongs don't make a right. This analogy fits the two of them perfectly.

Going overboard on drinking throughout the day to be prepared for this, he wonders if he should wait till morning instead, when he's sobered up. He thinks his mind would be a little clearer, and he won't risk somehow shooting himself incorrectly with his delayed judgment.

No, I'm doing it tonight.

He stares at his old revolver sitting neatly on a throw pillow beside him, loaded with one single round. He wants it to be quick and painless. He grabs the revolver, resting it against his lap. His grip on the handle is tight and shaky. He closes his eyes tightly, bringing the gun up and placing the barrel to the side of his temple.

However, the sound of his Jeep's engine starting outside makes him drop the revolver where it had just been. Only seconds later, music from his CD blasts from the car's speakers. He stands and rushes over to the window. He had parked unusually far away when returning from town after retrieving liquor. The headlights are on, and a bright light is directed at the window where he's standing, briefly blinding him. Regaining some sight, he sees a figure standing by the Jeep with the driver's side door open. It's hard to see, but the person is short and small-framed. Could it be — *Toni*?

He runs back to the couch, retrieving the revolver. In a hurry to see what's going on, he stuffs it in the back of his jeans. Unlocking his front door, he opens it and jogs toward his Jeep. He hasn't the slightest clue what he will say. He wants to be angry at her for being here and starting his vehicle, messing with him. But he also wants to hug her for stopping him from his end.

"Toni, what the hell are you—" he begins to say, but now only a couple yards from the vehicle and the light no longer directly in his face, he realizes it's not Toni but Heather.

She's wearing a skintight, yellow, lingerie-like nightgown with an innocent look as if she didn't just break into someone's vehicle.

"Heather, what the hell are you doing here?" Quinn asks.

Although he remembers that she's one of the few people he clued in about where he lives, there are still numerous questions about why she would be here now. There hadn't been much talking that night at the strip club when she had reluctantly given him a lap dance.

"I need to borrow some of your clothes. It's chilly out tonight," Heather says with a soft giggle, wrapping her small arms against her chest.

Quinn begins to scan her face to see if she looks distressed. She possibly got taken advantage of by a client — or Sunney.

"Sure, just give me a minute. Stay right there," Quinn says, not trusting the situation and slowly moving his hand to the back of his pants to reach the revolver.

Barely before he's able to get his hand over it, he feels something pressed against the back of his head — something familiar to him. The end of a gun.

"Sweet dreams, Robins," he hears a deep voice whisper before feeling the back of the gun bash against his head again, knocking him unconscious.

CHAPTER 31

Quinn Robins: Before

Quinn is woken up by a hard blast of water directly to his face. It's cold and smothers him almost immediately. He shakes awake, attempting to move his hands over his face, but they are bound behind his back with thick rope along with his ankles. Peering down, he notices he's shoeless. He's lying on his side on a flat ground of dirt. After the flow of water finally ceases, he opens his eyes. Sunney stands over him, wearing a pair of grey-colored boxers and a light pink robe with a ribbon tied around the waist, covering his shirtless body.

"Robins, right?" Sunney sarcastically asks, and Quinn instantly recalls it as the same line with the same condescending tone he had used at the strip club.

Wiggling his body frantically, Quinn yells, "What the fuck is this?"

"Ah, ah, ah," Sunney says, placing his foot on Quinn's shoulder and pressing down hard. "We both know how you've gotten into this predicament, Mr. Robins. It's not right, you know. Fucking other men's wives."

"Toni told you?" Quinn asks.

Chuckling and removing his foot from Quinn's shoulder, he says, "Told me? She didn't need to. I saw it all myself. My wife seems super dimwitted when it comes to drugging someone so she can sneak out. I, on the other hand, excel at it."

"No, this is between all three of us. You happily introduced yourself in our marriage."

Sunney's eyes widen as he stares down at Quinn and, inhaling a deep breath, kicks him directly in the abdomen. Quinn grimaces in pain. He feels the kick might cause him to throw up all the liquor he's had tonight.

"Sunney, quit it. He still needs to be able to walk," a familiar voice says in the background, and moments later, someone wearing a cop uniform is now at Sunney's side.

Deputy Adler, the homosexual cop who had pulled Quinn over a couple of days ago and had been struck dumbfounded by the namedrop of Sunney.

"I'm just having fun," Sunney replies.

"I found this on his coffee table," Adler says, handing the suicide envelope to Sunney, who looks it over before opening it up.

"That's private, you prick!" Quinn yells.

"Only fair as you helped yourself to my private belongings," Sunney says, unfolding the paper and reading through the contents.

His eyes and smile get bigger and bigger as he reads on. After finishing it, he begins to laugh hysterically.

"It's kind of a shame you were already planning on ending your cowardly, pathetic life as I had planned to do that for you. Watching you die with that in mind won't be as fun."

"What are you talking about?"

"You'll find out soon enough. I shouldn't even be talking to you about it. It might ruin the big secret. What I wanted to ask is, how many times did you fuck my wife?"

"Fuck off and let me go!"

Sunney, still grinning, gives Quinn another hard kick to the abdomen.

"Hey! I got an idea. One minute," he exclaims and over-dramatically prances away, retrieving a bottle of Crown Apple — the one Quinn had been drinking from earlier.

"A drink for every question you answer?"

Quinn remains silent.

"Come on. It was fun last time. Now, how many times did you sleep with my wife?"

Not knowing if his stomach full of whiskey can take another kick, Quinn answers, "Just once."

Sunney takes a brief sip and asks, "And how many times did you guys meet or hang out beforehand?"

"Sunney, it doesn't matter," Adler protests.

"It matters to me. Go on."

"Three times, I think."

Taking another sip, Sunney continues, "How did you make each other's acquaintances after the gas station?"

"She was out for a run the morning after. I convinced her to see me the next day. Then after I saw you at the stripper's club, I went to your cabin that night. I told her about your shady ass business and asked her to meet me the following night. Look, this is all my fault. Don't hurt Toni."

Raising his eyebrows, Sunney replies, "Look at you trying to be noble. What happened to the man who let his friend take the fall for him killing his ex-wife?"

Quinn tries to think of any way out of this and remembers his lucky lighter still in his back pocket. He slowly moves his tied-up hands down. Maybe if he can grab it, he can distract them long enough to somehow burn the ropes and free himself.

"And you, the wannabee drug dealer, will lecture me about my morals?"

"Lecture? No, it's just morbid curiosity."

Quinn's hand finds the lighter finally. He knows he's running out of time.

"Listen, it was just one time. Is it worth killing us both?"

Sunney is silent for a couple of moments. Quinn wants to believe he's hesitant to go through whatever it is he has been planning, but the small smirk on his lips says otherwise.

"Did you like her, or were you just trying to get laid? I won't judge you; I've acted all mushy and shit trying to get laid numerous times."

"What difference does it make?"

"Please don't make me kick you again."

That's the answer Sunney wants. He wants to know whether Quinn had just used his wife to get laid. Even though he may beat him to death, Quinn won't give him the satisfaction of that lie.

"To be completely honest, I liked her. I liked Toni a lot. She is sweet but damaged. She is a lot like me. I don't know how she ever settled for your bland ass."

Sunney bites his lower lip, clearly unhappy with the answer. Nodding, he takes another shot at the Crown Apple.

"For your information, she liked my so-called blandness. It's exactly what she needed at the time. Then she got bored and wanted something different — something I'd call shitty, but she'd call mysterious, like you."

"It's not your problem anymore. I've had plenty of women replace me in my lifetime. You get over it."

Sunney grins as if he'd probed those thoughts but turned them down.

"That's the difference between me and you, Quinn. I will not be embarrassed by some whore. She'll die knowing she hurt the wrong man."

"Look, if you're going to kill me, then fucking kill me already."

"I'm not going to kill you, Quinn. And because I think you're such a terrific guy, ready to be redeemed, I will do you a favor. I'm going to go back home to my wife. She's the one I'm out to skin alive. You can make a choice now. You can either save Toni and stop her murder or run far away from here and never return."

Quinn, unsure if Sunney is playing a sick joke on him, keeps his hands tightened on the lighter.

"Why should I believe you?"

"I want to give you a choice, Robins. The same choice you had the night your wife died. You can run from the truth and be a coward, or you can be a hero."

Sunney reaches into his robe pocket, pulls out a small pocketknife, and tosses it a mere twenty feet away.

"That's a gift from me if you don't want to stay in those ropes all night. Anyway, make a decision at your leisure; it's a big decision. I do, however, have the smallest catch. I feel it's only fair that you be just as shit-faced as you were the night you wrecked that car into the tree as you are now. Just to be in that mindset, you know?"

"Are you out of your fucking mind?"

"Yeah, that's what happens when your wife cheats on you."

Sunney opens the bottle cap and, leaning down, begins to pour the bottle and the entirety of its contents on Quinn's face. Half goes into his mouth, and the second half is wasted on his face and body. Thinking it's over, Quinn takes heavy breaths, tightly shutting his eyes against the liquor. When he does, another surge of liquid pours inside his mouth and all over his body. He begins choking, anger surging through him. Opening his eyes, he spits a mouth full of Crown directly at Sunney, who sits down, unfazed.

"Burn in hell!" Quinn curses at him, his eyes irritated.

The lighter idea won't work as he's drenched in Crown from head to toe. One spark of the lighter will land him a spot in an urn. He places it back in his pocket, hoping to find some use for it later.

Already drunk and not exactly in the spot to deal productively with this situation, Quinn has no idea what congesting this amount of alcohol will be to him. Alcohol poisoning might be possible if he doesn't find a hospital soon. *Get out of the ropes and save Toni or run as far from this place as possible*. As a survivor of domestic abuse, will she be able to handle herself or does she need him? Sunney is deranged and on a mission for revenge.

"Not before you, Quinn Robins. I hate to cut out, but I must return to my beloved wife. Good luck!" Sunney says, giving Quinn a quick salute with just his middle finger.

"That should buy us a little time," he says to Adler as if Quinn is already incapacitated and cannot hear them speak.

"Sunney, you psychopath! Get back here and fight me like a real man."

Sunney and the cop turn around and start walking away. Quinn notes which direction they are headed, fixing his eyes on them until he can't see them anymore. Sunney whispers something to Adler, who looks back at Quinn in return before nodding.

Once they're gone, Quinn crawls like a worm to where Sunney had thrown the knife. It takes him ten minutes to find it and another ten minutes to cut his bonds loose. Looking down at his wrists, he notes they're bleeding from rope burn, but emitting little to no pain. In most instances, it would be a blessing, but now it just means his senses are already numbed by the liquor. As he unties the ropes around his shoeless feet, nausea kicks in.

Once his feet are loose, he barrels over on all fours to dry heave, but nothing is ready to come out. Standing up is much harder, and he falls over four times. Once up, he stumbles to a nearby tree, looking around the wooded area he's in. His sight is blurred, as his eyes are still burning.

He attempts to run in the direction Sunney and Adler had walked. He only makes it a couple of yards before he stumbles over and pukes. Quinn makes it to the road several minutes later, quitting his attempts at running, knowing they will end with him on the ground. Now on the road, Quinn realizes it's the spot where he had last seen Toni. So that means she's only about a mile away. It would be an easy feat if it weren't for the fact he feels like he's on the verge of passing out.

He stares ahead at the right side of the road, where his feet feel compelled to go. Safety. But his heart beats heavily in his chest at the thought of not going left. To death, possibly.

She left you like nothing. Leave her the same, his drunk, muddled thoughts urge.

I can find someone more capable of helping her, he tells himself, walking to the right but only making a few steps before tripping again.

Images of Michelle's corpse flash in his head. Her dead body was laid face-first on the ground, never letting another breath out. Her blank eyes peer directly at him, and then her face transforms into Toni's, her beautiful, big blue eyes begging him to help. He is blacking out. Time is running out if he wants to do this before losing all control.

For once in your life, don't be a coward.

Slowly getting back up on his feet, Quinn turns around and, staying by the grass, makes his way down the road to Sunney's cabin. He feels the presence of his wife nearby, hopefully forgiving him for all he had done. Although he will never be able to forgive himself for the atrocity he committed that night, maybe saving Toni will redeem him in a way. It will hopefully put the constant self-hate and self-loathing to bed. If this were his end, he could at least die a courageous man.

It's another twenty minutes before he makes it to the end of the driveway to the cabin. Sunney's pickup sits in the driveway, Quinn notes, before realizing it can't be their getaway vehicle as the front tires are slashed.

Approaching the front door, he catches sight of something. His revolver. It has been placed innocently on the two concrete steps leading up to the glass front door. He bends down to retrieve it, almost falling over again.

Making it up the two steps to the front door, he hears music from inside. It sounds like a song from his CD. He peers through the opaque glass door to ensure Sunney isn't standing there. He isn't standing but sitting on the steps. He's all bloodied up. *Maybe Toni had been able to protect herself after all.*

What kind of shit am I getting myself into? Quinn thinks, putting his hand over the doorknob and turning it open.

CHAPTER 32

"—And then you stabbed him, and voila! You killed Quinn Robins. It all went according to my plan," Sunney says, sitting at the end of the sofa now, sipping from his glass.

I gulp, in shock over what I've just heard. Quinn had come here to save me, just to be *killed* by me. I wish I could know what had been going through his mind. All that forced alcohol into his system must've impaired his judgment completely. He might have just wanted to redeem himself for what he had done to his wife. I don't believe in heaven, but a part of me prays that's where he is right now. I can't even look at his still body near the stairs without feeling nauseated from the guilt coursing through me.

"How did you know he would come for me and not run away?" I ask.

"Guilt-tripping and persuasion, mostly. I wasn't completely sure even then, so just in case, I had Adler follow him the whole time. For Christ's sake, the man committed vehicular homicide and let his friend take the wrap. He, by no means, had a record for making good moral decisions."

"What about the revolver by the front porch? How'd you know he wouldn't check to see if it was loaded, let alone see it?"

"I knew his eyes would be on the ground, and again, he was wasted. He didn't think to check the fucking thing. Too much in a hurry to save you. What a simpleton!"

"Okay, so you psychopaths have crossed your t's and dotted your i's. So, what's the point of keeping me alive?"

"Why are we keeping her alive? Let's just kill the whore," Heather prompts, speaking for the first time in over twenty minutes.

She is not aware of the complete loop of the plan, I realize.

"You're calling me a whore? You? The stripper?" I accidentally blurt out.

Sunney immediately cracks an ever-so-small smile, the way he would when I'd comment about some of his coworkers or say some of our inside jokes in public. I call it the "I shouldn't smile or even laugh but want to" face. Heather's eyes immediately find mine, piercing them. I gulp as she strides over and slaps me hard. So much for trying to get this crazy broad on my side. The slap burns my face, but I keep my eyes on Sunney. I mimic his little smile to remind him that he still thinks I'm funny. Maybe instead of delusional Heather, he's the one who needs convincing to let me go.

"I'll kill the bitch myself," she says, seeing my eyes on Sunney.

She stridently walks over to the kitchen and pulls out a kitchen knife. Who knew calling a stripper a stripper would piss them off this much? Old Toni's smart mouth is going to get me killed.

Sunney immediately runs to her before she crosses the counter. He places his hands on her hips and kisses her lightly.

"You look so sexy when you're angry," he says, tightening his grip on her hips.

Blushing, Heather places a hand over his neck, drawing him in for a more passionate kiss. The kiss turns into a full-blown sloppy-looking makeup session until Heather drops the knife to place both hands over Sunney's neck. I look away, disgusted and angry. *Couldn't they kill me before making me witness this?*

Soon enough, Sunney slips his hands under Heather's nightgown to her panties, but before he can go further, she pulls away.

"I thought you said we couldn't do anything until we kill her? Until your marriage is over?" she asks.

I can't help but be surprised either, as cheating is a worse crime than murder in Sunney's psychotic mind.

Briefly glancing over at me, Sunney says, "It was over the minute she cheated."

Heather scowls, obviously not impressed with that answer.

"And I realized even long before that you were the one," he adds, kissing her wrinkled forehead.

I want to barf. He's so full of shit. *Shit you believed yourself, Toni.*

"You mean that, baby?" she asks, already smiling again.

"Without a doubt. You're amazing."

I've never wanted to puke and laugh at the same time. Listening to this garbage from a third-person point of view makes me see how easy it is for him to look at a woman and spew that romantic bullshit. I remember our second date when we had finally shared a real kiss. I had gotten goosebumps all over my body as he had looked at me. Then my legs had gone almost completely numb when he had said, *I don't think I've ever had a kiss that amazing. Who even are you?* "Amazing" — he sure did enjoy throwing that word around.

Heather obviously buys into it and launches her mouth back onto Sunney's, and they are at it again. It doesn't take long for him to remove her yellow-laced panties and lift her on the counter. As they continue kissing, Heather wraps her legs around Sunney's waist. She moves her hands down to his pajama pants until his bare ass is visible.

I want to look away, but my eyes force me to watch them. The anger and unwanted feeling of jealousy I have now are what Sunney must have felt as he had watched Quinn and me. Does he even truly like this girl in the slightest? After I'm dead, I wonder if he'll keep her around or toss her to the side as he's done to many other women.

Sunney starts thrusting himself into Heather, who, in turn, moans loudly with her hands still tight around his neck. It reminds me of a time he mentioned how he liked the way I kept my moans mostly hushed and only touched him gently. He doesn't like it when girls are loud and aggressive. He likes to take control, feeling like he is fucking a soft and weak woman. This is yet another reason he might toss her to the curb after I'm dead.

As they continue their loud, pugnacious sex right before me, a familiar song from Quinn's playlist plays. *Wild Horses* — the same song Quinn and I had gotten it on to. As if knowing this, with a flushed face, Sunney peers back at me with a small smirk. After that, I can look away.

Finally, five minutes later, both reach their climax in a big charade of moaning, and the sex is over. Sunney lifts his pajamas back over his hips, walks back to his drink, and takes a long sip. Heather stares at me like a high school girl would do when the popular boy chooses her over you. I stare back, keeping myself as calm and as unbothered as possible. I won't let her know the anger I currently feel. I know this will piss her off more than me cursing at her.

"How about one last game, huh?" Sunney asks after finishing his drink.

"Tell me. Does it involves killing her?" Heather asks, jumping off the counter to stand but not putting her panties back on.

"Precisely."

"Great!" she exclaims, bending down to grab the kitchen knife.

At this point, I don't know who I'd hate more to be the one to do it.

"But I think it's only fair if we cut Toni loose."

"Huh?" Heather and I both say simultaneously.

"Yeah, I don't think it's fair to murder someone who is completely helpless. So, we cut her free and then let you two fight it out. Let the better woman win."

This *HAS* to be Heather's breaking point. She must realize, *hey, maybe this guy is using me, and he's not worth murdering for.*

She's silent for a few minutes as if processing everything before asking, "What if she wins?"

"Come on, babe, as if she'd even have a chance. You get the knife. Just stab her."

While she looks doubtful, I'm convinced I can overpower this bimbo. Sunney, sensing my confidence, walks back over to her. He leans down to look at her, placing his hand to gently grasp her chin before planting a light kiss on her lips. I know logic can't beat that damn look and the way he's touching her.

"If I thought you couldn't handle this, I wouldn't even entertain the idea. But, if anything goes wrong, I got this bad boy for a reason," he says, taking out his pistol.

Great! So even if I can get the upper hand in this, I'll be shot anyway.

Sunney approaches me and goes behind my back. He bends down and begins cutting my ropes free. As he does so, I stare at Heather. *Is Sunney right? Would she easily be able to kill me? I have more height and weight than her; however, her body is far more toned. She also has a stainless-steel kitchen knife that could cut through me like butter. I know because I have just done that very thing to Quinn.*

"Always did love a good ol' cat fight," Sunney whispers in my ear before taking hold of my wrists, lifting me into a standing position then pushing me to the ground.

He quickly moves out of the way. Seeing the crazy look in Heather's eyes, I immediately get off the floor and stand behind the chair I was in moments earlier. This is my last chance to convince this woman not to do this.

"Wait, wait, wait! Heather, I can promise you he's not worth this. Please just think this through. He's using you to get revenge on me," I beg, lifting my palms in the air as she walks toward me.

"She knows she's dead. She'll say anything and everything to get you to believe her," Sunney says, dismissing my pleas.

"*He* will say anything and everything to get you to believe him. He's a narcissist and psychopath," I yell, my whole body shaking.

Sunney shakes his head when Heather looks at him, and I can see that Heather finds that to be assurance enough. She makes a growling noise and prances toward me with the knife aimed in my direction.

"You're dead, bitch!" she scowls at me.

"Sunney, stop this right now!" I plead, but he is preoccupied with taking a cigar out of his humidor box and lighting it with a match before sitting on the recliner.

"Quit talking to him!" Heather screams, finally leaping at me.

CHAPTER 33

Without thinking, I lift the chair and throw it directly at her. Due to my shaky hands, it's a weak throw that only momentarily stops her. Soon she is running toward me again. I run to the side of a tall bookshelf and stand against the wall, hearing Heather's footsteps behind me, her still growling like some deranged animal. I grab a book just in time to block Heather, who attacks me with the knife. I throw the book at her face, which causes her to stumble a couple of feet back. Seeing her standing directly across from the bookshelf, I push it forward. It smashes into her, and she crashes to the floor like a sack of potatoes.

However, the bookshelf doesn't keep her down long as it only held a handful of books and looked like it had been purchased on sale at IKEA. She flips it off her body with little to no effort, panting wildly. Not waiting for her to get back up, I run to the front door and desperately start unlocking one of its many locks.

I only get to the second one before I hear Heather running toward me again. I glance at the opaque glass and see her reflection as she comes near me. When she's close and preparing to dig the knife into my back, I drop to my knees so fast that the impact hurts. The kitchen knife collides with the glass from the door and clatters to the ground a couple feet away. While she's still shocked from my sudden movement, I shift my body around and punch her straight in the vagina as hard as possible. The punch isn't very strong, as I'm still shaking and shocked that I'm still alive. Her vagina wasn't the first area I had necessarily wanted to hit, but it was at my eye level. The face or stomach would have been a ten times worse blow.

Heather scowls in pain and attempts to punch me in the face, but her movements are so delayed that I manage to move my palms up, blocking the hit. Compared to any hits I've gotten from Tom, this is like a paper cut. *Maybe I do have a chance at this after all. I just need to get that knife.*

I spot the knife a couple feet away to my left and reach out to grab it. Once my fingers are only a couple inches away, Heather's foot steps on my hand before I can grab the knife. Although her stomp is somewhat weak as she's barefooted and visibly under pressure from my quick thinking, that one hurts. Realizing she has overpowered me, she uses her other foot to kick the knife out of reach.

Wanting her foot off me before it breaks my hand, I once again punch her in the vagina. Except this time, I mean to do it out of spite for her letting my husband's dick inside it right before my eyes. The old part of me who had been hoping she would switch sides and quit with the crazy is long gone. I am in survival mode now.

The punch causes her to kneel, her hands between her legs. I crawl away, my adrenaline pumping at full force through my veins now. My eyes frantically search for the knife and I see it only a few inches away from Sunney's feet, who currently has a cigar in one hand and the pistol in the other. He looks as amused as a devoted fan watching his team at the Super Bowl. I don't dare go for the knife, knowing it's now out of the question. There is, however, still a full set of knives in the kitchen. I can even hide behind the counter if Sunney shoots at me.

I start crawling toward the kitchen but only make it halfway before I feel Heather's teeth dig into my ankle. Instead of yelping, I scream, turning onto my back and kicking her in her face with my free foot.

"Not my face, you fucking bitch!" she screams, putting her hands over her face, her nose already gushing blood.

"Get her, babe!" Sunney cheers her on.

I glare at Sunney, who is enjoying this entirely too much. *Sick fuck.*

I shouldn't have been distracted as, only a moment later, Heather is on top of me, scratching at my face. Taking benefit of my weak moment, Heather reaches for the knife Sunney has kicked toward her.

"Finish her," he cheers her on again.

With both hands clasped over the knife handle, she lifts her arms and dives the knife down. Thankfully, my hands are already near my face so I grab her wrists, stopping her from plunging the knife into my cheek. Heather growls and pulls her hands free from my hold. She then attempts to slash the knife at me. Unable to grab a hold of her wrists this time, I protect my face. The knife slices my palms. I scream in pain as blood drips from my wounds into my open mouth. Heather, obviously shocked, weakly once again attempts to bring the knife into my face. I am able to grab her wrists but I feel my strength enfeeble from the pain on my palms. I can't hold her off this way much longer. I have only one viable option left. With all the spit and blood in my mouth, I hock a loogie into her eyes, momentarily blinding her. Once she lets go of the knife to wipe her eyes, I use all the momentum I have left to buck Heather off me.

Once she's off, I sit up and, gritting through the pain, grab the knife that had landed a foot away from me. I fling it towards Heather, but she slaps it away from my frail grasp before I can do any damage. It lands over five feet away, and I consider jumping to grab it but realize that'll give her more time to regain the upper hand again. I must end this now.

Feeling anger take over me, like it did that night I killed Tom, I know I have no other choice now. I swiftly punch her straight in the face with enough force to turn her whole body around.

As if time has slowed, I briefly make out the words to the current song playing over the speakers. *Tie a Yellow Ribbon Round the Old Oak Tree.*

The word "yellow" directs my gaze to Heather's yellow thong, which is on the ground a mere inch from me. *Tie a Yellow Ribbon Around This Bitch's Neck*. I grab it and jump onto Heather's back using my full weight. Then I wrap it around Heather's throat, choking her. She begins fighting and wiggling to get free from my grasp, but I pin her down with my weight overpowering hers. The more she fights for freedom, the more I tighten the thong around her small neck. I'm surprised they haven't ripped yet. They must be heavy-duty — Calvin Klein, most likely. I haven't felt this strong and powerful since I stabbed Tom repeatedly.

Instead of using her hands to get free, she extends them to Sunney, who is only a couple of feet away and still watching us like he's watching TV — just a viewer incapable of getting involved.

"H–h–help," she gargles out.

Toni, that's enough, a voice urges me. It must be New Toni's. But I don't listen to her. I choke Heather harder. It's either her or me. If I let her go, she'll waste no time to grab that knife, or Sunney will shoot me in the face. At least this way, I can get rid of his little girlfriend. Fuck him over just once more.

Her hands start to slowly move down. It brings me joy that the bitch's last sight will be that of the man she thought loved her so much just kicking back and enjoying a stupid cigar as she dies. I half-expect him to get up any second to help, but he doesn't. He stares at me, an evil smile on his face the whole time. I feel so angry at the sick fuck sitting right in front of me and letting this all happen that I don't even realize her body has gone limp.

New Toni finally takes over again. I let go, and her body drops to the ground immediately. I stand up, hands shaking as the pain from the knife wounds reappears. Sunney drops the half-gone cigar into an ashtray, stands up, and walks over to the body. He places two fingers over her neck, which already has red strangulation marks.

"She's dead," he murmurs.

"She's not dead," I instantly say, more to myself than him.

I couldn't have choked her for *that* long. It didn't even seem *that* long. However, when I had stabbed Tom, it hadn't felt like I'd done it more than twice.

I scream, realizing what I've done. I killed her. *It's what you had to do*, Old Toni reminds me.

"Why are you screaming now? She's already dead, sweetie," he says, laughing more.

"I–I didn't even want to do that. Why didn't you stop us?"

"I told her you deserved a fair fight. That wasn't in your favor, to begin with, and you still killed her."

I curl my body into a ball, putting my legs over my chest and shutting my eyes, unable to look at Heather's dead body or the smirk plastered on Sunney's face. I feel the warmth of the blood from my wounds oozing onto my legs, and the pressure between the two causes me immense pain, but I don't care. I know the time Sunney will kill me is near.

I sit there, weeping for a few minutes before feeling a hand grasp my wrist and a cloth-like substance being wrapped over the slices covering my palms. I jerk my hand away and open my eyes. Sunney has leaned down next to me, wrapping a white bandage over my right palm before dropping it to move onto the left.

"Stay still," he orders.

"What are you doing?"

"You're going to need those hands."

"What do you mean?"

"You kill her. You bury her."

"Please, Sunney. Please don't make me do this," I beg.

CHAPTER 34

Twenty minutes later, I watch Sunney place a plastic tarp over the counter while humming to Quinn's CD, which is still playing. At this point, we've been through the ten songs on the playlist more than twice.

I had been okay with the idea of burying Heather's corpse, thinking it might give me closure, but the minute Sunney brought out the plastic tarp, old newspapers, and hacksaw, I drew the line. My stomach took a flip and immediately favored the idea of being killed over what Sunney had planned. I couldn't even handle staring at her corpse, let alone cutting it up. Sunney explained it would be easier to bury her in a bunch of little holes rather than just one. How he knows this is a whole other terrifying question.

Sunney has ignored all my pleas thus far and has me tied up in the same chair. After explaining his plan with Heather's body, he's mostly ignored me, except when I complained that the gashes on my hands hurt and he gave me two tiny blue pills to ease the pain. I immediately recognized them as Fentanyl, my favorite painkiller back in the day. Sunney said he had found them at Quinn's place. It seems we both had the same liking for illegal prescription drugs. If the coroner finds the drugs in my system, Sunney will probably plant the pills in Quinn's Jeep.

Once the plastic is over the counter, Sunney lines old newspapers on the floor directly below it. While he always does important things carefully and precisely, now he seems to be rushing. We must be on a time hack. It's morning, most likely.

"What time is it?" I ask.

He says nothing.

I think, *maybe I can get him talking about something else and delay the inevitable*. "Why — why did you let her die?"

Still silence.

"I mean, I get it, fair fight, and all. But she — she trusted you. You have the right to judge me for betraying your trust."

"This is different."

He speaks, after all.

"How? How is letting her die versus me cheating on you different?"

"No one cheats on me, Toni. At least not without having to pay the price."

"Like you probably haven't cheated on every girlfriend you've ever had?"

"I've had three girlfriends, and I never cheated on them. The previous one cheated on me too."

Andrea. What psychotic shit did he do to get back at her?

"Why didn't you tell me about her?"

"Because that might have aroused unwanted attention. You might have tried to find information about her, asking my family or friends. I didn't want that happening."

"What did you do to her?" I ask, half-mortified that there may be a chance I'm not Sunney's first revenge plan.

He chuckles and stares at me, finally stopping what he's doing.

"She got what she deserved for betraying me."

"You killed her?"

"It was more than that. You want to know?"

I don't, but it's worth it if it will prolong time just a little. I nod.

He sighs, checking the time on his Louis Vuitton Quartz watch. He walks over to the cupboards and pulls out a bottle of whiskey. He then takes a couple side steps to the freezer and grabs a couple of ice cubes. Then he fetches his glass and makes another drink.

After taking a long, slow swig, he says, "Andrea was the second girl I ever dated in my lifetime. She was beautiful, of course, but lacked any real talent. Sort of like you, funny how that is. Anyways she was working at the club when we first met. She was a dancer and I was instantly mesmerized by her beauty and the trauma she held within her. She was lucky a guy like me would ever even glance her way but I did."

Is his story ever going to go anywhere besides him talking so highly of himself? I consider asking this but keep my mouth shut just so he doesn't get angry by my snide comment and not tell the story at all.

"We dated for some time and I was the best thing to happen to that piece of white trash. It must not have been enough though because I found out she was cheating on me with some client from the club. When I caught her in the act, just as I did with you, that was the moment I came up with my plan to make her pay. On the ride home, I acted completely relaxed. Calm and collected to the max. She sat there and apologized to me over fifty times. I acted as if we would just talk it out in the morning before giving her a glass of her favorite wine laced with the same sleeping pills you tried using on me. After she passed out, I was awake and ready to prepare my plan. Except, this time, I did it completely alone."

Sunney pauses momentarily, a thin smile appearing on his face as though he's telling a fond story of his childhood. Like his first time riding a bike, not the time he murdered his girlfriend. It gives me chills.

"Andrea had a fondness for animals and was even a vegetarian for a majority of her life. If she hadn't turned out to be a stripper, she said she would have wanted to be a vet. I decided to use this to my advantage. So, when she woke up, I had the cabin completely locked up. I boarded up the windows and the front door. She met me downstairs where I told her we would be playing a game. All she had to do was find the key to the back door and I would let her go. I gave her seven whole minutes.

"I then let a baby pig go, one that I had bought from a local farmer. I made it quite obvious I fed the pig the key. All she had to do was slaughter the pig, get the key and she would be free."

I hold my breath, wondering how afraid she must have been. Most likely how I am feeling now. Except I have yet to be given the option of escaping. Knowing Sunney, whether or not she passed his test, I doubt he would have let her go.

"So, I waited outside and watched as she pleaded and begged me not to make her do this. Then her survival instincts finally kicked in and she grabbed the only sharp object I had left in the house. A pair of kitchen scissors. I watched as she chased and chased that little pig around, crying like a little bitch as the animal kept scurrying out of her grasp. By the time she finally plunged the scissors into the pig and scraped around its intestines and organs finding the key she had less then ten seconds to make it out. Almost did but failed."

This story sickens me. I don't want to hear more but I know I have to buy time. I keep my face neutral, knowing if I show the nauseated sensation I'm feeling, Sunney will feel even more proud of himself and the depravity he had committed.

"What—what did you do next?" I ask.

"I let her know she failed. She tried running but I caught her on the road. Then I slaughtered her like the pig she was."

CHAPTER 35

I married a psychopath. He's been harboring this sick secret the whole time we've been together. I think about our first date and that devilish smile of his and how he carried himself so perfectly. I thought he was an angel made in God's eyes. Turns out he's a devil in disguise. He had murdered his girlfriend after forcing her to play his sick game only months prior. It's almost like the compulsion to keep the secret bottled up all this time had been hurting.

I had always found it odd that Sunney never mentioned any ex-girlfriends. That or even talked about all the women who swooned over him. I saw how they all looked at him and how he would simply smile before walking away. His buddies would always congratulate him for having such beautiful women all over him and he'd simply grab me and act as though I was the only one in his eyes. It was sweet but in reality, he wanted me to see all the women who wanted him. He wanted me to be the best I could be because of how easily he could replace me.

I had played that role nearly perfectly except the one time at the Christmas party. The one where I got drunk and took oxys in the bathroom. I had pictured myself as the one at fault in that mess. For letting my drinking get out of control. I remember Sunney grabbing me by the wrist as we were leaving and pulling me into the coat room alone. There he had kept a tight grasp on my wrist and told me to never drink like that again. Or embarrass him like that. I had regretted my actions so much so I had slept with him the first night, attempting to relax his anger.

Sunney is violent when his anger appears. He had just done so well at hiding it during our relationship. He is such a perfectionist. I had ignored the red flags because I had been so head over heels in love with him. He never really loved me, he just loved that he knew he had the upper hand in our relationship and that he could control me.

After he'd told me the story of the murder of Andrea, my first question had been what had he done with the body, but that had been promptly answered when I simply looked over at the counter covered in plastic with a hacksaw atop it. I feel sick knowing all the awful atrocities my husband can mercilessly engage in.

My second question had been how he even got away with the crime, to which, finally, he had an answer. He seemed to always have a plan for getting away with murder. He'd bought an apartment in her name in New York and dumped all her belongings there to rot. Then, when she didn't show up for work, he told everyone she had run away with the married man with whom she had been cheating. No one thought of trying to get a hold of her or find her. Her family had disowned her years ago for her drug addiction, and her only friend was Heather, who was too fixated on Sunney to care much about her friend's well-being.

As for the married man, his wife took everything (his house, kids, money) and the photographs were leaked to his boss, along with all the money he spent at the club with the company card. Sunney paid him a slim amount to disappear and never return to Rubico or attempt any contact with Andrea (who was dead anyway).

Goddamnit! It's not even that good a plan. So many possibilities of getting caught, but all Sunney had to do was play a broken-hearted boyfriend at the club to get everyone on his side. The police never got involved, as no one reported her missing. If I just disappeared like her, would anyone even report me missing? Or miss me? This last year I have put most of my time and energy into a man who can concoct a plan of killing anyone he wants within minutes.

I have at the very least successfully delayed him by another twenty minutes. Even if the cost was hearing that disturbing story, how he'd had gotten back at Andrea. I didn't love animals, so what would be my punishment? Cutting up the dead body of Heather and burying her? It wasn't even a game. At least Andrea had had the option to escape.

Before I can ask my third question, Sunney disappears outside for a few minutes. Once he's gone, I push and pull on the ropes over my wrists and feet but cannot even nudge them loose. Eventually he returns with a large bucket of tools, setting it on the table and taking out a power drill. I immediately think the worst. He surprises me, however, by starting to drill a hole into one of the corners of the counter.

"Would you have even let her go if she had gotten out in time?" I ask when Sunney walks toward me, lifting Heather's corpse to seemingly take it to the counter.

"Of course," he answers once he has set her down.

"Did you have a plan ready?"

"I didn't need one. Seven minutes wasn't exactly a plausible time to complete the task. It was just enough to get a good laugh while watching her fool around and, incidentally, it was one of the best whack-off sessions I've ever had. Just watching her cut up that innocent animal, knowing how much she adores them, was exhilarating," Sunney says, kissing the top of his fingers.

"You're demented."

I remember walking in on Sunney jerking off in the shower on the second day of our honeymoon and wonder if he had been thinking of something demented then, too, imagining doing something terrible to me. He had been uncomfortably upset after I had walked in on him. If I had been smart, that would have been the first and only red flag I needed before getting the fuck out.

"That may be so, but you aren't exactly an angel yourself, sweetie. I mean, you've killed how many people now? Three."

"I was forced, and you know that."

"Murder is still murder. Now shut up so we can clean up *your* mess," he says, pulling out a pair of handcuffs from his back pocket and walking toward me.

For the first time tonight, I don't want to be cut free.

"Get away from me, you psychopath!" I yell, shaking my body.

"Love you too, baby," he says, chuckling.

He moves behind me, leaning down and placing the cold handcuffs over my wrists and tightening them against my wrists. He cuts the rope binding my hands and feet to the chair. Then he grabs my armpits, lifting me. After I manage to stand up, I attempt to get loose from his grasp, but he aggressively pulls me back.

"Stop it. I'm not even going to make you do the dirty work. You're not capable of it," he orders, pushing me to walk forward.

Just then I discover the purpose of the hole drilled into the counter when Sunney undoes the handcuffs to loop the left end into the hole and leave the right on my wrist, binding me to the counter.

"What an innovator!" I comment, keeping my eyes fixated on the ceiling, not wanting to look at the dead body mere inches away from me.

"Why, thank you," he says, disappearing through the back door again.

I pull on the counter, attempting once again to break free, this time from an estimated $10,000 white marble granite counter — an effort that translates to fucking impossible. I would have had a better chance of getting out from the rope. Sunney could kill me, but he had another think coming if he thought I would cut up a dead body and help him bury it.

He soon returns with a clear-colored plastic tote on wheels. It's big enough to fit a body if it were cut up into small pieces.

"Whatever you think, I'm going to help you wi—"

"Don't worry, princess. I wouldn't trust you with a hacksaw anyway. I'm going to cut up the body into seven simple pieces. Nothing extensive. Separate the arms, legs, torso, head, and teeth. All you must do is toss the pieces in this tote, which luckily has wheels, so we can take it outside, where you'll be burying each piece in an area of my selection."

I keep my eyes glued to the ceiling, as the mere thought of doing any of that already churns my stomach.

"Fuck you, Sunney. You're killing me anyway. I'm not playing your game."

Only a moment after I say that, Sunney's hand goes over my throat, bringing my head back down to make direct eye contact with him, and he's so close to me I can smell the whiskey coming off his breath.

"This isn't a fucking game, bitch! This is real. You can help me bury this body, or I will force-feed you with her until you've eaten every piece, starting with the ass. The choice is yours."

I gulp, nearly choking from the tight grasp over my throat. His voice and the words he just spoke are burned into my mind. This is the most serious I have seen him tonight. Everything so far has mostly been a joke to him. He enjoyed watching me kill Heather, but he must've suddenly realized that her death could potentially cause him trouble.

"Capiche?"

My eyes feel so wide they might pop out of my skull. I nod.

"Lovely," he says, letting me go before planting a light kiss on my forehead.

He reaches into the tote, pulling out two plastic hooded ponchos. He places one over his body and the hood over his head before placing the second over mine. He must not want any DNA belonging to Heather on us so they aren't found during my autopsy, pinning any suspicion on Sunney.

Sunney hands me a pair of long blue latex gloves. He watches as I put them on before doing his own. I swallow once I'm done, knowing what's coming next. I close my eyes and keep my hands out. The harrowing sounds begin when Sunney grabs the hacksaw and cuts into Heather's limbs. Every second the hacksaw digs into her bones seems to go on forever before the weight of the leg lands on top of my arms. Foolishly, I open my eyes to look down at the carcass. Blood spills out from the amputated area and lands on the newspaper-lined floor and my feet. Gagging, I hastily toss the leg into the tote.

I expect to hear a chuckle out of Sunney, inspired by my disgust. But when I look up at him, his face is as white as a ghost. He's just as disgusted by this as I am. I hadn't expected that. I had thought he would be like those serial killers in movies who cut up bodies with just as much ease as they cut up raw chicken. I guess he had only done this one other time before.

"You okay?" I ask sarcastically.

Sunney forces an annoyed-looking smirk and ignores me, continuing to hack through the right leg.

It's silent momentarily as Sunney continues sawing away while I look out the window above the kitchen sink, doing my best not to gag. I hear Sunney swallow every other second, trying to maintain his composure.

"Just puke. It's not like my opinion of you matters now, does it?" I finally say.

Sunney finishes the second leg just as I make that remark, looking up to glare at me and then throwing the leg into my open arms unceremoniously. I half-expect him to strike me for showing attitude, but he does a complete 180 and jogs to the kitchen trash can, throwing up into it. After wiping his mouth, he takes one glove off before grabbing a nearby whiskey bottle, taking a large gulp and walking over to me, offering me a drink for the first time in our relationship. I want to say no, but if being buzzed helps me get through the sickening torture of watching this go down, then so be it. I open my mouth, not wanting to remove my glove. Cracking a smile, Sunney puts the bottle spout to my mouth, pouring the lukewarm drink into my throat. He doesn't stop pouring till I choke, lifting my hand in the air, my mouth too full to speak. He removes the spout from my mouth a second too late, and I gargle my mouthful, wincing.

"My first girlfriend's hobby was cheerleading, my second was obsessed with animals, and your vice is drinking. What the fuck am I supposed to do with that?"

Although Sunney is joking, it still strikes a chord with me. *My god, he's right.* I don't like doing anything. I have spent most of my life trying to please men or drinking my sorrows away. And now I will die with nothing to show for it besides a controversial affair with a teacher who killed himself and the history of stabbing an abusive boyfriend to death.

"Such a shame," Sunney comments mid-way through.

"What is?"

"She had such a rocking body."

"You're disgusting."

We continue the dismemberment of Heather, and thankfully, as time passes, I can control my stomach more. The alcohol is helping. Sunney, on the other hand, ends up puking one more time. It amazes me he can get off to a woman stabbing a pig or me choking out a woman to death, but this makes him sick. It must turn him on to watch women do horrific things but not do any of the dirty work himself.

CHAPTER 36

Nearly half an hour passes, and the only thing left now is the head. Sunney grabs the bottle of whiskey and allows me another chug before starting again. I look down at my bloody feet, unsure if I'm feeling dizzy from the alcohol or the sounds of Sunney gagging as the hacksaw digs into Heather's neck. He unexpectedly manages the feat without throwing up. After tossing her head over to me, which I hastily toss into the tote he grabs a pair of plyers from his bucket of tools, starting on the teeth.

"Why the teeth?" I ask.

"Dental records can help the police identify any person. One of the biggest pieces of evidence against Ted Bundy, which helped prove his guilt, was a bite mark on a victim."

"Forget I asked," I say, sickened he even knows that.

Having answered my question, he takes slow, steady breaths, and proceeds with the heinous activity. Once the first one is out, he tosses it in a white pearl jewelry box lined inside with wintergreen silk. He begins panting from exhaustion as he moves on to the remaining teeth.

"Why is it taking so long? I thought you were supposed to be strong?"

Sunney looks up and glares at me. "Care to give it a try?"

"No, please just hurry up."

"One second. I'm starving," he says, removing his gloves, throwing them into the tote, and heading to the cupboard.

"You're kidding."

He takes out a can of tuna, fetching an opener next. He's not kidding. He opens it, accidentally dropping the lid to the ground but not picking it up. He then begins picking out pieces of tuna with his hand and putting them in his mouth. I imagine her blood has seeped through the gloves and onto his hands, which he's now licking. How can he possibly eat after chopping up a body?

Once he's done, he discards the can and walks back to the table to finish the teeth extraction. When he's finished, panting like a wild dog, he walks closer to me and takes out a pair of keys to unlock my handcuffs. He undoes the right side, chaining me to the counter, and chains me to a hole in the tote.

"Be a dear and escort us outside."

"No, I can't carry her."

"Give it a try. You're not that weak, are you?"

"Can I have some water, please?"

Sunney stares at me, shaking his head in dismay.

"I need some hydration to do this. Please, Sunney," I urge.

I leave out the part that, along with water, I also need more time to stretch this out. I plan on taking more time to drag the tote to wherever he wants me to, but that may not be enough. The seconds count now more than ever. *Can I do anything to delay this?*

Rolling his eyes, he reaches for Jack again.

"No—"

"It's this or nothing. Now drink before I change my mind," he interrupts, lifting the glass.

I nod my head as he pours the whiskey into my mouth. I want to spit it in his face for being such a dick, but the alcoholic in me swallows it instead, savoring every drop. I can't tell if it quenches my thirst or makes me thirstier than before.

"You're welcome," he says, placing the cap back on.

I glare but begin pushing the plastic tote. *Damn! For a skinny bitch, she sure is heavy*, I think. I only make it a couple of feet before stopping to look at Sunney, to see if he expects me to open the door too.

As he approaches the door and opens it, my eyes flash at the tuna can lid only inches away. An idea pops into my mind once Sunney's back is turned. I push the tote, and once the front two wheels cross the door's threshold, I purposely trip. Landing on my knees, directly in front of the lid, I slip it into the palm of my hand that is not shackled to the tote.

I accidentally let out a squeal of pain. Its sharp edge has managed to dig through the gloves to the cut on my hand. Luckily, Sunney thinks I'm just whining from the fall and forces me to stand. As we walk on, I hastily stash the lid into my robe pocket and place my bleeding hand back on the cold plastic handle. I'm sure the lid will be more trouble than help, but at the very least, I have a weapon. A dull weapon, but a weapon, nonetheless.

Near the fire pit, I catch sight of a shovel and a black tube next to it. He must've placed them there when he went outside. Once at the stairs leading down, I glance back at Sunney. He has the pistol in his hand now, pointing directly at my back. I tighten my grip over the handles, pushing the tote down as slowly as possible. Just like I expected, the weight is too much and it slides down the stairs, taking me with it. Once at the bottom, luckily, the tote doesn't tip over, but my stomach collides with the handle, causing me to fall over for real this time.

"Be careful. There are steps there," I hear Sunney comment, chuckling.

I glare at him, getting back on my feet. We eventually make it to the shovel and black plastic tube. Sunney tosses the shovel into the tote and grabs the tube's handle, carrying it with his free hand.

"Where are we going?"

"Just keep walking. I'll tell you when to stop," he orders.

"What's in the tube?"

"Hydraulic acid. It's perfect for burning skin tissue."

Why do I have to keep asking questions when I know I can't bear to hear his answers?

Dragging the tote through the dirt is much more difficult than it was on the porch. The only good thing is that I start working up a sweat, which warns my body up, protecting it against the chilly late-night air. We walk straight for another ten minutes before Sunney tells me to stop.

"This should be far enough."

I let out a sigh of relief and look behind me. Despite ten minutes of dragging the tote, we aren't even out of eyesight of the cabin. I still see the kitchen lights illuminating the sliding door. Being this close almost seems like a sloppy move. I wonder how far he took Andrea's body before burying it.

"Okay, grab the shovel. Dig six, three feet wide deep holes and try to keep them a couple of feet away from each other."

"Okay, care to unshackle me then?"

"Why do you need two hands?"

"You expect me to dig six holes with one hand? Do you want this done by morning or not?"

Sunney stands there, seemingly thinking it through.

"For Christ's sake, Sunney. You have a gun. What am I possibly going to do?"

I'm trying to keep the helpless girl trope up and hopefully regain his trust. I now have two possible weapons in my possession — the shovel and the tuna can lid.

Checking his watch before letting out an exasperated sigh, he says, "Fine! But I swear if you try and hit me with that shovel, it'll be the last thing you ever do."

"Better keep your distance then."

Sunney moves to stand six feet across from me. Looking down, I decide I'll dig the first hole for the head since it'll be the easiest. It takes me around fifteen minutes, and by that time, the cold outside doesn't bother me due to the sweat I've worked up. But the hand with the reopened slit from the tuna can lid throbs from the shovel handle, slowing me down. Once the hole has been dug, I look over at the tote, dreading that I will have to riffle through the contents with my bare hands once again. It's too bad Sunney hasn't brought the whiskey along with him.

I close my eyes, taking a deep breath before reaching into the tote. Her head seems heavier now that I'm much more exhausted. I don't spend more than a few seconds with it in my hands before tossing it into the hole. I'm still unsure what had come over me in those moments, choking her. It's like I blacked out as my survival instincts had kicked in.

Looking up at Sunney as he grabs the black tube and begins pouring the acid into the hole, I am sure have never been less attracted to him. He looks exhausted and pale, with curly hair that is shaggy looking and drenched with blood. If he gets away with this, he will just continue murdering more women. Soon enough, cheating won't be the only reason he will kill. It could start being for more frivolous things like if they don't make him his morning coffee or don't take his suits to the dry cleaners'.

As I start digging the second hole, I try ideating my next actions. I decide to talk to him and make him feel a little warmer toward me. Our moment in the kitchen, with him pouring the whiskey in my mouth had seemed to ease him up. I mean, I had somehow gotten him to want to marry me. Somewhere deep inside that evil core of his, he still had to have some love for me.

"Sunney," I start, remembering I have always said his name when starting a conversation.

He gives me a blank stare and purses his lips, asking, "What?"

"Why do you choose to be with broken women?"

"I guess some part of me wants to fix them."

That seemed too obvious of an answer. "Are you lying?"

"I'm not lying. Now shut up and keep going."

Damn! Talking to Psychotic Sunney won't be easy if I continue playing New Toni. *Do I have to become Old Toni to get to him?* The last time I did that, I had blacked out and killed Heather.

More time passes, and now I have moved on to the third hole. About halfway into digging, an idea finally pops into my head.

"So did you have sex with that cop to get him to do all this for you?"

Immediately annoyed, Sunney says, "No, absolutely not!"

"It's nothing to be ashamed of. Gotta do what you gotta do."

"I didn't, so shut up."

"Are you going to suck his dick to make up for him having to cover up Heather's death as well?"

"If I do, I sure as hell am not taking your lessons."

I open my mouth, shocked.

As I work on the fourth hole, my body too drained and my hands too shaky to think much of anything, I continue trying to irritate Sunney. If I can get him mad enough to get closer to me, I can try attacking him then. That or he'll just shoot me from where he's standing.

"Are you going to take my ring and give it to the next troubled girl you find?"

"You think I can't just buy another?"

"You seem to like recycling your choices in women. Why not do the same for rings?"

"Why does it matter?"

"I'm just curious, Sunney."

"After you finish burying her, I'm going to kill you, and this is the shit you care about? God, you're so petty."

He's got to be joking. Feeling like I'm going to explode, I yell, "Me? Petty? You're kidding, right? You're killing your wife for being unfaithful one time. One fucking time."

"You betrayed me, and the worst part about it isn't just the fact we'd only been married four days or even that immediately afterward you returned and fucked me. It's the fact that you cheated with the first motherfucker to show you the slightest hint of interest. It didn't matter what he looked like, wore, or said because all you want in life is attention. You are an attention-seeking whore, plain and simple."

"You're wrong," is all I get out, my eyes watering up.

"What? You thought Quinn liked you. He was using you to get laid and had nowhere else to look. If not for you being my wife, I would have given him a high five at how fast he got you."

"I hate you," I say, a tear drop escaping from my eyes that I cannot brush away because I'm still wearing gut and blood-soaked gloves.

CHAPTER 37

Finally finished with the last hole and ready to throw in Heather's left leg, an idea dawns on me. Whether it works or not, I can hurt Sunney one last time.

"You know, you're wrong about Quinn."

"Which part?" Sunney says, chuckling, as he pours the last bit of acid into the hole.

"It wasn't because he was the first to give me attention that I liked him. We had a connection, it wasn't just getting laid that he was in for. He could have escaped when you gave him a choice, but he tried to rescue me instead."

"You think that was for you? The fucker just wanted to redeem himself for killing his wife."

"Okay, maybe that's true, but he wasn't just anyone to me. I've had plenty of opportunities to cheat on you. Half your friends would hump anything with a heartbeat. I didn't see anyone except you before Quinn. And you want to know why that is?"

Looking already on the verge of pointing the pistol at me and shooting my head off, Sunney shouts, "Not really, no!"

"He was actually into the real me, not some sugarcoated version of me I had to pretend to be to attract you."

Sunney hated not being in the limelight, not being the chosen one. Not treating him as such would piss him off fast, I knew.

"He was just there. Nothing more, nothing less," Sunney argues fervently.

"You haven't figured it out. We've hung out every day since we got here. Remember that day I went running? I ran into him and tried to avoid him because of you. I did, but I couldn't resist him. I liked everything about him. The way I could be myself around him without the fear of judgment. The way he smelled of cheap cologne, liquor, and chopped wood. The way he looked with his burly strong arms and wild beard. I was attracted to him and couldn't stop seeing him. We met again and got drunk together. It was the most fun I've had in a while. After he saw you at the strip club, he came over to the house and—"

"Oh, I'm fully fucking aware you let him in my house!" Sunney yells at me.

This is it. This is how I'll really anger him. He hates being chosen over someone else. It's time to let the bloody truth out.

"Yeah, and he told me every vile thing you said about your so-called business. We almost kissed, but you returned home just then. We met the following night, and he warned, no, begged, me not to be with you. I should've listened to him, but being an idiot, I returned to you. That is my regret — not leaving you for him at that very moment."

On the verge of blowing up, his body tenses, his brows lower, and his eyes narrow. Looking straight at me, he yells, "Okay! That's it. Drop the fucking shovel, Toni!"

"No!" I scream back.

Walking a couple of feet forward, Sunney commands, "Drop it, or I swear to God I'll shoot you in the stomach. Give you a slow, agonizing death."

He doesn't know about my trump card — the tuna can lid. I know if I drop the shovel, he'll think I'm completely helpless and come close to me. I throw the shovel to the ground, removing my gloves so my hands aren't slippery when I grab the lid.

Sunney comes near me, pressing the barrel of the gun to my throat. We're once again as close as we'd been in the kitchen when he was choking me. The gun barrel is cold and inflicts a sharp pain to my throat.

"You never deserved me," he breathes.

Borrowing a phrase from Quinn, I reply, "Don't flatter yourself, sweetie."

"Any last words?"

"Can I get one last kiss?" I ask, cracking a smile.

Knowing I'm being sarcastic, Sunney smirks and leans in. I'm stunned when his lips touch mine, but only moments later, the soft kiss turns into a prickling pain on my lips. He's biting me hard. I squeal and attempt to push him away, but he presses the gun harder to my throat, finally causing blood to spurt out of my bottom lip. Just when I think he'll bite it clean off any moment, he leans back. He then licks under his lips, where my blood is splattered in small red dots.

Disgusted, I reach into my pocket. Sunney looks down at the movement, but before he can stop me, I swiftly slash Sunney's throat with the lid. Once blood sprays out, I use my other hand to slap Sunney's arm, which holds the pistol, away from my throat. A mere second later, he presses the trigger, and it goes off only inches away from my throat. I slap his arm again but harder this time. Thankfully, his hold on it has loosened, and the pistol drops from his hand into the final hole.

"You bitch! I'm going to fucking kill you!" he screams, blocking the gash on his throat that's already leaking blood through his fingers. Sadly, it's not as deep as I had expected.

He tries to punch me — a mistake. I take a huge step back, falling on my ass, but avoiding the hit. I immediately sit up as Sunney does what he should have done in the first place — he tries to grab me. I do a half summersault to avoid his grasp and then stand up. I look in both directions, unsure which way to run. One way leads to the darkness of the woods that Sunney knows better than me. The other is toward the cabin and the road and I have a better chance of isolating myself or retrieving another weapon from there. The cabin it is.

It doesn't take long for Sunney to start running straight behind me. If it weren't for the fact he's wounded, bleeding from the throat, he would've caught me by now. Just when I approach the fire pit, I hear his steps get closer and closer.

"Toni! Get back here!" I hear Sunney's blood-hurling scream just behind me.

I look behind me, continuing to run blindly. That's my mistake, as only a couple of moments later, my body slams headfirst into an object. I realize it's the old shed that is currently unlocked. I grab the handle, open its door, and attempt to shut it behind me. Sunney grabs the edge of the door frame, trying to pull it back open. This is another stupid decision on his part as I get just enough leverage on the door, slamming it shut over his fingers. He screams, removing his hand from the frame for just long enough so I that can close and lock it.

"Toni, let me in! You fucking cunt! I'll kill you!"

Looking at the old, rusty wall-mounted lock, I know it won't hold long. The room is dark, and no light switch is in sight. I only feel around for a couple of seconds before the door opens further as Sunney pounds and kicks at it, screaming my name repeatedly. I find a cheap wooden bookshelf that gives me a splinter when I merely touch it. I begin pulling it toward the door that seems like it will give out at any moment. It gets caught on some sort of rug briefly before I can get it to lean against the door.

With a few moments to spare, my next step is finding a light switch. I reach out, feeling for a lightbulb with a hanging cord. Sunney has set those up in his garage, so I think he may have done the same here. With a pinch of luck, my hand goes over one. When I pull the string, a dim bulb turns on bringing light to the shed.

CHAPTER 38

The shed looks like any ordinary one. The walls are painted white or had been at some point. Most of the paint has flaked away to expose the brown plywood. There are multiple tall bookshelves and counters with different sorts of tools. As many are amiss, I guess Sunney had placed some in the black tote he brought with him into the cabin earlier.

I grab whatever I can get my hands on to put on the bookshelf leaning against the door to add extra weight. However, I already know it'll only buy me a short amount of time. Then I'll be screwed as there is only one tiny window at the opposite end of the shed, which doesn't look like it would allow me to squeeze through it. Running inside this piece-of-shit shed will probably get me killed. In the end, I know I wouldn't have made it very far with Sunney right behind me, anyway.

Thankfully, he has momentarily ceased the banging and screaming at me. I consider moving the bookshelf and trying to make a run for it, but I immediately worry he could be playing one of his tricks, pretending to be gone. He could be trying to retrieve his pistol that fell into the hole full of acid or tending to the slit in his throat. With any luck, he'll bleed to death before he can get to me. Remembering the small slash I had made, that seems highly unlikely. It seemed more like a gnarly paper cut than anything deadly.

While he's gone, I place another bookshelf against the window and nearly all the tools on the bookshelf against the door. Then I sit on a rickety stool, removing my gloves and looking at my mutilated palms. Using the shovel has caused the bandage to tear and expose my nasty, still throbbing right-hand palm.

With my first moment alone all night, I should be formulating an escape plan, grabbing a tool, and preparing myself to attack Sunney when he gets in, but instead, I sit and bawl my eyes out. Images from tonight's events flash in my mind. I begin praying to my mom and dad, urging them to watch over me and help me out of this mess. It's stupid, I know, the thought of them somehow hearing, let alone even wanting to help the daughter that got them killed. Maybe all this is happening for a reason. Maybe it's one last gruesome lesson to make me pay for all the pain Old Toni has caused others. My mom, dad, Mr. Nortec, Tom, Quinn, and Heather — all dead on my account.

The banging starts again suddenly, making me flinch, and the movement breaks the rickety stool I've been sitting on. Its legs snap and I fall on my back. In pain, I look to the left toward the door, catching sight of something peculiar. It's the vintage and very dusty rug I had run into when trying to move the bookshelf against the door. A corner exposes a square indent on the wooden floor. On a closer look, I find that the indent is a door hatch with a padlock over the handle — a secret cellar. I can't imagine what is beneath it, but as Sunney's banging becomes harder and harder, I realize I don't have a choice but to take my chances down there.

I stand up and uncover the full hatch. Dust comes wafting out from underneath, making me sneeze and cover my nose and mouth. It's small and can only fit one person through at a time. I grab a bolt cutter on the bookshelf and easily cut into the padlock. When I open the door, the complete darkness at the bottom greets me. I only see the top of a wooden ladder leading down.

I move the bookshelf leaning against the tiny window and push it to lean against the door. I then return to the window and break it with the bolt cutters. Possibly pulling the ol' *Fargo* trick will work. Sunney will break the door down, making the bookshelves tumble over the door hatch leading into the cellar, covering it up. He'll see the broken window, suspecting I ran into the woods.

Keeping the bolt cutters in my hand, I begin descending the ladder. My whole body trembles at the possibilities of what could be lurking beneath, especially the fact it may be housing the decomposing body of Andrea or that of other women.

This idea is foolish but maybe I can distract Sunney by sending him to the woods to search for me. I could actually take my chances out there but Sunney is faster than me. That and he knows these woods better than I. I can hold up down here and come up after I know he's broken through the door and gone.

Once I close the hatch, I slide one of the handles of the bolt cutters in between the steel handle to the hatch in case Sunney tries to come down. Now I am in complete darkness. I hold on tight to the wooden ladder as I carefully climb down it.

I can tell I've reached the bottom when my feet land on a hard area. It feels like pure sand or soft dirt. I stick my arms out, feeling for a string switch. Unable to find one, I wave my hands in the air, trying to reach the nearest wall. I only make it a couple of feet before running into an object. It feels like a metal desk with a bunch of crap on it. I feel around until my hand finds a familiar, soft, waxy object. A candle. *This means a lighter may be nearby.* I open the desk drawer; it seems to have one on each side. The first one is only filled with plastic bags, so I try the long drawer in the middle. Wedged in between a bunch of pens and pencils, I feel a lighter. I grab it and light the candle. It illuminates the room enough for me to find two others on the desk, which I light also.

Grabbing a candle fixed on a candelabrum, I raise it to gauge how large this room is and where it goes. It's a single room about five feet wide and twelve feet long. The opposite end of the ladder seems incomplete, as a large rock and dirt pile leads into a darkened crawlspace. One side of the room is lined with hay bales, while the other has a single desk. The walls are poorly cemented with cracks lining them and — photographs of all shapes and sizes strung up everywhere.

Unable to make them out, I walk over to the wall, pressing the candle near one of the larger photographs. It's a young woman posing for a senior photo, considering the formal stance and fake camera-ready smile. I recognize her forced smile from Sunney's prom picture. It's his first girlfriend. In sparkly pink letters, it's signed — *To my handsome Sunney, with love from Steph*. Taped underneath is another photograph of her, but she isn't paying attention to the camera here. A strand of blonde hair in a little Ziplock bag is attached to that photograph by a thumbnail. *Hers?* I cringe, wondering how or why he would need that.

Other surrounding photographs are also of her, obviously captured when she wasn't looking. Some look as though she had been followed and photographed. *By Sunney? Why? Why did he stalk his girlfriend?* I find a smaller photograph from the bunch that is not of her, but of another woman that resembles Steph. Her hair is also blonde, medium length, and she has soft youthful features. Underneath it, in Sunney's handwriting, the text reads "Maryam d'Abo in *The Living Daylights*." *A Bond girl? Why*? Right below that photograph, held up by a thumbnail with multiple other pricks and folds, is a nude photograph of Steph. She's laying down on a light orange and white (their school colors) locker room bench with no clothes on, smiling up at the camera. A pair of cleats belonging to the photographer, I assume, Sunney, is right at the end of the photo.

I move toward the right to other photographs that have been hung up. The next woman is classically beautiful, much like Steph. She's much less innocent-looking and wearing darker makeup, however. Her hair is a light chestnut, like Heather's, except she has a more serious tone. The next picture reveals she's lankier and taller than Stephanie, Heather, and I. *Andrea?*

Once again, the second photograph has a little baggie of hair thumbnailed to it. There are also photographs where it looks like she has been followed, unaware she's being photographed. However, unlike Steph, she has more than one provocative photograph. In most, she looks at the camera with a grim and tired expression. I'd recognize that sort of face anywhere. It's the one I'd see the mirror, high off my uppers. I find another woman who looks like Andrea. Sunney's handwriting reads "Ursula Andress in *Dr. No*," and the photo is of a woman in a white bikini who once again resembles Andrea heavily. *What's with his obsession with the Bond girls*? He clearly has some sort of fascination with dating women who resemble them. The last photograph at my eye level is the most alarming. The woman is asleep on Sunney's bed, wearing a sheer robe, red bra, and panty set. Like the set Sunney described when he caught her cheating on him and dressed her to play his game. She also has both hands bound with handcuffs, as he said.

I instinctively know the next on the wall will be me. I have never let him photograph me nude, so hopefully, unlike Andrea, there won't be numerous photographs like that. I take a deep breath, my feet feeling frozen and my body numb. Everything hurts, especially my hands and bitten lip. *Can I take what I'm about to see?* I have to, I decide.

Shining the candle up at the last area of photographs, I see the biggest one is a senior picture of me — one I remember now as missing from my school album. I didn't have many, so I had noticed the absence but not done anything when it had disappeared. It wasn't a time in my life I treasured anyway. In the picture, I lean against an old, red-painted barn, the vivid color bringing out my blue eyes and black hair perfectly. Of course, this is the one Sunney would choose to steal. Underneath my senior picture is one of Sunney and me. The only one with Sunney in it out of all the others. It is the first photo we ever took, our fourth date at some corny amusement park. I look so happy. By then, I had been repeating my first name with his last name hundreds of times in my mind. Little did I know the horrors of being this man's wife.

The next photograph is a bit more alarming. It's of me in my work shirt and khakis, walking to or from work. I can't tell. A Ziplock bag of my black hair hangs from it. In another, I'm standing by the window at my old apartment, removing my shirt. That same shirt had also been missing for a while now. As I move on to the next picture, I realize it's been taken out and then re-stuck to the wall many times. It is one of me sleeping on Sunney's bed. It's from the first night I slept with him. The blankets have been removed, and I'm not wearing any item of clothing. It doesn't end with just one, however. There are multiple photographs, all from the same night and from nearly every imaginable angle. It doesn't seem romantic. The gaze is that of a forensic pathologist photographing a murdered body. This makes me want to throw up more than when grabbing body parts of Heather's. I wonder how why I didn't wake up, then remember the pills I had taken during that night's holiday party. Of course, I had been in a deep sleep state.

Curious, I search past the twenty photographs on my side to find the photo that won't be of me. Catching sight of it, I'm unimpressed by his selection. It's Jane Seymour from *Live and Let Die*. No wonder he had forced me to watch it on more than one occasion.

I move to sit on one of the haybales in the small room, overwhelmed by it all. However, just as I sit down, I knock over an object. Looking over, I see it's a huge bottle of lotion and tissues. A small waste basket filled with used tissues is at the end of the haybale. I sit back up, disgusted with what Sunney has been doing here.

I turn my attention back to the desk, remembering all the papers I had felt, and walk back over. Here, there are multiple beige-colored folders in one pile with five plain black-colored journals neatly stacked right next to it. Setting the candle down, I open one of the folders first. It has multiple nude photographs of different women sleeping. I don't recognize any of them, even though they're all in Sunney's bed back home. Most have red ink slash marks over their body parts with their eye's X'ed out. The dates on the corners of the folders are as far back as five years. I drop the beige folders to the ground, the pictures scattering all over the floor. All the next folders are the same, filled with naked photos of women, showing two or three women in bed together. Again, there are red slashes through their throats or X's marked on their eyes. *My god! How many women has Sunney slept with and done this to?*

I start on the black journals next. I open the first one and see that the first page is blank, and it reads *2002* in the middle. That's the year we met, February to be exact. I turn the page and begin reading.

> *January 1, 2002*
>
> *Dear Journal: Finally, a new year and horizon are in sight. I'm happy to be putting 2001 and that nasty bitch Andrea behind. It's been five months since I got rid of her, but it still feels like yesterday. Women are a waste of breath. I want to work on myself this year. Become stronger physically and internally.*
>
> *Last night, I fucked this lovely innocent woman. Can't remember her name. Angie, Angela, Leah; it doesn't matter. I met her at a trashy cocktail bar downtown. She was dying to meet me. I could tell by how she stared at me with her Gollum eyes and bit those dick-sucking lips. These are two of my favorite qualities in women. If it had been any other night other than New Year's Eve, I wouldn't have remembered her, but I always remember the women I start the year with.*
>
> *As she slept after we got done fucking, too boozed and drugged up to wake up, I did my weekly rituals, taking photographs of all the deep hidden parts of her. With each photograph, I contemplated stabbing her to death mainly in the chest, near the heart. Just the thought gave me such a*

hard-on. Then when I turned her body over, I contemplated stabbing her in the back as I stared at her ass, but I couldn't. Like all the others, I couldn't get myself to stab her. Why God, WHY?

My whole life, I've wanted to kill. I think of it every day. It's the same for every woman — when I'm talking to them, fucking them, and then as they sleep. I want to stab them repeatedly. Something, however, stops me. I cannot explain it. Maybe I'm just too weak. The want has worsened since Andrea cheated on me. Now I see the cheating bitch Andrea inside all these women. I think I'm getting bored of the same old song and dance. Sleeping with them is getting tiring.

This year all I want is the will to do it.

CHAPTER 39

Holy shit! Holy shit! I think, slamming the journal shut. I cannot keep reading whatever the fuck this is. Sunney is a serial killer in the making, except it seems that, just like cutting up Heather's body, he has faced some trouble going through with it. If he gets away with killing me, that might be the impetus to start murdering indiscriminately.

Come on, Toni, you know you want to read what he was thinking after meeting you, Old Toni taunts. She's right. I am curious. Thank God I hadn't slept with him the first night. Is that all that had separated me from the others? It couldn't be. I know more women out there would have waited to sleep with him. So, what was it in me that made him want to give up his obsessive want to sleep with and then kill numerous women? Dating me had stopped him from playing around, so why was I worth that?

I shakily grab the journal again, skipping through a couple of pages. Most are merely days apart, with the same words written on them. He occasionally mentions how he feels depressed about not being able to kill and bored when sleeping with all these women. My suspicions are proven true when I read about some women more than once. He even went on dates with some of them. None of them made it after a third date, however, as he was soon bored of their normality. I see a pattern here.

Finally, after skimming through January, I reach the February entries. He had been out doing the same thing the night before meeting me. He was on a second date with a woman who only gave him a blowjob the first night. He didn't like that she didn't stay the night at his house. So, he planned a second date, did the deed, took photographs, and then sent her away. I get to the following day, the day we met.

February 7, 2002

Dear Journal: A regular night of prowling took an unexpected turn. Normally, I don't go out three nights in a row. Work is too grueling to keep up. But I was home and extremely horny, so I thought, why not do something about it? After more than two hours at my usual spots, finding nothing but overweight or butter-faced women, I decided to try the slums of town. Normally I wouldn't even imagine doing something like that, but a couple of buddies had said the druggies that hang out there are skinny and dumb enough that they remind you of models after a couple of drinks. I try avoiding women who do too many drugs because they remind me of Andrea, but I was a bit desperate last night. Maybe if the woman I found was pathetic enough, I thought, I could finally cut her throat. It's not like anyone would miss her anyhow.

Walking past the dumpster spitfire that was the Keelover bar, something propelled me into it. I want to say it's fate, but I think the flashing, half-out pink lights that made up the sign must've been it. They lent the environment a shitty neo-noir vibe I liked.

While sitting in that pathetic-looking bar, I met the madness that is Toni Lovette.

I think, swallowing, how I had never told him my last name that night.

She was not my type, not at first sight anyway. She certainly didn't light up a room like the women I'm accustomed to. It looked like she hadn't eaten or showered in over a week. Her face flaunted cheap old makeup that could not cover the obvious yellow bruises. To make a first bad impression worse, she nearly threw up upon speaking to me. But something about those deep, icy, evil-looking eyes kept me from walking out of that bar. They were bloodshot and looked like they'd seen some shit. I would love to have those eyes look up at me while she sucks on my dick. It gave me a wave of deja vu as I had found the same thing attractive in Andrea. Upon a long glance, as she ran to the bathroom, I noticed she has a nice-looking slim body. I could imagine myself fucking her from the back, and as it was already past midnight, that would have to suffice.

When she returned from barfing her brains out, I did what I usually didn't and made the first move, as she probably was feeling way too astronomically drunk and ashamed to. I didn't mention that I knew she had just thrown up. I played suave, naïve, and nice Sunney. That always works on the ladies. Upon ordering her a shot and talking, I realized I liked her. She is funny, and most, if not all, women aren't. She lacks any self-confidence. It was easy to see she hates talking about herself, which works for me as I can talk about myself all night. I knew that would wet her panties. But after some time, enough was enough, and I tried to get some information about her as there had to be some sob story behind those magnetic eyes. She nearly throws up on me again before saying anything.

To be honest, that had been enough for me. She was too drunk to fuck. I was about to head out, but then the bartender approached me. He asked if I knew what I was getting myself into talking to the freak show, Toni Lovette. Intrigued, I asked why, and he told me she had a drunk piece of shit ex-boyfriend who used to beat her. No stranger to straggly beaten women, I still planned to head out before I heard the end of the story.

He said that, not even a month prior, he had finally crossed the line, beating her to a pulp and attempting to kill her. I liked the man without even knowing him. Except I would never know him because Toni had stabbed him many times. So many times, that her sanity was questioned by the police. She was one of the first women I met who had killed another person, even in self-defense. That was the hottest thing I'd ever heard. None of the weak dumb broads I'd banged could come close to ever doing that.

I followed her out the back door where she had fled. Little did I know some drunk fuck would be harassing her about said killing, rendering me the ability to be the hero. I thought it would give me the ins to her, but it didn't. She walked off, ashamed again.

I walked her home that night. I wanted to fuck her so bad. But alas, for once in a very long time, nothing happened but a kiss on the forehead. I am not one of those sucker men who fall for the first girl who doesn't sleep with them. That is so played out. I liked that she thought something was off without fully knowing me and that I was too good to be true. That I reminded her of my favorite movie character — Patrick Bateman. That fictional man was living my very life. Is he a murderer, or is he not? I like her for what she saw in my eyes. I saw it in hers as well — a psychopath on the verge of ruin by the limitations of their psyche.

I will fix you, baby doll. Fix you to be mine.

I should've guessed he wanted my old version because I'd killed my boyfriend. He must've thought we were similar, as we had both killed our ex-lovers. Setting the 2002 journal down, I look at the first pages of the others, sorted by the year, ranging back five years.

Curious about what else I can find on the desk, I open the biggest drawer. Inside are a dozen articles of clothing stored in Ziplock bags, including t-shirts, bras, and panties. They're even labeled with a name. Most belong to me, a few others to Andrea, and the rest belong to random women. I even find the red bra and panty set, resembling what Sunney had told me Andrea was wearing the night he killed her. At the bottom of the pack of clothing, I find the sickest thing — a bag containing multiple pairs of my underwear, except they are stained with dried blood. I slam the drawer back, unable to take any more.

I look in the large drawer on the other side of the desk, but as soon as I open it, I quickly sit in the chair, unable to stand any more. It's a newspaper clipping from the obituary of Tom. Underneath it is another newspaper clipping of the first story written about the incident. It doesn't even have our names. How and why would he even want to have this?

As my eyes scan through the article, my stomach folds into knots as I begin to relive that night.

A sudden bang upstairs makes me jolt my whole body toward the hatch, and my elbow knocks over two lit candles in the process. I hastily try to fetch them, but they roll toward the hay bale, igniting it. My first instinct is to stomp it out, but I decide on plan B since I'm still barefoot. I look for a water source that has to be around somewhere. Half the hay bale is on fire when I spot a navy-colored titanium water bottle. I open the lid and splash all the fluid onto it. However, this move backfires and worsens the fire. How did I not realize this man would keep liquor as a replenishment in his dungeon?

I grab a dark navy-blue suit jacket from the desk chair and cover my mouth, attempting not to breathe in the smoke. I look around, wondering if I were to get out of this alive, what would I salvage for the cops? The smoke is already blurring my sight. I grab the 2002 journal and place it into the suit pocket. If I make it out of here, at least I'll have some proof of the sheer depravity that is Sunney Jameson.

CHAPTER 40

I head back up the ladder leading to the hatch, removing the bolt cutters from between the hatches pull handle and dropping them to the ground. I attempt opening the hatch, but it only lifts a couple of inches. It's blocked. I begin pushing with all my might, but it doesn't budge. My plan worked too well. The bookshelves and all the crap I piled over the door are now blocking my way out. Looking over, I see all the bales are on fire now, along with the photographs I had dropped on the ground, the fire only seconds away from spreading to the desk.

I descend from the ladder, my heart racing, unable to think of what to do. I cannot burn to death or die in this twisted cellar. I'm happy to let all this shit burn, but I will not go down with it. Looking around for anything that could help, I see the rocks and sand pile leading up to that crawlspace. It could be a dead end, but I have to take my chances.

I gingerly run through the ongoing flames. When I step on the photos on fire, the movement burns my feet but luckily it doesn't catch onto any of my clothing. The smoke from the room induces a coughing fit once I reach the pile. I try walking up, but as my feet sink into the dirt, I trip only a few feet up, with small, jagged rocks digging into my hands, knees, and feet. I gasp from pain but continue crawling. It takes me nearly three minutes after slipping down multiple times, but I finally manage to grab hold of the outer cement foundation of the window. The window is the size of approximately two cinder blocks. If I am even able to fit through it, it will be a tight one.

I pull the window open as I take one last look behind me. The whole room is now engulfed in fire and smoke, including the desk of Sunney's treasures. I smile, happy to have accidentally burned it all. I fit my head through the window, taking a deep breath of the fresh, early morning air. I feel water droplets land on my body. It's lightly raining out. The sky shows a beautiful pink and orange sunrise. After narrowly fitting my shoulders through the hole, I breathe in more air and slowly exhale the same. My smile widens the more and more I inch out. Soon enough, more than half of my body is out, leaving just my ass and legs behind in the room. However, before I can breathe a sigh of relief, a flashlight flashes on a piece of glass directly before me.

"I found her!" a voice cries.

The voice is male, but it's not Sunney's or that of anyone I know. They are not here to save me. I force my body out of the tight hole. Meanwhile, the flashlights continue to light me up.

"Sunney, hurry!" the voice yells.

Certain that I'm about to be attacked any minute, I pretend to be injured. I stay on my knees, breathing out all the smoke I inhale. I look up, finally seeing the man who is standing nearby. He's young, has dirty short blonde hair and blue eyes. He's in a beige jacket, a wrinkled dark green button-up shirt with a badge and a name tape on the breast pocket reading 'Adler'. This is the cop who is in love with Sunney. His hands shake while he holds the flashlight up at me continuously. There's a pistol at his side that he grabs.

I want to beg for help, but I remember what good that did me with Heather. So instead, I slowly stand, grabbing a clump of dirt and rocks.

"Freeze!" he says, pointing the gun at me.

I clench my fists, lifting them both in the air, staying as still as a scarecrow. I look at the woods, searching for a way I can run. Sunney could be anywhere by now, ready to catch me. I could just turn around and run for the house. This man has to have a vehicle parked up front.

"Don't shoot," I shakily plead.

The man and I stare at each other in agonizing silence. Watching his shaky hand on the pistol gives me hope he is too afraid to actually use the gun. I must do this now before Sunney arrives. Pulling my arm back like I'm about to throw a baseball, I chuck the dirt right at the man's face. He shrieks, foolishly attempting to cover his face. However, dirt still obscures his eyesight, blinding him momentarily.

Wasting no time, I turn around and sprint toward the house. As I run, I see two paths ahead of me. One leads up to the porch of the cabin, and the other one goes past to hopefully a vehicle parked out front. I take my chances and turn that way. Once I have almost passed the house, I see the back of a tail bed to a truck. I smile, only to crash straight into a body. Shocked, I drop to the ground while the body stays stiff, not moving a single inch. It's almost like they were waiting to surprise me.

I can only take a glance at the tall figure standing above me before he pounces on me, hands going over my throat.

"A fucking tuna can lid! Are you for real?" Sunney's furious cracked voice says as he starts choking me.

Looking up at the madman that I no longer recognize as my husband, I see his throat has a white bandage covering it. His eyes are bloodshot, and his face is still sprayed with blood. He's red-faced and either extremely sweaty or drenched from the rain.

I flail my hands, searching for anything to grab. They go over a pile of dirt that I immediately throw at Sunney's face. He flinches but remains unfazed, pure fury twisting his face. I lift my hands near his face, ready to scratch his eyes out if need be, but before I can, a pair of hands latch onto my wrist, bringing them back down.

"About fucking time!" Sunney yells at the terrified man.

"H–h–he—" I attempt to say to the officer, but Sunney's grasp over my throat is too tight. My vision is blurring by now, and everything I see is fuzzy.

"Hurry up and finish it. Your shed is on fire!" the officer yells.

"My shed?" Sunney angrily asks, turning his attention to the other man. "What the fuck did you do?" he screams, spit spraying my face.

Sunney looks like he had when cutting up Heather's body and is shaking profusely. By now, I know I have only a minute or so before dying. I widen my eyes and smile at the fact that I at least went down with a fight. I caused some noticeable scrapes people will take heed of and burned his cellar down. When the cops come, he will look extremely suspicious.

Looking down at me, Sunney's grasp slightly lets up. I can finally inhale air.

"What are you doing? Kill her!" Adler commands.

"I can't. I can't!" he screams, letting go of my throat.

My breath escapes out of my body even as I try to regain air. My throat burns with each breath inhale. My vision is still impaired and not showing any signs of getting better. I know I will pass out soon. Sunney stands up, bends over, and clutches his knees. I twist my body around, attempting to protect myself from getting choked again. It is no use as I feel my eyes begin to shut, and my brain goes numb.

"What the fuck!" Adler screams as my body goes immobile, and I close my eyes, passing out from the lack of oxygen.

CHAPTER 41

I wake up to a blinding light focused on my face and birds chirping in the distance. I'm sitting on the floor in the bathroom, leaning against the shower's glass door. It feels as though every part of my body is on fire. My throat burns from nearly being choked to death, my feet are red from the fire in the cellar, and my bottom lip is bleeding from being bitten. At the very least, my hands, although once again in the tight hold of the handcuffs, have been cleaned and re-bandaged. This means someone had taken the time to do so.

I assume it's mid to late morning by the looks of the bright light coming through the bathroom window. I've presumably been passed out for a couple of hours. My chances of escaping now have entirely vanished. Fighting against Sunney alone had been hard, but now, with two men, any desperate efforts would be futile.

However, after surviving everything I had tonight, it seems wrong to give up now. I mean, I outsmarted Sunney. What's to say I can't outsmart this Adler? All I need is a moment alone with him and explain that Sunney has been using him, except, when I had tried that with Heather, she had tried killing me.

I touch my unbound feet and look in the mirror above the sink. I look like a completely different person — like a lone survivor barely crawling out of a B-budget horror movie, except less prettied up and more traumatized. My hair is knotted in dirty clumps. My face bears remnants of dried blood and mud, and the rest of my body is muddied from climbing out of the crawlspace. I'm still wearing Sunney's suit jacket, which now reeks of smoke. I button up the jacket, covering the torn, blood-stained pajama set. Looking down at my scraped-up legs, I think of all the awful things I'd do to be wearing a pair of actual pajama pants, and not shorts. I pity Andrea, remembering she'd only gotten a lingerie set and a see-through robe.

Twisting my hair in a ponytail, I turn the sink on and wash the mud off my wrists and arms. Although I'm still shackled, to gain some semblance of dignity, I wash my face next as best as possible with my hands shaking uncontrollably as if I'm going through drug withdrawals. It must be the fear and trauma from all I've seen catching up. Once done, I look at myself again, still disgusted by what I see. At least the blood and mud had somewhat hidden the bags under my eyes and pasty white complexion.

I look around for anything I can use as a weapon, although that, too, seems pointless. Adler still has that pistol. It seems like the bathroom has been cleaned, with even the top toilet tank lid amiss. With my ability to use Heather's panties and the tuna can lid as a weapon, Sunney isn't taking any additional chances.

A couple of minutes pass before I hear footsteps approaching the bathroom door. I sit down where I had been originally positioned and breath in, ready for the worst. When no one comes in, I perk up my ears and hear a calm voice. Unable to hear clearly, I get back up and creep over to the door, pressing my ear to it. I hear Quinn's goddamn music still playing in the background and the voices of Sunney and Adler.

"We were going to take it tonight anyway. What's the big deal? Just let me have a little now," Sunney says.

"Do you really think now's the time for ecstasy? Besides, you've been drinking all night," Adler's agitated voice replies.

Ecstasy? I had never thought Sunney would be interested in that stuff, especially right now. It was a party drug you could use right before having sex. It made you undeniably touchy and happy. *Why would he even consider taking it now?*

"I need something to restore my serotonin levels right now. All I had was a glass or two of whiskey. I mean, for fuck's sake, I had to chop up a body. You think that's easy?"

"That's your fault for letting your psychotic wife kill Heather."

"I didn't think she could do it."

"Did you *actually* think she'd also get better of you?"

"Shut up! She — she caught me off guard at the most."

"Caught you off guard? Sunney, we are completely fucked! We must explain what happened to Heather and that gash on your neck."

"Heather quit the club and Kwikimart when I told her I would split Toni's life insurance with her. They'll all think she moved away."

"What about her friends and family?"

"No one knows about her and me. They'll think it's some whore's open and shut case. Happens all the time. She gets those ten seconds of fame she had always wanted when she was alive. People love mystery cases."

"And what about that gash on your neck?"

"It's just a nick. It'll heal up soon."

Sunney is in denial. I can tell by the way he gulps after almost every answer. The prick critiques people who use *Uh* and *Um* a lot when speaking but doesn't realize he has his own nervous ticks.

"Please, just one dose. I need it to deal with that — bitch."

"Fine, just hurry so we can finish your wife and clean this mess up. Have I mentioned that you owe me so much for this?" Adler says. His voice is flirtatious, and I hear them exchange a brief kiss.

"Soon, soon. Yeah," Sunney says, keeping the tenor of his voice normal, but I can tell he's slightly repulsed.

"I love you so much, Sunney. All of this is for you. Just remember that," Adler replies in a low, calm voice.

Poor Adler; he's just another pawn in Sunney's game. Having seen all the obsessive photographs of naked women in his cellar, I know Sunney is the least homosexual person in the world. I don't know how he's gone this long pretending he's attracted to this man. He does have a keen ability to manipulate whoever he needs to get what he wants.

I hear Sunney snort and then sigh with relief.

"Remember that woman is a master manipulator. Don't listen to anything she says. The bitch wants to be released and will say or do anything to get you on her side."

Funny how I had just been thinking of how much of a manipulator he is, and now he's calling me the same.

"Let's just get this over with," Adler prompts Sunney.

The doorknob starts to turn slowly, so I run back to the tub, staying on my feet all the while. The door opens and Sunney and Adler walk in. Adler is still sporting his police uniform, while Sunney has changed into jeans and a white button-up shirt with sweat marks seeping through at the armpits and neck collar. Although his clothes are fresh, he still looks like a holy mess. His hair is tangled and looks like he forced an old comb through it with some gel, and his eyes are deranged from all the alcohol and drugs running through his system.

"Shit! She's up," Adler says, making brief awkward eye contact with me before looking away.

"And she even cleaned up a little for her funeral," Sunney notices, not leaving my eyes like a hungry mountain lion waiting to pounce.

"Okay, let's do this," Adler says, taking out the pistol from his belt.

He points the gun in my direction, and I lift my hands in surrender, pleading, "You don't want to do this. He's not worth going to prison over."

Before I can beg anymore, Sunney snatches the gun from Adler's hand. He approaches me until he's close enough to press the gun to my temple. I realize, *he wants to demand answers about the cellar but doesn't want Adler to know what's down there.* He moves the gun from my temple to run the barrel through my hair, staring at it with longing eyes.

"I hate your hair up. Quinn was right. You know your hair does complement those eyes even more. Some would say it's the only thing that gives you some, if any, of that beauty you have."

I immediately remember Quinn complimenting my hair that night we had sex. So Sunney had overheard that entire conversation.

"Sunney, you promised. Kill her," Adler whines.

"I know, okay?" Sunney says, tightly shutting his blood-shot eyes.

"Did Sunney tell you what he accumulated in his little cellar?" I address Adler. *It's now or never.*

"Wha—" Adler begins to say, but before he can complete his question, Sunney hits me across the face with the pistol.

"Shut the fuck up!"

I fall to my knees. I taste blood flowing out from my bottom lip's bite wound. In anger, I spit it at Sunney's black loafers. He smirks, staring down at the blood.

"Take this. I have an idea," Sunney says, tossing Adler the pistol, who nearly drops it, looking confused and angry.

"He won't kill me. You'll have to," I say to Adler, who doesn't reply. "He's not worth it. I can promise you that. That man is as straight as they get."

"You're wrong, bitch," Sunney stresses.

I can't be mean again, not like with Heather. That episode had only ended in her death. I can't scream at this dim-witted cop to open his eyes and see Sunney has been playing him. I must be careful this time. I suppose Old Toni would allow me this small mercy. She surely had a way of convincing me to go her route.

"He never planned to be with you. Before I killed Heather, they were joking about it together."

Adler, unlike Heather, doesn't look completely oblivious to what I'm saying. It's as if he already knows it but doesn't want to believe it.

"Toni, I asked you to shut up!" Sunney screams at me, grabbing me by my shoulder and lifting me to stand.

"I know how it feels to be with him. Being with someone so well off, who is mysterious in terms of how he charms everyone he meets. It seems special and exhilarating that he would choose you. I get it. I was with him for over a year. But you must know he's a psychopath, incapable of loving anyone but himself."

"I'll be right back. Keep your eyes on her," Sunney orders before leaving the room.

Adler lowers the pistol, tightly closing his eyes. Old Toni wants to dash toward him and grab it, shooting Adler before running out the now-unlocked door to find and blast Sunney. I shake, trying to keep myself from doing so. I can talk some sense into this man. He doesn't have to die. I don't have to kill another person.

Sunney's journal! It has all I need to prove to Adler that Sunney will never be with him. I reach into my pocket, but just as I do, I hear footsteps near the door. I toss the book at Adler's feet.

"You don't have to believe a word I say, but that's Sunney's journal. It'll tell you everything you need to know about him," I say calmly, finally resigned to my fate.

Moments later, Sunney walks in with a glass of whiskey in one hand and a kitchen knife in the other. Adler looks as disturbed as I am by the contents of his hands. I worry he will snitch on me about the journal, but he stuffs it into his coat pocket instead.

"Sunney, what the hell?"

"She doesn't deserve a quick death."

"What are you going to do? Slit her throat as she did yours?" he asks, and although he isn't joking, I can't help but chuckle.

Sunney briefly looks at me over his shoulder, glaring at me. He then tosses the kitchen knife to the floor, which lands directly by the sink. We stare at each other, and I'm unsure what he expects me to do.

"Go on, grab it. Grab it before we blow your pretty head off," Sunney calmly instructs.

Believing Sunney is giving me another opportunity to save myself, I take the bait and hurl for the knife. But before I even make it a couple of feet, Sunney grabs me by my hair, pulling me close to him.

"Silly, stupid girl," he whispers in my hair, pulling me like a rag doll toward the sink.

I flail my handcuffed hands, banging his chest with them, but he rebuffs me by grabbing hold of my wrists and forcing them into one of the sinks. I look into the mirror at Sunney, who still has a hold on my hair and the same insane-looking face.

"This may sound creepy, but I can't stop looking at your icy eyes. They keep me wondering what's going on in that head. It's extremely difficult for me to tell if you're happy or whether you want to kill someone," Sunney says, petting my hair like I'm a cat.

These are the same words Quinn had said to me that night. *How does he even remember all this, especially with all the alcohol and drugs in his system?*

I wiggle more, attempting to escape his grasp, and he slams me harder into the sink in retaliation.

"If she moves, shoot her in the face," Sunney orders Adler, who still stands by, awe-struck.

"He's fucking crazy. You have to stop this!" I scream at him.

"When are you going to shut the fuck up, huh?" Sunney asks, aggressively pulling out some of my hair from the root.

He turns the faucet on full blast, pulling the lever to clog the water. Once it has been filled, I know he's planning to drown me. I look over at Adler, who slowly opens Sunney's journal. Hopefully, he'll read enough before I am killed.

"Look at yourself one more time, bitch!" Sunney screams.

I barely get a chance to glance at my tear-soaked face before he shoves it into the sink. I attempt to fight him off, wiggling my body against his force. I kick the back of his legs enough to bring my head above water. The faucet is still on full blast, flowing over the sink now. I only get a breath before Sunney plunges my head back in, stepping on my feet so they are immobile. The seconds feel like hours, and my body begs me to breathe in just a little air. However, I know that will make this process faster, as all I'll be doing is inhaling more water. I'm surprised that I don't feel much pain, only fear.

Moments later, the unrelenting force pushing my body into the sink lets up. Suddenly, there is a sound of a thump. I press my hands over the sink, breathing heavily for air as I choke out water. Once I regain my breathing, I look behind me to see Sunney unconscious on the ground. A few feet away is Adler with the pistol in his hand, perpendicular. The man who hit Sunney somehow looks just as shocked as I do.

I open my mouth to speak but hear a groaning sound beneath me. Sunney, already awake, touches the back of his head with his fingers.

"Ow," he murmurs.

"Come on!" Adler screams at me.

"Shoot him!"

Adler points the pistol at Sunney. He's shaking so incredibly badly I'm surprised he doesn't drop the gun to the ground. Seconds pass as Sunney regains more consciousness.

"I–I don't know if I can do this," he says, lowering the gun. It looks like he's on the verge of a mental breakdown.

"For the love of Pete!" I yell, jumping toward Adler, ready to take the gun from him.

As I reach to take the gun from his possession, he hands me Sunney's journal instead.

"Take this and run to my pickup. I'll be right behind you," he says.

I give him a distressed look.

"Please just go. I'll be right behind you, I promise," he says, reaching into his pocket and pulling out a pair of car keys.

The keys, which look like gold bars, give me the reassurance I need. I grab them, and just as I run out the door, I feel a hand grasp my ankle, nails digging into my skin. Sunney, still on the ground, looks up at me and the journal belonging to him in my hand. I think of him trying to drown me, feeling so in charge, and the thought fills me with enough anger to stomp him in the face. He cowers, and as I prepare myself for a second, Adler pushes me toward the door.

"I said go!" he screams.

I take one last look at the demon that is Sunney Jameson. I want to continue kicking his face and stomp on his body until it's lifeless, and then stick that knife in his back. It's the same urge I'd felt when I'd snapped with Tom — an overwhelming urge to kill and keep killing after they're dead. I blink hard, realizing how mentally ill that is. I then turn around, forcing myself out the door.

"Toni, get back here and fight me, you coward!" Sunney shouts.

Once out in the hallway, I run down the stairs as fast as my legs allow me. Not looking where I'm going once I'm downstairs, I trip over something, landing on my face. Getting to my knees, I look back to see Quinn's dead body. Although I've seen it multiple times, I still have to cover my mouth to muffle a scream.

"I'm so s–sorry," I mumble, shakily returning to a standing position.

I stand there staring at Quinn until the sound of a gunshot erupts upstairs.

CHAPTER 42

I want to feel relieved, but that could have been Sunney shooting Adler. I escape out the sliding door, assuming the front will still be locked. Once I'm outside, I see it's still raining. I catch sight of a white and brown pickup truck with the siren lights on top, which reads *Sheriff* across the doors. I unlock the driver's door, accidentally dropping the keys to the ground once before managing to get it unlocked. I get inside, tossing Sunney's journal on the passenger seat and inserting the keys into the ignition. The truck revs into life, and the stereo starts blaring music, almost giving me a heart attack. *Making Love out of Nothing at All* by Air Supply plays, which calms me because it's not one of the songs from Quinn's CD whose contents, I feel, are burned into my mind at this point.

I get the truck in park and am mortified to see it's a stick shift, which I have never tried to drive. My dad had wanted to teach me once, but I was a brat and refused to try. *How hard could it be?* I place the truck in reverse, and just as I am about to press my foot on the gas pedal, there's a knocking on the window. Peering out, I see Adler standing beside the truck, his fists banging on the driver's side window. I let out a sigh of relief, unlocking the door.

He opens it. Although he looks shaken up, he manages to say, "Get in the back. I'll drive."

I want to resist instinctively, but then I realize I can't drive a stick, and my hands are still handcuffed.

"Do you have the key to my handcuffs?" I ask.

"Sunney had those, sorry," he says, nearly pushing me out of the way to get in the front seat.

Once in the backseat, I see a glass prisoner partition separating the front from the back. This is my fourth time in the back of a police vehicle and first for a truck. The other times had been in a cruiser. The first time was when my affair had leaked, and the police had asked me to answer some questions. The second had been after my mother had drunk herself to death, and the third time had been after killing Tom. That time had been the most frightening one, as they had stared at me like I was a crazy person. They had walked into the scene of me just sitting on our loveseat smoking a cigarette with a black and blue bloodied face, and they had made their assumptions.

"What happened back there?" I ask when we turn around and drive forward on the dirt road.

Adler is momentarily silent as if he doesn't know the answer.

"Damnit, Adler. What happened?" I urge.

"I–I shot him. I did what I had to do, right?"

My heart, for some reason, sinks. I hadn't expected Adler to shoot him. My terror of a night is over, and I should be happy, delighted even. But I had so badly wanted to be the one to kill that motherfucker.

"Right?" Adler asks again, his voice cracking.

"Yes."

Why should I even have to reassure him?

Adler begins bawling his eyes out, hitting his head against the steering wheel repeatedly. Looking out the window, I realize we're moving at a steady pace of only ten miles an hour.

"What — what's wrong?" I ask, resisting the urge to scream at this man to get me as far away from this cabin as possible.

Slowing down even more to look back at me, a red-faced Adler replies, "I loved him, you know? Not like all those other whores. This was real. It wasn't just because of his money or status."

I don't have any sort of empathy left in me to deal with this.

"You did the right thing. Please just—"

"Was it? Was it the right thing? All he was trying to do was kill you so we could be together."

"He was trying to kill me to get back at me for cheating on him. It was all a revenge scheme. You and Heather were his pawns, helping him go through with it."

"No, we were real. Oh god! I killed him."

I realize, *I can't be too honest, or he'll turn on me. I must be nice.*

"You saw his journal. He would've hurt others — it was only a matter of time."

"Fuck the right thing. Even if I did the right thing, as soon as we get to the police station, you'll sell me out. I'll go to prison for aiding him in his schemes. I'll never be a cop again. My dad will find out. I'm — oh fuck!"

Finally, Adler starts speeding up, but somehow this worries me more. He's in no mental capacity to drive.

"No, I won't. I promise," I say as sincerely as possible, although I don't even know if that's true.

Adler looks back at me, noticing the doubt in my eyes.

Recognizing anger from his doubt-ridden face, I quickly say, "No, really, I won't—"

"You're a fucking liar, just like Sunney," Adler accuses, tightening his grasp over the steering wheel and pressing his foot on the gas pedal.

I place my palms over the barrier, getting my face so close that my breath fogs up the glass.

"Please, Adler, just slow down. We can talk about this. Whatever it is you are thinking, just take a deep—"

"I can't live without him. I can't go to prison. I can't have my dad finding out."

"Let's talk about this. Just stop the tru—"

I stop talking as I see Adler pull out his pistol. *Oh fuck! He's going to shoot me and then himself.*

"Adler, please—" I beg.

"Good luck, Toni," Adler says and then presses the barrel of the pistol to his temple.

"No!" I scream, but the sound of the trigger and the gunshot muffles my voice.

Blood spurts all over the glass barrier, and I flinch, pressing my back against the seat, already hyperventilating. Then Adler's body falls against the steering wheel, making the horn go off. I grab the seatbelt and buckle it over my body as the truck turns to the side of the road at an intense speed, Adler's foot is still placed against the gas pedal, so the truck goes off the road and, after hitting a large rock, goes airborne, flipping over. The temple of my forehead knocks against the window, making me black out.

CHAPTER 43

Just before knocking my head against the window, I thought I was going to die. That the vehicle flying through the air would be my final moments, but I regain consciousness to find myself sitting upside down, my fingers barely grazing the truck's hood. I have no clue how long I've been unconscious. When I can breathe again, I feel a warm trickle of blood move down from my forehead and into my mouth. I'm so accustomed to the taste of blood from tonight's experiences that the metallic taste doesn't bother me so much as the ache I feel from banging my head against the window. I sit there for a minute or so, repeatedly blinking as my eyesight goes in and out. The seat belt's nylon has already caused rashes against my lower abdomen as my body's weight prevented fatal injuries. I need to unbuckle myself, but I know the drop will hurt like a son of a bitch. I take long, heavy breaths, pressing my index finger over the button.

I use the still-playing radio to distract my mind before pressing the seatbelt's release button. I land on my right shoulder, forcing myself to crawl on my hands and knees. Once upright, I look through the rear windshield, which is nearly completely shattered. It's my best bet to escape the truck as both doors are locked from inside.

Here we go; more fucking pain, I think, getting into a position where I'm sitting on my ass, and my feet face the windshield. Thankfully, it looks like it's already on the brink of shattering.

I kick harder, and the glass shatters into a million pieces after only the fifth kick. It would have happened sooner I hadn't been so damn weak and wearing shoes. I yelp, feeling shards of glass splinter dig into my heels. Once it's broken, I turn over and crawl out, avoiding shards of glass on the ground. I hear a voice singing in the distance.

"Out of nothing at all! Out of nothing at all! Out of nothing at all!" a raspy voice sings Air Supply, which is still going on the radio.

No fucking way. This must be my imagination. There's no way that Sunney is alive and here now. Is this man a leper for the Grim Reaper? Is that why he keeps coming back?

I hear crunches on leaves as steps sound off nearby. I review the choices I have. One is to get out from my hiding place and run as fast as I can. Then again, with all the glass shards digging into my skin as I sit here, I doubt I'd be very fast. The second is to hope he does a walk-through but assumes I'm dead. It's feasible, as I might have died from the crash had I not fastened a seatbelt. The third option is to wait for him to get closer, get into the front seat, and retrieve Adler's pistol.

I like my odds best with the third option. I place my palms over the grass sprinkled with glass shards and inch myself farther out. Each shard that digs into my palms is torture. I can hear the voice still singing come near the collision spot until soon the he steps over the glass, and I catch sight of a pair of black Louis Vuitton loafers. I had peered down at the same pair when dancing on my wedding night. I remember thinking they matched so perfectly with my Jimmy Choo ivory satin pumps. Two overly expensive shoes to wear for only one night.

The shoes stand still in my view for a couple of moments, and I swear the beating of my heart can be heard miles away, it's so intense. After some long agonizing seconds, the Louis Vuitton loafers move on. The sound of glass crunching underneath human feet is in the air followed by some scavenging sounds. *Shit! He'll find the gun for sure.*

I wait until I hear the footsteps disappear into the distance. I look both ways for any movement before crawling out completely from the wreckage. Still on my knees, I move toward the front door slowly in case Sunney is still within earshot. I am positive that he has found the gun, but I decide to take my chances and still look. He's so high he might've missed it.

Once I reach the passenger door, I notice just how smashed the vehicle is. The door is jammed. I look around for a rock to break into the window. Once I find one as big as my fist, I carefully examine my surroundings for any movement before pounding the rock into the glass. It shatters, and I crawl halfway through it as fast as possible, truly feeling any moment could be my last. The smell of the dying engine and Adler's dead body consume the area. His body is slumped over on the hood, a giant pool of blood directly underneath his head. It's disgusting, but luckily enough, that is where the gun had landed. I close my eyes, extending my hand and then my fingers to grab it. Feeling the cold handle with the warm liquid makes my body shiver.

"What are you doing, darling?" a voice says and simultaneously hands plunge onto my lower waist, pulling me out of the truck.

I scream and turn my body around, finger over the trigger, ready to pull it at the messy blonde head of hair I see.

CHAPTER 44

My finger pulls the trigger that, just a couple of minutes ago, had been used for someone's suicide. I imagine that the trigger goes off smoothly, and I even hear a clicking sound. But nothing happens. It just clicks. I make a horrified face, the kind someone makes right before having a life-altering realization. The pistol had to have been loaded. I mean, only one bullet had been used. Unless, at some point, after the crash, it had been emptied and then replaced. Replaced directly in a pool of blood like some sick joke.

Although only seconds have passed, I am pulled out from the truck and into what is sure to be my death this time. The seconds slow down. It's almost like time freezes. That, or I'm going into shock. Either way, a brief flashback comes to mind as I am being pulled. It's a bullshit flashback, however. It's the night of my wedding, and my husband touches me gently with his hands, one over my lower back and the other tightly gripping my hand. At that moment, long before I discovered what a psychopathic crazy lunatic he is, I was completely smitten with him and submissive.

Once upon a time, I could've died for his faint smile and dazed eyes. I was obsessed with his vanilla bourbon aftershave, which tickled my nostrils whenever I was near him. It was the moment I'd looked forward to my whole life. Not the ceremony, not the first kiss after being married, and not even the night in the honeymoon suite. It was the first dance, our song playing as we held each other. Even if three hundred plus people were nearby, watching us, I felt we were truly alone.

A moment from the conversation we had shared earlier that night still struck a chord with me. I had had cold feet before our wedding, not in that I didn't want to marry him anymore but in a *what if he soon discovers he is so far out of my league and leaves me broken-hearted* way. I saw how his dad was with other women, and I recognized how it wasn't exactly a frowned-upon thing to be a cheating dirtbag when you had a lot of money. I was nervous that Sunney might turn out the same way once my looks started to fade.

While we danced, I asked him if this was really what he wanted. I tried my best not to blatantly beg him not to leave me for some young bimbo. However, with the way Sunney so easily perceived the hidden agenda behind our conversations, I failed to maintain a stoic front. He didn't get offended; instead, he behaved in a completely opposite manner. He reassured me that cheating was the ultimate sin in his eyes. I asked about how he perceived murder. He hesitated, making me gasp. Then we had laughed, joking about the whole thing. *Lord! If I had known he had been completely serious, it would've saved a life or two.* After that, I had decided to stop worrying, for then at least. I was still young and wouldn't have to worry about aging for another five years when I hit thirty.

It's funny now, that I had put so much thought into Sunney's cheating, as I had cheated on my partners again and again and again. I had cheated on my first high school boyfriend with my science teacher and cheated on Tom — yes, Tom. This is why he had reacted the way he had that night — prompting one of the worst nights of — well, now second worst nights of my life. Now I'd done the same with — Sunney. Maybe God is punishing me. It's His final straw for my disloyal habits. If this is indeed the case, cheating on

Sunney Jameson — a man who despised it out of everything else — is really the perfect lesson. He thought manipulation, torture, and murder were fair game in the face of cheating.

Now the light shines brightly in my eyes. I am a cheater, plain and simple. I won't say I'm a whore — as I've only been with ten or so men in my twenty-four years. When the forbidden apple came close to my mouth, I couldn't help but bite it. I am my mother's daughter, and she was the same way, wanting any man who made her feel special and different. Even if the one at home was doing just that, the exciting feeling of someone fresh felt too good to pass up.

With my mother in mind, a vivid memory pops into my head. I do not recall or even know if it's real or if my mind is just playing games with me. I'm little, about five years old, I guess, by the familiar, originally purple but now brown, teddy bear in my hand. He went missing for good when I was five. I never found out what happened to him. We were inseparable, me and that dumb bear.

While holding that bear, I see myself using my tiny hand to open my bedroom door. It's light outside; like usual, Daddy is at work. The sounds of moaning are coming from my mommy's room, which worries me as a five-year-old. *Is my mommy in trouble?* She has only been in Mommy and Daddy's room with the person she had introduced as an "old friend" for ten or so minutes. The old friend was so tall and mean-looking. I listened when my mommy told me to go to my room while they talked. But the moaning — the moaning scared me. As I tiptoe to Mommy's room, I hear she has stopped. Suddenly, with the sound of some sort of slap, she starts crying. I open the door, wanting nothing but to console her, hug her tight and tell her she will be okay. I did that often during the day when Daddy was away, and Mommy had been drinking her grown-up drink. I used to be such a loving, sweet little girl back then . . .

The pistol is slapped out of my hands as a hoarse-sounding laugh erupts. Time finally catches up, and I am back to reality. The unnerving yet beautiful face of my husband is before me.

His eyes are still bloodshot, and his pupils are dilated. I can't even question how he made it over here as fast as he has because I had blacked out after the crash. It makes it impossible for me to know how much time has passed. *He is supposed to be dead; Adler had said so himself, and I had heard the gunshot.*

I cover my face with my hands, knowing I will be stabbed, bashed, or shot at any moment. When that doesn't happen, I slowly open my eyes. Sunney has his head tilted, his legs straddling me with all his weight.

"Did you think he would kill me?"

I don't speak. My silence is answer enough.

"The idiot looked away as he aimed his shot. His undying love for me must've been too great for him to make a decent shot. I wish the same could've been said for the cold-hearted Toni Lovette. You just went for it, didn't you? How'd you do it, huh? First Heather, and now Adler. Wherever you go, people sure do die."

"I didn't do this. He thought I would rat him out when we reached the police station. To be honest, I would've exactly done that. But I think he was mostly broken-hearted about the fact you ended up being a total psychopath obsessed with the idea of murdering women."

"He did have a past of lovers breaking his heart. I must've been the last straw, I guess."

"Look, if you're going to kill me, just do it. This has gone on long enough."

"Aw! But we had such fun! I thought you liked me on top, babe," he says, humping me while laughing hysterically.

I squirm, attempting to push him off me.

"You're right, though. It has," Sunney says, standing up and fetching the empty pistol he slapped out of my hands.

Once he walks away, I attempt to stand up and make a run for it, but as if anticipating my move, Sunney immediately stomps down on my left ankle. Like a dog in trouble with its owner, I yelp in pain. I try to pull my ankle out from under his foot, but he presses down on it more forcefully. He reaches into his pocket with a couple of bullets in his hand

and loads the gun. Eventually, he moves his foot away from my ankle, releasing me. I bite my lip, wanting to stay strong in my last moments. I can try to run again, but what would be the use? He will just shoot me in the back of my head. Sunney, who can't seem to get himself to commit murder, might find it more difficult with me staring daggers into his eyes.

When the gun is again pointed in my direction, as fast as I can get the words out, I say, "I can — I can help you."

Intrigued, with slightly raised eyebrows, he asks, "Help me how?"

"I can tell you how to let go when you kill. That's what you are having trouble with, right? I can help you get over that."

Widening his eyes, he says, "Elaborate."

In all truth, I don't know if I can elaborate. Everyone I've murdered has nearly killed me on the inside. It's gut-wrenching, but there must be some sort of knack I have that Sunney doesn't. Something I've been able to overcome that he can't. Even if there isn't one, I will have to bullshit through it. *What was it that made killing possible for me?* I only did it when my survival instincts kicked in. I didn't want to do it for a euphoric sick kick like Sunney.

"It's like pulling a band-aid. You must get over that initial fear of pain — the fear of how it will be. You must let go."

"Let go?" he asks innocently.

"Like ignore all thoughts or feelings of empathy. Ignore the fact they are human beings. Imagine they are nothing. You did it with Andrea, right? After what she did, you thought she was nothing. You must imagine all women are nothing."

For a moment, I think he might be buying this.

"Well, thanks for the advice, Oprah," Sunney sneers sarcastically.

"No, no, no," I say, lacing my fingers together, begging.

I close my eyes tightly, feeling on the verge of wetting myself from fear. More moments pass. When I open my eyes again, I see Sunney, who still looks like he's ready to kill me.

His hands aren't shaking nearly as much as before in the bathroom. He looks nearly ready to do it.

"I actually have some questions to ask you," he says, dropping his hand with the pistol to his side.

"Questions?" I ask, not understanding what he could possibly want to know.

"Dance with me," he says, stuffing the pistol into the front of his pants.

"What?" I ask, dumbfounded, unsure if I heard the word "dance" right or if I have a concussion from the crash.

Using his free hand, Sunney grabs my handcuffed hands, moves them over his neck and lifts me to stand. I release all my weight on him, my head slumping on his bare chest. He's shirtless and sweaty. My ear rests right over his unusually fast-beating heart. It is pounding as fast as mine had been when I had finally finished stabbing Tom and collapsed over his bloody chest, feeling like I might pass out. His heart wasn't beating anymore, but mine had been doing enough for the both of us.

"Wh — why are you doing this?" I ask, mumbling, my body still limp against Sunney's.

"I'm not sure. Maybe it's the beautiful morning sky, my amazement at your efforts to generate sympathy, or the drugs making me feel euphoric."

"Maybe it's a mixture of all three."

"That's probably it."

"So, this momentary feeling of empathy. Do you care to explain what that's about?"

"You just — won't die. It's truly extraordinary that you survived everything I threw at you last night or this morning. Not even in a rollover. Don't tell me you remembered to put your seatbelt on in all that chaos?"

"I did. It was a last-minute decision. Smart, quick decisions like taking the bullets out of that pistol and placing it in a pool of blood for me to grab and try to shoot you with."

"Didn't think you were one for smart decisions, considering you fucked a man you didn't know on our honeymoon."

"When it's my brain making the decisions, and not my vagina, I can be."

He chuckles, his hand tightening around the fabric on my lower back. I can't tell if his laugh is an angry fake one or genuine.

"That is sadly true. Was he the only one while we were together, or were there more that slipped through?"

"No, Quinn was it. I promise," I say, regretting my words instantly, as if promising anything will make him spare my life.

"Was I the only man you cheated on?"

I sigh deeply and reply, "Sunney, I don't think it matters anymore."

"I'll take that as a no. Tom too?"

I nod, shutting my eyes tightly, not wanting to revisit that other horrible mistake of mine.

"And he tried to kill you over that too? Holy shit! You'd think that would've caused enough trauma to compel you never to do it again."

"I mean, yeah. For most people, it would've, but people also somehow rack up six DUIs in their life."

"So, you're saying some people never learn no matter how often they are punished for their crimes?"

"I wouldn't use the word 'crimes'."

"Then what word would you use?"

After contemplating that one, I confess, half-asking, half-stating, "Sins."

"And what a sinning whore you really are!"

"You know, as you pulled me out of the truck, time sort of stopped, and I was back at our wedding day. Dancing with you. Kind of funny how only a minute later, we're dancing."

"You really are special," Sunney says, chuckling as he tightens his arms around my waist.

"Yeah, I specialize in idiocy."

"It's a shame how true that is. I was so ready to start the rest of my life with you. Now I'll have to start the rest of my life mending my broken heart over you."

That's so cheesy, almost like something out of a romance movie. Too bad we're the farthest thing from that at this moment.

"What'd you think about my — cellar of prizes?"

My brain had blocked that out momentarily, but now, when he asks me about it, I remember it vividly — the nude photographs of so many women as they slept, along with aligned photos of the Bond women who Sunney had probably been pretending they were. I remember the dirty clothing of other women and mine and the article about Tom and Evan. There were so many answers I wanted desperately to know and yet made me sick.

"You really had an innocent man go to prison because you thought he liked me?"

"You should be grateful. I saw a potential man capable of taking you away, so I had him taken care of."

"Many men know if a woman is meant to be theirs. They don't need to take anyone out of the picture. What is meant to be is meant to be."

"I didn't want you to be taken away. At that time, I couldn't see clearly. But now I know that no matter what I do to other men, you will still find a way to be a cheating adulterous whore."

Did he have any other words in his vocabulary besides "whore"?

"Do I even want to know the reason behind the photographs of all those women, the used clothing, and the Bond girls?"

As if anticipating that question — even hoping for it to come up — he promptly answers, "James Bond had good taste in women. What can I say? As a young boy, I always fantasized about having women like he did. The rest are — were souvenirs, I would say. I've always been rather fond of the female body. The curves, dimples, feel, look — everything. All men are — so when I found myself unable to see a woman's unclothed body more than once, I thought it was normal to take photographs so I could keep a part of them forever. What you saw on the wall was merely the tip of the iceberg.

I have several boxes back at home. I didn't worry about my sanity until I wondered what it would be like to cut one open to see the real inside of those women. Apart from Andrea, of course, whose murder was easy on my conscience after what she did, but I couldn't get myself to do it. I didn't think I could get away with multiple murders like famous serial killers such as Ted Bundy or Robert Hanson so easily did. I didn't think I was intelligent enough. But now, if I get away with all this, there may be a chance for me."

"I think you're full of shit," is the first thing that comes out of my mouth without hesitation.

I know it's not exactly wise of me to say this to someone who is on the verge of cracking my neck, but it's the truth. Sunney has been bullshitting with me when he doesn't need to. He does not doubt that he is smart enough to commit another murder. He thinks the highest of himself possible. For Christ's sake, he thinks he's some diluted version of James Bond. He just can't get himself to commit murder. It terrifies him, almost like a young kid that killed animals but wasn't past the point where they could kill an actual human.

"You are far more in love with yourself than you will ever be with me or any other woman, for that matter. You are not killing women simply because something inside you is too weak. That is the only reason you decided to be with me, because I did kill someone. It made you think we were alike in some sick way for murdering our ex-lovers."

I anticipate Sunney to have another angry outburst, but he doesn't. He stops the slow dancing movements to stand still, holding me in his grasp. With his sweaty bare chest leaning against mine, this is the warmest I have felt since I was first awoken last night.

"Fuck! You really do know me better than anyone else."

"No, I just read your shitty journal entries. I could never even begin to know you."

"You've come closer than anyone else has, which makes this heartbreaking."

"Makes what heartbreaking?"

"The fact that I still have to kill you."

"What? Wait—" I begin to say, but my body is already being pulled up and over Sunney's shoulder.

"Where are we going?"

"Back to the cabin where it all should have ended in the first place."

"Just kill me if you're going to kill me!" I scream, my voice cracking as I beat my weak fists against Sunney's back.

"If I kill you here, your death will not fit the narrative. I want you to die thinking of all the harm you've done. It's the least everyone you've ever hurt or betrayed deserves if they are watching us from above."

"And you don't deserve the same? Adler and Heather's deaths are your fault. Heather died trying to impress you. Adler killed himself, believing he had killed the man who could never love him and that he would go to prison over it."

"I don't disagree with you, but you are still playing the blame game, turning the tables on someone other than yourself. At least I know I'm a bad guy."

His words make me shut my mouth and stop struggling with my fists. *He's — he's wrong. All those people I hurt had it coming. They did.*

CHAPTER 45

The walk goes on for some time. I assume we had crashed over a mile away from the cabin. Sunney's pace is slow, like a snail. I doze in and out, my eyes begging me to let them close, if only for a minute of rest. Occasionally, I'll peer up, straining my neck to look at the dirt road and pine trees spread all around us as far as the eye can see. It's warmer now, the sun finally partially out, heating the foggy sky from last night's rain. The more we walk, the more I see the dirt road drying in patches from the sun's rays.

I know we're near the cabin when the dirt road ends and the pavement appears. Sunney's truck, with its inflated tires, comes into view soon. I wonder how he's going to get out of all this now. It won't be easy to explain a crashed police truck and a policeman shot dead inside. However, he's right about one thing. In the unlikely event he gets away with this crime, murder will be a piece of cake for him.

Once inside, he immediately carries me up the stairs. Sunney huffs and puffs due to the strain and attempts to hide his out-of-breath sounds by breathing strictly through his nostrils. *He must be going through the same exhaustion my body is.*

Once upstairs and in the bedroom, he tosses me on the bed. He takes out what I suspect is the key to my handcuffs, uncuffing me momentarily only to re-cuff me to one side of the bed's headboard. I stare into his eyes and get an uncanny feeling that he's keeping me alive for only one reason. As if reinforcing my fears, he takes the pistol out of his pants and then takes them off, along with his underwear, becoming completely naked.

"Please, Sunney, you don't need to—"

"Get over yourself. I'm not a rapist. I'm going to shower," he says, rolling his eyes.

That's surprising, considering he had just mentioned famous rapist murders, wishing he was "like them".

"I have never really felt the need or want to rape. Would it be easy? Yes, but it just seems so desperate. Why rape when women are dying to fuck me consensually?"

I stare, not really understanding if he wants congratulations or a fuck you from me. I say neither and stare at him in disgust. *How did I ever find this man's over-the-top confidence sexy?*

"Unless you're planning to disassemble the whole bed to escape without me hearing, I'll be back when I'm done, hopefully not to punish you," he says, turning around and casually walking out of the room and into the bathroom.

After he walks out, I wait for the shower to start before standing up and pulling on the bed's headboard, hoping it breaks. It only takes a couple of minutes for my wrist, which is already scraped up, to start bleeding from forcefully pulling on it. If I had any more bravery or pain tolerance left in me, I would have attempted to pull the handcuff over my wrist, cutting away at my hand until it's free, but I don't. To add insult to injury, it's so tightly screwed on around my wrist that the amount of flesh I'd have to tear away at would make it nearly impossible for me not to scream.

Are you really giving up?

Once again, Old Toni is in my head, disappointed in the new me. Not that I blame her. New Toni easily gives up when things get tough. She prefers being a damsel in distress. Old Toni made all the quick and rash decisions to keep me afloat. Cutting out a person I'd so desperately tried to become for over a year now seems impossible to in the next twenty minutes. Before meeting Sunney, I had ideated this new character. I had pretended to be her as soon as I'd sat down in the dining room chair after killing Tom. I maintained the nice girl image for so long that I eventually started to believe that Sunney was at fault for forming such a weak-willed bitch, but it wasn't his fault. Our relationship had merely intensified the process of becoming her; New Toni had been birthed once I realized I had no choice. She should've emerged after the incident with Mr. Nortec, but I was still young and dumb then. I couldn't grasp how tragic my life would be without adopting New Toni's identity. It took years for me to realize how truly mad Old Toni was and even longer to realize I couldn't be that way.

Now, like my worst nightmares coming back, I realize I might need Old Toni to get me out of this. I just don't know how to bring her back.

CHAPTER 46

Soon, possibly ten minutes later, the shower turns off, and after a couple more, Sunney walks back into the bedroom with a teal-colored towel over his waist. I yearn to be as clean as he looks. I still feel the dirt in every crevice of my body, like when you're a kid leaving the beach. My eyes glare at his clean body, hating him for showing it off.

"See something you like?" he asks.

I get flashbacks of when he had said that to me early on in our relationship. We had gone swimming, and it was the first time I had seen him without a shirt. The moment had felt magnetic. My eyes had bulged out so much that I probably looked like a teenage boy seeing boobs for the first time. However, this time, his athletic figure isn't the center of my admiration. It's his clean, freshly washed body. Just mentioning water makes me feel thirsty.

"Can I have some water — p–please?" I ask, feeling as if just saying the word "please" to this man will make it burn my tongue.

Sunney ponders on the request for a moment and then walks into the bathroom, shrugging. He returns over a minute later with a clear cup we use to rinse our mouths after brushing half-full of, what I'm guessing is, sink water. He has another pair of handcuffs in his other hand.

"Must be parched after destroying all my prized possessions."

I roll my eyes, reaching over to grab the cup. But Sunney moves it away and stares at me, as if waiting for me to say something. *I had already said please. Does he want me to beg? At this point, I'll seriously consider it.*

"You are going to tell me why. Why you did what you did."

"I told you. Sleeping with him was just a rash decision. I didn't—"

"No, not that, Jesus! Why did you burn down my cellar? Was it merely to piss me off?"

Technically, I hadn't done that on purpose. However, I don't want to tell that to Sunney as it has been one of the few victories I've scored tonight during our whole battle. That water looks so delicious, though.

I take a deep inhale, hating myself more and more, not myself exactly, but New Toni. Old Toni would tell Sunney upfront it was because I did want to piss him off. New Toni was cowardly enough to tell him the truth — that she hadn't been quick-witted enough to do something so spiteful; it was a mere in-shock accident caused by the horror she saw before her eyes.

"I didn't do it on purpose, Sunney. I had lit a candle to see your little funhouse of horrors, and when you burst down the barrier, covering the entrance to the door, I knocked it over, and the rest — well, you know the rest. Please, just give me the water," I say, extending my hand toward it.

He grins, like he is subtracting one of my prevails in his head, adding it instead to his for getting me to tell him the truth.

"I knew you'd never have the balls to do that."

I bite my lips, fighting back the urge to cry or scream.

"Please," I beg, eyeing the water.

Looking at me with disgust, like I'm some pathetic crying toddler, Sunney ventures to hand the cup my way, but before handing it over, he instead takes it back and tosses it inside his mouth, nearly spilling half of it on his chin.

"Damn! I was parched. My bad."

I feel my body shake, and my anger and/or that of Old Toni takes over.

"You son of a bitch! I will kill you!" I scream, jumping out of bed and using my free hand to try and scratch at Sunney's face. He backs away a foot, getting out of my reach.

"You need some rest; you're looking a little tense."

I frantically pull on my handcuffed hand, screaming obscenities. My wrist burns and starts bleeding as I pull on the tightened shackle. Although painful, the anger I feel numbs it. I'm so fumed up that I can barely react when Sunney slips another handcuff on my wrist and pushes me face-first on the bed to lock it against the headboard.

Pressing my face hard against the pillow, he whispers, "I asked you to go to sleep."

Nearly suffocating me for what feels like an eternity before finally letting me go, I instantly start breathing in loud huffs. My cheeks are streaked with tears. I wiggle my body, desperately seeking to twist around. It doesn't work.

"I'll be back shortly, dear," he says before I hear footsteps exiting the room and the sounds of the door closing.

I peer up at my hands, gripping the bars to the headboard, trying to fight off the tears flowing from my eyes. I watch as my wrist bleeds on to the cream-colored sheets, staining them. Minutes that feel like years pass, and I feel increasingly sleepy as I'm on my stomach. I wish I could use my hands to force my eyes open because I know if I fall asleep, it'll let Sunney get the drop on me so much easier. I feel so drained both physically and mentally that it's hard not to slip away.

With my eyes closed and the darkness beginning to take over, a sudden voice is in my head. It's Old Toni.

Your DID is all that can save you. Please just let me through.

"I don't have DID," I say out loud.

Who do you think has saved you all these years?

"You didn't save me. You turned me into a monster."

You were pathetic. You needed to be me.

"You're wrong; you're wrong; you're wrong," I repeat until sleep finally overcomes me.

CHAPTER 47

More vivid life memories come to me in my dreams. I must've hidden them in the deepest crevices of my mind. The midday afternoon when I heard my mom moaning in her room, I had gone to check on her and opened the door accidentally without knocking on it first. I saw a naked man on top of her in bed. At the time, I thought he might have been hurting her. For reasons I'm unsure of still now, what had started as consensual had changed in a second. Most five-year-olds would have run away crying to their bedroom until a grown-up arrived to save them. God — if only that had been the case here.

Instead, I looked over at their clothes drawers. One made from cheap pine and the other an over-washed, faded beige color. My parents had broken the budget on my room, so theirs consisted of used thrift-store furniture. The bed even squeaked on most days. Daddy was always away at work when Mom had her many "old friends" over.

Atop this cheap drawer were specific items I had never seen there before. A pair of keys, cash, loose change, and a black pocketknife. Daddy had lectured me never to touch a knife as I had always had a shine in my eye for sharp objects — the way they gleamed bright until they cut into something that stained them a different shade. I grabbed the pocketknife, stretching my arms to make up for my small stature. If only the drawer had been another inch taller, I would've never reached that damned knife.

By then, the man was off the bed, hunched over my mom and screaming at her, completely unaware of my presence. Without any thought, I used the sharp object to stab the bad man repeatedly. The sight of blood oozing out of his skin startled me, so I dropped the knife. The bad man turned around, half in a daze, half-angry. Catching sight of the midget that was me, he pushed me as hard as possible. I flew across the room, knocking my head against the old dresser. After that, things went dark. Along with my favorite purple bear, I also never saw that cheap drawer again.

I woke up in a white room with people dressed in white who couldn't stop staring at me with droopy expressions. The bad man, my parents explained to me, was a burglar from whom I had protected my mother. My mother, once alone with me, informed me that he was not an old friend as she had previously explained. She couldn't stress this part enough for me to get it. I did as I was told until I understood the situation much later in life.

Everything changed that day. I was no longer the sweet, kind little girl from before. I had formed Old — then New — Toni. Knives had more of a shine to them than previously, and keeping me away from them was much more difficult for my parents. Little did my parents know that this Toni would wreak complete and utter havoc on their lives.

I remember so many hospital visits after that. Now thinking of it, they weren't harmless check-ups. My parents were worried about how I had drastically changed my personality in a day. Instead of giving them hugs and kisses in the morning, I cried and tried slapping them when they came near me. I threatened to hurt other kids frequently, telling them I'd done it before and would do it again. On other days, I'd be happy and loving again. It didn't make any sense; back then, I thought every little girl or boy was like that. They switched who they wanted to be that day.

After nearly a year of misdiagnoses, the doctor finally dropped the ball on my parents, revealing what I had. Dissociative identity disorder or *DID*. Old Toni didn't ever like saying the whole thing. It's just *DID*. It made it feel less serious to her. Tom was the only person with whom I had ever really felt inclined to talk about it after high school. As it's an unheard-of disease, he didn't take it seriously.

The feel of something light and soft landing on my feet jolts me awake. As I wake up from what feels like a day-long hibernation, I first smell a fresh but musky scent. I'm down on a rough sponge-like seat with my legs spread out in front of me. I'm wearing a long white cream-colored dress heavily wrinkled with a soft pink colored stain in the crotch area. With the creases, it takes me a delayed second to realize I'm no longer wearing the pink robe but my wedding dress. It's wrinkled because at the hotel room, the night before we headed to Rubico, I had accidentally spilled champagne on it. Sunney had been in too big of a hurry to tear the thing off, so we had never deposited it to the drycleaners. Maybe I am in hell, the Devil forcing me to wear the dress given to me by the man that killed me.

Besides the scent of champagne, I once again get the stinking odor of what I imagine a garden smells like. As my sight becomes less blurry, that makes sense as all I can see is dirt surrounding me, starting from my feet to up where the late afternoon sky sits. The sun is setting, marking the most beautiful time of day. I only concentrate on its purple, pink, and orange-like palette for seconds before realizing I'm not dead. This is not hell. I'm in an open hole in the ground.

My next startling realization is that my hands have been tightly securely behind my back by rope. I feel another pair of hands tied to mine. Their flesh is soft but icy cold. Almost like it could be a dead body. I turn my head to the side as far as it will go, catching sight of a plaid design resting against my shoulder. I know that plaid jacket and the feel of this spongey seat and its black ripped-up cover. Both had belonged to — *Oh, dear god!*

"Help, help!" I scream, looking up at the sunset sky, my voice so dry it hurts to speak.

A blonde head of hair appears at the top of the hole only seconds later. My husband has a large smile on his heat-red, sweaty face and a shovel in his right hand.

Wiping away a bead of sweat he exclaims, "Toni! You're finally awake and just in time. I was just setting up some tunes to play."

"Sunney, what the fuck are you doing?"

"Isn't it obvious? Wait, hold that thought."

Then he's gone again. A couple of moments of silence later, the whistling opening verse of a cheery cartoon-like song begins to play.

"Happy trails to you until we meet again," the opening verse sings, "Happy trails to you, keep smiling until then."

Happy Trails by Roy Rodgers is the song. I remember Sunney humming to it numerous mornings at his house while cooking breakfast for us and seeming to be in another world. I always got a Western slash Bugs Bunny vibe from it. He, on the other hand, was probably imagining murdering women.

"Who cares about the clouds when we are together," the song continues, and Sunney finally pops up again.

"So, I thought this would be the easiest way to kill you — by burying you alive."

"Are you insane?" I ask, beginning to wiggle my body.

"Now, before you get defensive, I did you a favor. I will bury you in my favorite spot with your favorite person."

It's Quinn's back seat and his dead body. I wiggle my secured wrists more, burning them through the rope.

"Don't worry. I secured the seat tightly so the both of you will be nice and cozy," Sunney says, digging his shovel into a pile of dirt and throwing it down into the hole.

Cozy is one hundred percent the correct way of phrasing the way things stand. It stays put no matter how much I try rocking the seat forward. I also notice my ankles have been duct taped, with what looks like a whole roll, to the seat.

This one I have no idea how to get out of, and by the looks of it, Sunney has already filled the hole nearly to the starting point of the seat.

"You won't get away with this."

Sunney shrugs and replies, "I'm sure I'll think of something. My wife and her lover, who killed his wife in a car crash, ran away and killed a cop hot on their pursuit. I haven't thought out all the details quite yet, but that's the gist of it."

"Sunney, let's talk this through. We can start fresh. It doesn't have to be this way. I love you, and I messed up, okay? I'm human."

Sunney chuckles, and leaning down, he says, "Goodbye, Toni. Happy trails to you until we meet again."

"Sunney, please just — just talk to me!" I scream, my voice cracking with every word.

"We've talked enough."

With an eccentric wave, Sunney disappears, and more dirt plummets down into the hole.

Let me in, the voice urges. I feel as if it's digging its fingernails inside me, trying to force itself out.

I tightly shut my eyes, chanting, "No, no, no — it's too late."

The least I can do is die a somewhat good person. I can't let the other me escape.

Hiding what you are does not make you a good person.

"I'm a good person," I whisper, sobbing as tears stream down my eyes.

Old Toni is silent, but she doesn't need to say anything. Her silence is loud enough. She's once again disappointed in me. I don't need her. I can't be her. I can get out of this as the new me. If I die, I might be forced to see Mr. Nortec, my mom, dad, and her "friend" I stabbed, or worst yet — Tom. All the ones I let down. *Not me, Old Toni. None of that was me.*

But was it me who killed Heather or Quinn? Who was that?

Sunney sings along to the song as he rapidly pours more and more dirt down the hole. Soon patches of dirt hit me as

I sob more. The smell of Quinn's decaying dead body and dirt make it hard to think of a last-minute plan. I think of any wishes I can ask of God. Not that he would give me any, but it doesn't hurt to wonder. Sunney gets caught and sent to prison. No worse than that. Sunney is caught, goes to prison, AND is raped by another inmate. Wait — no, 'cause then he still gets to go on living. How about Sunney's prized cabin somehow lighting on fire and burning down with him in it, unable to get out?

Light, light — light. Oh shit. *LIGHT. Light — er.*

I go back to that night with Quinn in his Jeep. It feels like so long ago. It's my last good memory. Even if I had ruined it by leaving him behind, his soft smile and dark beard were still etched into my mind. I remember wanting a smoke for the first time in forever due to all the stress. I had played it off cool, placing the cigarette in my mouth, looking over and asking for a light that I knew for certain that Quinn would have.

"I don't smoke much myself but always keep a lucky lighter on me," he had said, reaching into his back pocket to grab it before promptly putting it back in the same spot.

The fucking lighter. I'll show Old Toni; I still got this.

I thrust my ass in the air, shoving my finger into Quinn's jeans pockets. I fail on the first try and go too deep, my fingers going into his boxers. I try again, stretching my fingers out as far as possible, but doing so causes Quinn's limp head to press harder against mine. His smell burns my nostrils. He really does smell like death. The thought of my life ending makes me see how my demise will turn out to be if this plan doesn't work out. The dirt will envelope all around, slowly suffocating me. My body will decompose in Sunney's backyard while he becomes the serial killer he has always aspired to be.

My fingers finally brush the top of Quinn's back pockets and my middle finger grazes over the cold silver lighter. I hoist my body up more, stretching my fingers until my index finger goes over it. I use their tips to dig into the lighter, inching its way out of the jean pockets. Finally, after a couple of minutes, it slips out but falls out from my sweaty palms and into the seat cushion. *Fuck*.

The sound of Sunney singing as happy as he can be while he slowly buries me instills an overwhelming feeling of impending doom in me. *What will I even do if I am free?* I don't know if I can crawl out of this hole or fight Sunney. I could always wait for him to completely bury me, dig myself out when he's gone, and escape. One disaster at a time, I guess.

CHAPTER 48

It takes me ten minutes to grab the lighter that nearly got stuffed into the seat cushions. I also had to concentrate on not hacking up a lung as more dirt piled onto me, turning my white dress brown.

With the lighter in my hands, I flick open the top. Then with it turned toward the rope, I run my thumbs over the ignition. The first couple of tries barely sparks fire, and I realize it's low on fluid. However, when it does ignite, the flame burns my wrists more than the rope. I yelp and look up, fearful that Sunney may have heard the click. When dirt continues to fall, I start again. Burning myself is one of the worst pains I've ever experienced. I keep stopping, unable to go on, and the lighter is more difficult to turn on each time. The rope is barely freeing me, if at all. Soon, the lighter, seemingly empty of fluid, just sparks. Once I rub my numb thumb against its ignition, it finally stays lit. But the burns over my wrist are so painful I drop it.

I scream from anger and pain. I'm not sure I can keep this up.

Sunney finally makes an appearance, popping his head into view.

"Don't go screaming at me now. It's a little overdue."

"Sunney, please stop this—" I say, out of breath and in so much pain I can't even properly beg him anymore.

"I got one last song for you, doll. Hold up!" he exclaims, disappearing again.

Sea of Love starts blasting through the speakers — the song we had danced to. I get flashes of us dancing and of him playing the song when we first reached the cabin. I remember his gentle smile — the smile had made me feel safe. It was one that had made me oblivious to the evil man behind it. I guess you never really know someone. Like my dad never really knew my mother or Sunney never knew the real me.

Are you really going to die with that in the grave?

As if on cue, Old Toni is back. Like me, she seems to have given up. She makes one last request — to be shown one last time.

"What do you want me to do?" I ask.

"Let the truth free," I say out loud.

I'm officially talking to myself. Maybe Old Toni is already back. She's right about no longer being able to save me. But she doesn't want me to die a liar or a coward. Maybe letting the truth out could be the last good thing I do.

"I can't — I just can't," I cry, images of that night with Tom rushing into my mind.

"Do it! Tell him the truth. Let me in. If you don't do it, I'll do it for you," I shout at myself.

"I–I never wanted to hurt anyone."

"But you did."

"Fuck!" I scream.

Sunney's head reappears as our song concludes, causing a moment of silence, and he hears my scream clearly.

"Keep it down," he orders, his head popping above me.

Before he can disappear, I say, "Wait, wait!"

"This again?"

"Just please listen to me."

He sighs heavily and says, "Last words?"

"I'm — I'm not who you think I am. I just — I couldn't stop her."

"Couldn't stop who?"

"Myself."

"Couldn't stop yourself from doing what?'

"This rage. Rejection mostly caused it, but so did nothing. Sometimes a light switch would just go off. For the longest time, I kept the reason hidden deep in my memories, but now I know why. I hit my head and got injured badly as a little girl. It made me another person — one incapable of emotion."

"You're ridiculous. Do you know that? I've seen you express emotions."

"Because I killed the rage after I–I—"

My wrists still burn so bad it makes it hard to speak clearly.

"After you what?"

I tightly shut my eyelids and bite my lip, exactly where Sunney had already bitten it. For some reason, by voiding out the pain in my wrists, I can open my mouth to speak — to speak the truth.

"After — I killed Tom."

Sunney chuckles and says, "Wow, big shocker!"

"No — I killed — I killed Tom."

"I don't understand."

"It wasn't in self-defense, not really."

"Are you high?"

"I have — dissociative identity disorder. I was diagnosed with it at a young age after my first murder. I caught my mom fucking another man, and thinking he was hurting her, I stabbed him. He knocked me against this old wooden dresser, and I think that's when it really started. I became a menace of a child one moment, and then the other, I would be an angel."

Sunney's silence makes me push on with the truth.

"I didn't have an affair with Mr. Nortec. Not really. We had sex once, and I became obsessed. He didn't want to do it again, so I stalked him incessantly, following him and waiting for him in the school parking lot or at his house at night. He didn't want me and felt immoral for doing it in the first place. It was easy for me to manipulate anyone back then — but I couldn't coax him into loving me. That made me feel so rejected. I decided to get back at him. The day I knew my mother would go into my room to pick up clothes for laundry day, I left my diary with imaginary entries about Mr. Nortec and me purposely on my bed. I knew she would snoop into it, considering my recent behavior and habit of sneaking out. To add insurance, I snuck into his house and took a naked picture of myself, placing some of the photos in his bedroom and his desk at school. Everything went through to plan. He went to jail, but got bailed out. Before his trial, I went to his house one last time. I convinced him he was a very sick man who would go to prison and be raped due to sleeping with an underage girl and killing himself would be the easiest way out. I left, and he hung himself. For the first time in a long time, I felt such intense pleasure — the most euphoric feeling I'd ever felt. Then my mom started to catch onto me—"

"Hold the fuck up!" Sunney yells, halting my story. "Why — why didn't you tell me any of this? The accident when you were a kid?"

"A perk of the disorder. I forgot my trauma, but my trauma didn't forget me."

"So, you just kept everything about your life hidden from me?"

"I acted as though none of it was real. For you, I became a whole other person. I called her the new and improved me. The one good enough for Sunney Jameson. The New Toni."

When it's silent once again, I continue, thinking deep into the mush that comprises my old memories.

"Anyway, my mom demanded that I tell her what had really happened with Mr. Nortec. I decided to get back at her for cheating on my dad so many times. I threatened her that if she told anyone, I would tell my father about the so-called burglar from all those years ago. She agreed, but being evil incarnate, I decided to tell my dad anyway. He was the only person I loved in the world. He deserved to know. I didn't think he would even believe me, but thankfully once the whole story was out, how her infidelity had caused my erratic behavior made sense to him. She filed for divorce. I was sad — yeah, but I still had my dad. Until I didn't. He felt guilty for the whole ordeal. I felt guilty for being the sole reason everything had happened the way it did. I had stupidly told him the real story about Mr. Nortec and blackmailing my mom. I just wanted him to know it wasn't his fault. I wanted to bear all the guilt for him, and instead, karma reared its big head through my window. He killed himself, and I lost the only person I loved. My mom ended up drinking herself to death."

Recounting the past causes me more pain than from the burns. I wince. I must stop for a couple of moments. Sunney seems so into my story he doesn't even notice.

"You didn't feel a shred of guilt for any of that?" he asks.

"I did feel guilt — for my dad. With Mr. Nortec, I had fooled myself into believing that he was a very bad man and deserved it. As for my mom, I blamed her for how we were so similar. I hated her for giving me the crazy.

"Then — then Tom came along. I wanted him to be like my father, and when that didn't come to fruition, the evil in me awoke. I had never treated someone as well as I did Tom the first six months we dated. He was an ex-convict. He had spent time in prison for dealing heroin. Despite all that, he was among the kindest, warmest human beings I'd ever met. I wanted him to love me as much as my dad had loved my mom. I did everything I could to make him fall in love with me. Bought him gifts, played innocent, and let him move in with me. It was an ideal relationship for a long time until it wasn't. I took it out on him when he wasn't living up to the imaginary man I thought I deserved. I beat him up repeatedly. Whenever he tried to leave, I would warn him that I would contact his patrol officer and tell him that he had been using again. But the only reason he had been using it in the first place was to escape me. Everything was working out in my favor until I cheated on Tom, and that — that was the nail in the coffin. You remember that first night we met at the bar when that random man attacked me?"

Sunney nods, looking utterly flabbergasted. I still can't tell if he believes everything I'm saying or not. Either way, he's letting me talk.

"That man was telling the truth. I think Tom had confided in him about our toxic relationship several times."

"So, Tom finally snapped and tried beating you to death?"

"Not exactly."

"What do you mean 'not exactly'?"

"As I said, I killed him, but not in the way you think."

As the sound of silence drags on for a minute, I look at the crumbling dirt of the hole I'm in, except it isn't dirt I'm seeing. It's images from that night flashing in front of my eyes — the night I killed my second victim.

"It all started at dinner. I could tell something was off from the moment he walked in through the door. Once we started eating, it all went to shit."

CHAPTER 49

Before

Why is he always so fucking late?

This is the third time this month that Tom isn't here when he said he would be. He must be hitting the needle again, that junkie trash. It would be too over the top to think he might be with another woman. No woman would want him besides me. Still, my mind races and what I had originally planned was being turned to dust by Tom's tardiness.

I look down at the partially chopped-up onion and mushrooms and sigh. I have chopped them up like shit. Drinking and cooking don't mesh well, I realize.

Things between us have seemed strained and off lately. So, I'm cooking steak along with all the fixings to show him I still love him for all his flaws. I'm cooking dinner for someone other than myself for the first night in a long time. I work all day long, so I don't think I should have to cook for my junkie of a boyfriend. If he's hungry, he can cook for himself.

I finish chopping up the veggies and tossing them on the burner. Dark thoughts permeate my mind as I watch them sizzle in the pan, of making Tom pay for continuously being late. It's uncaring of him to make me wait when he knows I worry about him. I put a roof over his head and food on the table when he needed it. Sometimes I hurt him, but it's all a misunderstanding, and I'm not even that strong. Sometimes people do crazy things when they love someone.

This is what I get for thinking things could be different. I should have never thought things would get better. They don't.

Stop.

There's always that voice in my head, urging me to stop thinking the worst of any situation — to stop overreacting and feeling compelled to shift all my pain to the one I love the most. That voice convinces me that, even after years of suspicions, I'm not a sociopath. A part of me cares about a few people. I just have a darkness in me that makes it difficult for me to express my emotions.

Are you familiar with how a psychopath acts? Exactly like you do.

I hit myself on the head for such an absurd thought.

"Fuck off, won't you?" I ask.

You need help.

Sometimes I despise this inner voice that tells me to be and do better. I'm a good person.

If Tom had been here on fucking time, I wouldn't be stuck here, having to deal with my consciousness. This is another reason he needs to pay — inexplicably inflicting emotional pain on me. Hopefully, if I do have to strike him again, he'll strike back, making him feel guilty enough to stay.

I clear my thoughts and focus on dinner. Once the veggies are soft, I add the T-bone steaks to the griddle. I look at the time on the oven when I have finished cooking everything. It's 6:25. He's twenty minutes late now.

Our front door opens just as I start serving the dishes on our turquoise green dinner plates. Hearing that familiar sigh and slow walk into the apartment is like music to my ears. I tremble with anticipation as I listen to him unlace and remove his black boots.

Once he walks through the archway leading into our tiny kitchen, I can immediately tell something is amiss. His usual naturally pink cheeks are pale white, and he looks even more terrified of me than usual. He must be scared for being late again. His hair looks greasy and unwashed, and he's still wearing the clothing he has been wearing three days in a row. Referring to him as a disgusting human being is one of my most used insults, and this is exactly why.

He looks up at me, dark circles around his eyes. They look tired and more defeated than usual. I almost pity him at this point, but he hasn't even given me any excuse for his absence.

"Hey," he quietly says before walking to our tiny old wooden table and taking a seat.

"Glad you decided to show up. I made steak — your favorite," I say calmly, taking his plate and approaching him.

His eyes bulge from shock, but in a monotone voice, he replies, "Thank you."

I venture to grab my plate next, sitting next to him. I want to understand what is going on in that head of his. I have neither had an outburst in over a week nor hit him in two. He couldn't still be mad because he had hit me back, right? His abusive streak is infrequent but it does show up from time to time. I almost liked it, in a sense. It gave me more power than he thought, especially when he left marks. It gave me an opportunity to blackmail him in case he decided to leave me.

You can only manipulate someone for so long.

Now that voice is here when Tom is around. That's just as strange as his behavior. My intuition must be trying to tell me something. Did he know about — *oh shit!*

I did something atrocious a couple of nights ago. While out with one of my alcoholic friends, we had met a group of guys. Douchebags mostly, but one was decently attractive and kept buying me drinks. I didn't even ask for his name, nor did he ask mine. He just kept calling me "blue eyes". It felt nice to be complimented, as Tom rarely did anymore. That sweet name, along with all the free drinks, convinced me to fuck him in the back alley. I swear no one had seen us, but my friend kept insisting that one of Tom's friends had been at the bar all night, watching us.

I could always just say we were old friends. I had ensured not to touch or smile too much at him in the bar. At least that's what I remember, as I was trashed beyond belief and had popped a couple of Benzos so I couldn't make the greatest narrator for the night. Whether to lie my way out or tell the truth is the question now.

It's more like asking yourself if you want to be a piece of shit or be honest for once in your life.

This voice makes me want — no, *need* a shot. I stand, and even though I know Tom will roll his eyes, I walk over to our fridge and pull out a nearly empty bottle of our nearby liquor store's cheapest whiskey. I prefer Crown Royal, but I have had to improvise due to a tight budget (and already going through five bottles this month). I pour half a glass of whiskey for Tom, whose eyes are currently on me, but he doesn't chastise me. I pour another in my glass along with expired Coke.

"I have a headache," I say before he even speaks, taking a sip of my drink and returning to the table.

We sit in silence, eating for a while. I favor my drink over food, whereas Tom seems to be racing to finish his meal.

He wants to get away from you as soon as possible.

"Fuck off!" I mumble through my glass, which is nearly empty.

"What?" Tom asks, looking up from his plate.

"I just said I'm thirsty."

I get up and make another drink, this time with more whiskey.

Thankfully, the cheap liquor hits me fast. Soon enough, I'll be able to ask what is bothering Tom — or if he knows about my cheating.

"Is — is everything like — alright?"

This is when I notice Tom's hand, with which he holds his fork, shaking.

"No, it's just been a long day. Did a lot of thinking."

I take a sip of my drink while my brain buzzes on what thinking he could have possibly been doing. I want to say something snarky and mean, like "Thinking? Wow, that's a first!" But I stop myself, because I want to be as nice as possible for the first time in a long time.

"As long as you're okay."

Please let this be the end of it, God. Please. I promise I'll be better, I pray to myself over and over.

Being better would be to let him go.

As quickly as possible, I grab my drink and press it to my mouth, almost spilling it on my face.

Life without Tom is unimaginable. It makes me nearly tear up just thinking about it.

"Toni, I'm not okay. I haven't been okay in a long time," Tom says, setting his fork and steak knife down, his forehead dotted with a few beads of sweat.

I set my glass down and the drink flings out on to the kitchen tablecloth, soaking it. This is a stain I will never get out. I want to yell at Tom, asking why he would say something so abrupt like that to cause me to ruin our cloth.

"Can you explain?"

"Can I explain?" Tom asks, looking insulted that I don't know exactly what he's talking about.

"Yes," I say, gritting my teeth.

Tom looks from side to side before taking a deep breath.

"You know he saw you, right?"

He? I gulp. *I have to be calm.*

"Who saw me?"

Once again looking insulted, Tom replies, "Jason. My friend Jason saw you the other night. At the Keelover."

"When we were there last?"

"No, goddamnit! You know what I'm talking about, Toni."

Fucking Jason. A pathetic drunk who can't mind his own damn business.

"I don't recall. I was drunk, and when I'm drunk, I don't act like myself."

"Cut the shit, Toni. You are always drunk."

"I'm not always drunk. I drink when you stress me out like this," I say, gripping my glass to take the last sip.

"Do you also fuck random men in the back of bars?"

I feel like I just got hit in the gut. *He knows.*

"I don't — I don't know what Jason said—"

Tom stands up and, raising his hands in the air, shouts, "Don't lie to me!"

"Okay, okay, I fucked someone else," I say, standing up as well, my whole body shaking. "It meant nothing, I promise. I was drunk, and he was being nice, complimenting me. You never do that anymore," I say, approaching Tom with my hands extended to touch his cheeks, like we always do after we fight.

Tom flinches away from my grasp, taking a step back. It's not the first time he's receded from me.

"That's not an excuse."

"I know it's not."

"It's not just that, Toni. You are toxic."

I feel betrayed being called that word. I lower my outreached hands, rescinding my loving gesture.

"You're toxic too. Don't play innocent."

"I'm innocent compared to all the times you've been emotionally and physically abusive."

Before I can counter that argument, Tom throws his hands up in the air and adds, "I don't even know why I'm standing here arguing with you. No matter what I say, you will never take accountability for your actions."

"That's what couples do, babe. They fight."

Tom seems ill from being called "babe". I can see him attempting to steady his trembling hands by putting them over his hips. I wonder if he's trying to stop himself from striking me. I wish he would just get it over with so he can feel guilty and forgive me.

"I can't do this anymore, Toni."

Now the liquor in my system hits me like a blow to the stomach. I want to grab Tom's face, kiss him, and tell him to stop being ridiculous. If he stays with me, I'll change.

Working that manipulation tactic till the last beating minute, I see.

"Let's go on a trip!" I exclaim, using my fake happy sounding voice.

Tom scrunches his face and presses his lips tightly together. "What?"

"A trip. We can leave town for a few days."

I don't have the money for a trip, but I can work something out. Ask a friend to lend me some money or get a credit card.

"Do you honestly think that's going to fix everything?"

"I want to work for this — for us. I know what I did was wrong. See? There's me admitting I'm in the wrong," I say, reaching over to grab Tom's hand, and for a moment, the way he makes eye contact with me for more than a couple of seconds makes me believe I have successfully convinced him to stay.

"You'll say anything to make me stay."

Now I'm getting desperate. Time to go with Ole Reliable.

"It's just what happened when I was younger, you know? I'm messed up in the head."

"You can't use that bullshit excuse your whole life, Toni. Just because you had a tough childhood doesn't give you the right to beat up your boyfriend and cheat on him. I hope you get help; I really do," Tom says, removing his hand from mine.

I realize he is done in a crippling moment of silence. He's done with me. In other words — he's rejecting me. After this conversation, he'll pack his belongings and tell all his friends. If Tom and I have one thing in common, it's that they all drink heavily. They all see each other at the bar. That means my friends will also know about our break-up sooner than later.

"I didn't want to say anything, but I met someone else. I don't know if anyone will believe me, but I will tell my side of the story."

My face radiates anger now. I can't manipulate this man anymore. It reminds me of losing control over Mr. Nortec. As I aged and became an adult, I had thought all that anger had merely been my hormones, but once again, as a nearly twenty-three-year-old, I feel that burst of rage course through my veins.

I look down at the steak knife Tom had been using and contemplate how easy it would be to get away with murder. Not easy, obviously, but would it be impossible? Women don't kill as often as men; I can say it was self-defense.

Knowing me better than myself, Tom notices my eyes on his steak knife the moment I look at it. As I venture to grab it, he slaps it off the table. Before it can land on the floor, I plunge to the ground, trying to get it. I make it down on my knees to pick the knife up, but as I do, Tom punches me square in the face. He's retaliated by hitting me several times before, but nothing with this much force. I put my hands to my nose, which is now gushing blood.

Still on my knees and more furious than ever, I realize what a vantage point this is. I punch him in the balls. This is my first time hitting him there. I feel victorious until his hands are over my throat, forcing me to lie on my back.

"Why can't you just let me go?" he screams at me, heavy amounts of his saliva spraying on my bloody face.

I latch my hands to his wrists, using all my strength to release his hands from my throat.

Seeing my struggle, Tom stops choking me and begins punching me instead. He must be venting all those years of pent-up anger. The hits hurt but offer me a chance to save my own life. I didn't want to die — not yet anyway. I couldn't face my mom and dad if I did.

"Tom, stop!" I beg as he continues to strike me.

I beg more and more, but it's just a scheme to distract him. He believes I'm as helpless as ever. He's getting off on it, I can tell.

I stretch my hands out for that steak knife, hoping it's nearby. Tom stops striking me and starts choking me once again, still unaware of my truant left hand searching for the knife. My vision starts to blur, nearly going black, before I feel the knife handle.

CHAPTER 50

Before

I stab the knife into Tom's side with no hesitation, just a pure rush of adrenaline. The cheap and dull blade only goes halfway into his abdomen, but it must hurt enough that he ceases to choke me. Pushing his body off mine, I get up as quickly as my dizzy mind allows. I only make it a few steps before falling back to the ground due to an overpowering weakness.

Behind me, I see Tom in a fetal position, groaning while placing both hands over where he'd been stabbed. I crawl to the kitchen and use the counter to hoist myself up. I find the sharpest knife we own in the sink. There's no going back now.

Call the police and tell them everything.

"Oh, look who decided to show up right after I almost got choked to death," I whisper.

If I call the police, I'll be arrested for attempted murder. However, thinking back to all the events that just transpired, wouldn't it be hard for them to discover the truth? Tom had technically attacked me first. I went for the knife but didn't even get a chance to touch it before he punched me. With only one set of lips to tell the story, it would be much easier to turn the tables on Tom as the bad guy. I mean, here I am with a bloodied-up face and a bruised throat.

You are insane.

"That's the difference between you and me. I'm insane but not stupid."

Tom looks up to see me standing nearby. He lifts his palm in surrender after seeing the knife in my hand.

"Toni, stop. Please stop. Don't do this!" he begs.

I hesitate momentarily before realizing I had just begged him the same, and he had not shown me mercy. I look at his handsome but petrified face. It's like seeing death again for the first time since Mr. Nortec, moments before I had left his house that night.

"I have to. You broke my heart, Tom," I say, a small smile appearing on my face.

I know it's now or never. I lunge toward him, sticking the knife directly into his stomach. Now I am on top of him. I'm in charge here. I don't punch or strike him. Instead, my mind goes blank, and all I see is red. All I see is him with that other woman, him going behind my back, and finally, him trying to leave me.

I don't recall how many times I stab him before realizing he is dead. Once I am done, his blood covers my face and runs down my thin white t-shirt. I slowly stand up, dropping the knife to the floor. *Shit!* That might have been an overreaction.

I begin hyperventilating and walking back and forth, imagining myself getting imprisoned for this. I'm unsure if Tom had physically abused me enough to justify doing this. I must inflict more damage on myself — self-inflicted damage. I must make it look like he attacked me so crazily I had a total freak out, killing him to protect myself.

I could stab myself, but I doubt I have the wits to do that. I look at our cheap wooden table. Sitting nearby, unbothered, is Tom's empty turquoise plate. I could hit my face against the plate and table, breaking it and hopefully my nose.

Why would he do that, though? I would need a backup story of why he tried to kill me. I was leaving him. That's it. He has a bad history, and mine is nearly sparkling clear. I could say I discovered he was dealing heroin again and tried ending things, so he attempted to beat me to death. It seems probable that an ex-convict would kill his girlfriend.

I stand in front of the table, preparing myself to do this. I attempt smashing my face into the plate three or four times, stopping mid-way, unable to do it every time. I imagine prison and how horrible it will be if I don't convince the police without a doubt that I am innocent.

Finally, with all my might, I take one deep breath and crack my face into the plate, this time shattering it. It hurts worse than the punches and choking. I fall to my knees, grabbing my bleeding, crooked nose. It feels broken.

I want to pass out from all the blood and pain, but I know it's in my best interest to call the police, sounding as afraid as possible. I grab my Nokia, turn it on, and press the 9 and 1 keys.

Stop.

What could she want now?

"I have to call the police," I say.

Do you think they are going to believe you?

"What am I supposed to do?"

If you want to get out of this and start anew, I can help you.

"How? Please, I'll do anything."

You need to let me in completely.

That sounds horrible. She may have a point, though. I have screwed so much up in my life. The real me is a psychopath capable of committing murder multiple times. I should've listened to her all these years.

I'll call her the New and Improved Toni. New Toni, for short. She'll be kindhearted and innocent. Well, sort of innocent. She still needs to drink to deal with all the pain she's endured. Her parents are dead, and her boyfriend abused her before trying to kill her. At first, the police may be suspicious, like they should be, but she will play it off. She'll tell a heart-wrenching story about being groomed as a teenager and her parents both dying within a year of each other.

Unsure what to do, my mind continues racing with thoughts from Old and New Toni. I walk to the bedroom. Our cheap, navy-blue colored comforter and sheets are still messy from this morning when I got out of bed. I need to start making my bed every morning. I do just that, and like an old memory from my childhood, it calms my racing mind. New Toni will be cleaner and make her bed every morning.

After making my bed, I walk to a circular smudged-up mirror by the front door. I momentarily stare at my crazed face before beginning to fake cry while looking at myself in the mirror. "He-he t-tried to kill me, and I had no choice. I-I—" I whine, stopping halfway through to pinch one of my arms.

It's not convincing enough.

I trail back into the kitchen to stare at Tom again. I force myself to let out real tears, remembering how scared I felt when he was choking me. I go back to the mirror, ready to attempt this again.

"I-I was just so scared. His hands were around my throat — I begged him to stop. I thought I was going to die." I burst into more tears while gauging whether it would look real to the police.

Be a beaten girlfriend void of all anger and killing tendencies. Wipe those memories.

I cry a few more times in the mirror, each with a different fit. I should go with more frazzled and terrified, like how the women were in those lifetime movies after killing their abusive husbands.

I only wanted the best for him. I chant to myself after calling the police in the biggest snot-nosed crying fit possible.

Only five minutes pass before the police flood into the apartment. By then, I am seated on the couch with my arms wrapped around my legs with a blank expression, staring at the dead body of Tom.

As the cops escort me from the apartment to the police station, I look at my ex-boyfriend's corpse again. *Why did he do this to me* — the woman who loved him so unconditionally? Exiting the apartment, I also say goodbye to the Old Toni. If I want to get out of this as a victim, it's what I must do. It's time to get a fresh new start.

CHAPTER 51

As I finish narrating the truth of what had happened that night, finally coming to terms with what I had done, I know I have reversed from New Toni back to Old Toni. I had promised never to retreat from being her, but if I am to die, I want to die as the true me. My body feels numb.

I don't even feel anger towards Sunney anymore. He and I are the same. Both horrible, horrendous psychopaths. During this ordeal, I have tried convincing myself he is the bad guy. We have both been in love with two people who made us feel rejected. We've both resorted to murder for that rejection.

No one is the good guy. Not Sunney, not Heather, Adler, or even Quinn. Especially not me. As a little girl, I had loved all the heroes on TV, the protagonists who fought to stay alive. I even convinced myself I was like one of those bruised-up women in the movies. I longed to be like these main characters who did everything with the best intentions of others and were free of all guilt. I wanted to be them, but it just wasn't me. I'm not the good guy. I have an evil heart and a vile mind. I deserve to die.

A few minutes pass before Sunney finally asks, "So the police just bought your story?"

"Mostly, but I was asked to undergo a polygraph test, answering questions about that night and our relationship."

Seemingly unconvinced, Sunney asks, "You killed him. How did you pass the test?"

"I passed every question. I fully believed that he had been the abusive one in the relationship. Passing the test was easy."

Sunney drops the shovel to the ground and goes down on his knees. He stares at me dead in the eyes before placing his hands over his face. At first I think he is upset, possibly crying, until he starts cackling.

"How the fuck did I not realize this?" he asks through his laughter.

I look away, already knowing the answer. Manipulation is key. Old Toni doesn't believe in kindness. She believes it is a cutthroat world, and you have to be as tough as nails to get what you want. New Toni thinks the complete opposite.

"I became a better version of myself, capable of getting away with murder. One capable of getting you to fall in love with me."

"Did you ever even love me, or was it just a ruse to live a normal, somewhat extravagant life?"

Now there's a question I don't immediately know the answer to. It's safe to say New Toni has never been the real me, so does Old Toni love Sunney? She has been gone most of the relationship, so it is hard to know the answer to this question. I don't feel like lying anymore, not to Sunney or myself. My whole life had been based on lies, Old and New Toni alike.

I take a deep breath and reply, "No. But I think I could love the version of you I know now."

"The Real Sunney, you say?"

"Yes, the one who loves sick things. The one who, like me, hates rejection and leverages master manipulation to get what they want."

"Wait–wait–wait. Everything you discovered last night, you liked it?"

"New Toni was disgusted and repulsed, but me . . ."

I trail off, feeling sick at what I was about to say. I want to say what he did is not repulsive. Someone cheating on you and embarrassing you cannot be forgiven. Andrea deserved death. But she had done the same thing as me. *What a fucking hypocrite I am!*

"Sunney, I want you to kill me."

"What?"

"Bury me or shoot me dead. I don't care. You can chop my head off with that shovel if you want."

"Are you trying to fuck with me right now?"

"No, you did the same thing I would've done. If I feel rejected, I lose control. I can't handle it. If the person I married cheated on me with some fucking nobody, I would've chopped his fucking head off. I convinced Mr. Nortec to kill himself. I killed Tom when he said he had found someone else. I understand your anger, Sunney. I don't deserve you."

I look up at Sunney, and he looks down at me with longing for the first time since this all happened. It's not longing to cut my throat or choke me to death but longing to feel me. Although his face is bloodshot and exhausted, I still see a little of that glimmer from our wedding ceremony. It makes me imagine what could've been if I hadn't fucked it all up. We could've lived happily ever after for the rest of our lives. We could've had children — children with fucked-up problems, but still children that look like us.

"I cheated on you too, babe. I did you wrong."

"With whom?"

"You know. Heather."

"You said we were over by that point."

"But I was still married. I broke my own rule. I just wanted to make you angry; hurt you for hurting me. It meant nothing; I would've found a way to whack her as soon as she killed you."

I didn't think he had been planning on killing her, but I knew there was no way in hell he would've stayed with her in the long term.

"What? Didn't you want to date the stripper?" I sarcastically tease him.

Sunney chuckles and retorts, "What can I say? I wanted to piss you off one last time, and it worked."

"Yeah, I choked her out with her panties."

"That was incredible! You make it hard to be mad at you sometimes."

A couple of moments pass with both of us chuckling before he asks, "Did you do that for survival or — because she had sex with me?"

"A bit of both."

"I was going to save it in my mind for the spank bank."

"Gross!" I say, laughing.

"You're pretty gross, too, you know?"

"Physically or metaphorically?"

"Well, I mean, you are covered in dirt and blood right now. But, other than that, I'd say metaphorically. I've heard you're one sick fuck, no offense."

"None taken."

"We all are; every single one of us."

"In the world?" I ask.

"No, last night. Me, you, Heather, Adler, and Quinn. All of us."

"I've been trying to convince myself I'm a good person for a long time. I think they were too. We all do. We all spend our lives not taking the blame, thinking we are immune to the bad things we do and asking God for forgiveness. It's all just one pathetic, sad circle of lies, except you, Sunney. Sure, you hide what you do but you never apologize for being sick and deranged. In the end, you are the most real of us all, and I think that's why you'll be the lone survivor."

"I wish it didn't have to be this way, Toni. I loved — I still do love you."

"Why did you ask me to marry you? You could've married any other richer, better-off woman. Was it just because I had killed someone previously? Be honest. I deserve that."

"I mean, at first, yeah, I did like that about you, but that only interested me enough to want to fuck you. Then, as we spent more time together, and I couldn't put my finger on it, but there was something so dark, so mysterious about you that I found myself being constantly drawn to you. Now I know why. You're like me."

Sunney, deep down, wanted more than just to fuck the girl who's killed someone. I was the only person he thought he could ever connect with. Perhaps he thinks I'll be the last person with whom he will ever be able to share his feelings, which may hinder him from killing me.

I remember how, when we had started officially dating, he would slowly and nonchalantly ask about Tom. He asked about the details of our relationship and how I had felt about murdering him. At the time, I had thought he was sympathetic toward me, but now I know my words were fueling his sick mind. He wanted to paint a picture, but New Toni only fed him lies. She wasn't a killer. She was innocent and did what she had to do to survive. She thought she had no other choice but to kill him. Her identity and the story of the night had been fictitious this whole time. I had had so many chances to run out that door or call the police after stabbing him the first time, but I didn't.

"So Old Toni — is she back now?"

"Yeah, I had only negated her existence to get out of the murder of Tom and make you fall in love with me."

"She's been inside of you since long before that, right?"

"Yeah. I ignored her for a long time until I couldn't anymore."

"I'm glad you're back now."

"No, you aren't. I'm not the real one you fell in love with."

"I can love the real you even more. No one can understand you like me. Just think about it. Your idea from earlier can work. You can teach me how to kill without remorse."

Before killing Tom, I had spent a lot of time imagining what it would be like to watch life leave a person by my hands, but at the time, I had thought those were normal intrusive thoughts that everyone universally had. The act of doing it had made my skin crawl. Getting caught is usually inevitable. I don't want to go to prison. Even if Sunney does spare my life, I don't know how we'll get away with what happened last night.

"How will we even explain all that's happened? Quinn would be easy. He was already in hiding, but Adler's a cop, and people will come looking for him. Heather too."

"Quinn killed his wife and made his friend take the blame. We can say he became obsessed with you, used Heather to attempt to kill us, and they took out Adler together when he tried to arrest them. Heather was able to escape, but we took out Quinn. The knife you used to kill him has your fingerprints all over it."

My body feels so prepared for death that I don't even know if I want to explore this version of the future with Sunney. I had already made my peace with all the horrible things I'd done. Going through all that sounds exhausting, especially if there's a chance that we both might end up in prison. Sunney can easily throw me under the bus, or I can do the same to him. The plan still sounds utterly exhausting.

"I don't know, Sunney. You should just kill me. I'm sure your idea was more foolproof. You can commit murder on your own, I promise."

Sunney extends his hand toward me, pressing his fingers into the dirt.

"I don't want to be alone. I don't want anyone else. I want you. I can forgive you for your actions since you have shared your biggest secret with me now."

I want to believe it would be easy for him to forgive me, but cheating is a lasting hateful memory. You don't just forget and forgive in such situations.

"Would it be that easy for you?"

"Normal couples do it all the time."

Cute. I feel my eyes staring at his still outstretched hand, craving it in mine. Almost enough to give in to him, allowing me to live. So many lives can be saved if I die today. If he lets me out, I — we — will kill again. If I die, he may be unable to kill again. Alternately, this will give him the impetus to commit more murders, and without me keeping an eye on him, more humans will die. He could be the next-generation Bundy.

"We are the farthest thing from a normal couple."

"That's why we're so special. That doesn't mean we can't forgive each other. I can forgive you for cheating if you forgive me for putting you through hell."

That's a factor I hadn't put into perspective yet — all the hell this man has put me through. Normal people would consider all the shit I went through far worse than cheating. However, it does work in the same way in Sunney's and my mind. Cheating is an absolute sin.

"The two are equal?"

"Are they?"

"In our minds, yeah. Cheating practically justifies any punishment."

"Well, then, there you go. What do you say? Truce?"

Here we are at last. Sunney is the one trying to talk me into surviving when, these past two days, I've been solely trying to survive him. Funny how shit can turn out. I'm still unsure it is the right thing. Suppose more people die or live on account of this one decision? Do I even give a shit about the people Sunney will kill when it's evident?

"Do you think narcissists are even capable of loving another human being?"

"Are you saying I'm a narcissist?" Sunney asks.

"I'm saying I'm—" I trail off, then deciding to be honest, finish, "We're both narcissists."

"If it weren't completely true, my feelings would be hurt. However, I don't think you're a narcissist."

"You don't?"

"Tell me what you think a narcissist is?"

I want to answer, but I didn't know the exact definition. People throw around that word a lot. Those who had dated narcissists or were bad people tossed the blame on someone else (in my case). There were a lot of traits that could make up a narcissist. I had always thought the lack of empathy and the tendency of being a liar were the main ones.

"Someone who lies and lacks empathy," I finally answer.

"That's a part of what it is, but there's so much more to it. It's more than you are. They think highly of themselves. They think they have the utmost importance. They seek out attention everywhere they go. That's a small gist of it."

He's just described himself, I realize.

As if reading my thoughts, Sunney chuckles and says, "That's how I am. Not you."

That's accurate. I'd never really sought out attention or looked down on others.

"Can a full-on narcissist and a half-narcissist even be capable of love?"

"I may lack empathy and I don't give a shit about people who are in pain or dying, but you are my exception. I can't explain it, but we were meant to be together. Think about tonight and all that's happened. Everything happened for a reason. You survived everything for a reason. You told me the truth for a reason. You decided to retire this fake version of yourself for a reason."

"And that reason is?"

"We can be together, for real this time, with our true selves right out in the open."

"I once read a poem a long time ago. I thought it was cute at that time, but I didn't fully comprehend its meaning until now. Tell me every terrible thing you have ever done and let me love you anyway. Not many people reveal their secrets, except us, even to those with whom they are closest. We both know every terrible thing we've done. With that in mind, I ask you this — considering everything you know about me, can you still love me?"

Sunney hesitates for a moment, taking in my words. Eventually, he whispers, "Can you?"

I take in a deep breath, unable to control myself from smiling. Doesn't everyone in this world want someone around whom they can be their true authentic selves?

"I want to. It's just — what if we get caught for this? Will you throw me under the bus to spare yourself?"

That sounds harsh, but Sunney, seemingly not offended by it, shakes his head.

"I have connections. We can get out of this easily. I have over five hundred grand stashed in the cabin."

"They'll come looking for Adler soon."

"He's not expected to come into work for another two days. We'll figure this out."

I gulp, nodding. I'll have to accept that answer for the time being.

"Let me untie you, please. I love you; I love all of you."

My eyes dart to Sunney's fingers, which dig into the dirt. I want those fingers laced with mine. I want his dirty hand in my dirty hand. I want his fingers around my throat, not trying to kill me but gently throttling me. I want his fingers inside me, specifically his index and middle finger. I feel my body quiver like the first time we had made love in the cabin. We danced in his bedroom before he laid my body in bed, touching every inch. I want to have passionate sex with him in the dirt above Quinn's dead body. No more silly talking. We can sort everything out later. I want dirty sex with my sick, deranged, narcissistic, psychopathic husband.

"Come down here," I order Sunney, who jumps into the hole only seconds later.

I look up at this tall man standing directly in front of me. I want my hands free so I can unzip his pants and take him in my mouth. I normally don't yearn to do that, but now more than ever, I am down for anything and everything.

He kneels on the dirt, so we are face to face. He moves his face toward mine, and for a moment, I think he's going to kiss me. But instead, he moves his hands behind my back, grazing my waist. That touch alone, although against my clothing, makes my whole body tremble with pleasure. I feel the rope, which had been tightly fastened to my burned wrists just a few moments ago, release. It feels as though I've just been released from prison for the first time in years. I'm ready for a whole new world of freedom. I breathe heavily as if I have just run a marathon, and Sunney does the same. His breath smells of whiskey and I catch a whiff of body sweat as well. I want to lick it off his body and slide my tongue all over his whiskey-soaked mouth.

We stare at each other for a long time, the first time we've looked at each other with love instead of hate and longing to hold each other instead of trying to kill one another.

"I'm sorry I fucked him," I finally say.

"I know," he says, tucking a strand of my blood and dirt-ridden hair behind my ear.

"I want you," I say, basking in every second that I feel his hand on my bare skin.

"I know. Let me to bring you back to earth," he says, positioning himself to my side and placing one hand over my lower back and the other under my knees.

He lifts me into his arms, side-stepping across the hole's walls to lift me to the ground above the hole. It's so enthralling that, even after digging a hole in the ground, he can still lift me up so easily.

I peer around my surroundings at the cabin, only a mere eight yards away with the bushel of bushes and trees I'd thought I'd never see again. I realize that, if I wanted, I could make a run for it. I immediately dismiss it as a stupid thought. Sunney has so much more energy than me. It makes me feel sad that my survival instincts are still there. Sunney is ready to start over and let the past go. I should be grateful he's letting me live and forgiving me for the ultimate sin. Tom hadn't been so generous. Along with that thought, I also notice that running is still impossible as my feet haven't yet been untied. I imagine Sunney bending me over and leaving them on while taking me from behind. Yeah, no attempted escapes for me. I am far too horny.

Sunney pulls himself out of the hole to sit directly next to me. We both look at each other and, although cliché, I bite my lip, hoping to turn him on. It hurts from where he had bitten me earlier. I see his eyes wander down to my red wrists.

He looks confused momentarily, grabbing them to bring them closer to his eyes. I feel nervous, unsure if I should tell him how I had tried using Quinn's lighter to escape. However, on the downside, he could be agitated and toss me back in the hole.

"This from the fire?" he asks, kissing my wrists softly.

I gulp, preparing to lie, but ultimately decide otherwise. No more lying.

"Quinn had told me he kept a lucky lighter in his back pocket. While you were burying me, I tried to get loose with it."

"Was this some ploy to get more time while you told me about Tom?" he asks, mildly upset.

"No, no. It was before then. I couldn't get it, so I gave up."

"How do you endure that kind of pain so — effortlessly?"

"It hurt like hell, but at the time, I was trying anything I could to survive. When the lights went out, I realized maybe it was meant to be. I was meant to die. Old Toni came out and decided to let the truth out, at least."

"I'm glad you stopped," he says, continuing to kiss my wrists as if it would heal them.

"The truth does set you free," I say, faking a short laugh.

Sunney doesn't speak. Instead, he continues kissing my wrists and moving onward to my dirty arms. I get goosebumps immediately, my body continuing to quiver.

"I missed your body so much," he whispers.

"We had sex before all this."

"I had never felt angrier than when you hopped on to me. I wanted to choke you to death. It didn't count."

I don't blame him for this, as I'd just had sex with someone else not long before that, and he had watched the whole thing.

"Why'd you let me do that, then?"

"I was waiting to see if you'd admit the truth to me."

"And if I had?"

"I would've strangled you to death right then and there instead of concocting the plan to torture you to death. Let your death be quicker."

"Well, I'm glad I didn't do that then."

"It all happened for a reason."

We stare at each other for a couple of moments before his eyes wander from mine and down my body, which is still clad in my, now dirt-stained, wedding dress. Forgetting my ankles are still tied, he attempts to push my legs apart. We both laugh as he pulls a black pocketknife from his back pocket. He carefully grabs my legs and cuts into the rope before tossing the knife on the ground nearby. He tries to open my legs again, but feeling chilly, I stop him.

"Let's go upstairs," I urge.

"But I want you right now."

"In the dirt?"

"Yeah, there won't be another time like this."

He's right. There wouldn't, and I've been turned on for a while now. Maybe the goosebumps on my arms are more from being turned on, and not the chilly wind. I smile, opening my legs, getting an instant chill and knowing it'll be colder once my panties are off, but once Sunney enters me, it'll be warm again.

Sunney kisses my legs, slowly moving up. As he does so, my mind goes elsewhere. I remember when we first got here, the last time we had passionate sex, and the way he had touched me. It had felt like such real love then. I remember *Sea of Love* playing as he had pleasured me long before I had started on him. I remember all the times again. No matter how often we did it, it felt as special as the first time. Oh, how I yearned to have him every night! I never get bored of this man. I was a fool to have sex with another man when I had Sunney all to myself.

Soon Sunney is removing my panties. Tossing them aside, his mouth is soon on me. I gasp when his warm tongue touches my cold body. I soon begin imagining more of our special moments and the times when we made love. I remember the way he looked at me the first night we met. That morning I had touched myself, imagining his handsome, perfect-looking face on top of mine. All I wanted was to make him fall in love with me. Be done with all the pain from the past and stop being the one bringing pain into others' lives.

I remember his dark eyes looking into me as he held me tight our wedding night, barely ever an arm's length away. I wish I could go back to that moment. Get a do-over. It had felt like such an innocent, pure love. We both knew nothing of our sins. We were just a normal, deeply-in-love couple.

I could still be that person — after all this. I've already said that so many times — with Tom and now Sunney, but this time, I really could. This could finally be my life-altering moment. After surviving this, I could start afresh with a new view of life. Except there's one problem with that. We wouldn't be a normal couple. Sunney wanted me to help him murder people. He could hold it in while we adjusted to what we've been through, but it would be only a matter of time before he was ready to ravage other women with my help. We'd be the new Paul and Karla Bernardo.

I still feel pleasure from Sunney, nearly on the verge of coming. All the while, I still feel unsure about this whole murder partner dilemma. I love this man, but so did Karla. What if Sunney eventually got sick of me? Started abusing me, eventually killing me off too. I mean, that would happen if I rejected him right now anyway. This way would buy me some time at least.

As I feel my insides about to blow and every good feeling I've ever felt is about to erode from my body, a sight I hadn't expected to see comes to mind. It's not Sunney and his dark eyes staring at me but Quinn's green ones. They glisten in the sun like when we had met that second time I had been out running. There had been so much connection right away between us. I wonder what he would think of me doing this. He'd probably be ashamed.

We hadn't gotten a lot of time together. Not near as much as we deserved. I barely knew a thing about him. Yet I felt we could have had a happy future together. He had some past wrongdoings, as had I. We were both imperfect, but he wasn't a killer or a pervert. He had patiently listened to all my bullshit problems and understood the inner core of how I was. I can't imagine I would have ever cheated on him.

I wonder if Sunney had just left me, would Quinn and I have ended up together? Lived a secluded life in the woods? Been happy with the small things? Popular opinion had people believing I am a gold digger, but I wouldn't hate having a simple, not materialistic life. Did Quinn give up saving himself to go back to save me just for me to bow down to Sunney in the end? I would never have a future with Quinn now. So why was my mind still on him?

I couldn't let his death go down in vain, even if a gut feeling in the pit of my stomach felt like it already had.

I move my hand around the dirt, as I almost start to orgasm. I feel Sunney's eyes looking up at me as I moan loudly. I grab hold of his sweaty blonde hair, pulling it hard. He centers his eyes back down on what he's doing, chuckling. I don't want to say goodbye to that beautiful head of hair or charming laugh. *Oh God, it's not too late.*

My hand touches something cold — steel and very small. I grip it, getting flashbacks from when I was a child. That dreadful red handle, the old blade just sitting on the counter. Me getting on my toes and lifting my little hand to grab it. Sweat poured down my face then and now. My mom had been moaning, afraid of the impending danger. I got a hold of that knife and took it to her abuser. Stabbing in and out of him. Seeing his blood on my hand and wanting to lick it off. Curious about the taste of it. The dresser was gone when I returned home from the hospital. The memory of why it had been taken away had been erased from my mind.

As I lift the steel in my hand, I finally reach orgasm. One of my hands still has a tight hold on Sunney's blonde head of hair, which I tighten even more. My body goes numb for a couple of moments as I shout. It feels like my first orgasm. Shivers run rapidly through my entire body. It's almost like I've been rebirthed.

I lift the pocketknife high just in time to hear Sunney mutter one last sentence.

"I love you."

CHAPTER 52

I bring the knife down straight into Sunney's beautiful face. Blood spurts everywhere. It stains his blonde hair and splatters all over my face, soaking onto my chest and dripping down my wedding dress. I gasp, lying on the ground, finally dropping the pocketknife.

Sunney's unconscious body, still spilling blood, falls against me. His once carefully caressing hands over my legs begin to pull as his body is half in the hole. His corpse attempts to pull me into where I was originally meant to die. Still in shock, I twist my body around, grabbing a nearby lawn chair. As the chair starts to tip, his body falls into the hole, freeing me.

I lay on my stomach momentarily, breathing heavily but not remotely out of breath. I dig my fingers in the dirt, feeling tears sting my eyes. I turn my head to the side to see the pocketknife I just used to stab my husband's most prized possession, his face. He's dead. It's — it's all done.

I sit and stare at the darkening sky, listening for sounds around me. Breathing, cop sirens that won't be there, Sunney pulling himself out of the hole, but there's nothing except the faint sound of birds chirping in the background. I am alone.

Finally, nearly half an hour later, I pick myself up. I stare down into the hole. I see Sunney's dead body face down.

Quinn is still laying down, his closed, pale face turned up to me. I killed my husband to avenge this stranger's death. I've said goodbye to this man nearly a dozen times since meeting him, but I know this will be the last time. I kneel as if to get closer so he'll hear my words.

"Thank you for giving me the will to leave. Thank you for — everything. I'll be seeing you, friend."

With one last look at his face, I stand up and walk back into the cabin. Once inside, I drink three glasses of water in a row. I then search the freezer, finding a bottle of Jack Sunney had drunk most of. I find a pair of my white sneakers and slip them on. I walk outside again to stand on the porch, lifting the glass bottle in the air.

"To quitting bad habits," I toast, taking a large gulp and chucking it as far as I can.

I watch as it lands in the dirt, breaking into a bunch of little glass shards.

CHAPTER 53

Just as I finish burying Sunney and Quinn's bodies, I want to head to the back of Sunney's truck to dump the shovel in it. Instead, I collapse on my knees above the bodies into the dirt. My entire being feels sorrow, not from all the physical pain I feel but from the pain I feel inside myself. Tears begin streaming from my eyes, and I bring my fists down into the dirt, screaming as loud as I can. I hear birds rustling in the trees, flying away from the noise.

I lay there for a few minutes, bawling my eyes out and mourning Sunney or Quinn. I'm not entirely sure. Perhaps both. Quinn because he was the only one who truly liked me for me and all the fucked-up things about me. Sunney because I was thinking of what could have been. He would have spared me and taken me back even though I had cheated on him. We could've lived together in a happy fucked harmony. But I had to kill him before he killed others. I could never trust him, and he could never truly trust me again. It's what had to happen.

I wipe my tears away and take slow breaths. After collecting myself, I grab the shovel and take it to Sunney's truck to dispose of later. If I weren't on the verge of exhaustion, I'd change the two flat tires. It will have to be a chore for later.

I have two days until Adler is due back into work. I can get a trail between me and this town by then. That won't be possible until I find Sunney's stash of cash he had mentioned leaving around the cabin.

I walk back to the cabin, and before I even make it to the stairs, I have already removed my dirty wedding dress. Since it has Sunney's blood all over it, I'll need to burn it. I need a shower before hunting down the stash.

I turn up the hot water in the shower till my body nearly burns, soaking it all in. I clean every inch of myself, watching the dirt and blood-colored water go down the drain. I then shampoo and condition my hair. Once done, I turn the cold water up, attempting to wake my body up, so I won't be tempted to pass out after this.

When I'm out of the shower, I go to the mirror, using a towel to wipe the fog. Looking at myself, I realize I need to change my appearance, so I won't be caught. I take hold of my black hair in my hand. I always wanted to be a blonde. A short-haired blonde. With a towel wrapped around my body, I retrieve a pair of kitchen scissors downstairs. Back upstairs, I cut it off until my hair grazes my shoulders. I feel brand-new already. Once out of Rubico, I'll find a store to purchase some hair dye. It should last me sometime if I can locate Sunney's cash. When that time comes, I don't know what I'll do then. Be on the run my whole life?

I change into blue jeans and a cashmere plum-colored sweater Sunney got me last Christmas. Before my search for the cash ensues, I grab my dirty wedding dress and take it outside into the woods. As I sit and watch it burn slowly, I feel nothing. No memories of the night I wore it, or all the happiness and love I felt. Maybe I'll never feel love again. Not like with Sunney.

Once back in the cabin, I search the bedroom first, tearing the room apart. Nothing. I go through all the closets and am still unsuccessful.

I break down again in tears, this time over the thought of being unable to find the cash. I grab a throw pillow on the couch to scream into. If I want to find this money, I'll have to think like Sunney. Being a lunatic like him, it should be easy. He's smart and no fool, so it won't be obvious. He'll have hidden it somewhere to retrieve in an emergency.

I look around the cabin walls to see if I missed any secret doors. I recheck the closets for the same thing. Everything is completely normal-looking. I go back to the bedroom to do the same. Nothing. I collapse onto the bed, knowing that if I don't find that money, I'll be screwed.

Sitting up, I look up at the dresser. On it is Sunney's black leather wallet. I have already looked through it, only finding a couple twenties, his credit cards, and other useless things. I even found a picture he had taken of me on a picnic, and the autumn sky had hit my hair perfectly. There's a click on my mind just then. What did Sunney value more than his money? Pictures of his conquests. The women he'd slept with and taken numerous photographs of, so he'd never forget the look of them. The very pictures I'd accidentally burned down in the cellar.

I jump out of bed, run down the stairs and place on a pair of my sneakers in case the ground is still hot from being burned. I sprint past the burial site of Sunney and Quinn straight to the shack. The door opens, meaning the bookshelves and crap I threw down have been moved. Once inside, I see it's nearly dark, and clutter that had been forced toward the back of the room is piled everywhere. The carpet has been removed, showing the unlocked door of the hatch. I grab a nearby flashlight, knowing it'll be pitch black.

I take a deep breath before opening it up. My suspicions are correct; the ladder is too burned to use safely. I toss what remains down into the hole. It only takes me a couple of minutes before finding another wooden one leaning against the side of the shed. I place it into the hole and begin my descent down. Once my feet touch the ground, I turn my flashlight on, lighting up the blackened room. Everything is burned from the fire, including the metal desk, which is partly melted. This should dismay me, but I know Sunney would keep his cash inside an inflammable box.

I move the flashlight around the room before seeing a black box nestled underneath what was left of the desk. I grab it and see my suspicions are correct. There is a small 13-by-9 black box. It has an electronic keypad lock on the front of its door.

I must enter Sunney's mind once again. What would he use as a pin? I try his birthday first, but nothing. I try his father and mother's birthday next, and nothing. I sit and think for a couple of moments. Just to try, I attempt my birthday, but no success.

Maybe it's not a number. Maybe it's initials. I attempt Sunney's, his parents and mine to nothing. What would this man be so fond of to use as a pin? If it's Andrea's initials, I'm screwed. No, he wouldn't be dumb enough to make it a woman's. He was too self-centered. One more thing he's fond of that isn't a person or object . . . Wait — it couldn't be. I inhale the still smoke-filled air, typing in the numbers 782426. A green dot appears before the sound of a lock clicking emits. Rubico: bingo.

I open the box, which holds the heftiest amount of money I've ever seen. I move my hands over the paper Benjamin Franklins, loving the feel of them. After taking in what is finally a light in the darkness, I close the door. I attempt to take it up the ladder but realize it is much heavier than I can manage.

I go back up, leaving the lockbox behind. I just need some rope, and in my history with Sunney, I know he has some of that somewhere. I go to where he's buried now, remembering he had used some on my wrists and ankles. It doesn't take long to spot some on one of the nearby lawn chairs. I return inside the shed, tying one end of the rope to a nearby tree outside. I toss the other end into the cellar, following it soon after, and tie the other end to the box handle.

Once back upstairs, I want to shower again but I don't have enough time for that. I need to get as far away from this place as possible. I pull the rope with the box with all the strength I have to Sunney's truck.

Before my search for tires ensues, I pack some but not all my clothing. If I take too much, the cops will know much sooner that I ditched the area. I will take two days' worth of clothing I can buy some later.

That's not good enough, Toni.

I stop dead in my tracks. Who is this in my head? It's not New Toni. She's long gone. Whoever it is has worries about leaving here without evidence of me being kidnapped or killed, and she's right. I need to make it look like I am no longer alive.

Bleed.

"I've bled enough," I whisper, looking around the living room.

I can't tell the difference between Quinn's and my blood marks splattered all over the hardwood floor. Shit, the voice is right. I've done this before, breaking my nose after killing Tom. How hard could cutting myself be?

I go to the kitchen, grab a washcloth then wrap it around the handle of one of the sharpest kitchen knives. No fingerprints means the cops won't know this is self-inflicted. I grab a second washcloth and place it in my mouth to avoid biting my tongue off from the pain. A drink would be nice right about now. It must be somewhere away from my veins so I don't bleed to death. Forearm? I look at my scrapped-up but clean left arm. I tightly close my eyes, already biting down on the washcloth.

It takes some time to bring out my will to do this. When I do, I make one quick clean cut across my forearm, avoiding my veins to the best of my ability. Thank God for the washcloth in my mouth because I let out a scream of pain, biting my teeth deep into the cloth. Blood begins squirting from my arm. I slowly begin walking around the house, making a blood trail. Once enough has come out and I begin feeling dizzy, I set the knife down and cover my wound with the washcloth from my mouth. I find a roll of gauze and duct tape in one of the kitchen closets and after cleaning my wound, wrap it up. I take the knife out to the trash to make it seem like it was thrown out.

I go upstairs, grab a bottle of painkillers, and take double the recommended dosage. I sit down on the toilet grieving from the pain in my arm. I pray all this pain isn't for nothing. It's not too late to go to the police and try telling them the truth.

No, it's too late.

Fucking voice. *Who are you?*

Who do you want me to be?

That's a good question. Who do I want you to be? I can start brand new. No more New Toni and Old Toni. I stand up and go to the mirror. Who am I going to be from now on? Not the dumb broad who forced herself to be good for a man. Not the lunatic who did all this damage to her life.

"Tammy?" I ask, shaking my head afterward. *No.*

"Tanya?" I ask next, shaking my head, remembering a bitch in high school I hated with the same name.

The T is sticking out to me. Close to Toni.

"T-t-Taylor?" I ask.

When I don't shake my head but nod, this time I smile. I like that. Taylor. The name of a puppy my parents dog-sat for when I was just a little girl. A golden retriever who looked sweet at first, had to warm up to me before she'd let me pet her. That's how I will be from now on. Distant as possible to strangers. Can't trust anyone, especially handsome, sweet-looking men. Those are the deadliest. Hopefully, one day, if I get past all of this, I will meet another Quinn for Taylor.

With my bag packed, I search for the tires Sunney must've stashed away. It doesn't take me long to find them sitting against one end of the shed. Brand new tires. I don't plan on keeping the truck long, just long enough to get out of Rubico. I have enough money to find another vehicle.

After finding a wrench in the shed, I pack the tires into the truck. I thankfully find a jack and change both tires in under an hour. Toni wasn't much of a mechanic. She found men to do that job. Taylor would be different. She would learn how to do shit like this on her own.

Once I have everything I need in the pickup, I get in the passenger seat, finding the keys on the counter. I start the truck, turning the music up, but in too much of a daze to hear it. Instead, I stare at the cabin for a couple of moments, taking in the fact that I am finally leaving. Getting out of this hell house in one piece. I'll have to leave most of my sanity here. That and a lot of blood.

I pull out and drive down the gravel road, passing the spot Quinn and I had sex and his dirt road. Now I finally begin to listen to the music. It's a country station, but all I hear is the sad lullaby playing. From now on, I will live like Quinn. Start where he left off. Doing a terrible thing but attempting to forget it all the while being a better person.

I pass through Rubico, and although some want to drive around and see what peaked Sunney's infatuation with it, I don't. An inner part of me badly wants to stop at the strip club Sunney was doing business in. Catch a glimpse of the shit he was doing. I guess I'll just have to die not knowing what that man had been up to.

I drive for two hours until the truck's fuel light illuminates. I stop in a small town named Witiker. It's nearly as small as Rubico and smells like wheat and cow shit. Before fueling up, I run inside the gas station, grabbing as many carb-fueled snacks as my arms will hold. My body needs it after all the blood I've lost. As I'm leaving, I catch sight of an older man in his late sixties and overweight at the side of the gas station getting out of a maroon-colored Buick Century. It's a plain old car, but it catches my attention. The windows are darkened and could make a nice place to crash while also putting in more miles from Rubico.

I slowly approach him before he can make it into the gas station. I didn't need to wave my hands to get his attention, as he had already been checking me out from afar. He is probably curious about who the stranger he's never seen in his small town is. I look at his features as I walk over. He's wearing an old plaid shirt and worn-out ranger jeans. I doubt he's a farmer due to the fact he is driving a Buick and not a truck. Hopefully, he will not be some bible-thumping law-abiding citizen who will turn me in for suspicious activity once I make my offer.

"Hi — sir," I say once I'm only a couple of yards away, forcing a smile on my face.

"Hello there, young lady. What can I do for you?" he asks, tipping his beat-up ballcap and showing a small grin.

"Well, this is going to sound a bit off, but I like your car."

As if never hearing a compliment on his car before, he looks confused. "The old shit box? She ain't worth much, but thanks."

He's not wrong, but I'm glad he doesn't seem too keen on the car.

"What do you want for it?"

A wide-eyed gaze appears on the man before he says, "She ain't for sale."

I should give up at this point, but something about the glimmer of that unappealing car persuades me not to.

"How about a trade?" I ask, turning around to point at Sunney's truck.

Still looking taken aback, the man just says, "That's a nice pickup. You sure?"

"Absolutely."

"You didn't rob a bank with it, did yah?"

"No — it's my husband's — ex-husband."

The man looks on the verge of running away from the crazy women before him before glancing me up and down again. Shit, I think, knowing my short hair is probably exposing my swollen purple neck. That and the bandages wrapped around my hands. I'm only embarrassed for a moment before I realize the man now has a look of guilt in his eyes.

"I take it this ex-husband of yours is a real piece of work?" he asks.

I am, again, ready to play the same old abused woman. It's not who the new me wants to be, but I may have to for now.

"Yeah, can you see why I want to get rid of his truck so eagerly?" I ask, frowning while I place a piece of my short hair behind my ear.

"Look, I feel for you, I really do. He did a number on yah. I have a daughter who went through the same thing. But you and I both know I won't be driving that truck around long without getting some questions."

He's not saying no, but he's not saying yes. He wants something.

"I know a guy who will give me a little to dispose of the truck for parts and whatnot, but that won't cover a new vehicle on my end."

"I'll give you five grand," I blurt out.

Looking near being persuaded, I have one more card to play. An expensive card is sitting on my middle finger. One I had thought about burying with my ex-husband but felt it might be of more value elsewhere. I put my left hand in the air, pointing at my wedding ring.

"And I'll throw this in."

The man raises his eyebrows and chuckles.

"How much is it worth?"

"Not sure, it's eight carats. Knowing my husband, he probably overpaid for it."

"Now you're talking," he says, smiling and opening his palm.

I throw the truck's key in it, and then he tosses me the Buick's. I slip my ring from my hand, staring at it for a moment before handing it over. I bite my lip, knowing I could've got a pretty penny for it, but the longer I kept it, the harder it would be to give away. Besides, being seen at a jewelry or pawn shop selling it might cause unwanted attention.

"Just do me a favor and don't return to that man. My daughter did just the same and got even more battered up."

"Trust me. I won't. I'll get you your money."

CHAPTER 54

Another three hours later and five thousand, one hundred and twenty dollars spent, I am far away in my brand new — well, not new but new to me, Buick. I can't even remember the name of the town I'm in now, just that it's three hours from Witiker. I know it has a grocery store with a nice young woman working the front counter. There I purchased blonde-colored box dye and bleach, which cost me fifteen dollars. Then I gave the nice girl working a hundred for letting me use the employee restroom while I dyed my black hair blonde. Like anyone who dares use box dye and bleach, the ends are dried out and split to shit, but I still can't help but like the look of it. I look like a different person, and that was my sole goal.

While parked in the back of one of the town's only bars, the night now in full swing, I went through Sunney's chest of money to see if he might have any other things. Maybe some jewelry or, to my liking, some drugs. Nothing hard, but it was enough to calm my nerves. I take out a couple of stacks of cash till I get to the bottom. No jewelry or drugs but printed-out photographs and a — cell phone. I toss the cell phone to the side and grab the photographs, which are turned away from me. In one corner of a photograph, reads a date set back ten months ago. I hope these aren't more disgusting pictures. My curiosity peaks. They are the ones Sunney found important enough to keep safe.

I take a deep breath and turn one over. It's of a woman. She's fully clothed and standing in front of a window. It's hard to make out her features, but she has brunette-colored hair. She looks extremely familiar, but the photograph is too blurry to tell. The second one also has a date on the back, from eight months ago. I flip it over, and it's of the same woman walking down the street. She has a glum-looking expression and is wearing a large parka coat. I look closer at the photograph, still not recognizing who it is. I flip to another photo of the same woman, but she's in bed sleeping in this one. There are a couple more, but most are the same as the others. The dates all creep closer to today.

As I ponder who the woman is, I grab the phone and turn it on. The battery is nearly dead, so I must make this quick. I go to the messages. All are from some man named Brett. I click on the latest message from a couple of weeks ago. It reads *Money's been given to her*. Her? Who is her? Has to be the woman in the photograph. I go to the next message, which reads the same, and so do the other few. One from two months ago reads *need more money. The bills went up*.

Nothing says who this woman is. I click over to the contacts. There are only two. One is Brett, and the other — I nearly drop the phone, thinking I'm seeing things. It says "Andrea". Why would her number be in this phone unless she's the woman in the photographs? That must be why I didn't recognize her at first. In the other photographs, she was naked, but in these she is wearing heavy clothing. The dates on the photographs, though, are all from after Sunney said he killed her.

A sudden realization comes to my mind, and that's when I drop the phone onto my lap. Sunney could never kill. He told me Andrea was the only one he could, but what if he lied about that? He wanted to scare me more or lie to himself so he would have the guts to kill me. Whoever this Brett is must be someone he hired to keep an eye on her. With the money Sunney has and what he said he did to her, if true, it must've been enough to keep her from going to the police.

I grab the phone pressing the enter button over the name Andrea. I press it to my ear as it begins dialing.

When I am about to chicken out and end the call, a frightened female voice picks up, answering, "H-hello."

I open my mouth, but nothing comes out. What do I even say? The phone could die any second. She deserves to be set free.

"Sunney? What do you want? I've been good, I promise." The voice sounds utterly terrified.

"This isn't Sunney."

There's silence on the other end.

"Sunney's dead. You're free."

More silence, just heavy breathing.

"Who is this?"

"T—" I begin to say, but the line goes dead.

I look at the screen of the phone, and it's now black. I hope that she believes me. I feel a huge weight lifted off my chest as I step out of my car. It's lightly raining, and the drops as they hit my face feel like they're shedding away old skin to make room for the new me. To make room for Taylor. She'll be sweet, kind, and lighthearted on the outside, just like New Toni tried so hard to be but failed. Unlike New Toni, she will always be this way, not with the pressure of Old Toni trying to dig her way back in. I can never go back to being Toni.

I step into the bar, and although it's as cold inside as outside, I still feel warmth with the smell of liquor hitting my nose. I sit on a red-painted stool putting my arms onto the bar as I clutch the cuffs of my sweater, hoping no one will take sight of my bandages and ask questions. I look around the dimly lit room, which reminds me a lot of the Keelover where I met Sunney, which should unnerve me but does the opposite. I feel at home here.

There are around fifteen people in the bar in total. All in groups of five or more. Some are sitting at the booths in the back, and a group of three men are sitting on the stools at the other end of the bar. Only one bartender is working, who makes their way over to me only a few moments after I have sat down. I order a double cranberry vodka, and as the first sip hits my lips, I know where this night is headed. I'll drink until I no longer can and sleep in my car, then move on. After that, it's all up in the air. For now — until everything in Rubico is discovered, I am safe.

On my third drink, a man dressed in a navy-blue polo and khakis enters through the bar's front door. As he passes by, I keep my eyes on my drink but feel his staring at the back of my head for the entirety of his walk to the bar. His cologne smells of pine needles, and I enjoy the smell so much I try to take it in as long as possible. He sits down a couple of seats from me and orders an expensive bourbon. I glance his way and try to make out his features as discreetly as possible. He looks tall as his feet near the floor while sitting, unlike mine, which hang. His hair is dark brown and cut just below his ears. His jaw looks chiseled and has some scruff on it. Besides his clothing resembling something Sunney would wear, he looks like Quinn.

It doesn't take long for this man to peek at me, and as much as I want to keep my eyes on him, I instantly look away. I can't do this. I can't talk to men — or anyone. I need to keep a low profile. I untuck my hair from my ears, so it hangs over my eyes and blinds my sight of the man. I keep my mind busy with where I will go after this town while taking heavy drinks.

A group of men that have been here since I entered approach the man. They all sound drunk, which makes them talk loudly. I learn the man next to me is named Adam, and he must be known in this town as they all start bullshitting about his work. It seems that he's some owner of a lumber business. Figures. I sigh, seeing all the resemblance I had pictured him having with Quinn disappear. Just another Sunney.

I soon hear them start talking in hushed voices. They laugh loudly but whisper to each other while taking turns taking glances my way. Soon, however, Adam is the only one continuing to stare. His eyes show longing, and although I suspect he's another scumbag, it makes me feel warm inside. Taylor likes the attention. The feeling I look attractive in this man's eyes. A man who has power and appeal in this town.

Soon the other men are shooed away, and not long passes before a voice says, "What are you drinking?"

I glance up with a grin, slowly turning my head to look at this Adam. He has an attractive-looking face, tan glowing skin, with dark blue eyes. I had been nervous that my facial appearance might disappoint, but by the way his grin widens, it looks like it doesn't.

Placing my hand on my chin to lean against the bar, I say, "Vodka-Cran, nothing special."

"Nothing wrong with that. All vodka tastes the same. Cheap — good, whatever."

I don't agree with that, but I just nod my head. New Toni, as she did with Sunney, would force more conversation with this man. She'd think of anything to say to keep his attention, but Taylor wants him to work for it. She wants him to know she doesn't care whether we talk.

I look away, concentrating on my drink once again.

Taking the bait, the man gets up from his seat and moves closer to me.

"I hope it's okay that I join you. Seems rather lonely over here."

"I don't mind. Being alone or in company," I say, keeping my eyes forward.

"I like that. I don't think I've seen you around these parts before."

"You sure about that?"

"Yeah, trust me, I would've remembered eyes like those."

Always the eyes. They are my saving grace. The thing that pulls men my way.

"Same goes for you," I say, glancing back as I stare into his ocean-colored eyes. I must admit they're just as enthralling as my own.

"They're nothing compared to yours."

"Bet the girls still fall for 'em."

The man grins for the first time, exposing a group of white-shaded straight teeth. Another resemblance to Sunney. My hopefulness of meeting another Quinn is diminished. Taylor may have a different taste, though. She may have a taste for this man.

"Usually, but it's not as easy to pull that charm when someone as beautiful as you is around."

"Not everything is easy. That's the fun in it, right?"

Adam and I continue to stare at each other. My mind begins to wonder what he's thinking. I imagine his hands on me, searching to feel every inch of my skin. I imagine what it'd be like to love him, and he love me. I wonder what it would take for him to fall in love with me. How difficult it would be. What I'd have to do to keep his full attention my way. I'd done it before. How hard could it be when this man resembles my ex-husband?

Here I am again, getting a man to woo me. When is God going to punish me for my sins? If ever? Is he protecting me for a reason? Or is the Devil protecting me as I am one of his own?

Five lives, not counting my parents, Mr. Nortec or Officer Adler, have been taken by my hand. Doing it had never been hard. As a child feeling the tiny pocketknife go into that man's back had given me an incredulous rush. I had liked coaxing Mr. Nortec into killing himself for shutting me away. Liked my mother drinking herself to death after breaking my father's heart. Stabbing Tom repeatedly for leaving me for another woman. Even stabbing poor Quinn, who, at the time, I had thought was trying to kill me. Choking that whore Heather for fucking my husband right in front of me. Watching Adler point that gun at his head even gave me chills, knowing just because I would tell the police everything, he was willing to end things. Then finally stabbing Sunney in the scalp while he was down on his knees to pleasure me one last time. That had been my favorite.

I'm a sick woman. Not your typical crazy girlfriend but much more. I have seen the light of death so many times but somehow survived victorious.

After my thoughts of a sweet romantic relationship with Adam float away, I begin wondering what he'd let me get away with. He'd have to be in love with me to let me hurt him. I could let out my violent tendencies on him like Tom. If he ever stared at another woman, I imagine bludgeoning an axe into his chest. Lying with his dead body while letting his blood leak onto me. Letting it seep into my clothes.

I want to cry when I realize it was all their fault. It was never Toni's fault. They all had it coming. Toni was just a sweet innocent girl who let people use her until she could no longer take it. It's too bad she's gone now. I think she and I would have been good friends. I must, however, lay her to rest to make room for this new life. Possibly this new man. I just hope he won't end up like the others.

"I'm sorry I didn't get your name," Adam says, taking me away from my thoughts.

I bite my lips faintly and say, "It's Taylor."

THE END

ACKNOWLEDGEMENTS

I would like to give my warmest thanks to Joffe Books for taking my first novel and giving it a chance to be published into the world. I have waited my whole life for this moment. I have never wanted anything more, than to be an author and have my work read. Thanks to Joffe Books I have had my biggest dream made into reality.

I'd also like to extend gratitude to all my family, friends, and everyone in between who read my novel before it was published. I was terrified to release something I was unsure would be liked but thanks to all of you, I got the confidence to do so.

To anyone afraid to follow their dreams, no matter what they be take my word. You never know what you can achieve. Life in short so work hard and never EVER stop believing in yourself. It doesn't matter where you come from, you are entitled to live your life to its full extent.

Finally, I would like to thank my fiancé, Brandon, my sister, Makayla and my late mother, Carla. The first three people to read my unedited novel. I would have never believed in my work had it not been for you reading and giving me a tremendous amount of support. All of this is due in part to your love. My mother especially, for being there for me throughout life's many ups and downs, supporting me in everything I did. I am so grateful you read my debut novel, you are the reason I keep going and doing what I do. You are my inspiration, Mom. I miss you every day.

THE JOFFE BOOKS STORY

We began in 2014 when Jasper agreed to publish his mum's much-rejected romance novel and it became a bestseller.

Since then we've grown into the largest independent publisher in the UK. We're extremely proud to publish some of the very best writers in the world, including Joy Ellis, Faith Martin, Caro Ramsay, Helen Forrester, Simon Brett and Robert Goddard. Everyone at Joffe Books loves reading and we never forget that it all begins with the magic of an author telling a story.

We are proud to publish talented first-time authors, as well as established writers whose books we love introducing to a new generation of readers.

We won Trade Publisher of the Year at the Independent Publishing Awards in 2023. We have been shortlisted for Independent Publisher of the Year at the British Book Awards for the last four years, and were shortlisted for the Diversity and Inclusivity Award at the 2022 Independent Publishing Awards. In 2023 we were shortlisted for Publisher of the Year at the RNA Industry Awards.

We built this company with your help, and we love to hear from you, so please email us about absolutely anything bookish at feedback@joffebooks.com

If you want to receive free books every Friday and hear about all our new releases, join our mailing list: www.joffebooks.com/contact

And when you tell your friends about us, just remember: it's pronounced Joffe as in coffee or toffee!

Made in United States
North Haven, CT
04 April 2024